CRITICAL ACCLAIM FOR

An Obvious Enchantment

"A mystery whose clues are found in the pages of the Koran, a love story, and a quest that is nearly Ingrid's undoing. It's a stunning accomplishment for a first time novelist." —*The Seattle Times*

"As the island air thickens, Ingrid's academic universe collides with the reality of ancient feuds and modern compromises, making this novel, with its shades of Bowles, Maugham and Jacqueline Susann, an edifying—and, yes, enchanting—tale." —*Los Angeles Times*

"Ingrid is smart, driven and attractive, an amateur sleuth on the trail of her own obsessions. She's daring and determined, and a little naïve. She reminds me of all the reasons I once loved the fearless and compulsive world of Nancy Drew." —*Portland Mercury*

"An exotic tale of escape and adventure with a sexy, feminist twist. . . . it's an addictive book" —*The Hartford Courant*

"Other women dream of fleeing the country for a tropical island; anthropologist Ingrid Holtz does it—with a grant to follow her revered professor, Nick Templeton, to an island off the Kenyan coast. . . . You'll be riveted by this romantic adventure novel."

—*Glamour*

"A gripping novel pulls you in, keeps you turning the pages long after you should have turned out the light. Such a book leaves you feeling satisfied, yet wanting more. . . . Tucker Malarkey is a writer to watch. She writes beautifully . . . and has a way with words."

—*The Free Lance-Star*

Tucker Malarkey

An
Obvious
Enchantment

Tucker Malarkey grew up in San Francisco and lived for two years in Africa. She won the Michener Grant at the Iowa Writers' Workshop in 1995 and is a senior editor at *Tin House*, a literary magazine based in Portland, Oregon, and New York. This is her first book.

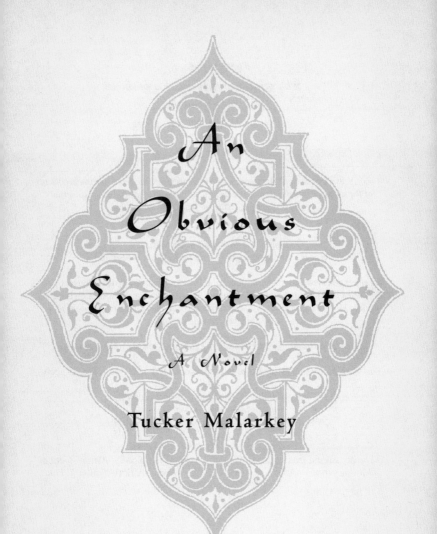

An Obvious Enchantment

A Novel

Tucker Malarkey

RANDOM HOUSE TRADE PAPERBACKS

NEW YORK

For my father,
who might have liked this book,
and for my mother,
who has been there all along

—————————

Copyright © 2000 by Tucker Malarkey
Reader's guide copyright © 2001 by Random House, Inc.

All rights reserved under International and Pan-American Copyright Conventions. Published in the United States by Random House Trade Paperbacks, a division of Random House, Inc., New York, and simultaneously in Canada by Random House of Canada Limited, Toronto.

RANDOM HOUSE TRADE PAPERBACKS and colophon are trademarks of Random House, Inc.
This work was originally published in hardcover by Random House, Inc., in 2000.

Library of Congress Cataloging-in-Publication Data
Malarkey, Tucker
An obvious enchantment : a novel / Tucker Malarkey.
p. cm.
ISBN 0-375-75820-8
1. Teacher-student relationships—Fiction. 2. Americans—Travel—Africa—Fiction.
3. Missing persons—Africa—Fiction. 4. Young women—Africa—Fiction. I. Title.
PS3563.A424028 2000
813′.54—dc21
99-055334

Random House website address: www.atrandom.com

Printed in the United States of America on acid-free paper

2 4 6 8 9 7 5 3

First Trade Paperback Edition

Book design by Caroline Cunningham

Contents

Contents

Part Three

Part Four

Part Five

Part
One

CHAPTER

1

Egypt

*T*hough the ground was hard and sharp, Ingrid knelt in the dirt. The dry surface layer, lifted by the afternoon wind, dusted her damp skin. She brushed the hair from her eyes, streaking her cheek with brown, looked up at the farmer who stood above her and placed her hands flat on the earth. "This is no good for farming," she said. "It's very, very old." The farmer's face was stubbornly blank. He did not want to understand. She began digging, jagged bits of rock tearing at her fingertips. Soon she found something. Holding up a shard, she smiled. "You see, antiquities. Good for tourists. Good for money." The farmer squatted and reached for the shard. After studying it, he threw it down and shook his head.

"This was a palace," Ingrid said, retrieving the shard. "A place where kings lived. Pharaohs."

The farmer motioned toward the north. "Giza," he said resolutely. "Kings in Giza."

"Giza is where they died. They lived *here*."

"Giza tourists. No here," the farmer said, waving a brown hand over the soil. "No here."

At a distance, a donkey stood in calm resignation, one hoof slightly raised. As the farmer approached, it opened a mournful eye. The donkey was hitched to a crude plow with rusted blades that cut into the earth as the animal again plodded forward in the heat.

Ingrid walked back to the jeep. "He won't listen," she said. "I think it's because I'm a woman."

"It's because he's fellahin," Louis said. "They've been doing this for three thousand years."

"Like you, the fellahin are impressed only by Giza." Ingrid chewed a fingernail and watched the farmer push an uneven row into the soil. "Damn." She got out of the jeep and stalked across the barren field. The farmer had turned the plow to start the next row when Ingrid stood in front of him. "You understand *maat*? It's very bad *maat* to plant here. Your crop will fail. You have a family? They will get sick. *Malaria*. Maybe they will die." The farmer stared at her through the donkey's ears. Then he clicked with his tongue, urging it on. "Wait," Ingrid said. "Just wait. I can get money for you, money instead of farming. How much money for this whole field of crops? How much for one year of crops?"

"Much money."

"How much?" she insisted.

"Enough for donkey." He pointed at his harnessed animal. "Two donkey."

"Two donkeys. Just wait, then. Do you understand? No more today. Tomorrow I will bring you money for two donkeys."

. . .

Louis was waiting in the jeep. "I need to get back to Cairo," she told him. "I've promised him two donkeys' worth of piastres. How much is a donkey worth, anyway?"

"Why are you doing this?" Louis said, starting up the jeep. "You leave in two days."

"Wait." Ingrid held him back. "I want to see if he starts again." They sat with the motor idling until the farmer led the donkey to a stand of tall grass into which he folded himself as the donkey began to graze.

"He's gone to sleep."

"He's dreaming about how with two more donkeys he'll be able to plow the field three times as fast," Louis said.

"We're going to have to dig after sunset. I need to find something tonight."

"You will get a bad reputation with the fellahin."

"I already have a bad reputation with the fellahin. But I have a feeling about this place. I could at least mark it for future work."

Louis' eyes traveled across the plot of land. "I know mudbrick is not my specialty, but to me it looks like an ordinary field."

"Be a friend and pretend it's important. Pretend there's an inverted pyramid under that farmer's plow."

Louis smiled and put the jeep into gear. "Because you are leaving, I will indulge you."

They followed a maze of dirt tracks dividing the planted fields. The side of the road was lined with papyrus, the reed used for centuries as paper by the people of Egypt. A few ancient scraps had survived: love letters, poems, lists—relics of undocumented lives of incidental men and women indentured to their pharaoh. This pharaoh was known by other titles: one of them was "king," another "god."

Ingrid thought, not for the first time, that it must have been a rotten life for them. Their crops and families were abandoned as soon as another temple or tomb was to be built. And something was always being built. Sometimes it was decades before they returned home, backs bent by the weight of monumental stone. She imagined the seeds of insurrection taking root and quickly withering again because any such feeling reflected a dangerous lapse in faith—a disbelief in the system of *maat*. And if you disturbed the balance of *maat*, you opened your life to danger.

They reached the paved road to Cairo and slowly picked up speed, the jeep lurching with each change of gear. Ingrid tied her hair in a scarf against the wind, chasing and capturing the skybound strands with one hand, anchoring the scarf with the other. She was momentarily blinded, trying to control the hair that, unbound, drew too much attention in this country.

"Why did you decide to study ruins that no one could see?" Louis shouted, his own hair a chaos of dark curls.

"Because there is no truth in temples," Ingrid shouted back. "It's propaganda. A king's story as he wanted it told. Glorified, altered, edited. It's unlikely that any of it actually happened. I want to know how the people lived, not just how the elite chose to die."

Louis swore in French as a motorcycle zagged in front of them. "The rest of the population catered to that elite, I can tell you that."

"Even the kings and queens of this country had to live, eat and make love somewhere. It's pretty damn clear it wasn't in the pyramids or the temples. It's unfortunate that they chose to build their palaces out of the best fertilizer around."

"They were temporary," Louis offered. "Life was temporary."

In the hotel lobby they paused, stunned by the sudden darkness. A few pieces of luggage leaned against the wall. An old paper lay on an age-stained table tinged with the neglect of rapid comings and goings. The places in between, Ingrid thought, are what you notice when you prepare to leave.

They moved slowly toward the back of the room, allowing their eyes to adjust. Up ahead at the reception desk, a letter waved at them in the dim light. "For the lady," the girl behind the desk said sullenly. Ingrid stepped more quickly, reaching the desk first. The girl blinked her kohl-rimmed eyes at Louis. "Nothing for the Frenchman," she said.

Louis guided Ingrid up the stairs while she studied the post-mark. "So your Templeton is not dead after all," he said.

She tucked the envelope away and groped in her bag for her room key. "You're not the least bit curious, are you?"

"About Templeton? Absolutely."

"About the mudbrick."

"Oh, that. A bit, yes."

"It's not very sexy, is it. I should have chosen something sexier. I'd have more funding. In the Cairo museum, I saw an old makeup case of Hatshepsut's from before the time she became pharaoh, when she was still a queen. The inscription on the case was 'God's Wife.' It wasn't found in her tomb because she died as a god, not as his wife."

"For some men, maybe this is not so sexy."

"That's why men don't write about Hatshepsut. They write about pyramids."

Louis laughed.

Ingrid stopped outside her door. "I need a shower."

"And a wash of the hair." Louis smiled sadly. "With the dust, the shine dies a little."

Light filtered through the thin curtains in Ingrid's room. She tied them open with ribbon she had bought at the bazaar. The street below was hazy with dust; the desert had again breathed on the city, covering its greenery with a patina of fine sand as if to say *Don't forget me—I can bury you as I buried the others.*

She sat down at her writing table, a faded map taped to the surface. She had learned the trick about maps from Templeton. They were like stories, he had told her, redrawn and reinvented throughout history. In Egypt, there were pharaohs who, after death, had been effectively erased from the map, their temples and cities destroyed, their names chipped out of the very obelisks that had honored them. Akhenaten was one such pharaoh, Hatshepsut another. Akhenaten had attracted more discussion and debate than almost any figure of ancient times, with his radical worship of one god and his visionary poetic writings. Much had been made of the resemblance of his god Aten to the Christian God: *"Thou hast made heaven afar off that thou mayest behold all that thou hast made when thou wast alone, appearing in thy aspect of the Living Aten, rising and shining forth,"* he had written. *"Thou art in my heart, but there is none other who knows thee save thy son Akhenaten. Thou hast made him wise in thy plans and thy power."*

Ingrid had steeped herself in these writings and in the writings inspired by him, drawn initially by his conflicting reputations as the instigator of monotheism and forerunner of Christ and as an atheist and a madman.

"Where there is argument," Templeton had said when she presented her thesis outline to him, "there is life. Akhenaten is a fine place to begin."

Hatshepsut had come later. Templeton alone had seen Ingrid's commitment to Akhenaten falter. "Your mind found a home in Akhenaten," he surmised. "But your heart found a better home with Hatshepsut. We must pay attention to what our heart prefers—for ourselves as much as our work."

Ingrid turned his letter over, inspecting the envelope. She bent it slightly and smiled: one corner was covered with late-night scratchings she would never be able to read. She placed the envelope above the map and picked up the shard. It had once been painted. She pushed the soft parts of her fingertips into its sharp corners and then placed it over the area on the map where she had found it. "I will find you," she whispered.

After he had showered, Louis came over with a bottle of wine. "What does Templeton say?"

"It's long," she said. "I'm saving it for later. Can you meet me and Mustafa at the field in a couple of hours?"

"If you'll come with me to the pyramids after."

"Fine, if we find something. If we find something big, I'll do whatever you want." When Louis raised an eyebrow Ingrid turned sharply and jammed a comb into her tangled hair. They were friends, but the friendship sometimes crossed lines.

"Here, let me do that," Louis said, reaching out with his hand. He positioned her at the sun-filled desk and began to carefully unsnarl her hair. "You shouldn't tear at it that way," he told her. "It breaks." Ingrid sat quietly with her hands in her lap. In the silence of his concentration, she began nervously pushing her cuticles back with her fingernails, watching Louis in the mirror. He was dark, someone who belonged in the desert. And she with her pale complexion, only slightly tanned by the Saharan sun . . . She tugged at the uneven ends of her hair.

"Someday I'm going to cut it all off," she said. "I've dreamed about doing it with enormous red scissors."

"French women do this usually later in life, when they are ready to be free."

"And I am not yet ready?"

Louis just smiled. He pulled the loose hair from the comb and let the fine yellow web float into the wastebasket.

Ingrid frowned in the mirror. "I wonder what Hatshepsut did to her hair when she became pharaoh."

"And what her lover did when she wore a beard." Louis ran the comb smoothly through her hair. "Voilà, you're all ready for digging. Tell Mustafa I will be around later, so he had better behave."

Mustafa was an old dragoman who had for decades guided tourists through the pyramids. He had made a good living for himself and, when he was hired permanently for the French project, revealed an aptitude for the digging process itself. His hands were said to be the nimblest in Cairo. He increased his prices as his reputation as a "finder" grew. He had endurance and, beyond that, instinctual knowledge. How else could he be so certain, so free of doubt? "They are *speaking* to me," he would say with inscrutable calm when locating a new relic. Mustafa was paid by the artifact. He lived close to the site and worked in the cool hours of the early morning and the evening, when the Europeans, who did not understand the desert, slept and ate.

In the evening sun, the windows of the perfumeries blazed with color, the deep light bursting inside the rows of tinted flasks and vials like jewels on an outstretched necklace. Incense and perfume had been manufactured by Egyptians for more than three thousand years, but all that remained was a cluster of cheap, honey-tongued vendors who could make any woman smell like a queen.

By the time Ingrid found his tent, Mustafa had been laid horizontal by his *shibuk*. The long pipe lay next to him like a lover.

"Sit, have some tea. I thought you were leaving."

"In two days. I want to check one last site."

"You are still looking for the woman pharaoh?"

"Yes."

"A woman who wanted to be a man, even dressed as a man. To me, she is not interesting."

"Her reign was prosperous and stable. Long, too, I might add."

Mustafa surveyed his guest, easing her into his consciousness with the hypnotic stroking of his beard. "You like her because she was a woman? But to find her, you will have to think like a man. Maybe wear a false beard as she did. And a pharaoh's kilt." Mustafa found this picture amusing and touched his *shibuk* as if nudging a friend who might see the humor.

"If she had reigned as a woman, Mustafa, no one would have listened to her."

Mustafa slapped his knee triumphantly. "Does this not teach you enough? A woman's place is not on the throne."

Ingrid smiled. "I am coming to you not to discuss politics, but because I want your opinion on something. There is a site, a field. I think it may have been one of Hatshepsut's mudbrick palaces."

"And you think this why—you have smelled her perfume?"

Ingrid ignored him and pulled out her map. "While she was supervising her expeditions to lower Africa, she would have had a palace built somewhere along the way to the Red Sea, which was where her boats set off. Cairo was close to the water. It would have been a good place to wait."

Mustafa stroked his beard in silence.

"The problem is there is a farmer who is ready to plow the field. I need your help. Maybe your hands can find something for me there tonight."

"There is a price for the hands," he said. "The opinion is free."

At sunset, Louis came in the jeep with a blanket and a basket of food. He waved to Ingrid where she stood in the field, uncorked a bottle of wine and drank from it, watching her as she bent down at some distance from Mustafa, her skirt blowing in the breeze. He whistled to her the way one would whistle to a horse and held up the bottle of wine when she turned. He had on a clean white shirt over his worn khakis. She came toward him, smiling. "Mustafa won't let me watch him," she said. "And he won't let me dig."

Louis handed her a glass of wine and held his in the air. "He doesn't like competition," he said.

As the light faded, they watched Mustafa in the field. The deepening shades of blue in the sky were ablaze with great streaks of orange and red. Louis set out baba ghanouj with bread and stuffed grape leaves. They ate in silence until the light in the sky was suddenly extinguished.

"I've been developing a theory about light," Ingrid said. "Have you noticed there's no twilight in Africa?"

"Yes, it's true. It is not a gentle transition."

"It must affect the way the psyche develops. I think it makes people here stronger. No gentle twilight to ease them into the darkness." Ingrid bit into a dolma. "Maybe it's twilight that makes Westerners so sentimental. They can sit on their porches and watch day recede as night approaches. It gives them time to consider what they're going to lose. It's like dying slowly versus being shot."

In the field, Mustafa lit his lantern. His robes hung around him like a shroud, his profile jutting from the smooth fabric. They watched him in the narrow glow of the lantern's flame.

"In France, we have twilight," Louis said. "*Le lit de lavande.* But we are not very sentimental."

"That's because you are a pompous people."

"Since we are being honest," Louis said, "the word I use for Americans is 'mushy.' It is not as dignified as sentiment."

"American mush is paying for your project, Louis. You should be grateful."

"According to your theory of light"—Louis toasted the sky with his wineglass—"I have twilight to thank."

Mustafa approached them, his lantern swinging. "Nothing," he announced.

Ingrid sat up. "Nothing?"

"It is late. I'm going to visit my cousin who lives near here. I will sleep there tonight."

"Thank you, Mustafa," Louis said. "For trying."

"My pleasure." He smiled and bowed. "Do not leave on my account."

They watched Mustafa's lantern bob across the field. "That farmer is probably his cousin," Ingrid said bitterly. "They're in cahoots."

"Before you go after him and start a civil war, finish your wine. I've brought dessert."

"Okay. Then tell me."

"Tell you?"

"About the project. I don't want to go back to Giza, so you'll have to tell me here."

"Lie back," he said. "You'll need to see the sky." Louis lay down next to her and turned onto his side to look at her. "You are a pharaoh. In death, you lie like this." He crossed her arms against her chest. "And this, this is your tomb. A huge chamber. But you cannot see all the stars we see tonight. You see a few stars only; they come into your chamber through long little tunnels, too small for a human. For a long time these tunnels were a mystery. We could not see where they went, what their purpose was. Now we have built a camera that travels like a rabbit down the tunnels and shows us what we could not see with our own eyes. Our little rabbit has found something quite incredible: through the tunnels, stars shine on you like beams. And they are not just any stars that shine into your chamber. Your ancient engineers have worked it out so that the stars of Osiris, the god of the afterlife, shine on your sarcophagus, inviting you to heaven. There, there and there, you see?"

"Orion's belt."

"And with your tomb, with the pyramids, you have mimicked the same constellation, creating a plan of heaven on earth, for they are placed in the exact position of the stars. A perfect mirror."

"I know this part. Tell me the really secret stuff. The stuff you haven't made public."

"Ah, not yet. For that you will have to wait." Louis touched her cheek with the back of his hand. The air blew softly across the field. They stayed close on the blanket while Orion chased his hunt to the horizon. Above them, the night was pierced with layers and layers of stars.

"When I was a girl, I used to think they were trying to break through a dome of black velvet. It was a prison and they were prisoners. They hurled the sharpest part of themselves at the fabric and stuck there, bleeding their light down to us. The night was there to tell us how hard they tried to break free."

"And you, what are you hurling yourself at?"

"I don't know," she said quietly.

She moved closer to him, resting her head on his arm. They stayed until the air grew cold. Louis wrapped Ingrid in the blanket and they drove through the darkness back to Cairo.

"The desert will lose a star when you go," Louis said when they reached the hotel. He dug into his pocket. "I will miss you. Your lady pharaoh will miss you. Even Mustafa will miss you." He opened Ingrid's hand and poured sand into it. "Take this with you. Think about us when you are surrounded by snow."

Templeton's Girl

*I*ngrid removed the copy of Professor Templeton's letter from her presentation folder, which was void of presentation notes. It wasn't what she wanted filling her brain twenty minutes before she was scheduled to stand in front of the senior members of the anthropology department to ask for money for a project she wasn't sure of. She tipped the spice bottle on her desk and Louis' sand angled and rested against two planes instead of one. Mimic the sand, she thought. Tilt and re-create yourself. Balance on an edge.

She chewed on the end of her pen and reviewed the letter. Templeton had trailed off in the middle and, by the looks of the pen marks, had fallen asleep. When he had woken, his mind was somewhere else. What had elapsed in that time—a dream, a drug or an hour—Ingrid didn't know. Templeton's mind was hard to track. It was why he was the best and, to a few, the most irritating scholar in his field. He was unapologetically cryptic in his communications from the bush, filing reports months late in longhand on paper stained with mosquito carcasses, wine rings, and God knew what else. It provoked a degree of hostility among the formalists of the department, particularly as his results were as good as his methods were bad. They tolerated him because they had to.

The rest of the letter was about a theory he had mentioned only once or twice before. She remembered it because of the way his voice changed when he spoke of it. He wrote:

What if we've been wrong about Islam on this coast. What if it didn't come with Persian traders, didn't sail on dhows from the East. What if the God that leads these people today was brought to them by the wisest and perhaps the bravest man this continent has ever known? And what if that man lived three hundred years before the date we've given for the arrival of Islam and, after being enslaved by Persian traders, he learned the religion of his captors and, filled with the glory of Allah, traveled to Mecca on his own two feet. As the story goes, he wore an amulet with both the languages of his captors and the language of his people. Its inscription read, *Every slave is a king with God in his heart.* What if there were proof of all of this?

Ingrid flattened the creased letter with her palm. A separate sealed envelope had been enclosed with the first. Inside were two photographs. One was of Templeton, toasting the camera, lanky and, it seemed, thinner. *My sixtieth* was written on the back. He had grown a full beard again and was dark from the sun. His sharp brown eyes and aristocratic features pierced her: she had not seen them in months. Another photo had him standing next to a tall blond man. Between them an enormous fish hung upside-down from a suspended hook. *Finn Bergmann and marlin at Salama Hotel.* Ingrid had placed the photos one above the other and stared absentmindedly at the images. Usually it was words he sent her, stories without punctuation like paintings without line, full of color, shadow and suggestion. It was through these stories that he continued to live in her mind. The detail of the photograph was somehow jarring.

On her way to the department meeting, Ingrid fell off her shoe and crumpled like a marionette. The hall was empty and her short cry of pain echoed down the corridor. The first body to round the corner was Henry Klingle's and, while it wasn't ideal, she smiled at him painfully. "Henry, I think I've sprained my ankle." She held her hand out cautiously. "If you could just help me up, I'm due for a department meeting."

"Ingrid! I didn't know you were back." He pulled her to her feet, where she stood like a stork. He looked at her ankle and then her legs. "Looks like you got some sun."

Ingrid winced and tested her weight on the ankle, taking a step back. Henry was insidious in a subterranean way. He was pleasant enough on the surface, but she sensed the root system of a tenaciously expansive weed underneath. Bending down, she shoved her foot back into her shoe. "Well, I'm off. Thanks for the hand, Henry. Good luck on your dissertation defense."

"I wanted to talk to you about that. I may need some help with Blackburn. Would it be all right if I came by your office?"

"No." Ingrid put her hand up like a traffic officer. "Call me."

On her way to the meeting, Ingrid ducked into an empty classroom and briefly recalled the points in an argument that was weaker for the five minutes she had lost, time she had needed for the inspiration pressure often brought her. She had no strategy. She was ill-prepared and now her foot throbbed. She had ten minutes and all she could hear was Templeton's voice, both mocking and instructing her.

"I have decided that you are going to make a good scholar because slavery," he had said, "is in your blood. Look at your father— a first-class slave. First-class slaves can ignore that they're slaves because they've chosen their servitude. Slavery becomes more obvious as you move down the socioeconomic ladder and the choices narrow. Freedom is knowing you are a slave and having the resources to choose your servitude. Not all slaves dream of freedom." Templeton stopped. He was drawing a picture in the rug with his cane. "You live in a country that is designed to relieve you of certain pressures by stimulating your senses and comforting you with material goodies, but you are smart enough to know that life is about more than that." The cane was in the air now, punctuating dangerously. "You will have to work against your culture to become free. Ignore the song of the sirens who tell you there is an easy way. There is no easy way. Besides, who would want an easy way? The more you know and understand, the more nooks you can wedge into to hoist yourself to a place of greater perspective."

Templeton lowered his cane and coughed into a handkerchief. "You have been born into the youngest, the least wise, the most precocious country on earth. Lucky, *unlucky* girl. My advice to you is to get out and steep yourself in a place that values the absurdities and fundamental mystery of human beings. A place that isn't always whistling and tooting to distract you. Start with the beginning. Start with Egypt."

"They've got scads of people working there." She'd learned the word from him, and had adopted it immediately. It sounded like *masses* and *scores* of healing wounds.

"Shame on you, Ingrid. There are scads of everything everywhere but no scad is the same. And you are occasionally a very intelligent scad. They would be lucky to have you."

"Lucky?"

"Lucky."

Lucky. When she entered the departmental meeting room, she managed to walk evenly to the head of the mahogany table. The pain was intense. "Gentlemen," she said, noting that the two female members were absent.

"How was Egypt, Ingrid?"

"Productive, interesting—hot. The Canadians have made progress on the reconstruction of Akhenaten's temple to Aten. Patterns are emerging, the symbols are starting to make some sense."

"It's only taken them twenty years," Dr. Blackburn sniped. Blackburn was a thin asp of a man whose blatant sexism went unchecked in the department. Ingrid dreaded all interactions with him. Like a petty dictator, he took every opportunity to preen and torment.

Ingrid forced herself to smile. "It's remarkable how thorough the Egyptians were in eliminating every trace, how terrified they were by the idea of Akhenaten's one god. I'm surprised the Canadians have been able to reconstruct as much as they have."

"Dr. Gregor told me he enjoyed your input," Dr. Reed said. "I'm looking forward to your report."

"You'll have it by the end of the week."

It was a small blessing that Jeb Reed was the chair of the department. He was balanced and relatively harmless. She remembered what Templeton had once said: "He's a family man, and families are messy. You don't want mess around you morning, noon and night, so he tries to keep things here as neat as possible. He's a peacekeeper. A bit soft. Think of him as an armored marshmallow."

Ingrid laced her fingers together behind her back. "What I'm here for today is not directly related to my work in Egypt," she began. "But the project I'm proposing is relevant to the event and evolution of monotheism in Egypt initiated by Akhenaten." She drew in a breath and looked directly at Dr. Reed. "I think it would be instructive to go to Kenya for a month to observe the particular brand of Islam on the Swahili Coast." No one spoke. "The question of how monotheism arrived," Ingrid continued, "and how Templeton's king, real or imagined, fit into all of this, would make an extremely interesting complement to the material I've already gathered in Egypt."

Dr. Araji tapped his empty pipe on the arm of his chair. Ingrid unclasped her hands and reached reflexively to open her folder and then stopped when she remembered that the only thing in it was Templeton's letter. She had nowhere to look. She decided to focus on Dr. Araji's pipe. Araji was the token foreigner, a man with unfamiliar and untouchable calm, reluctant to participate in departmental battles. He was private, subtle and, unlike his colleagues, not prone to envy. Ingrid liked him. He was not allowed to smoke in the meetings, so his pipe was unlit.

"Ingrid has been exploring the connection between ancient Egypt's worship of Aten and its later acceptance of Christianity," Dr. Reed explained. "Suggesting a trend and/or a predisposition to a monotheistic paradigm."

"The worship of Allah, or Islam," Ingrid continued, "is strong on the East Coast of Africa, also known as the Swahili Coast. What's interesting to me is why this particular god was adopted by the Africans—not only who brought him, but why he stayed. Why did Islam catch on and why so suddenly?"

"It's not your area, Ingrid."

"I realize that. If you'll remember, Professor Templeton has suggested that Islam was not brought by Arab traders in the twelfth century A.D., as has been reported, but by an African king, and not one, not two, but *three* centuries earlier. As far as we know, the king exists in oral mythology only. There is no solid evidence of his reign, of his pilgrimage to Mecca or of his return to Africa. But if we could find it, if Templeton is on to something, it could significantly change our theory of religious evolution. Imagine, Islam introduced by an *African* king. An African king's preparing the way for Allah is not so different from Akhenaten's preparing the ground for Christ."

"A tenuous parallel," Blackburn mumbled.

"Ingrid—" Dr. Reed raised his chaotic eyebrows and glanced at his colleagues. "And stop me if any of you disagree. That communiqué was vintage Templeton. He's an exceptional scholar but he's also immensely *creative.* It's been the bonus and the bane of his career. This last report was not unlike reports we've received in years past, when he's been in the bush for six months or more. He's susceptible to regionalization. He can let his mind wander too far."

"It was intriguing stuff," Dr. Goodman, a recent addition to the department, offered from across the table. "No question." Goodman was still playing his tenure politics safely and his input was invariably neutral.

"Perhaps not the end," Dr. Blackburn jumped in. "That was decidedly odd."

"I think there's something to his African king." Ingrid held her ground.

"There's often something to what Templeton hypothesizes." A token smile of acknowledgment passed over Dr. Reed's face. "Legitimate research is another issue. However unwillingly, Templeton is an academic, as are you. And a promising one, at that." Ingrid dipped her head in thanks. She slipped her shoe off under the table and rested her swollen foot on the arch of her good foot. "It's always best to stick to the facts," Reed concluded. "Especially at the outset of one's career."

Ingrid ignored the warning. "Dr. Templeton may have found substantiation to this African king theory. I think he's made a breakthrough."

"You seem to be granting this king more credibility than he deserves," Dr. Reed said. "May I remind you that we have no proof that he exists outside Templeton's imagination?"

Ingrid paused. Dr. Araji's head was bent over her dissertation summary. Was he asleep?

"Forgive me." Dr. Blackburn's voice bit into the air. "I'm afraid I've lost the thread here." He took out his handkerchief and wiped his nose. "Would it be out of line for me to suggest that in your desire to travel to Kenya, you may simply be a sheep in search of your shepherd?"

Ingrid looked at him levelly. "Yes," she said.

Blackburn cleared his throat to speak and Ingrid held up her hand. "If he's real, Templeton's African king brought a new god to his people—and, unlike the Egyptians under Akhenaten, the people were ready for it. Do you know why this excites Templeton? It's a better story, for one thing, but second, because Africa has been invaded and indoctrinated by missionaries for the last century and a half, we tend to think of it as a passive, under-planted terrain, perfectly suited for foreign gods to take root. This story sheds a different light, doesn't it? At the very least it makes us question what we assume we know. This, to some people's vexation, is one of Templeton's specialties. More water, please."

Dr. Reed refilled Ingrid's glass from the communal pitcher. She closed her eyes while she drank, momentarily allowing her current circumstance to lapse from her mind. Those seconds brought her professor to the fore with such vividness she felt he was actually in the room, tapping his foot with nervous excitement.

"You certainly sound like our man in the bush," Blackburn said. "Though you've developed your own flourish. I might add that it's six weeks before the term begins."

"Because Swahili Islam is based equally in Arab and African traditions, it's not as rigid as other Islamic societies. It's an ideal place to observe both the influences of Islam and the roots of African tribal culture as they coexist in a situation that is anthropologically unique. This will fit in well with the course section on African Islam I will be teaching next semester. An opportunity to observe it firsthand can only enliven my understanding—as well as my course work."

"How convenient it all turns out to be," Blackburn said.

Dr. Reed's beeper sounded. "My apologies," he said, punching numbers into a cellular phone. He listened and then hung up. "If it's all right, I'd like to reconvene in an hour or so. Say, four-thirty?"

Ingrid drifted down the hall to Templeton's office, where his secretary was getting ready to leave. "Hi, Maggie."

"Hello, dear. Just on my way out. You've got the key, just lock up after yourself."

Ingrid took Templeton's photo from her folder. "He's sixty, you know. This was taken on his birthday."

Maggie lowered her glasses to the bridge of her nose and held the photo to the light. "How unlike him to announce it. He must be enjoying himself."

"I don't think he's coming back."

Maggie smiled.

"Do you?"

"I try not to anticipate the man."

"I think he needs help."

"He would never ask if he did."

Ingrid glanced at his door.

"One always hopes that he is faring well," Maggie said. "And he usually is."

"Do you mind if I sit in his office for a while?"

"Of course not. Go mess up his papers some more."

Ingrid sat in Templeton's chair and swiveled around. It had been almost six years since she had first entered the war zone of his office to ask if he would be her advisor. What she had known of him at that time was as minimal as his presence at the university. She had chosen him after reading one essay.

"So you want me to be your advisor," he had said from behind a desk littered with papers, piles facing north, south, east and west. "You have come here with full knowledge that I have given up on advising. Why?"

"I think I could learn from you."

"Hmm," Templeton stalled. He pushed some papers around on his desk, as if looking for a way to discourage her. "Information has become the focus of our time. Maybe you're too young to have noticed."

"No, I've noticed." What she noticed was the lines in his face. She stared at the creases radiating from his eyes, the furrowed habit of compassion.

"Unfortunately," he was saying, "noticing isn't enough. Some chaotic sea threatens to drown me, because, it seems, I have neglected to build the necessary irrigation channels and harbors; file cabinets to hide it, drawers to make it disappear. I am looking for assistance, if you have any suggestions . . ." His voice trailed off.

Ingrid wrinkled her forehead and smiled. "Sorry."

"Well, it's a dangerous business. As a culture, we have allowed our once fertile soil to become so saturated with information that we must reject new rainfall, letting it run off willy-nilly down streets, through yards, collecting in leaf-cluttered gutters, upending the shallow-rooted foliage and weakening the deeply rooted so that the once straight trees that stretched for the sun lean and sometimes fall." Templeton stopped and closed his eyes as if to shield them from the vision.

"It's an apocalyptic picture," she said. What she was imagining was bad city planning, but she could see that Templeton saw something worse.

Templeton lowered his eyes. "As Thomas Eliot asked— Where is the knowledge that is lost in information? Where is the wisdom that is lost in knowledge?" He picked up his phone and stabbed a button. "Mags! It's as cold as a tomb in here. My blood has stopped circulating. Help me out with some tea here, Mags." He hung up the phone. "Come and see me in a week."

Ingrid had returned the next day and, when Templeton refused to talk to her, the day after that. She was fairly sure he had slept in his chair. He wore a loden coat and a woolen hat over his rumpled office clothes. Piles of paper had been dispatched from his desk and were now scattered around the room. He was leaning over a map. Next to the map was a drawing of what looked like a piece of jewelry, a decorative disk hanging from a chain. Ingrid cleared a chair and sat down.

"What's that?" she pointed at the drawing.

"That," Templeton pronounced, "is my Holy Grail. One can

have faith in something that may or may not exist." He tapped the drawing with his pipe. "What do you see here?"

Ingrid looked again at the disk. "Stars. Maybe some kind of constellation."

"In the ninth century, jewelry had a practical purpose. The Arab traders of the Sahara made a compass from these amulets. They drew maps of the stars, showing the way to water. The amulets passed from generation to generation, between families and tribes, because water in the desert was like God." Templeton smoothed his hands over the map and became absorbed with the details of the upper left corner.

"Do you know how *vague* borders really are? Kenya wanted a little more of the north country earlier this century, so they had mapmakers redraw their borders. One year Kenya got a little more of Somalia. By the time Somalia noticed, it was official. Why bother with the hullabaloo of regular channels?"

Templeton wrapped his coat more tightly around him. Moving like a much older man, he lowered himself into his chair. "So here you are again. Why, my girl, have you chosen this field? Looking at you, I'm not quite sure it hasn't chosen you."

"Why?" Ingrid challenged. "What do you see?"

"Barring alterations, what I saw the first, second, third and now fourth time you've come to my office. An attractive young lady with an overly severe hairstyle and unobtrusive clothing, on the gloomy side, I might add. You seem to favor flat shoes, and is it my imagination, or do you walk tentatively? A foot injury perhaps? No makeup save for a little lip color now and then." Templeton put his elbows on the desk and leaned into a pile of paper, as if to see her more clearly. "What's most interesting is that your physical attributes remain in focus only until you speak. Then your seriousness and your self-possession take over and a fellow realizes you are not here to be looked at, that you mean business. I find myself wondering what that business is."

Ingrid countered his offensive by leaning forward in her chair. "How did this come to be *your* business?"

"Me?" Templeton laughed. "Who knows. The story changes."

"What story, your story?"

"All stories."

"I want to know about yours."

"Oh, dear." Templeton emptied a packet of orange powder into a glass of water, where it sank to the bottom of the glass. He paled, as if the question had knocked the wind out of him. She watched him recede from her, pulling back until even his eyes had lost their focus. The shallowness of his breath made her wonder about his health. She wondered too why, in the face of his duress, she did not withdraw the question.

They sat in silence until he finally returned, leaning forward to stir the mixture with the end of his pen. "Well, I was in England," he said, "a country mired in its past. All great civilizations"—he paused and looked at the ceiling—"and there have been thirty-four to date, die. Some are mercifully brief in their final stanzas. They don't drivel on, trying to rehash old rhymes or match new ones in the old style. They simply end. Gone are the days of quick endings. England has outlived herself, and because death is no longer acceptable in the modern world, she has been kept alive by artificial means. I found her depressing, so I left. It has become a culture of manners, the substance long since eroded. Are you writing this down?"

"No."

"I see, you're sketching something. Is it me?"

"No."

"Good. The problem with England is that no one really converses anymore. As a young man I had to hunt for decent conversation." Templeton's fingers were in the air, working like castanets. "Chit chat chit chat. They are magnificent at chitchat. Like Chinese water torture. True dialogue transforms. We must work at it. No one seems to understand that, even in these hallowed halls."

"So you left England," she pressed. "Did you have a family?"

Templeton drank half of the orange liquid and dabbed his mouth with a handkerchief. "Awful stuff."

"You're trying to change the subject."

"The subject?"

"You. I'm asking because there's absolutely no biographical material on you anywhere."

"And this is important?"

"Yes, to me."

"I fail to see how it matters if I had a family or how my career formed."

"You're going to be my advisor. I think a little information is within bounds. You've been asking me questions of a non-advisorial nature."

"I don't remember consenting to being your advisor. Anyhow, it's how I think that should be of interest to you, not my personal history."

"I just want to know how you got here."

"You'd have better luck at Pompeii or Giza. Living human archaeology is deceptively hard, as the subject is in a constant state of change."

Ingrid looked at her watch. "I've got to go."

"We're finished, are we?" Templeton seemed both relieved and disappointed.

"No. We're not."

She returned to his office after her class. Outside the door, she put on lipstick, then wiped it off with the back of her hand.

"So you're determined," he said when she entered. This time she began with her elbows on his desk.

"Maybe."

"And you've got more lipstick on the back of your hand than you have on your lips." Ingrid blushed and stared at the mauve smear on her hand. "You're not sure you want to be a girl, is that it? Well, if you're not sure of that, how can you be sure of things less fundamental. Me, for instance."

"I just had a feeling."

"Expand, please."

"You seem to do things your way. And your work has . . . reverence. You come at things from unexpected angles. You don't simplify anything, nor do you claim absolute authority—like some people here." Ingrid paused. "I want to see what you've seen."

He was studying her with an unnerving focus. "This much you should know," he began. "The principal way I differ from my colleagues is that I see history not as a matter of facts but as a matter of meanings. We imagine facts as solid objects, totems with some kind of magic. They assume a life of their own and the relationship we create between them becomes a mixture of science and art. But there is always the artist. Man or woman, child or adult, among the living or the dead, facts began somewhere, with someone." The words swirled around Ingrid's mind like music. Inside, she felt a quiet elation.

"There is a seed," he was saying. "I am involved in the search for that seed. My current research involves the seed of Islam in Africa, which is not the seed we have been shown. It was planted much earlier, with roots deeper and more intertwined. But I am contesting what has become a fact. Facts sneak up on you. No one thinks of them as stealthy, and that's how they win. You know Abraham?"

"The Abraham who married Sarah?"

"Who could not initially conceive. Abraham married a sec-

ond time, to a black woman, Hagar, who promptly gave h..
son, Ishmael. Sarah conceived soon thereafter and brought Isaac
into the world. At which point she had her husband banish his
second wife and son. Hagar and Ishmael settled in what is now
known as Mecca and spawned the Arab people. Sarah and Abraham stayed in Palestine and ushered in the Jews. Do you know
what I'm thinking?"

Ingrid shook her head and waited.

"What I'm thinking is, perhaps the African blood was there
from the start. Perhaps the mother of what was to become Islam
was an African." Templeton chuckled and banged his shoe with
his cane. "What are you thinking?"

"I'm just listening."

"Listening to me rant."

"No."

"Well, it's a start, my girl. If this sort of thing doesn't drive
you away and you have the necessary resolve, you might be in for
the long haul."

"I think I'd like to be."

Templeton leaned forward. With his elbows on his knees, he
clasped his hands together and studied the crooked apse his fingers made. "Trouble is, I don't know why you'd like to be. If we're
to work together, I need to see it. Even if just for a moment."

Ingrid almost smiled. "That's a problem, I'm afraid." She held
up her hand with its lipstick smear. "I'm not sure what I want
you to see."

"Ah! She has a sense of humor. I was beginning to wonder.
Well, then, you must help me see."

Ingrid swallowed some of the pills Templeton kept around for
his malarial aches, and when the meeting reconvened, she stood

more steadily at the head of the table. The throbbing in her ankle had subsided and she felt generally more relaxed. Dr. Reed had tilted his chair back and was balancing on the two rear legs. He looked more relaxed, too. There were red spots in his cheeks. Maybe his phone call had been good news. Maybe he'd had a nip of brandy and a couple of pain pills of his own. "So, Ingrid," he said. "You're looking to put together some continental theories on the evolution of monotheistic cultures in Africa, taking the work you've already done in Egypt and expanding it to the East Coast of Africa, perhaps doing some comparative analysis between Christianity and Islam and a little African tribal culture as well?"

Ingrid almost smiled. "Thank you, Dr. Reed." The man was a soft-spined saint.

"I'm sorry if the argument eludes me," Dr. Blackburn's lips curved upward in what might have been a smile. Then, as he spoke, they flattened and came apart like a poorly sewn seam. "What is it you're proposing to do on the Swahili Coast for a month? Why not camp out in Templeton's office? It's much cheaper."

Ingrid sipped water from the cup Dr. Reed had pushed in front of her. "Outside what I've just proposed, I want to see what Professor Templeton has found. Compare notes. I think it might be useful for him to have some fresh eyes on material he's been saturated in for months."

"And it's your fresh eyes he needs?"

"I think he would benefit from another colleague's input. I'm quite sure he's uncovered something."

"Knowing Nick, it was a *bui-bui.*" Blackburn turned to Dr. Reed. "Come on, Jeb. Run interference, will you? We don't even know where the man is. We can't fund a wild-goose chase for a man who has made it his modus operandi to lose perspective."

Dr. Reed cleared his throat and smiled at Ingrid respectfully, indicating that, were he able, he would spare her the present unpleasantness. "I need to ask you candidly, Ingrid, if your reasons for traveling to Kenya are personal or professional."

Ingrid assumed an expression she had seen on her professor countless times. It was, she hoped, a calm and somewhat bemused expression intended to puzzle but not insult. Her eyes traveled the room purposefully, resting somewhere above Dr. Araji's head. She shifted her weight to her bad foot and the pain came shooting back. Instead of wincing, she dropped her eyes to the table, pressing her fingertips onto the mahogany finish and making smudges on the polished surface. Her fingertips were white with strain. "Gentlemen, Dr. Templeton is my advisor. We haven't heard from him in two months. He has survived his own odysseys before, I know. I also know his last letter sounded, in parts, delusional. If he is delusional, I want to be the first to know because I tend to take him seriously. He has not asked me to come, but I think he needs a witness. I think he's found something. If you think anything of his life or his work, you'll consider letting me go."

The room filled with the inaudible sounds of discomfort. A back straightened, papers moved. A pen tapped. Ingrid drew in her breath. "I'm confident that his research, however acquired, will help us understand why Islam found such fertile ground in Africa." She lifted an upturned palm in front of her, a movement that caught all eyes. How desperate they were for something to *chew.* She allowed her hand to float to her right, indicating an enormous framed map of ancient civilizations that hung on the wall. "Africa, with its primarily oral tradition, may have a history we do not know. It has not shared some of its greatest secrets with the rest of the world." Ingrid dropped her hand to her side. "But maybe, just maybe, because Templeton walks the line between worlds, Africa has decided to share its stories with him."

Dr. Araji, who had remained silent throughout the course of the interview, put his pipe in his pocket and rose. "Gentlemen, I think there are a few interesting ideas here, as diffuse as they are at the moment. I vote in support of Ms. Holtz's trip, necessitating funding for airfare and one month's research. It's not an expensive country. Ms. Holtz has already proven herself to be an exceptional scholar. And Dr. Reed, as you're well aware, it's not an unpopular area of research for some of the department's supporters."

Dr. Blackburn sighed loudly and visored his eyes with his hand. Dr. Reed's square glasses reflected the overhead lights as he glanced up at Ingrid. She could see he wanted the meeting to end. "Very well," he said. "Academia needs whatever passion comes its way. Come by the office Monday, Ingrid. Cynthia will have the paperwork."

Father

After locking up her office, Ingrid made a painful trek across campus to the physics department. The walkways were covered with colorless leaves, sodden from days of rain. Though they worked at the same university, it was unusual for her to see her father more than once a month. The past few years they had seen less and less of each other. They were both busy; weekly dinners had become monthly dinners. Her father had been relieved when Ingrid assured him that the decrease in contact was not a mortal blow to her social life. "Cut from the same cloth, you and I," he told her. "Too many other things to think about. Things, things and more *things*."

Her father was one of the few men at the university paid to think about *things*. Some days, between pacing and talking into the tape recorder, he tinkered with pencils or made folds in paper. She could see him now as she approached the old physics building, backlit as he paced back and forth in front of his office window on the second floor, like a rare animal in a drab, gray zoo.

Her father was notorious for a number of reasons, one being the fact that he'd been struck by lightning as a distinguished young doctoral student. He was newly married and it was summertime. He and his wife, Harriet, and his best friend, Jack, were walking by the lake discussing teaching jobs on the West Coast. California was still an academic frontier then, and Jack was all for trailblazing. "They've got money and we've got to tell them what to do with it." He wanted to get up and go, temper those rootless radical Californians with the sensible sobriety of a few stalwart midwesterners, take California the way they had taken Michigan. Jack was still single, it was easy enough for him to get up and go. Harriet was trying to talk him out of it. She was four months pregnant. Just wait a year or two, she told him. We'll come with you. They sat under a tree and watched a white band of rain move toward them from across the lake. The sudden summer storms of the Midwest. The heady electricity. Harriet said, "You don't get these in California, Jack."

The last moments before the bolt struck were vivid in her father's memory. A year ago, he had started talking about it. He remembered the white caps advancing across the lake like a herd of small horses. He remembered the feeling of the electricity in the air, the way charged particles made them all giddy. And Harriet's profile as she laughed at something Jack said. Jack could always make her laugh. What he didn't remember was the actual event, that one great flash of light and energy that cleansed him from the inside out. How he wished he had stayed conscious for it! Jack never regained consciousness. And why hadn't the bolt struck Harriet? It perplexed him until years later, when he understood that God had something else in mind for her.

It took Ingrid some time to understand why and how the plug of her father's reticence had been pulled. It had begun when he was contacted by a support group for people who had been struck by lightning. They met every week. Now her otherwise unsociable father drove two hours every Wednesday evening to talk to his new lightning-struck friends about their shared experiences. These days, he rarely spoke to Ingrid of anything else. He confided to her that he was sure the event had changed him on a physiological level. He thought, no, he *remembered,* that before the accident he was not a restless man. He was capable of having a conversation. Of course, Ingrid hadn't known him then. What she knew about him now was that he was paid to think and pace and talk into a tape recorder. He had published three highly respected and impenetrable books and was at work on a mathematical modeling of the fourth dimension. He didn't actually write the books, but narrated into a tape recorder, because his fingers could no longer hold a pen. Couldn't or wouldn't, Ingrid didn't know. "That part of my life is over," he offered by way of an explanation, as if further evidence that his life had been split cleanly in two by that single bolt. What had come before, Ingrid had no idea.

She knocked softly on his door. The steady, deep sound of his voice stopped. She heard the click of the tape recorder. The door opened suddenly. "Ingrid!"

"Hi, Dad."

He stepped back from the door to let her in. Today, as on most days, he had the slightly tormented look of a visionary struggling in an unfamiliar tongue. He was wearing slippers and a gray cardigan. "I'm writing a speech," he said. "Someone actually wants to know about my life. Seems I'm quite remarkable. What do you think of that?"

Ingrid smiled. "I think you were in the right place at the right time."

"Good, very good, Ingrid. What would I do without you to singe my wings and send me downward?"

"Disappear. Combust. I don't know."

"How did you get to be so bloody barbed? Did I teach you that? Should part of my speech include my failures as a father?"

Ingrid walked to the window. He had hung something in the branches of the tree. A glinting, spinning mobile of paper clips and something else she couldn't identify. "I've got funding to go on another trip," she said.

"Haven't you just returned?" Ingrid nodded without turning around. "Where to now?"

"East Coast of Africa."

"Now what's this African thing? Haven't you just been in Egypt?"

"Yes."

"Such wanderlust. Where does it come from?"

"Where does anything come from?" She could hear the shuffle of her father's slippers as he began to pace. "I don't know how long I'll be gone," she added, the thrill of escape suddenly coursing through her.

He began to hum a melody from a Mozart concerto she recognized as he paced back to his desk. Ingrid turned to go. The movement seemed to interrupt his thought process and he was aware of her again. He looked at her with agitated concern. These were the most painful moments, when he tried to make conversation with her. "You know there's a man in our group, he can't feel the cold. Have I told you about him?"

"No."

"Walks around in sub-zero temperatures in a T-shirt. It's actually quite dangerous. He's been badly frostbitten." He glanced at his daughter to gauge her level of involvement. "I'm sorry. This is probably of little interest to you. It seems the only people I can speak to comfortably are in the group." He smiled at Ingrid and said softly, "As odd as it sounds, I feel I have a place with them."

To make it worse, just when Ingrid mustered enough anger to fight back, to somehow hurt her father the way he hurt her, she was disarmed by his innocence. He was not trying to hurt her. But he did it easily and often. If she had attempted to explain he would have been befuddled and overly apologetic for something he didn't understand. It wasn't worth the battle. "I'm happy for you, Dad," she said.

He resumed his pacing. "What I've been thinking about today is how the lightning changed me. For instance, Jack and I are no longer friends."

"Jack's dead."

"Jack's dead. Yes. Well, I've been thinking that he was the better candidate for life. He was strong, honest, hardworking. A good man. Harriet, with her skills of resuscitation, chose to save me. Of course she did, she was my wife. What I've been thinking is, had it been up to God, I might have died. Jack was the better man. I think this is true because Harriet was taken from me so soon after. He evened it out. Ingrid, I think he gave her to Jack."

"Who, God? God gave her cancer, Dad."

"I always thought they made a good match. It's unfortunate you didn't know either of them better because we could talk about it some more. As it is, I'm the only one who talks, isn't that right? You hardly say anything, ever. I've often wondered whose DNA was responsible for that. Your brains could have come from either, but your silence—I don't know. Perhaps a touch of darkness from a generation or two back on your mother's side." Her father was the only person who accused Ingrid of silence. Depending on her state of mind, she thought it was either because he knew her well or not well enough. "It's a shame your mother isn't here to describe those old Swedish characters better. They were quite a cast." He bent over at the waist and attempted to touch his toes. "Argh! We men have no flexibility in this area. None at all. This is as far as I will go." He straightened, red-faced. "What about whosits, are you still seeing him?"

"Jonathan. I never really saw him."

"Why not? I quite liked him."

"I seem to keep going away."

"You must have decided against him. Not smart enough or something."

"No, I'm just not sure I'm built for these things."

Her father laughed. "Of course you are! Look at yourself!"

Ingrid looked out the window. "That tells me absolutely nothing."

"You're just like your mother. You are genetically predisposed to be loved, despite your efforts to hide yourself. The stuff will continue to be hurled in your direction—for a decade more, anyway. It's your nature. Did you ever just drink a nice bottle of wine with that young man? To fall in love you need, just for an hour or so, to forget the seriousness of it all. Christ, you and your mother remind me of two Swedes rattling around in a land where the sun never sets. While there's still light, the work is never done. How I fell in love with such a melancholy people, I don't know."

"Maybe it was the wine."

"Ha! Well, poor old whosits. I was hoping that might turn into something interesting for you."

"Were you?" Ingrid faced her father again. "Why?"

"I'm an old man." He seemed to have lost his train of thought and began to pace again. "You know, Harriet learned to relax after her childbearing years." Her father stopped and turned to her. "Do you ever think about her?"

"What would I think about?" Ingrid asked hotly. These occasional direct questions felt like an attack. "She's been dead for most of my life."

Her father started his pacing again. "Now, if we could only know that with absolute certainty, we'd all be able to find some peace. God keeps people alive. The God inside here," he touched his heart.

"Well, I barely remember her."

"Nothing?" The question was plaintive. She remembered her mother was beautiful, with a graceful height that drew attention. She had full, high cheekbones and clear green eyes that people who knew her still talked about. The eyes were what Ingrid remembered, what stood out as she fought her disease. In the end, they became grotesque.

"There was a way she touched the place behind my ear when I sat with her," Ingrid said quietly. "It put me into a trance. After she died I tried to do it on myself but it didn't work." She saw her father was about to cry. She tried and failed to smile. "It's interesting that God is suddenly figuring into things for you."

"Old age." Her father stepped off his worn pacing path toward her. He put his hands on her shoulders and touched his dry lips to her forehead. "Do you know the origins of the term *good-bye*? It means 'God be with you.' So, you see, God's been there all along." He turned from her. The conversation was over. In that moment, she had ceased to exist for him. As a child, she had wanted to weight him down with something; keep him from floating away from her like this. Clearly, she herself wasn't enough to keep him tethered. Now, as she stood watching him, she knew he had no idea she was there. As a child, she thought if he couldn't see her, maybe she wasn't really there. She would stand invisible in his presence and bite her lip until she could taste the warmth of blood.

※

The day had lost the fullness of light. There was enough of a wind to lift a layer of damp leaves into a brief, dispirited dance.

Ingrid hobbled across the quad again, this time to the history department. Jonathan's light was still on. She watched it from the walkway long enough to see that he was alone.

She entered his office without knocking and fell into his ancient, overstuffed armchair. Jonathan looked up from his desk and unhooked his wire glasses from behind his ears. "Hullo. Are you limping?"

"I twisted my bad ankle."

Jonathan stood and removed his blazer, rolling it into a sausage shape. He placed it on the ottoman at his feet, which he wheeled to Ingrid. "Here," he said, bending to lift her calf to the raised cushion. "You should keep it elevated."

"I got the money." Ingrid winced and adjusted her position. Jonathan gently moved her leg over and sat on the ottoman.

"When are you leaving?"

"Ten days from tomorrow."

"Will you have time to prepare your courses?"

"I don't know."

"Is this trip a good idea?"

Ingrid was chewing the inside of her cheek, doubting every idea that came to mind. "I'm not sure."

"Don't go, Ingrid. Not now."

"I think Templeton has found something he's been looking for for a long time."

"Good for him. Do something for me, will you? Think about moving in with me. You're hardly around anyway. That apartment of yours is going to waste. We'll be roommates."

"Don't be insane."

"Just think about it and try to remember the pickings are slim in our business—I think we're lucky to have found each other in a sea of myopic, sexually frustrated overachievers."

Ingrid laughed. "That's exactly what I am. I fooled you completely."

Jonathan's hands joined together and hung limply below his navel in a schoolboy posture that Ingrid called "the figleaf." He did this when he was unhappy. "Then I'll come to your place later?"

"No."

"No?"

"I'll call you."

Jonathan returned to his desk. "Here I've elevated your foot, given you my chair, proposed free rent, and my reward is the so-called Ingrid phone call, which rarely comes. How did my standing drop so suddenly?"

"Please, Jonathan. Don't."

"Don't what? Risk trying for more? You should do it once in a while. You might be happier."

Jonathan began to pack his briefcase. He was not only unhappy, he was angry; too angry to hear from her that it was no good, particularly when she didn't have the energy to tell him why. She felt both exhausted and giddy from the effort of the day, like an unfit soldier trying to complete an obstacle course. Jonathan now appeared to be the last obstacle. Let me go! She wanted to say. I am too weak for this! "My father has started crying," she said. "I don't know what's happening to him."

Jonathan wiped his glasses and rehooked them behind his ears. "Have you got something for the pain?"

"The pain?"

"Your ankle."

"Oh. Somewhere, yes."

"Take it. I have to teach now. Call me later."

"Will you let me stay in this chair for a while? I feel so tired."

Jonathan gathered his things, touched Ingrid's cheek and then bent to kiss it. When he left, he switched off the overhead, leaving her in the half-light of his desk lamp. She watched the reflection of the room in the window. The night beyond was invisible. She dug in her briefcase for a pen and wrote a note on the back of an orange campus flyer saying she was going to be busy this next week, that perhaps they should leave things for now.

Hotel Salama

*F*inn woke alone, although there had been someone there earlier. Thinking about what might have transpired between them, he slipped on his white plastic sandals and walked down to the seawall. It was not quite morning; the muezzin had not yet sounded the first prayer. The sky and the sea were flat, the houses he passed oyster gray and silent. His sandals slapped along the seawall that, in an hour or two, would be noisy with fish selling. Finn pushed his arms up into the air and yawned. He was still a little drunk. The girl had been drunker.

The tide had left his dinghy high on the beach. A few yards away, the anchor lay on the sand. He cupped his hands under the bow and swiveled her toward the surf, taking the rope over his shoulder and walking down to the water. The dinghy almost skipped behind him.

Knee-deep in the calm bay, Finn pushed the boat into the water. The surface rippled only slightly. He floated awhile before lowering the oars and then he rowed leisurely, letting himself shoot, glide and slow almost to a stop before plunging the oars in again. As the beach receded, the thatched roofs of the village came into view. He took in the island's changing composition sleepily, thinking of absolutely nothing until he bumped up gently against *Uma*. Jonah was asleep on her deck with a kikoi over his head. Finn pulled it off as he passed and Jonah mumbled something.

"Up, up," Finn said as he lowered himself into the cabin, closing his eyes to adjust to the darkness. Below, the galley was in order, the counters and cabinets wiped down, the floor swept. Finn cut two slabs of bread, buttered them, and boiled water for tea.

The two men sat as they always did, across from each other but not exactly, so both could see the water.

"I thought we'd go up to Kifi," Finn said in Swahili. "See what they've been catching."

Jonah stared ahead dully, still half asleep. "Not much there now. Not yet," he said, dropping his unfocused gaze to his tea, which he raised to his mouth and then scowled at. "Why you must boil the life out of water, I don't know."

"There aren't many big ones, but there're enough small fish for bait."

"We'll fish for marlin, then?" Jonah woke up a little. Marlin were the God and glory of the season.

"Mmm . . ." Finn swallowed his bread with a gulp of tea. "The season has to start sometime." They sat and drank their tea while the sun poured color back into the water. Finn leaned over to get a look at *Tarkar*, moored next to *Uma*.

If he hadn't known him all his life, Finn would have said that Nelson, *Tarkar*'s captain, was imported along with the boat. He was a good fisherman but recently he had grown lazy. His latest employer was a fellow European, but unlike Nelson, this man was a real *mzungu*. Under his guidance, Nelson's habits had changed. For one thing, he no longer rose with the sun. *Tarkar* never left at dawn with *Uma* because she could get out to sea in half the time. *Uma's* engine chugged along noisily as *Tarkar* blew by her, humming along at her own sweet frequency, leaving *Uma* upset and rocking in her wake.

Finn found he often viewed *Tarkar* from behind. This gave him a good perspective of her rig, on which *Tarkar's* owner, Stanley Wicks, had spent a small fortune. Last season Wicks had brought back carbon fiber rods from Europe, which were supposed to be more flexible and sensitive than fiberglass. Wicks talked about them like the second coming but Finn was skeptical of this worship of the new. Wicks' revered "product advancement" meant only that more and more of your work was done for you. Soon enough, your expertise was stolen from you. *Tarkar's* crew stood on deck like kings, but they were losing their feel for the fish and generally followed *Uma's* direction in the morning. High technology hadn't given Nelson the confidence he had always lacked; he still trusted Finn's instincts more than all that equipment.

Finn tossed the last swallow of tea into the water. He stood and stretched before going to inspect the engine. The hotel needed fish for the week. He studied the pale sky, slapped a flea from his forearm and momentarily regretted leaving Kip on shore. She was pregnant—might drop any minute—and was so big now he didn't have the heart to move her from his bed, much less give her a flea bath. She was a strange, water-loving cat, the only female that brought him good luck. It was useless trying to get rid of the fleas anyway; they were everywhere on the island. For a while, after visitors and various women complained, he had dutifully bathed Kip and flea-bombed his house every few weeks.

But he never really minded the fleas, and after Kip got pregnant, he forgot about them altogether. Besides, with the house infested, visitors were more reluctant to barge in. Instead, they yelled from the doorway. Finn heard the voices from inside but often kept quiet until they went away.

Finn reached into the supplies closet for the petrol funnel and poured ten liters into the tank. Not many people on the island attached themselves to cats, or even allowed them inside their homes. There were too many of them to be considered pets. The prophet Mohammed had liked them, so they flourished under his protection, eating and breeding and prowling along the beach. But they were nothing you wanted in your home. Most of the islanders were good enough Moslems to leave them alone.

In the local café, Finn often stared at a piece of driftwood that hung on the wall. Into its soft, sea-worn surface the owner had carved his own proverb, as if to give direction to the many discussions that took place under his thatched roof. It read: *Individuals divine history; some create and some destroy.* Over strong, sweet coffee, the men who frequented the café agreed without exception that Mohammed was a shining embodiment of the former group: he had given them the blessed Koran. Mohammed, a man who could neither read nor write, had transcribed the text of the Koran in its entirety, as it was told to him by the Lord. It was one of the miracles of creation. The other group, the destroyers, was represented by Satan and his legions of nonbelievers. This group was harder to determine, especially as their once simple island grew more complex. For instance, it was a matter of contention to which group of individuals Finn's father belonged. In his time on the island, the sacrilegious Swede had both created *and* destroyed. Shop owners, fishermen and hotel workers debated vigorously in the cool morning hours, tossing Henrik Bergmann's fate into the air among them like a coin. As a boy, Finn sat and listened. Fatima made certain that he was allowed to hear all the arguments. With her instruction, he came to understand the honor of being told the truth about this man who was many things, the most distant and least probable, his own father.

Shop owners, who had the most time to debate, often raised the topic. "Bergmann knew about the cats, yet he did not understand."

"If he did not understand about the cats," another continued, "how could he understand Mohammed?"

"Had he understood," still another said, "boss man Bergmann might still be around." About this, there was consensus and, for a moment, peace.

"Bergmann was ignorant, not evil," a hotel worker volunteered when the peace grew dull. (Hotel workers were more generous with Bergmann than the others. After three decades, they still prospered from the industry he had created.)

The orthodox and elderly opposition refused to accept this. "Bergmann was possessed by *majini*," an old man croaked. "The evil spirits of Satan."

The man next to him nodded and spit. "He was infected with *ghaflah*."

"The Lord has mercy," a hotel bartender said. "So should you. Forgive the man!"

"He has suffered enough," someone else murmured.

"It is *we* who are suffering under his legacy," a hotheaded youth asserted. "Our island is crawling with the unfaithful."

The conversation turned into a pell-mell forum for general opinions, many of which were spoken simultaneously. "We work to increase their pleasure. And what of our pleasure?"

"Our pleasure is with our faith. Only those who look away from the Lord are weakened."

"We have gotten stronger since Bergmann, and richer. How

could I afford two wives before I worked at Salama? I toast to Bergmann!"

"We are their slaves!"

Later, in the dead afternoon hours on the beach, a few fishermen still argued. They lay side by side under their long thatch shelter like cigars, their voices swelling and floating back into the village.

Finn heard all the stories in time. On such a peaceful island, stories of conflict were welcome. Each story pushed Finn's father further and further from his own life until he became a fable that even his son could tell. It went something like this:

When Henrik Bergmann first arrived on the island, his face had aged enough for strangers to know what kind of man he was. It was a face on which everything was written: distant burrowing eyes, so deeply set they were sensed more than seen; a high brow that fell in bony planes down to his stubborn cliff of a jaw; thick, blond hair brutally and unevenly cropped. (Later, the islanders were not surprised to see Bergmann hack away at his own hair with a pair of blunt shears.)

But the tall blond man came speaking Swahili, which made it hard for the islanders to remember what they had seen in his face before he spoke. He came wanting to build something large: a hotel, he said. A nice place for foreigners to stay on vacation. A place for them to renew themselves.

"A holy place?" one of the men asked.

"Sort of," Bergmann answered. *Sawa sawa.* The men nodded. Some of them smiled. He needed one hundred men. He would pay them to work for him. The wages he offered were high. Men volunteered. They had never made such a wage.

Materials arrived from other places. Doorknobs, plates of glass, things never seen before on the island. At the docks,

Bergmann sat under a broad-brimmed hat and waved a long mangrove branch as if he were a conductor. As crates were off-loaded, he married the strongest men to the heaviest boxes and then rode at the rear of the groaning donkey train, humming all the way back to the building site. Forty more men were sent by dhow to Tomba Island to cut blocks of rag coral, while the remaining forty hauled baskets of sand from the dunes. In one month, the men completed the sprawling foundation that included ten luxury bungalows as well as a central structure with additional rooms, an expansive dining room, a kitchen and indoor and outdoor bars. The men realized with some unease that they were building a structure bigger than the biggest mosque.

This *mzungu,* this white man, was rich. Very rich. In the wooden crates that came on the big dhows from Mombasa were linen and silver, yards of fine white cloth and exquisite glass bottles. In the heaviest crates were mahogany and brick. Chocolate and chewing gum started drifting back from the site into the village and the children quickly devised a barter system for these new delicacies. Bergmann's ability to produce such goods gave him a status that rivaled that of any of the three village chiefs. For a year, he continually produced things no one had known existed.

It was two years later when Bergmann left the island and returned soon after with a small, yellow-haired child. He gathered the island's male volunteers and, holding his curly-haired infant, announced that he needed workers, permanent workers, for the hotel: men to cook, clean, serve, sail boats, pour drinks. The first hundred volunteers had priority if they were willing to learn a little English. There was some mumbling of protest about this. English was the language of the unfaithful. Bergmann disarmed the men by smiling. He went on to explain that the men who had contact with the guests would have to be able to say a few things—they would have to be able to greet and answer basic questions. Nothing much. A few of the men nodded in understanding.

For the sake of simplicity, Bergmann continued, they'd have to make up names for themselves that English-speaking people could pronounce and remember; easy names like Jackson, Johnson, Hamilton. They weren't *real* names after all.

"What is the name of the child?" one of them asked.

"Finn," Bergmann answered.

"Finn?"

"A name from the north."

"Can we be named Finn?"

"I'd rather not," Bergmann replied.

"So there will be only one Finn on the island."

"Yes, just one."

"Here we share names! Many of us have the same name. Abdul, Habib, Ali."

"And you can do the same with your hotel names."

Most of the men shrugged and chose the same few names Bergmann suggested that sunny afternoon.

"Who is the child?" they wanted to know. "Where is its mother?"

"The child," Bergmann told them with his eyes on the sand, "is my son. His mother is no longer with us." Then Bergmann turned and walked away.

After they were trained, the men shuffled to work in white uniforms and shoes they had crushed at the heels. They didn't fasten their pants properly. Bergmann told them they looked like delinquent hospital workers. They shrugged—what did they know of hospitals?—and neither fastened their pants nor pushed their feet all the way into their shoes. They respected

Bergmann, but there was a limit to the compliance he could demand. The pants were not so comfortable between the legs and the shoes made their feet sweat. Though the work itself wasn't hard, the pants, the shoes and the unfamiliar hours made it strenuous. The hotel didn't operate on the same clock as the village. Late nights were like the pants and the shoes. So were late mornings and the occasional missed prayer. A few months later, so was the occasional late-night beer. All these things traveled from different places, but arrived together somehow. Alcohol wasn't normally allowed for Moslems, but working until eleven or twelve at night wasn't normal. Together, the beer and the hours formed a nucleus separate from the life the men shared with their families and their village. Around this hard little seed, a new organism began to grow.

Bergmann called his hotel "Salama," the Swahili word for peace. It sat perched above the Indian Ocean like a tropical bird, with the bulk of the structure flanked by two wings of private bungalows. Each bungalow was surrounded by lush, exotic foliage that blocked out everything but the sea before it. Sweet frangipani, jasmine and wild orchid scented the air. Above, coconut palms swayed and rustled like gentle protectors.

No one had really believed "guests" would come to the hotel, or that people would come to Salama from so far away, arriving by yacht and by seaplane. The word spread in Nairobi among the expat crowd and soon weekend forays to the coast became fashionable. From farther afield, Europeans and Americans came to swim in the warm sea and rid themselves of safari dust. The hotel workers sniggered at the pith helmets worn by these pale, perspiring hunters.

Bergmann paid his workers every week, and one hundred

steady incomes launched the island into its first complex econ-
omy. Two more shops opened up and carried, along with grains,
flour and sugar, the kinds of things the people at the hotel liked.
Once or twice a day, rich hotel guests would wander back into
the village, where they explored the mosques and bought things
from the shops. Now some of the crates from Mombasa went
back to the shops in the village, where they were stocking Fanta,
Big G bubble gum and four kinds of Cadbury chocolate. Island
children learned to run to the beaches when they heard the distant hum of a motor.

Bergmann trained his five most responsible employees to run the
place in his absence, teaching them about telephones, accounting, ordering forms and the many strict standards to which
Salama would always adhere. In beautiful italic script, Bergmann
himself inscribed two handsome pieces of wood with meticulous
lists in both English and Swahili. The lists hung in the office like
manifestos, describing everything from room cleaning to the
slicing of breakfast fruit. Finally, he showed them how envelopes
came from Sweden with papers inside that represented money,
that the money came from his partner at the bank in Stockholm.
The men marveled at the fact that this single piece of paper
transformed into one hundred salaries. They wondered among
themselves if this could be called magic. "Everything is set up,"
Bergmann told them. "All you must do is keep perfect records
and you will continue to get your money from the bank. If you
do a good job, that money will increase and you will become rich.
But," Bergmann said gravely, "if you break a single rule or neglect to follow a single instruction, the whole system will fall
apart and the first thing that will happen is you will be fired. My
partner at the bank has all your names and knows everything

about you. If I am not here to fire you, he will. But you will do nothing to deserve that. You are the proud chiefs of this hotel. You have power that you must use wisely. If you are wise, nothing will go wrong. You will all go to heaven," Bergmann added, "or wherever it is you want to go."

After two years of smooth operation, Bergmann's vigil over his workers eased. They performed admirably. Bergmann rewarded them generously, according to merit. The rank-and-file system had turned them into conscientious, industrious members of hotel society, leaving Bergmann finally free to smoke his Dunhill Partagas and spend some time with his guests. It was at this point that he let himself relax and reconsider aspects of the island he was living on. One troubling aspect was the encroachment of felines on the hotel kitchen and garbage area. They had recently started to invade the bungalows through open windows, spreading their fleas and contaminating the polished floors with their damp, sandy paws. They had started lapping up the milk left on early-morning tea trays outside the bungalows. It was both unhygienic and unacceptable.

Islanders believed that it was often in peaceful, idle moments that the *majini,* the evil spirits, crept into the human soul. They must have invaded Henrik Bergmann in this way, slipping into his daydreams, singing lullabies into his lazy ear as he lolled in his hammock. *Build something else,* they whispered. A structure much smaller than the hotel, so simple one man could build it by himself. When the idea took hold, Bergmann set up shop in a hotel storage shack, where he worked alone when the rest of the island was either sleeping or praying.

"What is it?" his houseboy, Abdul, asked.

"It is a raft," Bergmann answered.

Abdul considered this. "A raft for what?"

"A raft for the water."

"Small enough for baby Finn," Abdul suggested.

"No, it's not for Finn."

Abdul watched, squatting, arms crossed. After a while he got bored and went away. Bergmann had cut down twenty evenly sized mangrove poles and bound the long, lean trunks together with twine, rope and banana leaves. No one knew what he was doing, or how he was doing it. They only reconstructed it later, after it was too late. Boss man Bergmann worked at night, his craggy brow furrowed and, at times, demented with purpose.

At the end of the week, the raft was completed. Bergmann constructed a large box next to the raft, with the leftover mangrove poles, with roughly the same surface area as the raft. He covered it with a thick layer of banana leaves, which, bound to four horizontally laid, 90-degree mangrove poles hinged by sisal on one side, served as a lid.

Bergmann owned a racing yacht that had won an Olympic medal for the Danish sailing team in 1928. The boat was flawless. Bergmann kept it moored in the harbor, where it swung with the tide like a dancer. He planned to charter it personally for the guests, take them for sunset meals and serve them fresh prawns and endive salad. But when he rowed his dinghy out one choppy morning, he gave the boat only perfunctory attention. He had come for something else. For those who might see him from the beach, he put on a deceptive little show. He wiped a few surfaces, polished the wheel, a few brass fittings. When he left an hour later, he took along with him a thick canvas sail bag, which he folded into a square and sat on while he rowed back to shore, as if to cushion his behind.

It was with this bag that he stalked the cats that night, finding them where they ate, slept, and shat around the hotel, picking them up by the scruff of their necks, dropping them into the bag. He collected cats until they became heavy and noisy and then he headed back to his hut. By the flicker of a storm lantern he emptied the contents of the bag into the pen where he had earlier dumped hotel dinner leftovers and a couple of fish he had bought from little Boni that morning. Bergmann closed the lid and waited. Screeches quieted into guzzling, chewing sounds. He went out for another bagful.

He gathered forty-two cats before he nailed the lid shut. It was a sizable number, a respectable first load. With the thick rope he had attached to two sides of the raft, he dragged the weighty box to the sea like an old mule.

It was a moonless night and a dark sea that swallowed the raft. The current of the ebb tide was as strong as a river, and the raft picked up speed and moved swiftly away from him like a shadow. Watching it, he sat back on the sand and lit a cigar.

Henrik Bergmann knew a lot about the island, but he did not know everything. He had only heard about a *mganga*—a healer more powerful than a witch who lived in the village. He did not know that the *mganga* was an albino woman. He had not looked into her pale eyes or seen her hair in the sunlight. Even in the village, few saw her. As a child she had escaped the traditional communal attention village children received. The baby with crossed blue eyes had been kept inside for as long as possible. Eyes like that cursed whatever they looked at. No one but the family saw the child and even then they did not look her in the eye. The fate of the child was determined one silvery night when she wandered to the center of the village and stopped in front of the head chief's hut, where she stood in the doorway, moonlight shining on her bright hair. She stood a long time in silence and then started to make a faint whining noise. The chief's wife woke and saw the white-haired child with its crossed eyes and closed mouth. The whining sound emanated from somewhere around her head. Her ears? The chief's wife covered herself and tried to rouse her husband. Their baby was sick with malaria and was sleeping for the first time in hours. When the child stopped whining and went to the back of the hut, the baby started to cry. The baby's mother leapt out of bed, but the child reached the baby first and put her pale, ghostly hand on its forehead. It was hot with fever. The mother watched, her hands at her mouth. Soon, the baby stopped crying. The albino child curled up on the ground and slept. By morning the baby's fever was gone.

The next rainy season, when malaria came again to the village, the child was sought out by the head chief and taken from her home. After she had saved two more infants from fever, a large hut was built for the girl, and those with fever came to sleep in the hut. What had been suspected was true: the child was a *mganga,* a healer. She went from mat to mat and held her dry hands on burning cheeks and foreheads. She slept occasionally, wound around herself like a salamander. In the day, she vanished to the alcove in the back of the hut and saw no one.

As she grew older, the chiefs requested her counsel often. They were happy just to have her sit quietly in the dark corner of the meeting hut. Even stone silent, the *mganga*'s presence on the island was formidable.

⚜

From what he had heard about this *mganga,* Bergmann assumed the village had a taste for drama. He also assumed that all of the cats on the island were the same. It hadn't occurred to him that the cats, two in particular, would be missed.

The *mganga* did not need to find the abandoned hut where the remainders of the raft building were still in evidence. She did not need to see the strange geometric tracks to the sea. She knew where her cats had gone.

She pierced the night with a wail that she sustained for a quarter of an hour. Then she fled from her hut at the edge of the village with a chalk-white face and ran through the center of the village, stomping the earth in front of the chiefs' huts. She was livid. They were all in danger of the white evil that lived in the *mzungu,* Henrik Bergmann. The white evil would ruin them, incur the wrath of wandering spirits, make their own spirits wander after death. There would be no peace.

No one had ever heard her say so much. The chiefs stood before her with their eyes lowered. They waited for her to finish. After a long silence, the head chief said, "Bergmann gives us jobs." The *mganga*'s blue eyes grew wide and crossed even more. The head chief stared at her, unable to look away. She stared back at him for a long moment and then screamed a heart-stopping scream that chased his hand to his chest. She began running around and around in a circle, making grunting noises and kicking up dust. She came to a sudden halt in front of the chiefs.

"He gives you only hunger for things you did not need before," she told them. She stared at each of them, forcing each in turn to raise his eyes to hers. Each chief looked from one of her eyes to the other, unsure of which one was looking at him. "He steals your souls," she hissed. "And he has stolen my cats."

The chiefs did not entirely understand why the *mganga* was so upset, but they didn't press her. Her cats were missing. Do what you must do, they said. And they went back to their huts to sleep.

Henrik Bergmann was warned.

"Nonsense," he told Abdul. But he watched where he walked, checked his bed for snakes and poured all his own water. He survived that day and the next and then on the third day carried on much as before, putting the *mganga,* the cats and the curse out of his mind. On the afternoon of the third day, Henrik Bergmann rowed back to his yacht to return the canvas bag. His dinghy stayed tied to the yacht all day and through the night. When Bergmann hadn't returned the next day, Abdul took a dhow out to the yacht, but there was no trace of his employer. The boy sat down on the edge of the boat and stared into the water, trying to imagine what might have happened to Bergmann. It was the *mganga*'s curse, he was sure.

"His heart stopped beating," he announced back on the island. "He fell overboard." Abdul walked down the long beach every morning for a week, hoping to find a body to confirm his story. But no one ever saw Bergmann again. The islanders were sad for little Finn. They were also sad that Bergmann didn't live to hear that the raft of cats had landed safely on neighboring Tomba Island, which, in a short period, they proceeded to colonize.

Soon after, the sister of the *mganga* appointed herself to take care of baby Finn. She was called Fatima. Some referred to her as *Mama Salama,* or "mother of peace," because she had been called by Allah to mend the tear between the Bergmann family and the islanders. The islanders came to respect Finn as he matured under Fatima's native influence, trusting the towheaded child was, in some ways, like them.

Finn reached for the Tusker beer bottle under Jonah's sleeping berth.

"Jonah," he called up the stairs. "You were drinking last night?"

"You know how it is," Jonah answered from above. Finn put the bottles in the rubbish bin and sat down to check the rods.

"And your wife, did you see her?"

"No, not this last night."

"She was looking for you. She said she doesn't know where to find you anymore."

"Of course not." Jonah threw him a thick rope from the roof of the boat. "You know how it is. When you drink you do not always go home."

"Brother, the difference is, I have no wife."

"Were you to take a wife, you would have big problems." Finn waved his hand by his ear. It was an old conversation. Jonah jumped down from the roof. "And last night? There was someone? I saw you and Danny at the hotel bar, up to no good."

"Maybe. I don't remember." The girl had left by the time he woke up. He could not picture her face; he did not try. "The next trip will be a long one, Jonah."

"A long trip. Next week? I did not tell my wife."

"I told her."

"So we will go for marlin." Jonah grinned.

Finn nodded. "More marlin than last season, hopefully." This season had started out well, but then engine trouble grounded them for weeks. Getting parts for a Ferrari boat engine—getting parts for any engine in Africa—was problematic. For *Uma*'s part, Finn contacted a dealer in Mombasa who contacted the Ferrari supplier in Milan who had the part shipped, supposedly by air freight. Technically, it should have taken no more than two weeks for the part to reach Mombasa. It would stop in Cairo and then proceed to Nairobi. From there, one of the puddle-jumper Cessnas that made regular trips to the island would get it to Pelat. But once on the African continent, the part slowed, ceasing to obey Western laws of efficiency.

Finn no longer expected even relative timeliness. He had been through it too many times. When *Uma*'s cooling tank had ex-

ploded last season, Jonah scrambled to the engine while Finn sat
down and closed his eyes because, for all intents and purposes,
the season was over for them. Finn clenched his fists and un-
clenched them. He let his head roll around on his neck and then
stood up and stared down at the boat's planks, down to the engine, to the soul of *Uma,* and climbed into the dinghy. Once on
shore, he had pulled the dinghy only a few feet up onto the beach
and then walked home, trancelike, leaving Jonah to swim. Jonah
was happy enough to swim. He had known Finn for many years.
He knew his temper.

Being separated from the sea had profound effects on Finn. He
stayed in his house, became totally inert. He drank and smoked
cigarettes, pot, hash—anything he could get his hands on. In his
altered condition, he read airport novels that tourists had left at the
hotel. Every day seemed to bring him closer to death.

Half-naked on his veranda, he'd sat with a paperback folded
over his thigh, Kip on his lap, the telephone and an overflowing
ashtray on the table next to him. From where he sat he could see
the hull of *Uma* beached below. He was waiting. When the phone
rang he picked it up, keeping his eyes fixed on the boat.

"It's Ramin," the caller said. "Mr. Bergmann, it seems the
part was sent from Italy three weeks ago. That's what their
records show, but you know the Italians. I wish I could tell you
where it was."

"It's probably in front of you," Finn said quietly. "I know how
you run things down there, Ramin. Don't give me this about the
Italians; you wouldn't know your ass from a generator. That place
of yours is a mess. The part has been there for a week, at least.
Take another look."

"Mr. Bergmann, the part is not here. My workmen have
looked already. Twice."

"Offer a reward—from me. They have no reason to find the part for you, you don't pay those poor s.o.b.'s anything. If I were them, I wouldn't bother looking either." Finn scratched behind Kip's ears. "Offer whoever locates the part a thousand shillings."

Finn heard Ramin draw in his breath. "That's very generous, Mr. Bergmann, but I'm afraid you'd be wasting their time."

"I know something you don't, Ramin. Offer it. Call me back when you find it, because you will find it, Ramin." Finn hung up the phone and lit a cigarette. He continued to stroke Kip while he stared at the sea.

When the part arrived three days later, Jonah called Finn from the door. Finn stubbed out his cigarette, draped Kip around his neck and strapped on his sandals. It was almost the end of high season. After they put *Uma* back together, they brought in another marlin, in addition to the two they had caught before the boat broke down. *Tarkar* had seven marlin and sailfish.

This year would be different. After he made a quick trip to Nairobi to pick up a new carburetor, *Uma* would be in good shape; Finn had inspected every inch of her. Nothing was going to blow. *Tarkar* wouldn't know what had hit her. She would have to start getting up and out before dawn if she wanted to have a chance against *Uma*. Finn had been dreaming about big fish; he knew he would find them.

The Second Hotel

*S*tanley Wicks was jolted awake at dawn by *Uma*'s gunshot start. He lay awake until sunrise, then got out of bed. His wife mumbled into her pillow and stretched a sunburned arm to the place Stanley had vacated.

"Sleep some more, darling," Stanley said. "It's still early."

"Mmm. Be down soon." She was never down before ten-thirty or eleven.

The Wickses' house was fully staffed for high season, which they had for years spent in Africa, missing the English winter completely. Stanley had taken up some projects that kept him busy and justified the time away from home. Now they had come for good. Leaving England was a liberation. After farming out his estate responsibilities, he governed his little province in absentia. Anyone was welcome to visit them on the island; the Wickses could not be accused of isolationism. A few friends did visit, flying to Africa on a drunken whim. One or two liked it so much they never left.

Stanley generally rose between nine and nine-thirty in the morning. It was the least complicated, most satisfying time of his day. The unwavering regularity of his morning routine set him right, no matter how severely he had polluted himself the night before. He often forgot when he came to bed, and so, rather than risk waking before his requisite six hours, he slept until the sun reached the top third of the crack in the wooden shutter on his side of the bed. Daisy slept longer. She wasn't fully awake until lunchtime.

Stanley wrapped an orange kikoi around his waist, native-style. Over it he buttoned a pale pink cotton shirt and then lowered himself down the steep stairs to the capacious main room where their long wood dining table was set for two, with sliced papaw and lime, a thermos of coffee and a smaller thermos of warm milk. He smiled and pressed his hand into the softness of his stomach, creating the waistline he'd had at University. Three pairs of tall wooden shutters were opened to the sea. The water glistened before him. A vivid, sparkling day with a soft wind blowing the bright flowers and palms. The view never ceased to enthrall him.

"Good morning, Jackson." Stanley cheerfully greeted his new houseboy and eyed an envelope to the side of his place setting.

"Good morning, Mr. Wicks. This letter has come under the door for you."

"Thank you, Jackson. Call me Stanley, will you? I prefer it."

"Yes, sir."

"I think I'll have fried eggs this morning, sunnyside up. Bacon, two slices of toasted brown bread and juice. Grapefruit, if there is any."

"Yes, Mr. Wicks." Jackson bowed slightly and disappeared down the stairs to the large kitchen below. Stanley leaned back in his chair and let his eyes idle on the water. He sat in silence for a minute and then poured himself some coffee and yawned. "Melissa!"

"Mr. Wicks?" A voice rose from downstairs.

"Bring the baby." Stanley sipped his coffee until a young woman entered the room, holding a child. "Hello, Harry." Stanley held out his hands to receive the child. "Have you been behaving yourself? Have you?" Stanley cooed and bounced the baby on his knee. It laughed until he reached with one hand for his coffee, gripping the child too tightly with the other. The baby howled.

"Ohhh, Harry, don't cry. Why are you crying? What's wrong, my little boy? Are you hungry?" Stanley turned to Melissa. "Is he hungry?"

"He's had his breaky."

"Why is he crying?"

"He's in a bad temper, that's all."

The girl was unhelpful. "Here, take him." Stanley handed the child to Melissa. She stared back at him with characteristic impudence. Stanley smiled. "You do a much better job with him." The baby continued to cry. Stanley raised an eyebrow at Melissa, who hadn't moved an inch. "Is this the best place for him?" Melissa got the message and walked to the corner of the large room and set the baby down into a bouncing chair on wheels. It had a tray and an abacus with colored beads. Harry's face was pinched and red. He sat with his legs hanging. He looked like a suffocated little frog. "Poor little chap is miserable," Stanley said, squeezing lime on his papaw. "What on earth makes them cry like that?"

Melissa was busy gathering toys from around the room. "Lookie here, Harry, look at this." She shoved a blue rabbit in his lap.

"Perhaps you should take him to the nursery. He might need changing."

Melissa scowled and lifted the baby from the bouncing chair and took him away. The sound of his wails grew rapidly faint. Stanley lit a cigarette and sipped his coffee.

By the time breakfast was served, Daisy had descended in her silk kimono. She sat across from Stanley at the table. Her face was puffy and as red from sunburn as Harry's was from crying. Stanley poured her coffee. She reached for his pack of cigarettes.

"Who's the letter from?"

"No idea."

Daisy put her hand out for the lighter. "So what's on for today?"

"I thought I'd take the speedboat to Kitali, see how things are coming. I haven't seen Gus for a while."

"I don't know how you talk to that man." Smoke billowed from Daisy's mouth. No elegant, side-blown emission, but an industrial smokestack. "But it's a lovely day for a ride."

"So you have no interest in joining me?"

"Can't. I'm lunching with Judy at Salama."

Stanley studied his wife. "Let's say hello to Harry, shall we? Melissa!" Stanley bellowed. "Bring Harry back!" A door from the back of the house opened and there was the sudden noise of wailing. Melissa entered the room with Harry, whose shrieks were now ear-piercing.

Daisy put her head in her hands. "Oh God, not now, Melissa." Melissa stood at the far end of the table, bouncing the baby. She looked from one parent to the other with the enthusiasm of an indentured servant.

"It's fine, Melissa. Daisy?"

"Stanley, please, I've got the most horrific headache." She put another cigarette between her lips and lit it with the last, extending her free hand for the envelope. Stanley slid the envelope out of her reach.

"Maybe not so much wine next time," Stanley advised quietly, folding and stuffing the envelope in his pocket.

"Melissa," Daisy said. "Take the child away. I'll look in on him later." Melissa and the child disappeared. The noise died out. "I'm sorry, darling, I'm just off-color this morning."

Stanley walked along the seawall to Salama, trying not to think about how off-color his wife was. He could not imagine what color she was, except sunburned. He waved at a passing dhow and felt cheered. The justice of it was that here, in this place he had discovered and come to love, it didn't matter what kind of woman, what kind of mother, Daisy was. She could do what she liked. She could keep eating like a cow and get as big as the *Hindenburg*. She could see her son for no more than ten excruciating minutes a day. No one here watched like they did in England. No one cared. Stanley had done what he could do. He had hired a nanny for Harry and had battened his own hatches.

As he rounded the bend in the seawall, the hotel came into view, splendid and white in the morning sun. This was the island's civilization, Stanley's lifeline. He ate at least one meal a day there, usually lunch at the outdoor grill. He could spend hours at one of the sturdy white tables, his toes dug into the sand and a canopy of bougainvillea vines over his head, the slight stirring of ocean air all around him. What an extraordinary feeling to have one's feet in the sand while eating a fresh lobster offset by crisp white linen. Daisy would be there for lunch that day. By the time he got back from Kitali, she'd be sleeping off the wine.

In front of Salama, floating in a blinding patch of sunstruck water, was the dark shape of *Tarkar*. Stanley shielded his eyes to better view his boat. From where he stood, he could make out Nelson's unevenly tanned bulk, moving around on the deck. A few darker bodies, too, all hard at work. Good. Stanley would have to go out with them for a few days, give his new rods a try. There was something better than carbon fiber now— aluminum oxide. Straight from the U.S. space program. Higher sensitivity, greater flex. They had lost three fish last year. This year they wouldn't lose any.

The rod came with a video on its use and maintenance. Stanley and Nelson had watched it together on Stanley's video machine, the only one on the island. Nelson sat in front of the screen and inched forward, narrating the demonstration. "Gaff the monster," he exploded. "Not that way, you idiot, both ends of the tail!"

Nelson had a passion for the sport. It was the only subject he could talk about at length, not because he was shy, but because it was all he knew. Matters unrelated to fishing left him quiet, with an uncomfortable, slightly confused expression on his face. Because fishing was the business they shared, Stanley found Nelson excessively talkative. The man was excessive in other ways too. He ignored Stanley's warnings about his food and alcohol consumption and Stanley found himself caught between annoyance and humility. He knew better than to condemn someone for his weakness. Nelson's weakness was harmless; his indulgence hurt only himself. Besides, his homeliness was a cockeyed blessing: there had been no complications with women, no parties on *Tarkar* while Stanley was away in England. Nelson was too fearful to take advantage. In that way he was unlike the other European men who lived on the island. To his friends back home, Stanley described these white Kenyans as African, through and through. They were unruly, particularly the men. Their lack of any sense of time would have ruined them in a first or even a second world country. How would they survive, open bank accounts, catch trains, when they could plan for nothing beyond the present and whatever appetite was tempting them at that moment?

At the hotel, the walkway was blocked with a crowd—Boni and his morning's catch, negotiating prices. Stanley stopped to watch. He seemed to have an endless supply of fish in his boat. Stanley peered over the side, looking for his tackle.

"Boni!" he called. "What are you using?" Boni grinned and stepped to the back of the boat. He held up a block of wood with nylon line and a hook attached to the end. Stanley shook his head. The man did everything with his hands. One had only to look at them; they were scarred with white lines, tough as leather. If he did this well with block and tackle, imagine what he'd do with something better. Stanley made a mental note to show Boni a wire line.

On the quay, Abdul was waiting for Stanley with the speedboat. Together they swept up the wide channels of the archipelago, passing between the white sands of Pelat and the green banks of neighboring Tomba, dense with mangrove. The trip to Kitali took roughly an hour, depending on the weather. This morning the air was still, the water calm; it would be a fast trip. Regardless of wind or weather, Abdul stood to steer the powerboat. The man had remarkable posture. Even with the boat at full throttle, he was as straight as a plank. Stanley found the combination of white noise and motion regenerative—thankfully, there was never an attempt to speak on the boat. He stood up when a clearing of *makute* roofs came into view.

Stanley mused, as he often did, about how this end of the island had a different feel to it. The quality of light and the exposure was softer and, perhaps because there weren't as many colors to distract the eye, the effect was often soothing. When the low rumble of the motor quit, Stanley felt disoriented. It was too quiet. Instead of calm, the place seemed lifeless. For an anxious moment he questioned his judgment. "Too late," he said to himself, but loud enough for Abdul to overhear.

"Bwana Wicks?" Abdul asked.

"Nothing, Abdul. Just a touch of buyer's remorse." He peered through his binoculars. Under an expanse of *makute* roof, the walls of his hotel were just beginning to rise. Around the periphery of the sheltered open spaces were a few meters of waist-high thatch. He found no movement under or around the roofs.

Abdul beached the boat and Stanley plodded up the steep dune to the half-finished huts. He found his contractor, Gus, and a few of the workers in the shade of the largest hut—what was to be the central dining area. Gus had come to the island from England to recover from the loss of his wife in an automobile accident. He had been driving. Though Stanley knew him only superficially, he was jarred by his transformation. In two years, Gus had gone from a soft-spoken, well-mannered Brit to a vulgar recluse. As Stanley approached, he found him sitting against one of the slender mangroves that anchored the walls in four corners, rolling a cigarette.

"Gus!" he called cheerfully.

Gus glanced up before licking his cigarette. "Hello, Stanley. You're perspiring."

"How's it coming?"

"It's not at the moment. We're out of nails."

Stanley touched his forehead. "Nails?"

"That's right."

"Good Lord, didn't we just get a shipment a few weeks ago?"

"It's going to be a big hotel."

Wicks said nothing. Gus cupped his hands to light his cigarette. "They've gone to good use, every one of them." He shook out his match. "It's a good thing you came today. I was figuring on two or three days before I made it to your side of the island. We're getting hungry over here. Slows things down."

"You need provisions, of course," Stanley said. "Tell me now and I'll have them sent down tomorrow."

"Potatoes, bread, long-life milk. Any produce you can muster. Tobacco and coffee."

"Potatoes, bread, milk, et cetera. Right." Stanley looked around. Gus waved a hand at him. "Have a sit-down, Stanley. Take a vacation from your vacation."

Stanley smiled, propped his sunglasses on his head and sat in the sand. "Do you have one of those for me?" Gus put his cigarette between his lips and began rolling another. "How's life in the bush?"

"Well, Stanley, it's quiet. No wine, no women. No trouble." Gus licked the cigarette, lit it and handed it to Stanley. "Come to think of it, that professor fellow was through here. Asked a few questions about your hotel. Good questions."

"What's he on about, any idea?"

Gus shook his head. "Funny fellow. I like him. He drank me under the table last night. Not easy to do. He's got some interesting ideas, none of which I remember."

Stanley dragged on his cigarette and decided that Templeton's ideas were not a conversational priority. "Tell me, Gus, do you miss England?"

"Not really. It's like a dream. I can't remember it clearly."

"Hmm, yes, it fades down here." One of the workers interrupted them to reach for Gus' tobacco.

"I just hope this place gets finished before the rains," Stanley said. "The walls and the plumbing anyway." He held his cigarette up and smelled it suspiciously. "Have you put stuff in these?"

"Just a bit."

"Hmm." Stanley exhaled and closed his eyes. A bit of hash meant a nap. Realizing he didn't really mind the thought of a nap, he scooted himself against a palm tree and waited for the sensation of loosening to begin. Against the darkness of his eyelids, he imagined the hotel building itself, rising into the air without the aid of human hands, as if by divine will. "Like Stonehenge," he whispered.

"What's that?" Gus asked.

Stanley opened his eyes and found Gus in his field of vision. "It's going to be a magnificent hotel, Gus," he said softly before drifting off to sleep.

An hour or so later, Stanley woke up, his head clotted with thick, slow thoughts. Gus was gone. He sat up and dug his knuckles into his eye sockets, wondering where Abdul had got to. To distract himself from the unpleasant feeling that, by napping, he had somehow transgressed, he pulled the envelope from his pocket and settled into the constructive business of reading.

To Stanley Wicks:

Do you know about the power of belief? Maybe you believe in God, in the old gray-haired man upstairs you once pictured as a child. Quite possibly you haven't thought deeply about him since because at about the same time you came to understand that comfort and security come from somewhere closer, that you could manufacture and purchase your deities. Belief, in your life, is just a word.

Perhaps I misjudge you. If so, don't take offense. As a fellow

Englishman I ask you not to make the mistakes others from our country have made, thinking the intellect and the pound are stronger than belief. You are farther from home than you imagine. It's a lovely island but it is also an angry island.

Here they believe in witches and ghosts and curses and more than any of it they believe in the existence of evil. Real evil. Not devils with forks but invisible wisps that easily pass through solid matter. These innocuous little wisps begin to cloud the soul. It is when God is no longer visible in the soul that the presence of evil is known. Evil takes the form of an obstacle. A roadblock. We in the West would not necessarily recognize it, but for these people, evil is as frightening for what it takes away as for what it can become. It is surprising what can become evil.

While you feel like a pioneer, alone out here on the edge of the world with a resplendent vision—know there has been another, that you are not the first. Be careful. If you choose to ignore me, know that the dreams you have at night, the feelings of doubt that visit you in the course of a day are to be heeded. Do not continue to build. We are all limited, but we are not all conscious of our limits. Pay attention to doubt. This is a friendly warning but I would suggest you heed it as a threat.

> Sincerely,
> Nick Templeton

By nightfall, with the help of a little wine, Wicks was able to forget the letter. He slipped into bed with his wife almost happily. That night he dreamed he was asleep. He must have been sleepwalking in his dream when someone asked him to make a decision. Something urgent. But his eyes refused to open. He could not see what he needed to see in order to make the decision. *Damn it,* he thought, *I'm asleep.* Who can be asking me to do something when I'm asleep? He woke too early and went downstairs gloomily, wondering who the hell Nick Templeton thought he was.

The Chichester

As his base, Templeton kept a room at the Chichester Hotel in Nairobi. It was the only information Ingrid had, the only contact he had left with the department. His last letter had been postmarked from Pelat, an island roughly two hundred miles north of Mombasa, which she would reach by plane after catching the overnight train to the coast. With luck, she would arrive the next day.

She landed in Nairobi at dawn, dropping through a cloudless melon-colored sky that seemed larger than Egypt, larger than any sky she'd ever seen. She instructed a cabdriver to take her to the Chichester and collapsed into the thick torpor of travel. The air was mild, and even at this early hour, there were bicycles and people along the roadside. She realized that by an act of pure will, she was once again far away. As soon as her funding was secure, she had pressed to leave Michigan ahead of schedule.

The night before she left, she had wrapped herself in a woolen blanket and lay on her couch in the dark while Jonathan stood on

her doorstep. Finally, he had stopped knocking and slid an envelope under the door. She had watched it from her cocoon until she
was too tired to be curious. In the morning, she pushed it under
the rug with the toe of her slipper. Then she packed a duffel bag
with clothes and a backpack with her PC, a hardback notebook,
Templeton's books on Swahili culture and a few others on the roots
of Islam, a copy of the Koran in both English and Arabic, two lip-
sticks and some chewing gum for the plane. When she was done,
she called a taxi and sat on her duffel to wait for an amount of time
that was too short to read and too long to think about anything but
what she might have forgotten. A faint voice inside her made her
leap up and turn on NPR. *I think I am afraid. I think that's what this
is.* In the middle of the hourly news report, the voice grew louder.
She waited nervously as it grew louder still. It seemed on the verge
of actually saying something, something unpleasant. When the
taxi honked, the voice rocketed out of her.

On her way out the door, she retrieved the envelope from under
the rug and held it all the way to the airport, tapping its sharp corner against her knee. She waited until she was on the plane to open
it. It was a photograph of the two of them taken by some waiter at
a restaurant. They were laughing at the camera, a bottle of wine between them. On the back Jonathan had written, "Hard evidence of
happiness." She slid the photo into one of her books on Swahili culture and for the remainder of the flight used it as a bookmark.

The Chichester was a converted estate run by an elderly British
couple, a sprawling structure with a comfortable lobby, dining
room and bar in the main house, and guest rooms that unfolded off
an open-air wing that bent around the garden, forming a horseshoe
with the main house. As soon as she arrived, Ingrid went straight

to the hotel's office to see if she could book a seat on the train to Mombasa. An elderly, slightly confused British man in his pajamas informed her that there were no trains available until Wednesday. This was Sunday, he noted with some surprise, removing his glasses to clean them. "It's rather easy to lose track," he explained. She thanked him, slung her bag over her shoulder and went off to find her room, having no idea what she would do for three days.

The rooms were no more than a large shoe box with a door, a window and a bed. Most of them had makeshift closets; a few had sinks. At the end of the walkway there were two communal bathrooms toward which guests shuffled in flip-flops or untied shoes.

In room eleven, Ingrid had the longest, most perilous passage to the bathrooms. Insects patrolled the walkway: large spiders and beetles. Trapped at one end of the horseshoe, she experimented her first night with warning sounds and discovered that nocturnal insects weren't threatened by clicking or hissing. They scurried across the rust-red tiles inches from her feet, darting out of nowhere as she passed, slithering into the darkness of the garden beyond the lit walkway.

The garden was more tropical than tidy, which was why, Ingrid guessed, it was so infested. In the morning, she wandered through its cheerful chaos, past the lacy mimosa trees to the purple blooms of a jacaranda. Along the trail were passion flowers and hibiscus roses. Trained along trellises were vines of bougainvillea, their clusters of magenta blossoms hanging heavy and bright against the white walls of the main house.

Ingrid sat on a stone in the garden with her journal, waiting for breakfast. Unfamiliar smells surrounded her. Meat was cooking in the kitchen, masking the sweet smell of the garden. She wrote: "I am here. I am early. I am tired. I am trying not to think beyond the facts because I am too tired to understand why I am here early." She suspected that she wanted to catch Templeton making his final escape—to witness how he would do it, and toward what.

"I'm not trying to escape," he had insisted before he left. "I'm not running from anything. You can't presume the motives for the things I do—you can't even guess at them."

"You're not coming back, are you?"

Templeton smiled. "Now, why do you say that?"

"Because I've been watching you. You know you're not going back to the university. You're ready for something else. I want to know what it is."

Templeton's eyes lost their focus. "It's a feeling, really. That's all it is at this point. I would like to tell you more but I can't. It's in the periphery. Sometimes I catch sight of it when I'm looking at something else. But then it's gone."

"Describe it."

"Dear girl."

"How will I find you?"

"I'll send you something. But you've done well, Ingrid. You can take your own direction."

"No. I can't. The department doesn't like me."

"You mean they don't like *me*."

"Same thing."

"Well, it's time you learned to survive alone. Nothing worse than depending on something or someone for direction. Things and people can disappear overnight."

"So you're going to disappear. That's what's going to happen."

"I didn't say that, Ingrid. Calm down, now. Some days I wonder if I've taught you anything."

Ingrid had nodded to avoid crying. "I'm sorry to be so pathetic." *Don't leave me,* is what she wanted to say. *I'm alone here.*

In the garden, birds screeched and Ingrid sketched a hibiscus rose. She added a bee at the center of the flower, though she had yet to see one here. A voice from behind startled her. "Go-Away birds," it said. A gray-haired woman stood barefoot on a stone next to Ingrid's. She was dressed in a flowing dress covered with embroidered butterflies. "Those are Go-Away birds," she repeated. The woman swayed slightly as she looked up and pointed. "You can see them up there in the acacia, high up. Big black-and-white brutes with enormous beaks. And then there are the ibises, which fly over and make the most dreadful racket at six in the morning and six in the evening. Worse than Swiss clocks, those bloody birds. *Kubwa dingi,* as they say here. Big bad birds."

"Are you Christa Chisham?" Ingrid asked.

The woman smiled girlishly. "Am I famous, then?"

"Your brother was a friend of Nick Templeton's, from school. I've come to meet him."

"They must have been at Oxford together," Christa said. "With all those horrid spires. European architecture is so aggressive, don't you think? So insecure. Always having to assert itself against God or whatever scared it most that century. I'm glad to have left such a passel of fear behind. I don't miss it in the least. In Africa, there's no fear at all. People live in mud huts. I've given up wearing shoes."

"Do you know Nick Templeton? I think he stayed here."

"Oh yes," Christa said vaguely. "Tall man. Walked with crutches."

"Crutches?"

"Well, maybe that was some other friend of my brother's. The hotel business is such a flurry of faces, I've long stopped memorizing them. There are only so many things a brain can hang on to. You've got to choose what you want circulating in your dreams at night. Strangers confuse the memory—every face can look so familiar." She looked more closely at Ingrid. "You're not a friend of Danny's, are you?"

"No."

"Danny's our son. Mine and Henry's. Women trickle through here looking for him. Lovely creatures, like you. He's gone, I tell them. Swore off Nairobi years ago. Personally I think he's *hiding*." Christa winked. "I think he learned that from me."

The night was impossibly loud, a constant din of insects, frogs, and, more distant, monkeys or birds. Something howled from a mile, maybe ten miles away. Ingrid was woken by a sudden cacophonous burst that left her wide awake, watching shadows travel across the walls. Light slanted into her room—a headlight? house lights?—backlighting a canopy of leaves and occasionally illuminating the pale transparency of a gecko migrating across the ceiling on its sure, sticky pads to the wall and back across the ceiling again. Trying to keep the gecko in view, she allowed herself to consider the viability of her proposal. The evolution of continental monotheism; how cultures around the world had all, in their own time and way, come to decide on one god. Perhaps something would come of it. Perhaps not. She felt none of the urgency she had felt in Egypt, the driving impatience that obviated sleep and food, proving what Templeton had suspected: that she was capable of hard, original work. She had carved herself a niche in an ossified department that was 90 percent petrified male. Templeton had urged her forward: "As quickly as possible, you must establish your credibility. The real work begins when they stop watching you like hawks. Remember, we live in a small, jealous kingdom with a few paltry treasures. You must rise above the squabbling and the envy. These geezers are threatened by the energy of youth. They're busy signing autographs. They don't want to be reminded that the work continues—and you, for one, must continue it."

And she had. She had done what she had said she would. She had done it for him, for the challenge and then, later, for the subject itself. No civilization she had studied engrossed her like Egypt. That such integrated intelligence had existed so long ago and had subsequently been buried confirmed to her that evolution was not a continuum, but something that occurred in isolated outbreaks, splendid accidents. In the case of Egypt, the miracle of the pyramids had been started by an incidental alignment of precise engineering, a potent belief system and fearless imagination. And where had it all gone? *Where?* Ingrid found herself nostalgic for a culture that had the will and passion to construct such monumental temples to its own hubris and insecurity.

She sat up in bed and pressed her hand against the solitary shadow of her head on the wall. If she were to live as long as her mother, three quarters of her life was over. Was it a triumph to have the years move at such a speed? If so, where were the rewards, the evidence of its passage? *Where?* No husband, no child, no pyramid. At the moment, no career. It felt like a trick had been played on her. At least I haven't married out of fear, she thought. "That won't be your mistake," Templeton told her once. "Nor has it been mine—yet. But I'm older than you, and fear approaches suddenly." Ingrid lay back down and watched the trees replace her shadow.

Before Templeton had left for Africa in June, she had taken him to Lake Superior. He had composed a strange, unexpected picnic for her. He was quiet throughout the drive, maintaining a contemplative silence for over an hour. In the weeks before Ingrid left for Egypt, he had given himself over to an awkward, last-minute education, things he might have missed telling her over the years. "I'm trying to show you the bread crumbs you keep asking for," he explained. "To show I didn't just arrive at this place in my life as the crow flies—nor can you."

"But the chapters are linked. You can make sense of them."

"Well, fine, but you cannot get a summary statement about life—yours, mine, a toad's—and get the whole picture. That is why I don't like my own biographical information floating around. We believe we can locate ourselves and each other with a few scratches on a page. The only way we can locate ourselves is to look at where we are. The quality and amount of light, the minerals in the tap water, the weather and the way it impacts us—because we are every bit as much animals as a herd of cows mooing when the air pressure drops, sensing rain." Ingrid enjoyed watching the rare event of Templeton relaxing, overflowing with an unobstructed sense of well-being.

He lay back on the grass and stuck a blade in his mouth. The lines in his brow softened. He sighed between olives, alternating between pungent Greek kalamatas and fat green ones stuffed with garlic. He spit the kalamata pits onto the ground and said a brief prayer in Greek for future olive trees, the first in Michigan. "Have you seen an olive grove? It's like a shimmering ocean. The leaves are dense and silvery green. From the mountainside of Delphi, you can see olive groves melt into the Aegean, one glimmer replacing the other and stretching on and on and on." Ingrid was spreading what looked like pâté on a slice of miniature rye. "Don't forget the cornichons," he instructed. "There's a bottle of them in there somewhere."

He continued to ruminate in silence. Ingrid bunched up her sweater and lay down on the grass. The sky was buoyed with high, white clouds. She began to tell him then about how she had almost been killed as a child when the nanny her father had employed after her mother's death drove them over an embankment into a tree. Her father blamed himself for hiring someone from the South, where they didn't know about braking on ice. The young woman had died instantly. Ingrid, who was seven, held on to her hand and did not cry. Seven bones were broken in her foot and ankle; and pieces of them still floated around like driftwood.

"Six years I've known you," he had said, "and I can confirm that you are still a woman of secrets. A little flotsam isn't so bad. A good reminder that we are all so many bits and pieces." He dug into the picnic basket and extracted a pomegranate. "A very dangerous fruit," he said, tucking his napkin into his collar. He offered Ingrid a section and then said a short prayer for her nanny and then another for poor old Persephone and her approaching sentence in Hades. The smooth crimson seeds stained their fingertips. Templeton popped a handful into his mouth. "Did you know Zeus swallowed his first wife, Mita? It was prophesied that Mita would bear a son who would one day overthrow him. So down the hatch with Mita. She lived inside his head, poor thing."

Ingrid had since thought about the possibility that she had similarly ingested the man who told her the story, that he lived inside her. She couldn't pinpoint when she was suddenly able, in his absence, to hear Templeton's voice.

"When you get back," he said then, "I may be gone."

Ingrid frowned. "When you go," she said. "Do you always go alone?"

"Lord, yes," and then a rare smile. "Practice what I preach."

Colin

There was a man at the Chichester who, like Ingrid, sat through the dinner meal alone, reading or writing at his table. He was young and sober-looking, though he drank three pints of stout with his meal. She noticed him because his slightly stooped posture, agitated intensity and clean haircut suggested academe.

On her second night she watched him from her corner, tapping her pencil on another blank page in her notebook. His head shot up and he laughed almost maniacally at the empty place across from him. "Remarkable," he said out loud, not exactly to Ingrid, though there was no one else in the room. "Hatched his wings right there on the table, dried them off and went off to see the world."

After that he introduced himself and they spoke across the room. His name was Colin. He was a doctoral student from Cambridge, an entomologist who spent most of his time with army worms down in Makindu. "Nasty pests that wipe out crops every three years. They've just done their work again so I've come down ahead of schedule. The alternative was to wait another three years in the stinkin' lab. You can learn more from a week in the field than a year in the lab. Least with army worms." Colin finished his pint of beer and held up an index finger for another as the dinner waiter emerged from the kitchen, coffee in hand. The waiter, a simple man who had many times proven his inability to deviate from the set menu, was confused. "British Mister wants coffee and beers?"

"I know it's bad form, but yes." The waiter shrugged and scuffled off to the bar. "Always feel like I'm keeping the bloke awake."

"You are."

"Tried talking to him yesterday. After a few weeks with the worms, I'll talk to anything."

After dinner, Colin refilled his stout at the bar and led Ingrid to the garden, where he pushed his glass into the dirt and knelt in the darkness. "Listen," he whispered. "Can you hear that? The steady undertone to our screeching. Bloody musical they are. Most people can't hear them even when they're squashing them underfoot. They're like the bass in the band, thrum thrum thrum. Don't know it's there but you couldn't do without it."

Ingrid saw his long fingers join to make a spade and scoop the earth between the passion flowers, sifting through it nimbly, looking for worms and larvae. She sat on the tiles of the walkway and kept her eyes on his hands, which caught the light from the walkway when he held them close to his face to inspect the black soil. "Astounding proliferation of insect life here," he said. "Enough nocturnal activity to keep you up till dawn." She thought about how academics lost sight of themselves and saw only their subject, how this liberated them from their own scrutiny. It was an inadvertent act of self-generosity; allowing one's self to be, uninterrupted by observation.

"You haven't met a man named Nick Templeton here, have
you? He would have been staying in room nine. He comes and
goes from the coast, but uses the Chichester as his base."

"Ah." Colin smiled. "Is he who you're after?"

"No. I'm here doing fieldwork, like you. Cultural anthropology."

"Great stuff, that. Don't think I know your friend."

"He's a colleague," Ingrid explained. "I'm trying to get myself to the coast to find him."

Colin paused in his digging and took a swallow of beer. "You
in love with him?"

"He's my professor."

"Ever been in love?"

"Hmm."

"Hmm what?"

"I'm one of those people who get asked that question a lot."

A room opened down the walkway and they turned to see a
tall, barefooted man walking away from them, headed toward
the bar. Ingrid stared after him.

"He's wearing a skirt," she said.

"That's a kikoi. Native garb. The men on the coast wear
them."

"But he's white."

"Probably a white African. Born here from European parents,
raised by the African help. Played with African children. Fascinating, conflicted group, especially for a cultural anthropologist.
They don't know which tribe they belong to."

"Maybe he knows Templeton."

Colin finished his beer. "Have you seen Nairobi?"

"Not much. It hasn't been highly recommended."

He dusted off his hands. "While you won't find anything too
ancient, it's still good to see a country's cities. Let's go for a drive.

I wanted to show you my worms but it seems they're lunching somewhere else."

❧

They walked in darkness to an ancestral jeep, parked at the side of the hotel. Its edges were jagged with rust and it had no doors. Colin helped Ingrid into her seat. "How are you getting to the coast?"

"Train, in principle. But I couldn't get a reservation until Wednesday. I wish I could get there sooner—I don't have much to do around here."

"If you don't mind the vehicle, I'd be happy to give you a lift."

"Why, are there army worms on the coast?"

"There's everything on the coast. It's a great festering petri dish of insects."

"Great. Well, if you're serious about the ride, I'll take you up on it. I'd love to leave tomorrow."

"First thing, then," Colin said. "You'll get used to the doors."

Colin drove fast. Too fast. Ingrid clung to the edges of her seat when he made sudden and reckless turns that led them to what Colin called "the underbelly" of the city. She studied his profile as they drove slowly down a poorly lit street. He was handsome: boyish but strong. She turned away sharply when he caught her staring.

Outside, there were women standing on the sidewalk. Some of them walked alongside the jeep, touching Colin's leg as he drove by. "Hello, jeep man," they said, smiling. "Where have you been?"

"So they know you," Ingrid observed quietly.

A particularly thin woman came up alongside the car. "You got a woman now, *vunjika mtu?*"

"You shouldn't be here," Colin told her. She smiled coyly and licked her lips. He turned to Ingrid. "I knew her sister. They're dying, you know." He turned to the woman in the street. "You're dying." She winked and followed a car going in the opposite direction. "Here and in Mombasa where they work the sailors. French and American naval bases. They don't understand what's killing them. No one in the country will use a freaking condom. In Uganda they do. For some reason they understand there. Here it's about virility and fertility and the unmanliness of a latex barrier; an undermining of the strength of numbers. The oldest rule. It will kill them. The disease will beat the birth numbers. The babies will be born diseased." He pressed his foot to the accelerator, leaving the women behind. Ingrid turned back and could see only their silhouettes. "I tried to tell her, that one's sister. She laughed at me, called me *vunjika mtu,* which means, essentially, limp penis. She thought I preferred to talk instead of fuck. Another cultural difference. I'm a good Catholic boy, you see."

Colin took a joint from his shirt pocket. He held a match to its tip and the pungent smell swirled around the jeep. "Do you smoke this stuff?" Ingrid shook her head. "When in Rome . . ." He inhaled the weed and held the smoke in his chest. "Malawi Gold," he exhaled and smiled into the headlights of an oncoming car. "Magic."

Ingrid had never seen a man hold things the way Colin did. Simple objects; a joint, a pint of beer, a handful of soil. His fingers were long and flat and they adhered to bottles and glasses of drinking water with the solidity and semipermanence of warm wax. She took the joint from him and held it in her own stiff fingers. The wind in the jeep made the ember burn red, specks of color flew from the tip as she held it out in the open air. "Let's go back," she said.

"You ever get lonely?" Colin asked when they pulled in to the Chichester.

Ingrid hesitated. "Of course."

"Come," he said. "I want to show you something."

Ingrid sat rigidly on the edge of Colin's bed while he relit his joint and flipped through a Gideon Bible, licking his finger lightly and turning the onionskin pages to find passages and scan columns that he read to himself and not to her. The motion of his fingers and the soft crinkling of the paper mesmerized her. She had closed her eyes when she felt his fingers on her shirt, gently exploring the shape of her breasts. "No," she said, instantly regretting it because the word sounded somehow violent. As it hovered between them, Ingrid considered taking it back, retrieving it. But then what?

"No," Colin acknowledged soberly. "Of course not."

Ingrid stood abruptly. "I'll go now, Colin," she said. "I'll go."

He held his hand out to her. "There is a kind of frog in the desert. He lives underground and creates a shell of saliva that hardens around him and keeps him moist. When it rains in the desert, once, maybe twice a year, he comes out, jumps around, finds a female to fuck and then goes back down." She looked at his fingers extending toward her, the pale fingers of a ruminating saint. Pressing them quickly into hers, she stepped past him. "She died, you know. Sheba's sister. That's how fucking stupid they are here."

Something crashed against the wall after she shut the door behind her.

❧

The man she had seen earlier was sitting in the doorway of room number eight, his bare legs extended. Above his legs, which were long and tanned, was a yellow kikoi, and above that the white plume of cigarette smoke. Ingrid slowed as she approached the doorway. When she turned to look at his face, she saw only shadow. Nothing in his posture registered her arrival. She stopped and took a step backward so that she stood in front of him. "You're from the coast," she said.

"Yes."

"I'm looking for someone there."

"Then why are you here?"

"He kept a room here. I was thinking you might know him." The man closed his eyes. He seemed to be dozing. "Do you have another cigarette?" she asked.

His shirt pocket rustled with cellophane and a cigarette emerged from the darkness. "You'll have to come down here for a light." The voice was barely audible.

Ingrid leaned toward him and was immediately blinded by a flame. She sat back on her haunches with the cigarette, blinking the image of the flame, the damage of its brightness.

"I've just had the strangest conversation," she said.

From him another exhalation, no promise of sound. She waited.

"Before now," he finally said. The two words were a concession.

She held herself to one. "Yes."

"Another drunk stranger?"

"Yes, I suppose he was."

"You came from his room?"

"We were reading the Bible. Or he was. I was watching." She moved closer to the doorway. Now she could make out the outline of his face.

"There are better ways to seduce a girl." He brought a beer bottle to his lips and then dropped the cigarette into its emptiness, where it hissed and died. "What he probably meant to do was this." He leaned over and kissed Ingrid softly on the lips. Cigarettes, beer, salt and, somewhere below these other flavors, the man. She closed her eyes as her body started to burn, wanting the kiss to last until she could taste only him. Before he moved his head away from hers he whispered, "You should probably try my room."

She was equal parts shock and desire. The most she could manage was an echo: "I probably should."

He closed the door behind them and they were in darkness, a crack of pale light at the bottom of the door. She wiped the palms of her hands on her skirt, knowing she should not have entered. Then she moved slowly forward in the darkness. "I won't stay for long," she said, though the darkness was delicious. "I have to be up and out by dawn." She stepped toward where she thought he might be, no longer needing to see him, not caring who he was.

It was not sex. He held her and she let herself be held until she could feel the breath move in his body. Then she started to touch him, moving her fingers lightly from his cheek to his neck to his shoulder, resting them finally on his chest. When he moved on top of her, she held his face in her hands and without taking off their clothes, they began pressing into each other, pressing so hard Ingrid felt the bruising bones meet—and still she pushed harder, her pelvis rising to meet him. She pulled his face to hers and laid her cheek against his until his stubble burned her skin. When she could no longer stand it, Ingrid rolled over and fit her back into his chest. "This is hard," she said. "It is harder than it is strange."

"Is it?"

"Because of the wanting. Because I don't know you."

His hand was on her hair, stroking automatically, moving more clumsily as sleep approached. "Shhh. Wanting is good. Knowing is not so important." He fingered the fabric of her blouse. Consciousness slipped a bit and then a bit more. They fell together, as if sinking simultaneously into the unknown was something they had done before. A slow, vague idea brought her back to the surface. "What happens next?" she whispered.

His voice was as faint as his breath. "You will have to imagine it."

"I may never see you again."

"Have you seen me?"

"I would know you if I saw you."

"Hmm."

"I am good at finding people."

"Are you, now?" In the dark, she thought she could hear him smile.

Ingrid waited to move until his breath slowed into sleep. To separate her curve from his when they held each other so neatly seemed a violation. She waited in his arms, the darkness surrounding them like thick, sweet cream.

Then, in the isolation of sleep, he released her. She rolled away from him, reaching for the floor with one arm and then standing on all fours like a cat, searching for her shoes, arching with the memory of his body imprinted on hers.

Back in her own bed, she touched herself. He was here, and here. This part of him was hard, this part soft. *His shape is in my skin,* she thought. *I will know him.*

❧

The next morning, the man in room number eight was gone. Colin and his jeep were also gone. Ingrid asked Kipo at the front desk. Kipo, who was small, fastidious, and, it seemed to Ingrid, mildly disapproving, had no answers. "Away," he said, as if this were enough. "He has gone away."

"What do you mean, 'away'?"

"Off somewhere, wherever he goes when he goes. I don't know."

"Has he gone to look at the army worms in Makindu?"

Kipo squinted slightly. "The army what?"

"The worms he's studying, for his dissertation."

"I don't know about research. He likes bugs. This I do know."

Ingrid was at a loss. "Well, how long does he go for?"

Kipo shrugged. "A few weeks. A month."

"He told me he would help me get to the coast. We were going to leave today."

"Maybe you should speak to Henry. Possibly he knows more."

Ingrid found Henry, Christa's husband, in the bar, a small dark room of varnished wood. He had finished his lunch at a small table and was folding the daily newspaper in half, creasing it precisely with his index finger. He smiled up at her and, when she continued to stand there, stopped smiling and motioned for her to sit down. "Kipo told me you might know where Colin has gone," she said.

Henry blinked. "Colin, is it?"

Ingrid nodded, taking a seat. "It seems he's gone. We had plans to drive to the coast."

Henry drank from his pint glass of beer and seemed for the first time to consider its color. "Yes. Yes, you should probably make other arrangements." He broke his gaze and focused on Ingrid long enough to politely dismiss her.

"Why?" she asked, ignoring the dismissal.

"Why. Why anything in this country?"

"Please. We're friends, Colin and I."

"Are you?" Henry raised his glass and then put it down. "He's been with us two years now."

"Two years?"

Henry took off his glasses and wiped them with a handkerchief. "Colin's got the bug. Does unexpected things to a person."

"The bug," Ingrid repeated.

"Thin. Skinny. They call it all sorts of things. The AIDS, I think you call it in the States." Ingrid's eyes fell to the table.

Henry lit his pipe. "Had a girl in town, I think."

She closed her eyes to the smoke. "Is he getting treatment?"

"Treatment?"

"There are medicines."

"No, no." Henry shook his match out. "He's not getting any treatment."

"Why the hell not?"

"For starters, he doesn't want any. Second, he couldn't if he wanted to. Hasn't got a farthing." He tilted his glass to the ceiling and neatly placed the empty glass back on the table where his fingers encircled it, sliding its moisure-slick base a fraction to the right and then a fraction to the left. "No. We take care of him. For the time being."

"That's kind of you."

Henry looked Ingrid in the eye for a brief moment before he waved his empty glass in front of the bartender and stared obdurately at the table until his refill was delivered. "I'm not Christa's first husband, you know. She's not my first wife." Ingrid said nothing as he tucked into his new beer. "Danny's not my natural son. He's never had much use for me."

"Ah."

"And Colin," Henry smiled sadly. "Colin's different. Colin was married back in England. Decided he couldn't go back."

"He's lucky to have you," Ingrid said.

"And I him." Henry looked back at the newspaper. "Nothing lasts for long, you know. You can see that more here."

❧

At breakfast the next morning, Ingrid brought the material Templeton had sent her over the past months and spread it out on the table. The dining room, a warm wood room with garden-facing windows and rough tables, was full at breakfast, the quickest, most reliable meal. Sunlight fell through the windows onto the tables and steam rose from the coffee and pitchers of warmed milk. Henry Chisham came to her table in his flannel robe. "Kipo tells me you're off to Pelat today," he said.

"Hopefully." Ingrid smiled. She had slept poorly, imagining insects in her bed. Twice she had thrown off the sheets, switched on the light and inspected the bed down to the corners. The morning sun was too bright for Henry's eyes. He blinked uncomfortably.

"It's been nice having you here. I hope you'll visit us again."

"On the way out. In a few weeks."

"Pelat's quite beautiful. Do you have a place to stay?"

"Not yet."

"I'll call and book you a room at Abdul's guesthouse. The rates are decent."

"Thank you."

"Look out for our Danny. He's been living there for a while now. Nice chap. Spends too much time at the bar, I suspect." Henry looked at the pages Ingrid had spread out on the table. "Ah, you have a little preview here." He put on his glasses and leaned toward the photo of the blond man standing with Templeton and a large fish. "Well, well"—he smiled—"Finn got a nice fish."

"This is Finn Bergmann, isn't it?"

"You know him?"

"I think I met him last night."

"Quite possible, as he was just here, picking something up for his boat. Left this morning. Finn's father built the hotel on the island." Henry picked up the photo. "I met him once, way back.

Anyway, you'll see the place when you get there. Salama. Hard to miss. Man named Wicks is putting up another one on the other end of the island. All sorts of hoopla about that. Seems one hotel on Pelat is enough for some." Henry returned the photo of Finn and winked. "Watch out for this one. He and Danny are mates from way back. Up to no good with the ladies." Henry cleared his throat. "If you come upon Danny, tell him we're expecting him for Christmas."

"Christmas," Ingrid repeated.

"Last year it slipped his mind. Hurt his mum's feelings."

Ingrid wrote down the names in her notebook: Danny, Wicks. After a cup of coffee, she added Finn.

Part
Two

An Unexpected Guide

$\mathcal{T}$ he first man Ingrid saw on Pelat Island she saw from the sea. Her body knew him even from a distance. His hair was bright with the sun as he moved along the stone wall above the water.

Two elderly British women stood in the dhow in front of her, straw hats clasped to their heads. The three of them had flown together in a four-seat Cessna from Mombasa, the two ladies chatting like sparrows, their knees touching in the small plane. (The landing strip was on a neighboring island, where a dhow met the passengers and took them across the narrow channel.) They were silent now as they watched the island come nearer. Palm trees bent like lashes above the white beach. The sun was like a glorious warm liquid that touched the pale skin between the leather straps of their sandals, the soft protected backs of their necks.

The green water of the bay splashed below the turquoise eye painted on the prow, giving the ancient boat a steep profile, a stern mouth gulping warm salt water. The thick handmade sails were full, the billow of their downwind tack obscuring the view of the quay. Ingrid leaned to keep the man in sight. There were details now: a rust-red kikoi, wrapped around his waist, hung below his knees; his back was broad and brown. It seemed, at the speed they were traveling, that they would intercept him perfectly, that the two paths of motion would connect.

A crowd had gathered on the stone wall along the quay. Children were waving. The man wove his way through the throng of bodies, and by the time the dhow bumped against the stone steps, he was gone. Ingrid eased her disappointment into relief by telling herself it was too soon to see him, that it was better first to see his island, have a shower and change her clothes.

The quay was alive with fingers pointing and hands reaching for the luggage stowed in the bow of the boat. From above, a hand appeared in front of her. With the sun in her eyes, she could not see the face. The British women were laughing. The dhow rocked as they disembarked and she grabbed the hand so she wouldn't fall and was pulled up to the stone wall to face a brown man with tea-colored eyes and the face of a cherub, an odd combination of bleached curls and dark skin. "You are staying at Abdul's guesthouse, yes?"

"Yes."

"Point to me your bag," he said. He swung it onto his shoulder and beckoned to her. "Come." Then the British ladies were gone and the crowd was gone and she was following him on a narrow path of sand that led to other paths of sand, weaving through the village. Ingrid kept her eyes on the cherub's back. He was singing, leading her along through the warm island air. His kikoi was worn thin, his back barely covered by an ill-fitting tank top. His curls still dripped water, which snaked down his neck in dark rivulets. "I am Ali. Anything you want to see, I will show you. I will collect you in an hour for a drink at Salama where you can get food. Signal me and I will take you home. I am to be trusted."

"How much?"

"No. The pleasure is mine."

"I don't think I can afford you, really. I'm not a tourist."

"No?" Ali smiled.

They stopped in front of a windowless white house with a large wooden door. "An hour to freshen." Ali pulled a rope that rang a bell inside the house and disappeared around the corner.

The door opened slowly, and a flesh-bare, wizened man squinted and gestured her through a shaded stone courtyard with chickens and children. Laundry hung on a line. In the motionless air was the faint odor of fish. Pliant from the heat, Ingrid followed him, relinquishing any expectation of control.

The roof of the guesthouse had been transformed into a comfortable lounging porch. Hammocks hung in the corners and colorful, sun-faded pillows were piled under a sunken thatch shelter. The old man spoke to her over his shoulder as they ascended a flight of narrow stairs. "It is coolest up here," he said. On the back third of the sizable roof was an addition to the main house, with two rooms. The roof looked over the tops of palm trees and the thatch of village houses to an expansive white structure that must have been Salama Hotel. Beyond it, the Indian Ocean stretched to where on the horizon it was reflected back by the late-afternoon sun. The old man gestured to a door and stood by as Ingrid looked in.

"Are you Abdul?"

"I am."

"My name is Ingrid."

"Yes," the old man said indifferently.

The room was simple: three paneless windows covered by sun-faded fabric that blew in the cross breeze. In the middle was a rough wooden bed with a tented mosquito net. A single sheet was pulled tight across the narrow mattress. The floor was bare and a wooden chair stood in the corner, on three of its four uneven legs. There was nowhere to put her things. "Thank you," she said. Abdul nodded and retreated.

Ingrid pulled the mosquito net aside and lay down on the bed, sheltering herself with the mesh net. Templeton had laughed the first time she had returned from Africa with malaria. "Don't run from mosquitoes, malaria jogs the brain," he had told her. "Some of my best thinking has been done with a fever." She closed her eyes. The cloth curtains flapped softly.

Later, from below, she heard the sounds of children laughing and a goat. Later still, a prayer call from a nearby mosque, sudden and deafening from a loudspeaker. Then, as the light began to fade, a knock at the door. Three soft knocks. Ingrid watched the door open through the mesh of the mosquito net. A man in white appeared as if in a vision: Ali had changed his clothes. He was elegant now, in a white kikoi and button-down shirt. He took in his breath when he saw her lying there. "So sorry," he said. "I will wait."

Ingrid knelt to unzip her duffel and stared blankly at its neatly folded contents. The laundry boys at the Chichester had pressed even her jeans. She pulled on a floral skirt and a white cotton shirt. Fishing in her purse for a lipstick, she called out to Ali. "Has someone asked you to look after me?"

"You are Miss Holes, the American."

"Holtz." Ingrid closed the door to her room. "How do you know that?"

"This is an island. Come."

"Where are we going?"

"To the hotel for a drink. You will meet other foreigners there. There is a telephone. They serve dinner. You will be wanting dinner, yes?"

"Has a man named Templeton sent you?"

"The professor?" Ali smiled. "No."

"You know him?"

"Of course," Ali motioned beyond a few rooftops. "He stays over there."

Ingrid almost tripped following him down the stairs. Ali turned to catch her. She could see his smile gleaming in the darkness. "Is he there now?"

"I don't know," he said. "I haven't seen him." Ali paused to open the front door for her. "You are what, his daughter?"

"No."

"What, then?"

"I am his student."

"His student." Two women draped in *bui-bui*s turned the corner and cast their eyes downward at the sight of Ingrid. Their black robes covered all but a swatch for the eyes. As they approached, their quiet talk ceased. Ingrid turned to watch the sway of the dark cloth and caught one of them staring at her, her eyes thickly outlined with kohl. "Two weeks ago I tried to call him at the hotel," she resumed. "I was told he wasn't here."

"I remember. I took the message—I was working in the hotel office that night."

"So you knew I was coming." Ali chose not to answer and they lapsed into silence. "You say the professor lives on that side of town," Ingrid tried. "Do you know where?"

"He must stay somewhere else now. I haven't seen him lately."

"You might have told me that on the phone."

"I had not seen him. I told you as much, Miss Holes."

"Just Ingrid, please." She had stopped to empty the sand from her shoes. "Did he go to the hotel?"

"No, not much." The path had emerged onto a neatly swept patio. "Here we are," Ali said. He motioned ahead to a bar under

a *makute* roof lit with small candles. "There is the outside bar. But
we will go to the indoor bar. Danny must see you. Then, whenever you want to go, I will take you." He paused, running his
eyes over her. "You are lucky to have me," he said. "You could
have ended up with any number of scoundrels."

"And you're not a scoundrel?" she asked.

"No, I am an angel," he said, opening the door for her. "You
have been a queen, yes? It's in your face. You are proud."

"I can't give you money, Ali."

He shrugged. "Do not get upset. I'm only naming what I
see."

The bar was elegant: panels of dark wood set against pale yellow
walls. The room was small but the high ceiling made it feel spa-
cious. Candles flickered from the breeze of a languorous wooden
ceiling fan. On two adjoining sides, French doors opened to the
night. Ingrid followed Ali to a table where a man sat, drinking.
"Hello, Danny. This is Miss Ingrid Holes. From America."

Danny at first did not respond. His long limbs were bent over,
crisscrossed against a slender frame. His head was large, with dis-
concertingly pronounced features: enormous blue eyes, a generous
mouth, a thick mop of hair falling over his forehead. Ingrid was
struck by the incongruence of the substantial head and the van-
quished spine curved miserably against the wall, the shoulders
collapsed forward, protecting an invisible sphere of space in front
of the sunken chest cavity. Danny's blue eyes were on her now and
his lips had turned in a kind of smile. His hand reached for hers.

"I have this boat." His voice was soft. Ingrid watched his
thumb stroke the veins of her hand. "If tomorrow's nice we could
sail it to Kisu Island. I've never been there but I've always wanted
to go. I'll have Hamilton pack a lunch. It's a little boat, but seaworthy. Will you come? Please don't say no. I can't tolerate no."

Ali's voice was in her ear. "Say yes, he won't remember."

"Your parents want you to come to Nairobi for Christmas," Ingrid said. Danny's head crumpled over her hand. His lips, soft and slack, pressed hard against her hand. A few moments later, the weight of his head followed. He seemed to be asleep. Ingrid signaled Ali with her eyes.

"Good night, Danny," Ali said.

Danny's head rose like a balloon. His eyes were shot with red. "Yes, yes, good night." Ali offered him a hand and pulled him to his feet. He was well over six feet, his starched kikoi bunched above his swaying knees like a diaper. "Until tomorrow." He bent to kiss Ingrid's head and then staggered off into the night. She watched him through the windows as he was joined by another shorter, darker man whom he propped himself up against, as if the man were a crutch, and left the stone terrace for the sand;

"That's Hamilton," Ali said. "Danny's houseboy."

"What a sad man."

"This sadness is charming, no?"

"I met his parents in Nairobi. They told me to tell him to come home for Christmas."

"They say that every year." Ali smiled. "Danny hasn't left the island for years."

CHAPTER

9

The New Arrivals

$\mathcal{S}$tanley Wicks had started to dream. He had not dreamed since he was a child, and he had almost forgotten about being a child when these dreams brought back the terror and the wonder of uninhibited, uncontrollable situations. The difference of late was the subject matter. His dreams now had aspects of reality, characters he recognized, places he had been. But all jumbled and mixed and horribly changed: vivid narratives that made so much sense they threatened his waking hours with their palpability. It could have been the heat, he thought, that made the days more dreamlike and dreams more like something real.

That night he had dreamed of Daisy. In the morning she seemed to know it too, watching him through slitted eyes as he poked an egg yolk and cut his toast. "How about spending time with Harry today?" he suggested, without looking up.

He sliced into his egg white and placed it on top of the toast. Daisy turned from her husband to his plate and stabbed his egg with her fork. "I'm ravenous. Where's the boy? Jackson?" she called, pouring milk into her coffee. In a voice that was more like a low growl, she said, "Don't start with me, Stanley."

"I just thought it was natural for a mother to want to be with her child."

Daisy made a sound, almost a snort. "What's natural? You tell me, Mr. African Primitive. Isn't it natural for husbands to want to fuck their wives from time to time?"

Stanley reddened. "We're discussing Harry, darling. I'd like to continue, if you don't mind."

"And who appointed you to the motherhood police?"

"Daisy—"

Daisy held up her yolk-covered fork. "If you keep on, you'll ruin both of our days. I want you to leave it alone for now, all right? Can you do that for me?"

Stanley studied his wife. She was fat. She had been fat since the pregnancy. The extra weight had done nothing for her face: the delicacy had been ballooned out of it. With a sunburn, it looked almost blistered. Her eyes were puffy from sleep and the blue color of the irises shot out in small, angry rays. "Jackson!" her mouth yelled harshly. "Damn it, where is that boy? They jump when *you* call, you know. They don't seem to hear me at all."

Stanley had married beneath him. The knowledge of the mistake was still settling in. He had been stuck in a leaky capsule with Daisy for seven years and finally felt he was being forced to escape and swim up for air. He had been warned by his mother and gently pitied by his peers, and he had shunned them all. All the family propaganda he had ignored haunted him now. They had been right: his wife was proving to be somehow deficient.

For the last few months, he had been considering their marriage. Outside the bedroom, they had always had little in common. Daisy had feeling only for status, not people. What she wanted was to get above positionless people and stay there. She had the unpleasant habit of avoiding the eyes of her subordinates, giving them orders without looking at them. To a degree, Stanley understood. Daisy sprang from the dangerously amorphous middle class, the class as big as an army, rabid with envy. These were the people who worshiped the royals and criticized them simultaneously, speaking with a frightening intimacy. There was unity without loyalty in their ranks. As soon as she secured her place above them with her marriage to Stanley, Daisy had denied ever knowing they existed.

Things had more or less held together until the pregnancy, but Daisy had panicked when she began to lose her shape. She had fought with her weight most of her life, and her figure, while good when she met Stanley, was newly won. Much to Stanley's surprise, in the natural process of getting bigger, something happened to Daisy's emotional stability. She disowned her body. It was as if a few layers of skin had fallen off and a vulnerability had been exposed, a grotesque weakness that disgusted her. Stanley watched the transformation with morbid fascination. Her vanity seemed to sharpen and then puncture her ego. What made him want to run was her response to her pregnancy, how easily and artlessly she had let herself go to ruin. There was nothing underneath to support her, no structure or fiber to prevent it from happening. She was common after all, common in her self-loathing. It was only when she had abandoned all pretense that he had allowed himself to recognize his mistake.

That night, he dreamed that she had trapped him in a dank underground place with rats and filthy pools of water, the ear-shattering noise of trains running above, one after another, shaking the ground and disturbing the putrid pools. But there was no train below to take him out. He was stuck with only his wife. And she was there, sitting in bed with food laid all around her, laughing. Laughing and eating. "How do you like our home, Stanley darling?"

Stanley shivered, despite the heat. He unzipped his hip pouch and rubbed some of Daisy's Elizabeth Arden sun factor 35 on his nose. Both were fair and burned easily, only he didn't want to blister.

By two o'clock, Stanley still could not think of a reason to leave the bar at Salama. It was too hot to visit Kitali, and the workers would be sleeping, anyway. At home, Daisy was waiting feverishly for the afternoon flight from Nairobi. By now she would be sitting on the roof, slathered in sun-tanning oil, scanning the sky for the Cessna. The Cessna brought essential things from the mainland: mail, booze, American cigarettes. Today it was to bring a larger "essential," ordered and bought sight unseen—a masseur named, Stanley couldn't remember, something ridiculous like Adolpho. Not just a masseur, Daisy insisted, but a body worker. He was, she declared, a healer. "He's going to heal me," she said.

"Of what?"

"I'm not well, Stanley, in case you hadn't noticed. Look at me! I'm fat and unhappy. I haven't been myself since the baby was born. Relaxation and physical manipulation through touch is the best, most natural way to heal. I've read it in many magazines. The curative powers of touch, the touch of someone who knows how to touch. Adolpho has told me that he can stimulate my thyroid gland and boost my metabolism. I can get back to normal shape in no time. And if you're worried about the money, think about the savings on food and booze. I will be adding years to my life. No more cigarettes, either. That should save a load right there. Do you know what we spend on cigarettes alone in a year?"

"Probably less than it costs to have an in-house body worker for the season."

"*Far* less."

So there was no argument.

Stanley lit a cigarette and perused an old paper. After a while, Ali sat next to him and had a beer. "A beautiful woman has come to the island," he announced.

"How do you know?"

"I have been escorting her. She may belong to the professor, but I don't think so."

"So, Ali, are you going to lie in wait, like a shark?"

"Sharks never stop moving. They can't lie in wait," Ali said, remembering that Wicks was, unlike Finn, a real white man. A real *mzungu* who knew nothing of fish.

Finn arrived and ordered a sandwich and a beer. After greeting each other, they sat for a while in silence. "How's it, Stanley?" Finn finally said.

"Oh, fair."

"Hotel coming along?"

"Rather like a snail. Do you have snails here? I don't think I've seen one. They're delicious with butter, bit of garlic and parsley." Stanley rested his eyes on Finn's food.

"Hungry, Stanley?" Finn asked, offering his plate.

Stanley helped himself to Finn's sandwich and ordered another beer.

"Finn, aren't you friendly with that professor fellow?"

"Friendly, I don't know."

"Is he right in the head?"

"A fair question."

Because it seemed Finn might impart something more, Stanley swallowed his bite of sandwich and washed it down with half a bottle of beer before he moved on to the next question. "What's he doing here, anyway?"

Finn finished his meal and wiped his face with his napkin. "What's bothering you, Wicks?"

"A longish story." Stanley had kept Templeton's letter in his pocket, where it stayed because he could bring himself neither to reread it nor to throw it away. Templeton's words had disturbed him, transforming the otherwise innocent happiness of island life to something potentially sinister.

"Is it your hotel?" Finn was asking.

Stanley shook his head, finished his beer, and proposed another round. "My wife has bought a masseur," he said miserably. "A man who rubs naked bodies with oil. He's arriving today."

Ali chuckled. "That should help things at home."

"I'm going to avoid home, I think."

"You already avoid home," Finn said.

"I suppose I do. Just now I wish I could find another place to sleep."

"Sleep on your boat."

"Now there's an idea. But Nelson farts like a hippo." Stanley picked at the Tusker beer label. "She calls him a *healer*, of all things. He has a ridiculous name. *Adolpho* or something. Where do you suppose a man named Adolpho comes from?"

"It may be just the thing, Stanley, this Adolpho," Finn said. "Take the pressure off you, anyway. And he's a professional, isn't he? Let him do his job and see what happens."

"It makes me unhappy, the whole business."

"Oh, now, cheer up. The sun's shining, and look, here comes the dhow from Tomba."

"Adolpho is on that dhow."

"But I also see some long hair. A new batch of women, looks like."

Ali grinned. "If Daisy can play, so can you."

"It's not how I thought it would be." Stanley turned backward on his stool and faced the approaching dhow. Perhaps they were right. "Have you seen that girl on the terrace?" he asked.

"Yes," Finn said.

Ali piped in, "That's the one I was telling you about."

"I like the looks of her," Stanley said. "She's decently dressed anyway. What happens to women here? They come and the first thing they do is rip their clothes off. It's as if no one's watching because they're in Africa. Someone should tell them it isn't decent. Not even here."

"You won't get much help on that, I'm afraid."

"Do you enjoy seeing women bare their goods for the world, Finn?"

"I don't even see it anymore."

"But does it *appeal* to you as a man?"

"Depends on my liquor intake."

"You know, I don't think I've ever seen you with anyone steady."

"Yes, well, I haven't gone hungry, Stanley. Don't worry. The girl on the terrace—I think Danny's made a bid on her."

"Danny? Is he capable?"

"That's not the question. He likes her. I think she reminds him of England. Like you. She's all buttoned-up."

Stanley stayed at the hotel through dinner, which he ate alone on the terrace. How ridiculous that someone could bid on a woman! If he had the opportunity, he would ask her to dinner. He wouldn't hesitate for a moment.

He lingered over his coconut ice cream and coffee, and when they were gone, decided it was a cognac night. The deep amber color of the liqueur returned him to the memory of cognac nights past and the rich expanse of a life that was still unfolding. *His* life. He took out Templeton's letter and studied it in the candlelight. Manufactured deities, for Christ's sake. What did he mean by that? The church had always been a political institution. It had no choice. It was that way in all civilized countries, England being the first; church and state vying for a limited amount of funds and power. Of course there were moments of malfeasance, ignoble but necessary. Perhaps this man had missed out on the lesson of realpolitik. Perhaps he had missed a century or two.

At midnight, he headed home to where Adolpho was being paid to sleep in his house. He sniffed around the house, convinced it already reeked of foreign matter. To his horror, the refrigerator handle was covered with grease, as was the handle to his bedroom door and the bathroom faucet. Stanley smelled the oil residue on his hand. It smelled vaguely like marzipan, a sickly-sweet almondy smell. When he turned the light on he saw there were oily footprints on the floor. Daisy's feet and larger Adolpho feet. Stanley felt ill and angry. This oil might corrode the varnish on the floor. Harry might somehow ingest it. It was unclean and it smelled vile. Where would he sleep? In the bed with his oil-coated wife? Think of the sheets!

Stanley paced as he smoked. He had been subtly ousted from his own house. Like Tsar Nicholas, whose place had been usurped by Rasputin when he was off at war. Noble Nicholas had been replaced by a smelly, hairy yeti of a man. Rasputin had also claimed to be a healer. Sure he had special powers, Stanley thought. Screwing his way to the top. An old story. Sling the wife a big oily sausage when her husband's away, see how her allegiance shifts.

What could he do? Where could he sleep? He went to his

bedroom and stood over the nebulous shape of his wife, half-covered in sheet. There was barely any room for him anyway, the way she was sprawled. He bent down to smell her. Yes, it was stronger here. The smell of sloth, betrayal and corruption. "Why have I been so loyal to you?" he whispered. He extracted his pillow from under Daisy's arm and set himself up on the window seat in the living room, where he could almost stretch out. He could hear the ocean, tamed by the coral reef and so quiet at this time of night. He thought about how long his marriage might have lasted in England, where Daisy had the comforts of home and there was enough noise to prevent anyone from thinking. Before he dozed off, he thanked Africa, where nothing could stay hidden for long.

Templeton's Room

The next morning Ali interrupted Ingrid as she was slogging through Templeton's book on Swahili culture. She put up her hand for him to let her finish a particularly succinct paragraph, and then read it again to commit it to memory. In the Swahili world, God was all-powerful. Under his compassionate eye, human beings were blown this way and that by forces both visible and invisible. God's world (perhaps not as compassionate as God himself) was ordered by a strict system of rank and file. Those of high birth and pure lineage were better positioned for the afterlife, though all earthly souls were threatened daily by corruption and pollution and were continually faced with new opportunities to gain or lose power in the battle for purity. This power, while desirable, also brought one dangerously closer to God and the ultimate sin of seeing oneself as his equal.

Paradise, lost to the earthbound, was to be regained only in death, on the Day of Judgment. With effort, a modicum of happiness and peace was possible before that day, though the never-ending war against evil and defilement wore souls thin. Every member of every community had to be vigilant in the fight against them, purifying him- or herself with ritual prayer and ablution. Evil lurking in one soul was a threat to everyone who came in contact with that soul.

While Ingrid marked the page and closed the book, Ali spelled the title out backward. "You need a book?" he asked. "I will tell you everything you need to know." He motioned to the sparkling water. "Come, Miss Ingrid, see the island from the water. Before it gets hot. The tide is high and the wind is blowing. It is perfect."

Ingrid could not see why she should put up a resistance to Ali. She had made her status clear on money and if he understood that she was going to give him nothing in exchange for his attentions, the rest was his choice. It was possible he had nothing better to do. It was equally possible that he genuinely wanted to share the island with her, a sort of self-appointed ambassador. Whatever the motive, she was comfortable enough with him, and a sail around the island would help her get her bearings.

"Is a skirt okay?"

"A skirt is best. Don't bother with shoes."

Ingrid tucked her hair into a sun hat and put on her sunglasses. She was suddenly eager to leave her roof and get out to the water, to touch the sand with her feet.

Like the other island dhows, Ali's had a slightly tilted mast made from the trunk of a mangrove tree. He demonstrated how the yard could be slid up and down the mast to adjust the height and angle of the sail. The hull was deep and damp with seawater. Ingrid sat on the salty planks while Ali unfurled the sail and swam the boat away from the shore. When the sail luffed with the beginnings of a breeze, he heaved himself back into the dhow and smiled. "You are enjoying yourself?"

"Very much," Ingrid said, leaning her head back to see the sky. "I grew up sailing little boats."

Ali clenched a sheet between his teeth as the sail filled with wind. He steered with his foot. "Come back here and steer the boat," he said after a lull. "I think you like steering, no?"

Ingrid held the thick wooden rudder in her hand and experimented with the boat's responsiveness, gauging whether it liked to point into the wind or fall off.

"Few things are as nice as sailing," Ali said. "Using what God gives you in nature; the wind and the water. And with the wood that God provides, we build the boat. We build it so it will go where you tell it to go. How many things go where you tell them to go? Not even I can tell myself to go somewhere I want myself to go. At the hotel bar after a few beers I tell myself to go home to bed and then I don't. I have another beer and I see a pretty girl and I am out all night."

"Doing what?"

"Don't worry, Miss Ingrid, I am a good boy. I tell you these things because you understand, coming from the West."

"Understand what, Ali?"

"Understand a split in the self."

Ali closed his eyes and trailed his hand in the water. "Too many desires is like too many children for an inheritance. No one gets enough money. Every child is left wanting, hating the other children for taking the money that could have been theirs. I know, this happened in my own family. Desires are like that, like greedy children, jealous of each other. Mean sometimes. Sometimes they even want to kill each other."

"Maybe not everyone has as many desires as you."

"No? On this island I see strong desires. Fighting desires. The desire to pray and the desire to fuck, for instance. These desires fight."

"Is that the word they use here, 'fuck'?"

Ali shrugged. "I myself like the word. It's a strong word for a strong act. Like the verb *nataka,* 'to want' in Swahili. *Ninakutaka.* I want you. *Ninakutaka* fuck. Ha ha."

"And Western women respond to this approach?"

"They love it. Western women like savages. They like bad words and crazy fucking all night with savage African boys."

"You know this firsthand, I assume."

"I know it but I am a good boy. Don't worry. You are a little frightened, you think you should be a little cautious, but you don't really want to be safe. Maybe it's because you are not often with men, not often fucking like a savage."

Ingrid laughed. "Now, how would you know that?"

"You can see these things. A woman fucking every night is very different from a woman fucking once a month or never fucking. It is the difference between a mango and a coconut. The coconut is hard and dry but if you work hard there is sweet milk deep inside. A mango, well, you know mangoes. You just have to smell a mango to know how sweet it is." Ali straightened. "Ah, you hear that humming? That is Wicks' powerboat. He will arrive shortly from around that corner."

A boat swept around the sandbar, angling with speed. Ali stood ceremoniously and raised a hand in greeting. The two men in the speedboat, one black and one sunburned white, waved back. Ali sat down and watched the boat pass. "Wicks is going to his hotel. He's a rich man. His children will fight over his money." Ali's dhow rocked suddenly with the wake of the speedboat. "You see, this is the problem with powerboats. They make noise and they make waves. It is hard to sail calmly past such a boat."

※

It was two days before Ingrid saw Finn Bergmann. They made way for each other on the seawall; she going to the hotel, he leaving. High tide slapped against the stones of the wall, spraying mist into the air. His eyes met hers for a moment and she smiled in recognition. He looked down quickly as he continued past her. She turned to watch him walk away, jolted by the possibility that she was a stranger to him.

That night she put on her white dress and lipstick and went to the hotel bar. She sat at one of the dimly lit tables with her notebook and an envelope full of receipts and began to detail her expenses to date. Templeton had said in his letter that he would be at the hotel for Christmas. It had been a mistake, Ingrid now realized, to expect him on arrival. She had been forced to recognize that she knew little of his methods in the field—too little to respond appropriately to his absence. She had ten days until Christmas. In that time, she would establish a basic outline for her course.

She was beginning to understand that the Swahili saw themselves as morally superior to the peoples of the mainland, a bastion of godliness in a land of heathens held high with the pillars of prayer, ablution and proper family and community behavior. At the center of it all was the Koran. Though few Swahili spoke Arabic, it was still regarded as a sacred tongue. Even without comprehension, its words strengthened and purified the listener. It was the language of the Koran that even Ali claimed he would speak on the Day of Judgment, when his soul was called up from the grave.

Ingrid was penning numbers into her receipt book, wondering if Ali really believed his soul would be saved, when Danny cajoled her into joining him at the bar. People came and went, a blur of good-looking men and women: sun-bleached blondes with brown skin, a few with darker coloring. An exquisite woman sat on the other side of Danny, dangling her bare legs from the barstool. She wore no shoes. Carved mangrove sticks secured her long brown hair. A petite blonde was passing out jasmine flowers from a basket. "Put it on your pillow at night," she whispered in Ingrid's ear. "You will dream of a prince."

Danny explained that a small community of *mzungu*s, or whites, had taken up residence on the island. Some were European-Kenyan, some just European. Some lived there year-round, some just for the season. Danny knew them all. Names floated around the room, circulating with the smoke and the sweet smell of jasmine. Ingrid felt displaced, a prude in the land of the lotus-eaters. When she heard Finn's name spoken, the molecules in her body churned. "Where's Finn?" she asked Danny.

"Finn? Finn isn't here."

Before she left she put her hand on Danny's arm. "Is there anyone here who might know Professor Templeton or where he lived—anything about him?"

"Anyone know the professor gentleman or where he lived or anything about him?" Danny boomed to a response of blank stares and silence. "He's a bit out of our age range, you see. Doesn't come here much—and when he does, I have noted with regret that he is neither a talker nor a drinker. Spends most of his time in the office, doing what, God knows. It's a mystery to us barflies."

"It's curious," Ingrid said. "That there can be any mystery on such a small island."

"A matter of attention!" Danny declared. "And mine isn't generally directed toward elderly gentlemen." He planted a messy kiss on her cheek. "Come by tomorrow. There's a chance I could rustle something up for you. I do know a thing or two about your old professor." He smiled and turned back to the bar. "There is an advantage, you know, to spending so much time here."

Ingrid woke with the second prayer call, the sour taste of alcohol in her mouth reminding her of why she had slept through the first. After covering herself, she walked through the village toward Danny's house. The cool morning air buoyed her spirits and she boldly smiled at an old woman who paused to stare at her with distaste, her knuckles tightly gripping her walking cane.

Ingrid continued past her (somewhat chastened), slowing again as she approached an unmarked structure that murmured with voices too controlled to be conversation. Through barred windows she could see rows of boys sitting on the earthen floor, fingers traveling right to left across scripture, small bent heads whispering the Prophet's words into memory. She lingered until a small boy saw her there and nudged his friend. The two started giggling and she left the window, stooping to pet one of the cats that lay resting in the shade of the building. The other cats eyed her distrustfully while the one she stroked seemed too tired to purr. They were strange, sinewy creatures that looked both sickly and strong. "You're very tired," she said, picking the cat up and holding it to her. "Aren't you."

Hamilton was outside Danny's house, sitting on his coconut stool, a surprisingly strong structure for its size. His heels were dug into the dirt for leverage. He held the coconut to the ground like an animal that might escape. "Miss Ingrid," he greeted her with a wide smile. He was younger than she had expected, with a pleasant, open face. "Danny told me you would come."

"Is he all right?"

"Don't you worry about Danny."

"Does he need anything? He was drunk last night. Very drunk."

Hamilton looked up from his perch. "You are a nice lady, Miss Ingrid." She watched him husk the coconut, shaving out the tough white meat and piling it into a stone mortar. "He's cut his feet again," Hamilton said. "It's because of the cats. He is trying to kill these cats by throwing dishes. The dishes break and five minutes later he has forgotten he has thrown the plates and there are broken dishes on the floor and he steps on them. He cannot learn from this mistake. Every year it is the same."

"You have been with him a long time?"

"Many years."

A bell rang from inside the house. Hamilton held up a finger and trotted inside. His bare feet slapped across the stone floor and up the stairs. Ingrid picked a shaving from the mortar and laid it on her tongue.

Hamilton reappeared with a chipped ceramic bowl. "He knows you are here," he said, transferring the shavings to the bowl. "I think he hears your voice. You have somewhere to be this morning?"

Ingrid smiled. "I'm fairly free today, actually."

"Then you are to follow me. Danny wants me to show you something." He set the bowl inside. "Fish curry tonight," he said, closing the door behind him. "It's what brings the cats."

Hamilton was a foot shorter than Ingrid. He wore what must have been an old T-shirt of Danny's with a Trinity College emblem embroidered on the chest. His shorts were tattered; white threads hung down against his muscular brown legs. Ingrid kept her eyes on his bleached heels as they padded down streets and between houses, deep into a part of the village she had not yet seen.

Hamilton paused at the entrance to an empty courtyard, veiled on all sides by thick foliage. A trickle of water fell from the mouth of a clay fish arched in a fountain, an otherwise comforting sound made somehow ominous in this deserted place. The rooms on both sides of the courtyard had numbers carved into their painted doors. Hamilton motioned for Ingrid to stay put. He crossed the courtyard and slipped into a side room marked off by a faded curtain. A moment later she heard his voice, suddenly authoritative. He returned with a worn wooden block in his hand. Painted crudely in white on one side of the block was the number three. Attached was a key.

Ingrid stood behind Hamilton as he opened the door. "Templeton's room," he announced and then made his way to the room's only window. He opened the wooden shutters and stood silhouetted by light.

Ingrid's eyes immediately darted to a dark figure on the sunken bed: a wooden statue of a fierce man with African features. She stepped deeper into the room. Hamilton traversed quickly to the bed to inspect the statue. Even from a distance, she could see it was some kind of warrior totem with a spear and shield, and teeth filed to points. Resisting the pull of the statue, she squinted in the uneven light at the rest of the room, which was larger than hers but just as plain. The walls were white and peeling in some places, the floor cool and bare. Opposite the bed was a bureau that Ingrid gratefully began to rummage through while Hamilton continued to eye the statue uncomfortably. Most of the drawers were empty. Outside of a handful of shirts in the top drawer and a scattering of old papers, Templeton had left few traces of his occupancy. She looked around skeptically.

"How did you know he was staying here?"

"Not long ago I brought him something, a letter from the hotel. He was not here. I put the letter under the door. But now it is gone."

"Who was the letter from?"

"I don't know. America maybe."

On top of the bureau was a pen she recognized from his office in Michigan. "I know people here talk," she said, turning the pen slowly in her fingers. "What do they say about him?"

"That he is a *mwalimu*. That he—" Hamilton hesitated. "That he has special powers."

"Don't worry, Hamilton," Ingrid said with a smile. "I know he does."

"Yes?"

"We call it something different where I come from." She allowed her mind to wander back to their last meeting and then finally turned to the bed. "What about the statue?"

"Maybe a guard."

"You're guessing," she said sharply.

"Yes, but it's from the mainland, not here."

"Professor Templeton was looking for evidence of an African king who is said to have brought Islam to this coast. Have you ever heard of such a king?"

Hamilton shook his head. "I know nothing of kings."

Ingrid joined him at the side of the bed and dropped to her knees. "Where are his things?"

Hamilton crawled around to the other side of the bed, peered under it, and emerged empty-handed. "I think we should go now," he said. "This room is not wanting visitors."

Ingrid reached under the mattress with her hands, her eyes now level with the statue, and searched from just under the pillow to the bottom of the bed. Near the foot of the bed she felt something hard, and hesitating only momentarily, she pulled out a thin leather briefcase. Hamilton whistled. She sat down on the floor and placed the briefcase in front of her. The leather was scratched and of poor quality. The sides were sewn loosely to-

gether with thick cord. Ingrid rested her fingertips on the briefcase, noting the marks on the leather, where it had worn thin.
Then, watching Hamilton, she slipped her hand inside and with-
drew two notebooks.

"Those are from Habib's shop," Hamilton pointed out.
"They're for schoolchildren."

Peering inside the now empty compartment, Ingrid found an
interior side pocket and pulled out a passport. "He's still here,
then," she said, flipping through it. The photo had been taken
years ago, long before she met him. His face was not wholly familiar to her. She glanced at Hamilton, her hand on the notebooks. "I have to look at these," she said. He nodded reluctantly
and sat on the edge of the bed as she leafed through the notebooks.

The first one opened with a sketch of an amulet that made her
think of Templeton's "grail." Only instead of stars, she could make
out the faint outline of an inscription and, beneath it, rows of symbols. At the bottom of the amulet were three uneven lines.

On the next page he had begun his notes. They started with
a row of numbers that quickly dissolved into text. Ingrid passed
her fingers over the words, feeling the slight indentations on the
paper where he had pressed his pen.

*In the creation of the heavens and earth; in the alternations of night and
day; in the ships that sail the ocean with cargoes beneficial to man; in
the water which God sends down from the sky and with which he revives the earth after its death, disposing over it all manner of beasts; in
the disposal of the winds, and in the clouds that are driven between sky
and earth: surely in these there are signs for rational men.*

She read on, entranced by the bold insistence of the lines, not
knowing what it was she had found.

By the dust-scattering winds and the heavily laden clouds; by the swiftly gliding ships, and by the angels who deal out blessings to all men; that which you are promised shall be fulfilled.

We opened the gates of heaven with pouring rain and caused the earth to burst with gushing springs, so that the waters met for a predestined end. We carried him in a vessel built with planks and nails, which drifted on under Our eyes: a recompense for him who had been disbelieved.

He stood on the uppermost horizon; then, drawing near, he came down within two bows' lengths or even closer, and revealed to his servant that which he revealed. He beheld him once again at the sidra tree, beyond which no one may pass. (Near it is the Garden of Repose.) When the tree was covered with what covered it, his eyes did not wander, nor did they turn aside.

The Lord of the two easts is He, and the Lord of the two wests. Which of your Lord's blessings would you deny? He has let loose the two oceans: they meet one another. Yet between them stands a barrier which they cannot overrun.

This is a declaration to mankind: a guide and an admonition to the righteous. Take heart and do not despair. Have faith and you shall triumph.

Ingrid flipped through a dozen or so blank pages after this before coming across what appeared to be a diary—a scribbled assemblage of brief and disjointed notes. The first entry was undated.

F tells me leaders are sent from God to mend the tears between men. My king was not the first, will not be the last. This with a puzzling smile: I can't possibly understand the great pattern God weaves with our lives. I am only a single thread. Unattached, subject to winds. But winds come from God, I say. Like currents. God is the air, F says. He is the ocean—

July 15

The Persian sailors were terrified to be blown off course to the land of Zanj because Zanj in those days was thought to be ruled by Barbarians. But what they found was generosity and food such as they had never tasted— a hospitality and readiness to trade that suggested these were not the first visitors from afar. A banquet was prepared with tender fish cooked in the milk of coconut and fruits with delicious nectars, all in abundance springing forth from the arid land. And at the center, handsome and well-formed, a born leader to whom trust came naturally. Come aboard our ship, the Persians said. He went with delight. He had never seen a ship so large.

This is the story they tell of his abduction—always the banquet, always the ship, and the false promise of trade. It was only as an afterthought that they took him and his men with them. He didn't utter a word of protest, but was silent for the entire journey. Silence cleared his soul for the task of faith.

Years later, the same ship was blown off course to precisely the same shore.

July 31

Softened by his kindness, how quickly they moved from terror to greed. Instead of gratitude for trade and safe passage, they rewarded him with captivity. They knew he would fetch a fine price in their markets and carried him off, unafraid of trading in the lives of men.

His pilgrimage would start with a new language and eventually lead him home, along the Nile, through a desert where men found water by the stars, back to his own kingdom, where his people were waiting for him and where a new god was waiting to be born.

Aug. 20

The second hotel is here to stay. M tells me there is nothing to prevent. His denial burns like a prediction of fire.

I tell him the enemy has changed its face and his methods and God has been traded in for the false idols of money. The place must be protected, with or without his consent. Evil is that for which they have bartered away their souls.

At this point, the dates broke off abruptly and the entries became harder to read. Ingrid drew the notebook closer to her and continued.

Humankind is made of haste. I will show you all My signs, so do not try to hurry Me.

Each year, a current has brought crates to M's beach, providing them with seeds and flowers unknown to Africa. The current is called the Agulhas. Agulhas is the palace, the haven he repaired to. It is the spring that nourished his kingdom. It is the warning and the revelation of a new king.

M says God provides for the faithful, issuing sweet water from rock, a clear pool in a desert of sand.

Swahili proverb: Tellers there are. Listeners there are none. He who wants all will miss all.

Luqman: 31:27
And even if all the trees on earth were pens, and the ocean ink, backed up by seven more oceans, the word of God would not be exhausted, for God is infinite in power and wisdom.

It has begun. M's niece will not speak to me, will not look at me. M will divulge no details but I know it must have been a white man. Gus? Wicks? She will heal, M says. But there is no healing from such a wound.

Al-Baqarah: 2:81
Truly, those who commit evil and become engrossed in sin shall be the inmates of the fire; there they shall abide for ever.

I tell myself it is only a man's dreams that have disturbed the peace. If the man could see the folly of his dream, perhaps he could alter it. I must do my part to help him see....

The words trailed off into Arabic. Ingrid showed them to Hamilton, who shrugged and shook his head. She stared at the pages one at a time, at the dance of swirls, dips and arcs and suddenly she could feel him again. She touched the letters, wanting to know them, wanting to breathe them as he had onto the page, wanting to be with him through his words as she had so many times before.

"We come back," Hamilton said. By now he was uneasy. "The man with the key said only ten minutes."

"Can't I take these?" Ingrid asked.

"It's against the law."

"What law?"

"They don't belong to you. They belong to the professor. In his absence, they are protected by the man with the key. Habib."

"That's the law?"

Hamilton nodded.

Ingrid leafed through them quickly. "They're mostly empty. That's not like him."

"Come, then, Miss Ingrid. Leave everything the way it was."

She returned the notebooks reluctantly to the briefcase and slipped it back under the mattress. Again the statue caught her eye. She lifted her arm to touch it and then changed her mind and turned for the door. "I suppose he prays," Ingrid said as she emerged from the room, gesturing toward the courtyard. "The guard, I mean."

"Of course he prays," Hamilton said.

Ingrid spent the warm afternoon hours on her roof, thinking. If Hamilton was right, Templeton had been in his room on or around the day she had arrived. The coincidence was disturbing. The island was too small for him not to have heard of her arrival. How was it that no one had seen him—and why were Ali and Danny so certain he was not around? If he had truly gone off somewhere, why had he left his notes behind?

In the strangely portentous world of his diary, it was impossible to make out his sources. Outside of a few marked passages toward the end, which she took to be from the Koran, there were no documents, no pointers, nothing concrete to go by—none of the precious facts she had promised the department. And nothing to indicate what, if anything, he had found.

Ingrid could not decide what to make of the inscriptions, at once menacing and promising, that filled the early pages of the notebook. She resolved to search her Koran to establish whether they too were quotations.

Only after determining this slender course of action did she allow herself to consider that something could have happened to him.

She got up and walked around the roof. It was odd that Hamilton knew nothing of an African king. Templeton had always given her to understand that the legend was one of the island's central myths of origin. He had told her once, in a rare moment of intimacy, that this was why he had chosen Pelat as his base for so many years.

Ingrid stopped at the washbasin and splashed water on her face. Perhaps she had been wrong to read his personal writings. She hadn't even tried to stop herself, hadn't considered that it might be a violation. When it came to him, she had made blunders of enthusiasm before. That he did not seem to notice one way or the other was one of his generosities toward her.

Settling into the hammock, she draped a scarf over her eyes and made an attempt to recall his journal entries in full: the earlier entries suggested a ratification of Templeton's hypothesis about the story of the African king. But she couldn't make out whether the story as transcribed was authentic, a local legend, or the product of Templeton's own imaginings. It seemed someone had helped him fill in the details—but who? Then there were the later Koranic verses, for which Templeton had been good enough to scribble down verse and line numbers. Even these were unsettling. Their words offered not only specific guidance, but prophecy. They seemed to dictate an incisive response to something or someone. But to what or whom? And why?

Templeton's African king was some kind of a touchstone for a more complicated confluence of events. Though he was somewhat eclipsed by the stronger presence of an angry God, Ingrid was reluctant to let the king recede. However immaterial, she did not want to lose hold of the one element of Templeton's thinking she could still grasp.

She found some level of comfort in thinking about the new details of the story, details that did not diminish the epic quality of the king's journey of faith, but instead made it more real. Ingrid found this faith both extraordinary and appealing. Perhaps the ultimate freedom it granted had intrigued Templeton too.

It was clear that the second hotel made him unhappy. Someone he cared about had been hurt. He was angry. In years of academic challenge, contention and competition, Ingrid had never seen Templeton angry.

She flipped through her English-Arabic translation of the Koran, reading a passage in English and then studying the crescent shapes on the adjacent page. The ancient writing excited her imagination. She took notes, struggling to keep her mind on track. He had found answers in this text. Perhaps she would too.

This book is not to be doubted, she began. *It is a guide for the righteous, who believe in the unseen.* It was not long before she came across a passage similar to the one she had read in the opening pages of Templeton's notebook: *In the creation of the heavens and earth; in the alternations of night and day; in the ships that sail the ocean with cargoes beneficial to man . . .* She read on past the section he had transcribed in his journal: *Yet there are some who worship idols, bestowing on them the adoration due to God. But when they face their punishment the wrongdoers will learn that might is God's alone, and God is retribution.* Ingrid's happiness at locating the verse was instantly tempered by its content. Retribution? For what, she wondered.

When the day grew too hot for her to continue, her thoughts became fluid, melting into one another in a sluggish brutality she couldn't direct. She watched the ocean from her hammock. The unreality of its color both soothed and disquieted her. Fighting off sleep, she started and then abandoned a letter to Dr. Reed. Composing coherent thought was like trying to climb the steep sand dunes in the back of the village, sinking and sliding back to where she began, more tired with each effort. She continued to force her attention outward, resorting, finally, to her own journal. She began writing down her observations, pinning herself down like an insect on a cork board. She would record everything from objects to emotions, as Templeton had once taught her. *Think not only about what you are looking for, but specifically where it has taken you. Details details!* The relief was immediate, and, for a few minutes, she was free of him.

My current residence, she wrote, *is a traditional Swahili stone house, built from rag coral. These patrician houses look much the same from the outside. Their character is within the walls, which are hard to penetrate. Even as a paying guest, I am hurried through the family area of the courtyard. It seems that outside of Abdul and a few small children, there are only women, but it's hard to tell because the women lurk in closed rooms off the courtyard as dark as caves. I have seen one old and humorless enough to be Abdul's wife, and a few younger ones. Daughters, maybe. They don't seem to mind if I watch them on my way upstairs. One even smiles at me. Abdul doesn't like it and rushes toward me in a greeting that is more of an interception.*

*But he is a good Moslem and is gone for all five prayer times, when I
can meander in peace.*

*Ali tells me Abdul is a rich man; he has two wives. One of the
young women is a newly purchased wife, going these days for about ten
thousand dollars. She mostly stays in her room, across the courtyard
from the rest of the family. She seems alone and not terribly happy.
(But maybe she's perfectly happy—God knows I've been unfairly accused. Some people can only look glum. In photographs, my mother is
smiling but maybe the glum photos were thrown away. This is something I will never know.)*

She put her pen down. It was only three-thirty. The slowness of
the hours had a discombobulating effect, like a car braking suddenly at high speed. Things behind her flew forward, landing
jumbled and all together at her feet; events she had forgotten, objects, memories, desires. She thought briefly of her night with
Finn at the Chichester, and then quelled the memory, pushing
herself back further, to Jonathan's soft kiss and her father's
strange parting words. She had called him from the airport.

"I'm sorry I'll be missing your birthday." She was sitting in a
phone booth and already feeling far away. She stared at the floor
while a blur of bodies passed her line of vision, a turbulent river
of legs and feet. So many kinds of shoes, in so many states of el-
egance and disrepair. Ingrid closed her eyes. "Are you angry?"

"Of course not."

"Isn't the department giving you a big seventy-year bash?
And your one family member won't be there. It makes me look
like an ungrateful brat."

"You've long been beyond reproach, Ingrid. Mine, anyway."

"Let my birthday present be that I'm enough like you to survive. Let lightning strike."

"Ingrid, darling"—she could hear him smile—"you're a woman. You're not like me at all."

What did that mean, exactly? She considered her shoeless feet and wondered at the shape of her toes. Had her mother's toes looked like this? The second toe nearly as long as the first, the fifth toe barely there, wedged against the fourth. She bent down to pry her fifth toe free. "Be your *own* toe," she instructed it.

As the afternoon wore on, her waking state became bare, a step away from sleep. Ali appeared, like some hallucination materializing out of the heat. He sat with her on her rooftop and peeled the bark of a bundle of little sticks with his teeth, wadding them into his cheek where they bulged and distorted his speech. Ingrid would have asked him to leave but she was fascinated by the sticks. "So," he said, sucking his bits of bark. "You have been married?"

"No."

"You seem to me like a widow. Sad like a widow."

"I'm not sad. I'm trying to get some work done."

"You are alone, then?"

"No. I'm not alone. Not exactly."

Ali smiled, pleased with the ambiguity of her answer. "I will call you my widow." Ingrid pretended he wasn't there. *Not exactly.* She had to do better than that. I've been too engaged with the bones of the dead to find a partner among the living. And Templeton had been there all along, very much alive next to the dead and the lovers she had occasionally had. *Not alone exactly.*

When Ali left, Ingrid changed her clothes and went down to the street. The muezzin had called for the final time that day. The rose light of sunset fell through the silent village and she walked alone through the streets: the men were in the mosque; the women were preparing dinner. She stopped at the village store and bought a stout white candle and a book of matches. As she made her way to Danny's, clouds gathered above the ocean and the sun pushed through in narrow rays, dimming the day's light to a silvery minimum. She thought if she started from Danny's, she would remember the way to Templeton's room. But the light had changed the feel of the village and she was no longer sure of the direction she and Hamilton had followed.

After two wrong turns that ended in shadowy culs-de-sac, she found the courtyard again. She walked as Hamilton had walked to the office with the keys, reminding herself she had a right to be there, that this was the reason she had come.

The wooden blocks hung from nails on the wall, crooked and randomly placed. She reached for number three and wished for a sound besides the relentless trickle of the fountain. She knew she had at least fifteen minutes—the guard would stop at the coffee hut after evening prayer along with the rest of the men. Quietly crossing the courtyard, she practiced her excuses. She didn't know it was against the rules. She had left something there earlier and had come to retrieve it. She knew Templeton and meant him no harm.

The room was dark. She moved tentatively toward the bed where the shape of the wooden figure lay dark against the mattress. To calm her imagination, she touched its face with her hand. Just wood—a dramatic prop to protect a passport.

Relocating the leather briefcase, she removed the notebooks and placed them on the floor. Then she struck a match, remembering too late to close her eyes, and blinked for a moment without seeing. When her eyes adjusted, the room, alive now with shadows, had become unfamiliar. Beyond the shadows, there was an object in the middle of the floor. She crawled forward with the candle. The room around her warped with shapes.

Alone in a circle of meager light, Ingrid noticed the comforting boundaries of walls and corners had melted away. In front of her, on a plain white plate, was a yellow starchy substance, a simple piece of meat and some kind of wilted green. She put a finger on the meat. It was cold.

Nothing else in the room seemed to have been altered. There was no sign that Templeton had returned. She moved back to the bed and tried to ignore the plate. Who else had access to this room? She pulled out a sheet of tracing paper and held it over the drawing of the amulet. When she had finished copying the inscription, she looked at her watch. Ten minutes had passed.

Adrenaline propelled her next transgression: she located Templeton's last few entries in Arabic and tore them out. After folding them into her pocket, she turned to the remaining pages of the journals, which were mostly empty. Toward the back of the notebook, she came upon a hand-drawn map with an arrow pointing from the Arabian Sea to the Indian Ocean. Along the arrow was the word "Agulhas." An island had been outlined, with two dense areas of crosshatching on either side. Another arrow came from the interior of the smaller of these, originating in the middle of a tight circle of stars. The two arrows met at an intersection with a third line, cut off not far from this point. Ingrid brought the map closer. On one side of the island was a light drawing of a small crescent moon. On another was a Christian cross.

At the bottom of the page were two lines in Arabic written in red ink. Or was it ink? She held it to her nose instinctively, as if to detect, as an animal would, the presence of blood.

Outside she heard something stirring. It could have been nothing more than wind in the trees, but a palpable fear rose in her. *You don't know this place, these people.* Then she added to herself, *You don't know this man.* Ingrid blew out her candle and quietly ripped the map from the notebook.

Finding Finn

$\mathcal{A}$li came looking for her just before noon. She had grown restless on her roof trying to decipher Templeton's unreadable Arabic script and was glad when he called up the stairs for her. Ali had become a pleasant irritant which, for the time being, she tolerated. He was her only regular company, and while he did not speak Arabic, occasionally he taught her things.

Ingrid had searched Templeton's books that morning to find a possible explanation for the plate of food. She marked a paragraph that described something called *Kafara,* a Swahili rite intended to purify a polluted or dangerous place. The source of pollution and danger were *majini,* invisible spirits that could possess or haunt humans. Where angels were made from light and humans from clay or dust, the *majini* were created by fire. They were thought to be the first inhabitants of earth and were said to have once lived in paradise alongside Adam. When their leader, Iblisi, refused to bow to Adam as God had instructed, he and his followers were driven from paradise and made invisible to man.

> *And when God said to the angels,*
> *"Bow to Adam," they bowed,*
> *except one, Iblisi:*
> *he refused, and showed arrogance;*
> *and he was of the ungrateful . . .*

Majini could be either good or evil, male or female. They could assume startling human dimension and even cohabit with people, becoming spirit husbands or wives who would participate in the raising of spirit children. The majority of Swahili people believed these *majini* were real, living in the same villages, walking the same paths. To Ingrid, this seemed improbable and she allowed herself a measure of incredulity, which, on this island, seemed like necessary protection.

The rite of *Kafara* was performed to expel an evil *majini*. A plate of food was left to absorb the pollution and, after doing so, was thrown out into the bush or the sea. What Ingrid didn't know was if the pollution they were trying to purge from the room had come from Templeton or from her.

Ali took her down to the beach to show her the sea eagles. As he had predicted, they found an eagle balancing on the wind above the shoreline. He whistled to it and produced a fish, which he waved in the air. The eagle cocked its white head as Ali stood poised to hurl the fish into the water, the round muscle of his shoulder smooth and tense. When he let the fish fly, the bird tucked into a dive, plunging swiftly toward the waves. It slowed itself with sudden outstretched wings and extended its talons, snatching the fish from the water and flying off behind the dunes, the dark shape of its catch dwarfed by its tremendous wingspan.

Ingrid looked away from the eagle to Ali, who bowed. It was a strange triangle of death and deliverance, and something about it was unsettling. Because it was so clearly a performance, Ingrid applauded.

They walked back to the village in silence. The tide was low; hundreds of sand crabs scuttled sideways, their bulbous eyes darting in confusion. Ali chased them, corralled thirty or so into a herd where they danced on the hard sand, creating round little beads with the frantic mechanical scratching of their claws. He ran them in a final dash into the waves and returned, panting and smiling at his mastery over nature.

"Tell me, Ali, have you ever heard stories about an African king? A great leader who lived hundreds of years ago and was the first to bring Islam to the Swahili people."

"Never," Ali said, after some thought. "And I know many things."

"So how do you think the Koran found its way here?"

"The Koran comes from Mohammed, Miss Ingrid. Mohammed brought Islam to the island." Ali's tone was annoyingly robotic.

"I don't suppose you know any Arabic numbers," she asked offhandedly.

"You are wrong," he said proudly. "These I learned in school."

"Do me a favor, then," Ingrid slowed her pace. "Write them in the sand. I want to see what they look like."

The idea appealed to Ali, the showman. He pointed his foot as he drew shapes in the hard sand with his toes. "One to ten," he explained. Behind him, Ingrid had taken out a pen and was copying the numbers on the palm of her hand.

"Is this satisfactory?" Ali asked when he had finished.

"Perfect, Ali. Thank you."

Ali looked up and down the beach. "Someone might think it strange," he said, raising his arms. "I give these numbers back to the sea!"

They resumed their walk in silence. Soon they were approaching the hotel. "Where does Finn live?" Ingrid asked.

"Who?"

"Finn Bergmann."

Ali made a sound with his tongue and kicked the sand with the ball of his foot. "You know him?"

"Not really."

"Then you shouldn't care where he lives."

But Ingrid had decided she needed to find Finn. She decided this with full knowledge that he was taking on the dangerous form of an answer to a question she hadn't yet fully formulated.

The next day, Ingrid went to the hotel and had coffee and papaya on the veranda. She squeezed a lime over the fruit and ate it slowly with a fork and knife, allowing the sweet astringency to blossom in her mouth. Templeton's pages were in front of her, still untranslated. Her own attempts had been futile, and Arabic, it seemed, was not widely read on the island.

She had copied Ali's numbers into her notebook and then compared them to the inscription on the amulet. There was not even a vague similarity. Her hunch that they might correspond to the Koranic verses in Templeton's notebook had been wrong.

In the afternoon, she left her books to explore the village, parts of which were broken down with crumbling walls and ancient topless pillars. She saw no cars in the narrow streets, only donkeys and cats and the occasional child on a stoop, staring intently, too curious to smile. There were areas of the village that

seemed deserted. Houses and streets were empty. Ingrid walked
with some fear through these abandoned patches. Soon she was
lost in a maze of small alleys that at last gave way to a square full
of sun and sky, azure against the whitewash of the stone houses.

Off to the side of the square, a child played with a kitten, a
dirty handkerchief tied loosely around its slim neck. Ingrid
squatted and smiled, pointing to the handkerchief. "Did a
mzungu make this a gift to you?" she asked. The child held the
kitten close. Templeton wasn't the only white man to carry white
handkerchiefs, but Ingrid began to study the houses on the
square anyway, so she might know it again.

From her roof, Ingrid could see the minaret of the celebrated Friday Mosque rise above the tallest houses, rounded and curving to
a point like a spear bound for heaven. At the top, near the point,
windows had been cut for the muezzin's speakers. Below it, most
of the village's tall stone houses had partly thatched roofs laid
with pillows or beds, where the wind cooled the hot hours and
one could hear the village below, and, beyond that, the soft lapping of a sedated sea. In the best houses, the rag coral had been
shaped into decorative porches and an outdoor staircase. Bougainvillea was trained to climb the bright outer walls, its intense
pink flowers catching the eye like jewelry.

Ingrid dozed with the rest of the village. She was learning the
island's rhythms: low tide fell in the afternoon, in the hours when
heat muted all life. The dance of wind began in the early evening,
with flower petals skittering and palm fronds glinting like
blades in the sun.

She spent the evening at the bar with Danny, who told her tales
of the island and its strange population. He himself was an is-

lander. But was he? "It is my home and I will die here I suppose. Perhaps what I like is that it is so definitely not my home. It couldn't be a worse place for someone like me. That's what makes it so perfect."

"It's far from your parents."

"Blessedly so. They can't stand the climate here, which is an added bonus."

"Have you always avoided them?"

"They're not my true family. My true family is here."

The French doors let in a late-night breeze. The great wooden fan circled lazily, mingling the new air with the smoke and heat of their bodies. Drinking three drinks to her one, he told her the story of Henrik Bergmann. "You've got to consider that a northerner built this place and he built it to escape. What drove him all the way here, God knows. Whatever it was, he wanted to forget every last bit. I can testify as a fellow northerner, that's what the island is best for. But things worked out badly for him." He smiled privately into his glass. "We watch his son's progress with hope and fear."

"Finn is Henrik Bergmann's son?"

Danny nodded. "Don't be fooled by the European features," he told her. "Finn is African."

"I gather he's a fisherman."

"He catches all the fish for the hotel. This time of year he's stocked the freezers and is off chasing game fish. Marlin, and the like. There's a whole fleet of these ninnies competing against each other to see who can catch the biggest fish."

"Does Finn live here in the hotel?"

"God, no."

"Where, then?"

"So many questions, Miss Muffet. Before it's too late, you should know it's quite common for women to fall in love with Finn."

"I'm not in love with him. I've never met him."

"You've seen him, though."

"I think so."

"Well, it's a dull and predictable fate."

Ingrid raised her glass and tilted it as if about to drink. She didn't know why she felt compelled to lie. "Why is that?"

"The only place you'll find Finn is at the hotel and the only thing Finn likes about the hotel is the bar. What he likes about the bar is the booze. You will always find him drunk. Me too, for that matter. These are our limitations as men. It's strengthened our friendship enormously. The point is, for Finn to approach any significant emotion he has to be sober, and you and your kind will never catch him sober. He's too quick."

Danny drained his tumbler. "As for the other man you're after, the older gent, you might not catch him either. As I said, he rarely comes here to Salama."

"Where else is there to go?"

"Nowhere as far as I'm concerned. But there are other *settlements* on the island. Nothing as friendly as what we have here. Jackson, come over here. Tell our girl Friday what goes on over in Kitali."

Jackson ran a soft rag over the gleaming wood surface of the bar. "Which part, Mister Danny, would she like to know?"

"What the old *mzungu* Templeton might be doing over there."

"I have heard stories only."

"What stories?" Ingrid asked.

"That he was there."

Danny pointed again to his glass. "That's a brief, unsatisfying story, Jackson."

"That he is often there."

"Have you heard anything else?" Ingrid asked.

"Just stories." Jackson moved down the bar to serve a lone hotel guest.

"Why doesn't he want to talk about it?"

"These people are very superstitious. Maybe your professor is bad luck."

Ingrid waited until Jackson returned before she asked about Templeton's king. "Stories, fables, anything you might have heard about such a man would be helpful."

"My memory is short on African kings," Danny said. Jackson simply shook his head and turned away.

❧

On her way back, Ingrid found the beach down in the village where the fishing dhows rested on the sand at low tide. A tribe of cats sat in the wet sand and watched impassively as a fisherman painted shark's liver oil on the bottom of his boat. The smell was rank; the fisherman tied a scarf around his face. The cats waited patiently. Another dhow approached the sloping beach and the cats pivoted to face it. Ingrid sketched them sitting fearlessly on the shore. They were shaped like Bastet, the Egyptian cat goddess, thin and royally arched. Their fur was a motley blend of tortoise, calico and tabby and every variation in between. They made absolutely no noise. Off to the side, a particularly regal cat sat facing the sea.

When she finally decided to head back to Abdul's, Ingrid ran into a cluster of beach boys watching a soccer game in the sand. The sand changed the dynamic of the game, deadening the bounce of the ball. The legs of the players were taut as they dodged and feinted, effortlessly trapping and controlling the ball's erratic movement. A particularly young player wove his way around a less agile defender and tapped the ball through two pieces of driftwood. He let out a victorious whoop before he was tackled by the eluded defender.

As she continued to walk, Ingrid almost tripped over Finn. He had been sitting a few meters down the seawall, watching the same game. She was so startled by the sight of him that instead of passing him by, she stood, catching the hair blowing in her eyes so she could see him. Finally he looked up. "Hello."

"I think we met in Nairobi."

"Yes. The Chichester." He smiled distantly as if the memory were insufficient to warrant more. He squinted up at her. "You here alone?"

"Yes. I'm looking for someone. The man I asked you about at the Chichester. He was my professor."

A sudden, brief smile and a clear look at his eyes. "I hope you find him."

Ingrid smiled back, paralyzed by his disinterest. "Thank you." She walked past him and the beach boys, whose conversation had halted as soon as she had approached and now resumed behind her, their laughter carried forward by the wind.

She followed the seawall back to the hotel, where the stone terrace was deserted, and sat alone above the bright ocean. She ordered tea and, when it arrived, hypnotically dipped the teabag. She couldn't forget what she had seen in Finn's eyes—pride, loss, something like pain—any more than she could decide if he had chosen to show it to her or if it was just there, for everyone to see.

Ingrid pushed away her now undrinkable tea. In her notebook, she wrote: *I've finally found Finn.* She couldn't love a man she didn't know. Desire, she thought, was another thing.

An Obvious Enchantment

*I*ngrid could not sleep in her room for the four or five hours of the night when the air was completely still. That night, the heat drove her outside to a bed of pillows. She was woken before dawn by Abdul, whose sinewy hand was grasping her shoulder like a claw. He wanted her to return to her room. It wasn't safe to sleep outside. Or proper. He sat on his haunches, waiting for her to get up. In the darkness, she could see his bare feet gripping the smooth ground. From downstairs came the sound of wailing; mournful, weeping female tones. "What is it?" she asked his silhouette.

"It is Sari, my wife. She is singing."

"That's a strange sort of song. It sounds like crying."

Abdul didn't answer. Ingrid watched him in the dark. Finally he said, "Maybe it's just a song you don't know."

"You can leave now, Abdul," she said. "I will go inside."

She stepped into her room and reemerged a few minutes after

he had gone. A candle in a hurricane lamp allowed her to continue reading even as the breeze picked up. She flipped restlessly through the Koran, impatient with the endless invocations and the disturbing sense that language was scattered by these repeated mentions of the Lord, like clouds parting around a mountain. The text both defied the power of words and depended on them. A paradox, Ingrid thought, that would have appealed to Templeton. Unlike the Bible, the text of the Koran did not build into stories. There were no escapes of narrative. Just as soon as a story began, it was leveled by an injunction of faith and the always lurking threat of admonition. She searched its pages anyway, copying characters of the Arabic script into her notebook. Her hand formed the soaring loops awkwardly and paused with uncertainty at the unclosed circles. Templeton had traveled this road, she thought, considering the passage in front of her: *Humankind is made of haste. I will show you all My signs, so do not try to hurry Me.*

The word *Allah,* she found, was like a breath that barely disturbed the lips . . .

Abdul woke her just before dawn, when she had again fallen asleep on the pillows. This time she told him in Swahili she was not afraid. Allah would protect her. The old man was stubborn but she waited him out. She lay with her eyes closed until finally he left and she drifted off until the first call to prayer.

In the morning, there was no water. A lukewarm trickle escaped from the tap. Ingrid cupped her hands underneath it and splashed the brackish warmth on her eyes. Downstairs, in the courtyard, were signs of washing: a bucket of precious water, soaked rags hanging over its rim. Sheets blew in the slight breeze of the sheltered space, suspended from a cord tied to two pillars. The smell of laundry was trapped in the enclosed space and, somewhere, someone was cooking: a sweet, sugary smell of dough, possibly the source of the unfamiliar pastry shapes that had begun appearing on her doorstep, wrapped in clean white cloth.

Passing through the courtyard, Ingrid paused and smiled at Abdul's young wife. Ali had told her that Sari was Abdul's second wife, come from down the coast. Other than Abdul and his family, she was alone here on the island. A mail-order wife.

Ingrid discovered that Sari stayed in a room by herself, a room not unlike Ingrid's own, but with no windows. No light. Sari would sit at her door sewing, bent over the fabric she was mending as the sun fell on her hair and the cloth of her *bui-bui,* disappearing like water into a sponge. Her movements were economical to the point of being imperceptible. Ingrid watched her sitting, still as a root, and wondered how many times she had passed by without seeing her at all.

When Abdul was gone, the energy in the courtyard took flight like a helium balloon cut loose. Ingrid tried to smile encouragingly when she walked in on the unchecked laughter of these women left alone. *Don't stop, it sounds wonderful.* Sari was rarely among the merrymakers. It was Abdul's daughters who formed a phalanx around their mother, whispering between bursts of laughter and stories related with theatrical gesticulation. Ingrid slowed her step so her eyes could adjust to the shadows of the courtyard. She could not see beyond the threshold of Sari's door, but from time to time, she heard her singing inside.

Sari—Ingrid said her name softly because it was as soft as her own name was harsh. From the fear in Sari's eyes, Ingrid knew that Sari had been instructed not to talk to her. She bent down next to her and smiled. There were things she needed, Ingrid explained in broken Swahili. Washing powder. She held a soiled dress in her hands.

No. Sari shook her bare head. Me. She pointed to herself. Me. I will wash it. And then her fingers, long and thin, went out to the cloth of the dress and her mouth opened slightly at the shape of it as she held it before her in the air. Ingrid shook her head and took the dress back. No. She smiled in apology. Me.

When Ingrid was certain that neither Abdul nor his first wife was around, she unfolded one of Templeton's pages from her copy of the Koran and held it up. "Can you read this?" she asked, watching Sari carefully. "It's very important."

Sari took a quick step back and glanced quickly around the courtyard before continuing in halting English. "It is not possible for me to read," she announced, and turned as if to go.

Ingrid held on to her wrists. "I am worried a friend of mine may be in danger and this is all I have to find him. Please, Sari, I need your help. I know you know Arabic—I have been listening to your singing."

Sari hesitated before answering. "Maybe I know someone," she said at last, holding her hand out for the page. "You let me take it to him?"

Ingrid removed the rest of the pages from the book. "Take these too. Be careful with them—and please tell no one about this."

"Of course," Sari said, tucking the pages into her *bui-bui*. "No harm will come. My friend is a good man, a teacher. I will bring them tomorrow."

The next afternoon, Ali made his daily trip to the roof of Abdul's guesthouse to visit Ingrid. "You are working. I will just sit here in the shade for a moment."

Ingrid wasn't working. She was sketching rooftops and palm trees, waiting for Sari to deliver her translations. While she continued, Ali sat and stared at her until he broke her concentration.

She gave him a brief, ferocious look and then chewed on the end of her pencil. She had found that nothing but time could make him leave.

"Now are you finished with the work?"

"It's not the kind of work you can finish."

"No? How terrible. How tragic. How terribly tragic."

"You've learned a new word."

Ali grinned. "There is a nice British lady at the hotel. She is teaching me."

"I'll bet she is." Ingrid went back to her sketch and shaded the fronds of a palm tree. She wanted Ali to go away.

"You think I am bad. A bad boy."

"I'm teasing you, Ali. Anyway, I don't care."

"You should care."

"Why?"

"Because it is what women do."

"Now you're teasing me."

Ali bared his teeth in something like a smile. "I would like it sometimes if you laughed."

Ingrid frowned deliberately. "Ali, is there something wrong with Abdul's second wife, Sari?"

Ali glanced toward the stairs. "She is not well," he confided.

"Why not?"

"I don't know. What I have heard is that she has a *pepo.* A bad spirit inside of her. It is a kind of sickness."

Ingrid remembered the term from her reading. A *pepo* was a *majini* that possessed someone, making the person either deranged or zombielike. "I have heard her crying at night."

"A bad *pepo* can ruin your life."

"How does one get a bad *pepo*?"

"A *pepo* grabs you when you walk out in the bush, or by large trees. Sometimes they grab you in town."

"So a *pepo* can grab you anywhere. It's not Sari's fault she has a bad *pepo*."

"She might have invited one."

"Why would she have done that?"

"Who knows? She is a woman."

"Now, Ali, that's not enough of a reason."

Ali grinned. "It is more than enough. Didn't you know women have faulty souls? Just hearing the voices of other people can be dangerous. That's why we lock them up."

"You can't be serious."

"No, it's all a joke. Our island is a joke. Sometime you must start laughing."

When Sari came up the stairs, she seemed exuberant. Her face was flushed as she extracted Ingrid's pages from inside her *bui-bui*. "They are now in English," she said proudly. Ingrid realized that Sari was quite capable of happiness.

"Where have you been?"

"Dancing at Riyadh Mosque. The Imam there read your pages."

"I thought women weren't allowed in the mosques."

"This one is different. This the mosque of Habib Salih." Sari's face lost some of its light. "But please tell no one I have been there."

"Don't worry, Sari. Thank you for this." Ingrid's eyes were already scanning the translated passages, which were penciled in a neat script. The first was from a chapter in the Koran called *"Al-Nur,"* or "Light."

> As for the ungrateful who do not have faith,
> their works are like a mirage on a plain,

which the thirsty man thinks to be water
until he comes to it and finds nothing there—
but he finds God in his presence,
and God pays him his earnings;
and God is swift in his accounting—

or like the darknesses in an ocean deep and vast
covered over with waves,
upon them waves,
over them clouds.
Darkness one on top of another;
If one stretched forth a hand,
One would hardly see it.
And whoever God gives no light
Has no light at all.

The verse stopped there. The next passage came from "Saba," or
the "Sheba" chapter, which occurred later in the Koran.

Thus on that day none of you
will have power over anyone else,
whether the helpful or harmful.
And We will say to those who did wrong,
"Taste the torment of the fire,
in which you do not believe."
And when Our clear signs
are recited to them, they say,
"What is this but a man
who wishes to deter you
from what your fathers worshiped?"
And they say,
"What is this but a fabricated lie?"

> *And those who deny the truth*
> *when it comes down to them say,*
> *"This is obvious enchantment."*

The lines in red below the map repeated the middle part of the passage:

> *"Taste the torment of the fire,*
> *in which you do not believe."*

At the bottom was a note for her from the Imam. *"Come to Riyadh Mosque,"* he had written. *"I must hear the story of these pages."*

"Taste the torment of the fire . . ." More than to explain the story of these pages, she wanted this Imam to dispel her worry over the vengeance of his translation. Reluctantly, she matched the Imam's translations to passages in her Koran and found them to be almost identical. She left the guesthouse abruptly, heading for the hotel.

Ali was in the office. "I have been hearing about Habib Salih," Ingrid said.

"Habib Salih is famous," Ali's voice turned mellifluous as he instantly transformed into an expert tour guide. "He founded the Riyadh Mosque. It is a mosque for the people. Slaves, workers, fishermen. He had them sing and dance *maulidi,* since they were not educated enough to read it. Also it was not proper for them to read it because they were slaves and workers and fishermen," Ali added with a flourish. "But Habib Salih believed that what people did was more important than who they were and the position or parentage they had."

"According to one of my books that you think say nothing, Habib's mosque took the people one step closer to Allah. It says that with ecstatic dance comes ecstatic rapture, which is where God lives. What do you make of that?"

"I think you have been reading too much, making your own philosophies."

"Maybe," Ingrid said, laughing. "But I am beginning to believe in my own philosophies. I think they merit research. Could you take me to this mosque?"

"This," Ali said. "I will have to see."

※

Under Ali's supervision, Ingrid ransacked the office for maps. "Why didn't you tell me where Templeton stayed that first night?" she demanded, suddenly irritated by Ali. "I think he might have been here."

Ali shrugged. "I didn't care where he stayed. I only knew the direction he walked when he left the hotel." They finally found one old map. The layout was similar to the map Ingrid had found in Templeton's notebook. "This is where the other village is," Ali pointed. "But this map is no good."

"What other village?" Ingrid asked. "Kitali?"

"Yes, where our people have gone. The crazies. Mad as rabbits."

"Mad as hatters," she corrected. "But what are you talking about? What crazies?"

Ali shrugged. "I won't take you there. They cast spells, make you lose your lunch."

"Can you please explain more fully?" she asked patiently. "This is important. Tell me what you know about this second village."

"Before I was born there was a split in the island. Chief Mohammad took his people away because there were so many evil *majini* at Salama. Now, right near them, there is a second hotel and again there is talk of splitting, though there is nowhere for them to go—except back here. I don't want them to come back here. I have heard they don't talk."

"That's ridiculous."

"You might think." Ali inspected the map. "But this map is wrong. This isn't where the village is at all."

"You've been there?"

"No. But this is not where it is."

"Is there another map somewhere?"

"The professor took all the maps."

"More news! And where might he have put the maps?"

"Once he had them spread all over the office floor. He was crawling around them like an infant. Then he took them away."

"Took them where? Where in God's name are all these things he might have had?"

"I think he had a lady friend on the island. Maybe he took them to her."

"Why would he have done that?"

"A gift, maybe."

"Do you really think he took all those maps to a girlfriend, Ali?"

"I think he is no longer on the island, Miss Holes."

Ingrid went back to the guesthouse and sat on the roof with her two maps of the island. The location of the other village was not exactly the same on both maps, but it was close enough. "The second village is Kitali," she wrote. Covering the hotel map with Templeton's, she added, " 'M' stands for Mohammad."

The walls of Templeton's house in Michigan were papered with maps: layers of them, like geologic strata of his life, his work. Once Ingrid had pulled back the loose corners, sliding her hand between the smooth surfaces, trying to see what had come before. She was still looking for bread crumbs then, some way to understand him empirically so she could say to herself, "See here, this is what makes him worth my while. Look at his background, his experiences, his choices . . ."

"Have you or have you not been married?" Ingrid had demanded.

"Married!" he erupted and then folded into a fit of coughing. "Why, are you considering it in the near future?"

"No."

"Good girl. Get more work done. Tell me something, are you a lover?"

"What?"

"Do you consider yourself a passionate person?"

"Yes. No. You're asking about relationships, aren't you?"

"If that's what you're passionate about."

"Well, I'm not, really."

"No need to fight love, girl, it dissolves quite readily on its own. I say let the piercing notes of passion and pain ring out— there are only so many of them in a lifetime, and they are a joy to hear. Can you imagine a symphony without the violins?"

"But you never married."

"Marriage is for the truly heroic. If done properly, it is probably the single most worthwhile undertaking in one's life. But one needs vast amounts of humility and patience. I am expecting these virtues to arrive at some point."

Ingrid predicted that he would evade marriage the way he had evaded other norms of human behavior. He could even do without basic human needs of sunlight, sleep or food, staying locked in his office for days at a time, with Mags faithfully guarding his door. She would shake her head ruefully when Ingrid stopped by. Not yet. Ingrid waited because the vigor and resolve with which he broke his fast thrilled her, bursting up to gulp the air, the light and the joy of discovery making his appetites suddenly ravenous—"Give me bloody red steak and red wine—I need life pumping through me!" She had heard such declarations before when he bounded out of what Mags referred to as his "deathbed." Really it was a deep meditation, a hibernation in which the information he had gathered and consumed settled inside him and began to make sense and something more.

Once he had dictated to Ingrid because his hands trembled too much to write. Another time, when Mags had sent him home to bed, he tied his robe when Ingrid came with provisions and, barefoot, led her to the gravel in his driveway where he drew pictures with his cane. He whispered emphatically as he scratched the images. "Tell me you can see it." Ingrid's eyes were on the winter-pale light that lit his tangled gray hair like a halo. "I think you should put your shoes on," she said, with a real fear that he would catch his death through the soles of his feet.

"Dear girl"—Templeton laughed—"you're trying to calm me down."

"You've been ill. Or something."

"This is who I am," he smiled, a strange old man-angel sweeping his wand through the morning air. Triumphant.

"Well, then," Ingrid conceded.

"Do you see it?"

"Maybe. Yes."

Templeton's cane flew into the air like a baton. Ingrid leapt toward it to keep it from cracking his head. "You needn't have," he told her. "I almost always catch it. If I don't, it's a sign from above that I need more rest."

. . .

If Templeton didn't return by Christmas, she would go to Kitali. That gave her three days. Ingrid tossed her pen above her head to see if she could catch it. She did it twice, dropping it once and catching it once. She started to play a game. If, out of ten tosses, she caught more than five, she would go to the bar and treat herself to the newfound pleasure of an afternoon beer.

The Body Worker

$\mathcal{A}$fter a few long nights on *Tarkar*, Stanley stole into his house one afternoon for his mail and a change of clothes. His floating haven of peace had recently been threatened when one of the crew members had made Nelson translate a curse on both Stanley and his hotel. It made Stanley think he should be supervising them more carefully at Kitali; curses were a good excuse for bad behavior. But late at night and in the early morning, the beginnings of fear nipped at him like little dogs. He became prone to overactivity, haunting the hotel bar after hours and micromanaging affairs on *Tarkar* he barely understood—further endangering the goodwill of his crew.

Stanley crept down the path to his house, listening for Daisy's voice from the rooftop. Satisfied that she was either asleep or away, he pushed open the front door. Jackson, coming from the kitchen with a broom, jumped when he saw his employer standing on the doorstep.

"Jackson!" Stanley exclaimed in a loud whisper. The sight of the boy seemed to make him overjoyed.

"Mr. Wicks! You frightened me."

"Are you alone?"

"Yes sir. Melissa and the baby have gone to the beach." He paused, his face full of anguish over whether to report on the other half of the household.

"Don't worry, Jackson. I don't need to know about the others." Jackson smiled in relief. "At least they're not bonking upstairs." The smile dropped from his face like a stone. Jackson, Stanley realized, was on edge. He could not think of what to say. Almost anything that came to mind would only make the boy more nervous. He was peeved with new reason at Daisy. Our little community has been damaged! To be fair, while Jackson's young mind was being imprinted with Daisy's immoral behavior, Stanley had quite dishonorably abandoned him. He felt ashamed and then angry with both himself and Daisy. We could have been such good influences, he thought. This all could have gone so differently. Perhaps it wasn't too late.

Stanley went to the bookshelf and perused the titles. None of the books had moved since he'd put them there. They were collecting dust. Was Daisy simply not interested in literature? He pulled out E. M. Forster's *A Passage to India* and settled into the window seat. Jackson was sweeping the floor, clearly trying to remain industrious in the face of his household's decline. Stanley felt he owed the boy something. Instead of suggesting that he dust the bookshelf every now and then he asked, "Ever read, Jackson?"

"Not often, Mr. Wicks."

"But they teach you in school, don't they?"

Jackson smiled and moved his head to the side a little to indicate that school might not have been his peak experience. "Well, if you're ever interested, I'd be happy to teach you."

"Teach me?"

"To read, Jackson. There's a whole world inside this book. See how small a book is? There are ten different places inside these pages. It's an amazing trick. Listen to this: 'Except for the Marabar Caves—and they are twenty miles off—the city of Chandrapore presents nothing extraordinary. Edged rather than washed by the river Ganges, it trails for a couple of miles along the bank, scarcely distinguishable from the rubbish it deposits so freely . . .' " Stanley glanced up to find Jackson still standing and motioned him to sit. " 'There are no bathing-steps on the river-front, as the Ganges happens not to be holy there; indeed there is no riverfront, the bazaars shut out the wide and shifting panorama of the stream. The streets are mean, the temples inef-fective, and though a few fine houses exist they are hidden away in gardens or down alleys whose filth deters all but the invited guest . . .' " Stanley looked over the book at Jackson, who sat rigidly at the table. "What did you think of that?"

"I think India sounds like a very dirty place. I would not like to go there."

"You see?" Stanley put down the book and flipped through a stack of mail. "Chandrapore is not one of the better places. Now what do we have here. Bill, bill, bill, boring, bill, letter. Ah, it's from my father. Let's see what he has to say." Because Stanley had not yet released him, Jackson remained motionless. "Blah blah, oh, now this is interesting. Listen to this. Here is a taste of my home in England. My father writes: 'Took the train into London for the opera opening. *La Bohème,* this year. I find these surtitles unfortunate; the performance loses something when you learn that these characters are just a bunch of lazy, melodramatic *artist*

types bellowing about how cold it is.' " Stanley paused to laugh.
" 'But the bubbly at intermission was nonpareil. I treated myself
to a medicinal dose and slept through the second half.' That's my
father, the old grouser. Loves the bubbly."

Jackson smiled and waited for his dismissal. When it did not
come, he asked, "What is bubbly?"

"A terrible, wonderful drink. It can make you very happy."

Jackson brightened. "We have some here?"

"No. No bubbly," Stanley said regretfully. "It doesn't keep
very well here."

Jackson's brow furrowed with concern. A moment later it
smoothed out. "Would you like some tea?"

"That would be lovely, Jackson."

Stanley's tea had steeped to perfection when Daisy's shrieks of
laughter became audible. They shattered the delicate silence of
the afternoon, driving India, the Marabar Caves and lovely Miss
Quested into the ground. My *God,* Stanley thought, the woman
can make noise. Jackson and Stanley glanced at each other like
fellow warriors about to be taken in their own fort. To the side of
Stanley's anxiety was annoyance that the highly agreeable mood
in the room had been dashed to pieces. Jackson, who had relaxed,
was noticeably nervous again, his eyes pivoting from Stanley to
the door as if he were preparing himself to watch a jousting
match. He stood looking stricken as the shrieks grew louder.
They were almost at the door. "It's all right, Jackson," Stanley
said. "Adolpho must be sidesplittingly funny."

The enemy burst in, packages in hand. She was wearing a thin
dress that didn't cover her well enough. Stanley noticed she wore
no brassiere. He stared openly at her breasts, where he could see
the round darkness of the areolae, the slight hardness of her nipples. "Hello, Stanley, it's been ages. We've been shopping. Can

you imagine? I didn't think there was anything to buy here." Stanley put down his book and feigned interest as she pulled objects from her bag; a package of henna, a cloth of some sort, chocolate, gum and something wrapped in a banana leaf.

"Have you gone and bought *miraa*?" Stanley was appalled. "Lord, Daisy!"

"Oh, don't be so pious. At least it's a natural high."

"So is heroin."

"Oh, *please,* it's not as if you can OD on it. It's a native ritual—right, Jackson?" Jackson had been extricating himself slowly from the room. He had almost reached the kitchen door, poor fellow.

"Leave Jackson out of it," Stanley said.

Daisy was unwrapping the banana leaf. She held the bundle of sticks to her nose. "Smells perfectly harmless."

"I can't smell anything but *body oil* in here," Stanley lied. "I just hope its not affecting Harry."

"Don't be ridiculous. Come, Adolpho." Adolpho had posted his bulky frame at the window, where he stood with military stoicism. This was just another "operation" for Adolpho, the professional masseur. At the sound of his name he came to life and lumbered like a mastiff to his owner. After he had heaved himself up the steep staircase, Daisy glared at Stanley. "We're not *doing it,* you know. I'm sure you'd like to think so."

"I don't think about it at all, Daisy."

"Ha! I know you think about it because you *talk* about it, Stanley. Do you think I'm a complete noodle? To your friends at the bar, 'Oh Daisy, she's off bonking her masseur.' It makes hating me easier, doesn't it. Well, I'm past caring what you think, Stanley. I'm just grateful to have a companion who values my company."

It was the moment for rebuttal, but Stanley was mute. Did he want to hate his wife? What sort of husband was he? Daisy stood across the room from him, seething. Looking at her, he realized she was angrier than he'd thought. Attempting reconciliation now would be like tangling with a wounded ferret. He could get hurt. "I suppose it's not the worst thing that could have happened," he said, more to himself than to her.

"*What?*" He watched with some anxiety as the color in his wife's face deepened. "What did you say, Stanley?" She seemed to tremble, like a volcano. She's going into pulmonary distress, Stanley thought. The best thing to do was leave, immediately. Remain calm, he told himself. Move slowly. He collected his book and his mail and rose, yawning as if he had all the time in the world. "Lovely letter from Dad," he said easily. "Seems the weather in England is unseasonably warm." Crossing the room, he gave himself some distance from Daisy because it occurred to him that, if she could, she might kick him.

Once out of the house, Stanley felt light as a cloud. He decided to go visit Harry on the beach. He spotted the little tyke from far off; a lonely little form sitting on the sand. A few yards away was a slab of horizontal flesh that must be Melissa. As he approached, he saw that Harry was playing with a dead jellyfish while Melissa tanned on her stomach, topless and asleep. "Crikey, what've you got there, Harry?"

Harry gurgled and flung the jellyfish to the sand. Stanley noticed a number of jellyfish in the vicinity of his son. He bent to pick Harry up and considered dropping a jellyfish onto Melissa's bare back to wake her. Impulsively, he decided not to wake her at all and instead took Harry to the hotel bar for a juice. That would teach her a better lesson.

Things were astir at Salama. The veranda was filled with lounging hotel guests. Stanley pulled up a chair to the small, familiar
crowd in the corner. He and Harry were greeted warmly by
Onka, who was extremely pregnant, and Lady Emily, who didn't
have a maternal bone in her body. Stanley had known her in England, where her family and his attended some of the same parties. She petted the top of Harry's head abstractly and lit a
cigarette. Danny arrived with a trayful of drinks from the bar.
"Splendid!" said Lady Emily, extending a long arm for a glass.
"Don't give any to Onka, she's about to burst."

"It doesn't matter anymore," Onka said. "He's all finished in
there."

"Aren't you *terrified*?" Lady Emily asked. "I would be. I mean,
what sort of *real* painkillers do they have here?"

"We're going to try to do it in the water. Sabo read a book
about it. He says babies can swim right after they're born. It's
supposed to be less traumatic."

"In the *ocean*?" Stanley wrestled to get his son comfortably
situated on his lap. Harry pulled his hand out of his mouth
and reached, trancelike, for Onka's protruding belly. Onka
squealed and pressed a hand to her side. "He's kicking! I think
he wants to talk to Harry." Onka was Danish-Kenyan and
had been on the island for ten years. To Stanley, she looked
like she was sixteen. He found an enormous belly on an otherwise nubile body somehow obscene. He shifted Harry away
from her bulge and turned to Danny, whose face was all but
hidden by an absurd-looking lady's sun hat covered with pink
flowers. Stanley could think of nothing to say to Danny, who
could be unpredictably acerbic, so he turned his son around to

face him and, affecting deep involvement, bounced him on his knee.

"How's married life, Stanley?" Danny asked. "Daisy getting along all right?"

"Managing nicely, thanks."

"You know, I don't think she likes me."

"Who, Daisy?"

"Yes, I get that distinct feeling."

"I'm sure you're wrong. Daisy's a very nice girl at heart."

"To me she seems a bit hostile."

"Well, maybe a bit of postpregnancy temper, that's all."

"Did you hear that, Onka? You should prepare your husband for some postpartum bitchiness." Onka smiled serenely and put her hands on her belly. "We're lucky not to have to go through that, aren't we, Stanley?" Danny asked.

"I think it's terribly unfair that you *can't* go through it," Lady Emily said. "It would help gender relations considerably. I wish Staz could have *my* baby. I have no interest in going through the ordeal myself. Yuck and double yuck."

"Besides, you'd lose your fabulous shape, like Daisy did. It would become an *epidemic*," Danny said. "Can't have a bunch of fatties lying around in bikini land. It would ruin all the fun."

Stanley looked around the veranda, wishing he could talk to the hotel guests instead of being mired in another inane conversation with this licentious group of dissolutes he called his friends. It wasn't that he disliked them, it was that everything they spoke about was contaminated by fiendish contempt. He wasn't sure how the malice crept in, but it did, always. He motioned to the waiter and ordered a mint julep for himself and some diluted papaya juice for Harry. He held his son close to him.

"Where's your new friend, Danny?"

"Oh, yes." Onka clapped her hands. "I heard you have a crush."

"Miss Muffet? I imaging she is reading her books. Anyway, I wouldn't think of subjecting her to any of you. She's far too innocent."

"Well, sometime you've got to introduce us properly," Lady Emily said. "Have a party or something. So we can *observe* her."

"She's not nearly as beautiful as you, Emily, so no need to be vicious. She's actually quite awkward-looking."

"Vicious?" Lady Emily laughed. "I'll be sugar sweet, as always."

"Is this the American girl?" Stanley asked. "I rather like the way she looks."

"Well," Danny said. "May the best man win."

"I think you misunderstood me," Stanley said, focusing on tipping juice into Harry's tiny mouth.

"Did I? Well, I'm not surprised she hasn't captured your fancy. She's not exactly dripping with sexuality. She prefers to read."

"Like you," Onka said.

"Yes, like me."

"Now I do want to meet her," Lady Emily said.

"You'd only scare her, Emily."

"More than you, Danny? I doubt it. Let's have a party. When Staz and I get back from safari. It must be somebody's birthday this month."

"Stanley, I think your nanny has arrived," Danny said. "She looks like a mad cat."

Melissa was stalking toward them, inflamed with sunburn. She stood behind Stanley and put her hands on her hips in her now familiar stance of domestic rebellion. "You might have *told* me where you were off to."

"You seemed quite peaceful there," Stanley replied. "I decided not to wake you."

"I nearly fainted with fright." Quite suddenly, Melissa burst into tears.

"Oh, now, it's all right," Stanley said, relenting. "Here, take Harry. You see, he's happy to see you." Melissa buried her face in the child's neck. Stanley was quietly pleased with himself. His plan had worked. "He's had a little juice but he's probably ready for some lunch."

Melissa was tenderly stroking the back of Harry's head. "Well," she said wearily, "I'm off, then."

"Good-*bye,* Melissa!" Danny boomed as she walked away. Melissa spun around, confused. The baby started to cry.

"See what you've done, Danny," Lady Emily said. "Big ogre."

Stanley rose. "Well, I'm off too," he said, not yet knowing where he was off to.

❧

As he left the hotel, Stanley spotted *Tarkar* coming in and went to the beach to signal Nelson. He sat on the sand and waited for Nelson to ride in to shore. Scanning the beach, he looked out for the American girl. If he saw her again he would approach her, if only to save her from Danny. She read books, damn it. Why couldn't Daisy read? Books alone could save a failing marriage; he was suddenly and wildly certain of it.

Stanley watched as Nelson neared the beach in *Tarkar*'s dinghy. Nelson held both sides of the boat as he teetered to his feet and launched himself into the shallows, dragging the dinghy behind him. He stumbled, dripping, onto the sand and settled himself next to Stanley.

"I think you should take more men next time out," Stanley said. "*Tarkar* can handle it and that means more lines, and more fish."

Nelson seemed unusually pensive. "If you think so," he said reluctantly.

"Why not?"

"Finn only has Jonah. Seems like enough. Don't want to overdo it."

"Finn couldn't take another man if he wanted to. Doesn't have the room or the engine."

Nelson looked a bit happier. "True."

"I'd like to keep a gun on board."

"A gun?"

"In case of emergencies. Say you hook a wild fish, or if you get in trouble and run out of flares. You can hear a gunshot for miles." Stanley paused. "Maybe the crew takes a swim and the sharks are out."

Nelson was nodding his head. "I can see that."

"For safety," Stanley confided. "Can you shoot a gun?"

Nelson's face peeled into a smile. "I'm Kenyan. I can kill a bull elephant with one bullet."

"All right, then, great white hunter. I'll bring one out this afternoon. I've got a derringer."

Nelson was impressed. "I wonder what Finn will think of a gun on board."

"I don't think you need to tell Finn, Nelson. This is *Tarkar*'s business."

Part
Three

A Night Swim

*T*hree days passed like one long afternoon. It was as if the heat had softened the shape of time, resculpting its passage. Ingrid's clothes were always damp, either with sweat or from washing. She no longer knew what was clean and what wasn't: everything had started to smell the same. She sat cross-legged on her roof as the muezzin's call sounded for the third time that day. Time, she decided, was broken and divided and reconnected by calls to prayer. Odd, dissonant melodies five times a day, more than any one thing she had ever experienced in a twelve-hour period. It was a day shaped not by the customary peaks of breakfast, lunch and dinner, but by many rolling hills in between.

Like most of the island, Ingrid rose and fell with the sun. Only the bar at Salama defied the rule and rhythm of the days. The bar ran *contra natura,* as Templeton would have said. Against nature. But above nature on this island was God.

God causes the dawn to break,
And has made the night for rest,
And the sun and moon for reckoning . . .

Ingrid put down the Koran. It was Christmas Eve. Soon, she allowed herself to hope, Templeton would be available to discuss this God, among other things. They would have a drink and she would tell him about the trouble she'd had in tracking him. He would rant about the dangers of an overactive imagination and she would settle back to listen to a long story.

Ingrid stared across the bay at Tomba Island and decided she would swim the channel to its beach. It was safe; Ali had done it many times. "You see these arms?" he had said. "You can't get arms like this just from walking in the sand." Ingrid had pretended to ignore his arms, but they were noticeably well-formed. She circled her own upper arm with her fingers and decided she wanted to be stronger—wanted to make herself do something hard. Besides, her body's temperature had begun to annoy her; it was first too hot and then too cool. Physical exertion might excite her nerve endings into some kind of release.

Ali followed her to the beach and stopped her before she stepped into the sea. "There is a jellyfish tide, Miss Ingrid. Not good for swimming." Ingrid looked down. Around her ankles lay dozens of transparent carcasses, their fringes undulating lifelessly with the tide's pull. She stepped out of the water and saw she had walked through a graveyard of dead jellyfish. The sand showed right through their gelatinous bodies. "The water is no good for another day, maybe longer," Ali informed her. "The jellyfish are poisonous."

"I have never understood how something transparent can be dangerous."

Ali shrugged. "Many poisons are clear. I discovered that at the Salama bar."

Ingrid sat on the sand and pulled her knees to her chest. Ali sat next to her. "Don't you have anything else to do, Ali? It's prayer time, isn't it?"

"I'll pray here, with you."

"Why are you watching me so closely?"

"I like watching you. In addition, you are my responsibility."

"Since when did I become your responsibility? In America, it's fine for women to be by themselves."

"I would like to go to America," he said, playing with a piece of driftwood.

"It would ruin you. But at least you would learn to leave people alone."

"I will sit over there, on that log."

"No. I don't want to stay here."

"You are not grateful I told you about the jellyfish?"

"I don't know. Maybe I wouldn't have noticed them." Ingrid began walking quickly back to the village. Ali followed at a distance.

After they had discussed the Koran and its complex instruction of both violence and peace, they would approach the subject of faith on Pelat. She would ask Templeton about the men who neglected their worship and the women who, as if governed by a different set of rules, danced themselves into joy.

Ingrid took care in preparing herself that night. After a long shower, she drew the curtains in her room and let herself dry naturally, brushing her hair until her scalp tingled. She slipped on a skirt and blouse before smoothing her hair back from her face and fastening it with a clip. Finally, she held up her smudged compact mirror to apply lipstick. Maybe, after everything else, Templeton would explain the enigma of Finn—about whom she had achieved partial resolution. Their brief encounter had stirred her imagination, encouraging a tropical fantasy that had sprung to life in the rich soil of too many empty hours and no Templeton. When Templeton returned, these other thoughts would dissipate. Until then, she had no need to see a man whose indifference to her was insulting.

Her position changed when she saw Finn drinking alone at the hotel bar, his broad back hunched to the room. She wanted to approach him. Instead she went to the end of the bar and stood in his arc of vision, hoping he would see what men sometimes saw in her. She told herself she would not move toward him unless he moved first.

She paid for her drink and carried it away from the bar through the open doors to the stone terrace, where a week-old newspaper sat on a wicker chair. She held the paper in front of her, her back to the bar. This is how strong I am, she wanted to tell him. I can wait and if you don't come I will be fine because I don't need you to come.

She read an article about Daniel Arap Moi, the president of Kenya. She followed the article to the jump page, reading to the end. There was internal strife in Kenya's government. Tribes were competing for power and position. Kikuyus, Luos, the occasional Masai. Maybe she could approach him directly, ask him if he had any news from Templeton. Ask a legitimate question and get it over with. But then it would be over and she did not want it to be over so soon.

She had started another article about the ban on ivory when a man with pressed white pants sat near her on the terrace. She heard him order a bourbon on the rocks in his perfect upper-class English accent and kept reading. His cologne drifted toward her, finally forcing her to look up from her paper. He was fortyish and attractive in a safe way, like a well-executed painting by a cautious artist forever aware of his patron. He caught her staring.

"It's Christmas Eve, you know," he said. "That's what I love about Africa. Here it's just another day."

Ingrid folded her paper. "Why do you love that?"

"One gets a chance to do things differently, I suppose."

"What do you do differently here?"

"Forget my manners, for one thing. My name's Stanley Wicks."

"Ingrid Holtz."

"Pleased to meet you." A waiter arrived with his bourbon, which Stanley Wicks rushed to his lips. "Dining by myself on a holiday is different. Asking a stranger to join me is also different."

"I've never minded eating alone," Ingrid said. "I'm sorry— was that an invitation?"

"An obtuse one."

"I can't. Not tonight."

"You're not alone?"

"No, not exactly."

"I see." Stanley paused over a long, almost meditative sip of bourbon.

"I'm expecting someone," she explained. "A colleague . . . I didn't actually come here on vacation."

"How refreshing. No one works around here. But on Christmas Eve?"

"As you said"—Ingrid smiled—"it's just another day."

"Yes." Stanley's nose wrinkled in disappointment. "I was beginning to hope it wouldn't be."

Ingrid rose. "Maybe another time."

"Can I hold you to that?" Stanley Wicks stood and held his hand out. "I'd love to hear what your work is. Conversation can be limited on this island; I haven't had a decent chat in weeks."

"Maybe we'll have one sometime. Merry Christmas, Stanley Wicks."

"Yes, to you as well."

You see, she said silently to the man behind her at the bar as she walked away from Stanley Wicks, I don't need to be with someone. It's not why I'm here. I'm not some floozy looking for sex in the tropics. Trust me. I'm walking away from him. Are you watching? I am doing this for you. If you weren't here I might let him take me to dinner, feed me from your precious sea.

As she passed the bar she glanced sideways and saw that it was empty. She had been conversing with no one.

Ingrid did not understand the adrenaline shooting through her like buckshot or the panic that followed. She looked back to the terrace where Stanley Wicks had been. The terrace, too, was empty. Instead of continuing back to the guesthouse, she sat down at the bar and ordered a whiskey.

She sipped the tepid liquor, so wrong for this climate, and took out her tracing of Templeton's amulet. She studied it for a long time, absorbing herself in the smallest detail. Because the placement of the characters was so irregular, she discarded the possibility that the inscription itself was anything but a collection of symbols. She could not conceive of a way to begin analyzing them. Putting the tracing aside, she started writing on a paper napkin. "Templeton, I need you. Please appear."

She let the ink of her pen bleed onto the words until they were illegible, suddenly certain that he was not coming. She finished her whiskey and, when she felt the panic surging back, ordered another. What are you afraid of, Ingrid? Tricks of momentum? Why have you come all this way? *You've come to help him when he did not ask for help,* she thought. *He has every right to disappoint you.* Near the end of her second whiskey, she allowed herself another thought. *Maybe you didn't come here for him at all.*

She didn't hear them enter the bar. "Hello, Miss Muffet," Danny said as he sat on her left. Finn settled to her right, his shoulder to her, his forearms resting on the bar. Ingrid swiveled toward Danny, who had straddled her stool and now fingered her watch. With his other hand, he finished her whiskey. "Jackson, make her a breeze." Behind the bar, Jackson dutifully scooped chunks of mango and pineapple and ice into a blender. Over the mixture, he splashed dark rum. Danny held a hand over Ingrid's eyes to shield her as he nodded to Jackson, who was familiar with the order and jigged an extra shot of rum. "Have you met Finn?" he added with mock formality. "Finn, this is Ingrid."

Finn turned his head in her direction and raised his beer bottle. "Ingrid," he repeated. "From where?"

"From heaven," Danny said, leaning back and surveying her legs. "God gave her those gams so she could walk here straight from heaven."

Ingrid made the mistake of looking directly at Finn. She faltered as his features seemed to harden into a mask of contempt. "I'm looking for someone," she said. "But then you knew that."

"Did I?"

"Professor Templeton. Nick Templeton."

"Nick, is it?" Finn smiled. "Well, well. I see."

"I'm a student of his," Ingrid said evenly. "A colleague from university."

"Isn't she lovely?" Danny said. "Who sent you here, angel?"

"He told me in a letter that he'd be here for Christmas. I came to find him, to help him with his work. The department hasn't heard from him in months."

"Enough about the professor," Danny said. "Tell us about you. I need to hear it all again. Make her another breeze, Jackson."

"No, thank you."

"Well, then, pour me another whiskey, Jackson. And in a moment another breeze for the professor's girl."

"Not his girl."

"No, of course not. Finn, another Tusker? Another Tusker for Finn, Jackson. It's all on my bill tonight."

"In that case, I'll take some rum with that, Jackson," Finn added. *"Asante sana."*

"Ingrid," Danny mused. "What are you? American? Canadian? Scandinavian? European women love the black boys on the island. Is that what you've come for? A little white mischief?"

Ingrid took her lips off the straw of her drink. "I told you what you need to know," she said impatiently. "I've come for Templeton."

"And I'm sure he's come for you." Danny smiled. "More than once. That rum looks damn nice, Jackson. Much better at this hour." Danny slid Ingrid's whiskey glass down the bar, where it tipped off the edge and shattered on the floor. "Drink your beer, Finn. Where's that bloody rum, Jackson?" Jackson was staring at the shards of glass on the floor.

They were playing with her, like two boys chasing a fish in the shallows, standing above her with nets. As soon as one came into focus, the other stepped in front. Ingrid started in on a new drink and taking longer sips, wondered what Finn might possibly gain by denying knowing Templeton. Music from the forties played over the speakers. "Heaven . . . I'm in heaven . . ."

Finn drank his rum in one swallow and stood up. "I'm off," he said.

"No," Ingrid said firmly, without looking at him.

"No?"

Ingrid bent down for her bag and extracted Templeton's map. She placed the map on his vacated barstool and watched closely as Finn stared at it and then at her. Danny rambled on.

"Have I told you, Finn, that we're taking the boat to Kisu to-morrow?" Danny said. "Miss Muffet and I? It's going to be lovely. A Christmas excursion. Bring a hat, Miss Muffet, you're as fair as I once was. We don't want to lose those peaches and cream yet. They're just too delicious." Danny rested his head on her shoulder. "Haven't seen such a ripe peach in ages."

"Sounds nice, Danny," Finn said. "I hope you two enjoy your-selves."

Finn moved his friend's head from Ingrid's shoulder to the bar. Danny grunted in protest. Ingrid pushed her drink away and searched for bills in her purse, satisfied that Finn knew more than he was letting on. She replaced the map in her bag and looked at him with composure. "Are you off to bed, then?"

"After a quick swim." Finn turned to go. A moment before he disappeared into darkness, he turned. "Come if you like." And he walked out of the bar.

Before Jackson swept her drink away, she gulped down half of it. "Thank you," she said to Jackson.

"You're welcome, miss."

"*Asante sana,*" she added.

Jackson smiled politely.

She trailed Finn's shadow down to the fine white sand. On the beach he walked ahead of her without looking back to see if she was there. She stopped at the edge of the dark water to reconsider, letting the distance between them grow.

Ahead, she could see the white of Finn's kikoi as he unwrapped it from his waist and dropped it to the sand. His body joined the water and then he was immersed. Gone. Ingrid stared as a green glow lit up the water. The light shot toward the center of the channel. She pulled up her skirt and knelt in the sand, running her hands through the water and watching as green lights trailed the motion, sparking up around her hands like fireflies. Ingrid agitated her hand until the shape of her fingers was clearly luminescent against the dark water. "I am here," she whispered, submerging her other hand. She made her hands zoom and flap and explode from fists. Under the water, light was everywhere, surrounding, adorning and falling from her hands. She played with the phosphorescence until the question of Finn subsided.

Feeling almost tranquil, she walked along the beach to where he was standing waist-deep in the water. "Are you coming in?" he asked.

"I don't have a bathing suit."

"Don't need one." He stood without moving. On the beach, a nervousness invaded her. He had grown stronger in his watery domain. In the darkness he looked magical, terrible. She took a small step backward. "What about the jellyfish?"

At this, soft laughter.

Though she could not see him well, Ingrid could hear that he hadn't moved, that he was standing there watching her. Her feet felt unstable. She stepped out of her skirt gingerly, not wanting to lose her balance.

Holding her forearms over her breasts, she hunched over as if suddenly cold, walking like a cripple to the shore. She was going to show him something of her, but she didn't want to show him everything. Then, submerged in the brilliant warmth, she forgot her fear and swam to him in the shallows, laughing at the beauty of the water. She wound herself around his legs like a seal. He stood above her when she surfaced, and offered her his hand.

She held on to him from where she was and then let go. "I want to swim for a while." She dunked her head under the water and pushed the sandy bottom with her foot, shooting off like a neon bullet. When she turned back, she was far away. She could see him resurfacing in the pale light, his shoulders and back glistening wet. He was leaving.

"Wait," she said, paddling back.

He turned and watched her walk out of the water, pressing her arms against her breasts again, but no longer doubled over. He ran his kikoi over his body and then tossed it to her.

"What's Agulhas?" she asked, not allowing herself to look at his naked body.

"An ocean current."

"A current? That's all?"

"As far as I know."

She wrapped herself up in the thin cotton and then draped it over her back while she pulled her skirt over her knees. The kikoi covered her like a tent. She hesitated before buttoning her blouse and, taking the kikoi, walked to where Finn stood.

"Why do you pretend not to know Templeton?" The moon shone from behind him. "He's got some sort of plan," she pressed. "What is it? Where is he?"

She could not see his eyes as he brushed the backs of his fingers lightly over her breast, against her nipple. His hand was coarse against her skin. Ingrid stepped closer to him, letting his hand drift down to her abdomen, press into her skirt, briefly explore the area between her legs, as far as the material would allow. "Oh," she said, recoiling at her own sensitivity. He stepped away and wrapped his kikoi around his waist. "Come," he said.

She recaptured his hand while they walked and held on to its dry roughness as they passed the hotel and the path that led to her guesthouse. A whistle sounded from the trees near the outdoor bar. Ali. Ingrid slowed, trying to see where he was. Finn gently pulled her forward. She continued on, fingering the calluses on his palm, pressing her soft fingertips into the thick layers of dead skin, wondering if he could feel her. He pulled his hand away when they reached the seawall. Disconnected, she followed him.

Later she couldn't remember how they had gotten there, only that she was glad when he walked through the open door of his house and, without turning, went to the bed. She stood barefoot on the cool tile floor while he ducked under the billow of his mosquito net and then under a single white sheet. She listened for his breathing as she crept into his bed and hesitated before lowering herself to him. His eyes were open, looking up at her. She saw his face fully before he stopped her with his hand and turned her head to the side, so she saw only the wall. He kissed her cheek before he rolled over.

He was tired. Sleep came to him within minutes.

Ingrid lay awake, her blouse still open. The gauze of the mosquito net obscured the room: she could see the outline of a sisal mat, a wall hanging, a large wooden chair. She inched closer to him, until her breasts were against his back. There was something tattooed on his shoulder. With her tongue, she touched the dark, salty shape. She stayed pressed to him like a leaf until she knew he was sleeping. Then she rolled away. The mosquito net rested on her hair when she sat up. Before she left him, she stared at his back, thinking she had never seen such a tangle of beauty and sadness.

Christmas

Sari was waiting for her in the courtyard, a dark shadow that detached from a pillar and floated toward her. She took Ingrid's hand and put her fingers over her lips. Then she pointed. Abdul was sleeping on a mat at the bottom of the stairs, his thin arms wrapped like ribbons around his body.

"He's waiting for you," Sari whispered, motioning for her to step over him. "You should be in bed by now. If you are with men at night he might make you leave this house."

"He cannot stop me from visiting or having visitors, Sari. I'm paying him to stay here."

"He can be mean."

"Is that why you cry at night?"

Sari shook her head and stepped back, rejoining the shadows. Ingrid caught her hand to reassure her. "I know I am lucky to have such a home," Sari whispered, her eyes on Abdul.

Ingrid held her hand tight. "You don't have to say that for me."

. . .

Upstairs, Ingrid lay in rigid exhaustion, trying to imagine sleep as a distant continent she had to reach. Her bed was hard, and instead of absorbing the electricity flowing through her, it acted as a conduit. She was still lying there when Finn appeared in her doorway that afternoon, holding an envelope. She had been trying not to move. Christmas was almost over; there was no reason to move. "It was left on my doorstep," he said, walking around her little cell, peering out the windows.

The letter was addressed to Ingrid Holtz, care of Finn Bergmann. Ingrid reached her hand under the mosquito net to take it from him, avoiding his eyes. She could smell the alcohol on him.

Dear Ingrid,

Welcome to Pelat. I am sorry I cannot be there to act as your guide. Knowing you, I can guess that you have come to find proof of both my own existence and, I have heard, the existence of my theory. You seem to have made progress of a kind—I never imagined that I would be investigated by my own best student. The search for evidence, however, need not involve trespassing. To trespass against the dead is not the same as trespassing against the living. On this island, where the living commune with the dead, I would strongly advise against it. As with any place in transition, my dear, Pelat is volatile. I cannot take responsibility for what you may or may not understand.

Sadly, we are not always able to locate the thing we need most to exist. I have learned that the worlds we people create can overtake the ultimate work. There is, you see, *life* to be lived. Don't forget about yours in pursuit of mine.

Finally, you must trust that you would not benefit from finding me just now. I have nothing of substance to offer you and pray you will make your way home safely. Go back to Egypt, Ingrid. Pick up with Hatshepsut. As for my king, you will not find him here.

Yours as ever,
Nick Templeton

Ingrid stared numbly at the page. Across the room, Finn was watching her. She folded the letter and forced herself to meet his gaze.

"How did he know I was here?" she asked lightly.

"I have no idea."

"It's dated the twenty-first. Where has it been since then?"

"Traveling, maybe." Finn smiled. "He's a clever man, the professor."

"Why?"

"He knew I had found you."

"You found me? You didn't find me."

"I did. Right away. I saw you get off the boat. Saw Ali whisk you off."

"But you waited for me to come to you." Ingrid was up on her elbows. "Why?"

Finn pulled the curtain over the window he had been posted at. "It's an island. We were going to meet."

"What has he told you about me?"

"Look"—Finn gestured outside to the roof—"you have a visitor. Another admirer."

"What does that map mean?"

"That your professor has an imagination. I have no idea where it's taken him but I'd rather not follow."

"Why?"

Finn chose not to respond.

"Will you please answer me?" Ingrid insisted.

Finn kept his silence, watching the door.

She propped her pillow behind her and glared at him from behind the mosquito net. "Is proper communication really so loathsome to you?"

"In some cases."

Ingrid ignored him and reread the letter as Ali made his way up the stairs. Finn leaned against the wall, as if waiting. He registered Ali's momentary loss of composure with a dark smile. "Forget to knock, Ali?"

"Hello, Finn, Miss Ingrid." Ali's smile was sloppy as spilt milk. "The door was open. I'm sorry."

"Ingrid is a guest here," Finn said.

Ali bowed his head. "As I said, I am sorry."

"Her friendliness should not be mistaken for something else."

Ali remained silent, his hands clasped in front of him. When Finn left, Ali uncoiled like a snake. "So you have met Finn," he said. "Son of Henrik Bergmann, the cat killer." For once, he did not elaborate. Ingrid waited for more, but there was no more; no anecdote, no history.

"He knows the professor," Ingrid urged.

Ali only nodded.

"Does he?" she pressed.

Ali looked at her. "You like him."

"I don't know him."

"All the women like Finn."

Ingrid waited. "And?"

"He doesn't care about them."

"Don't worry about me, Ali. I have work to do."

"I think it's a very good thing that you have work to do. Why, may I ask, are you in bed?"

"Because it's so damn hot. Don't worry, I know what kind of man he is." Ingrid turned over onto her stomach and rested her cheek on her forearms. "Where does a man like that go when the bar's closed?"

Ali shrugged. "Maybe his house. Maybe to sea. Maybe it's good that you don't care one way or the other."

She went to the swimming beach that afternoon and sat alone, watching the wind meet the waves, dusting their crests with spray. The sea was rough and the sails of dhows crossed one another rapidly in the bay. There was some sort of race going on. Young boys clung to wooden planks jutting out from the upwind keel and hung over the open water for ballast. Ingrid took a handful of sand and released it gradually at her knee. The grains cascaded along her shin to her foot, where some of them collected. Templeton was not coming. He had slapped her wrist and then urged her to leave in an obliquely protective note that did not even sound like him. Had she not seen his notebooks, she might not have needed to know what it was he was trying to protect her from. But leaving was no longer a possibility until she had found out. She had come too far.

And then there was Finn the messenger. He was both a part of this and separate. She could not guess at his involvement with Templeton, but she knew it was more significant than he was letting on. Direct interrogation had not advanced matters. Finn was someone who could not be badgered. It seemed she had no choice but to watch him.

She raised her eyes to the water. The sharp triangles of the dhow sails cut across the water, capturing and ferrying her eye to another place in the sea. Tireless children threw themselves into the surf. Sometimes a woman in her dark robe waded in cautiously, delight on her face as the fabric grew wet and floated freely around her legs. "Merry Christmas," Ingrid murmured.

❦

Later that night the door to her room groaned on its thin hinges and she could hear the coarse sound of a man's breath. She felt someone standing in the dark. Ingrid sat up and pulled the sheet around her. "Who's there?"

"It's Finn." Then a cough. The smell of cigarettes and alcohol wafted through the small room. "Boys were out late tonight. You're lucky it's me." He cleared his throat. "There are no locks on these doors. It could have been anyone." Ingrid tried to make room for him as he approached her narrow bed, tilting like a prop plane touching down in a strong wind. He was very drunk. As he reached out for balance she wanted, somehow, to slow the whole process down, to prevent him from crashing. "Why am I lucky?" she asked.

"I won't hurt you."

"Hurt me how?" she asked, when he had sat down.

"Did you find what you were looking for in that letter?"

Ingrid paused. "No."

Finn lay down, suddenly and terminally exhausted. "Are you the professor's girl?"

"No."

"Danny's girl?"

"No."

"Whose girl?"

"No one's girl."

"Mmm." Finn lowered his head to the pillow. "Me either."

When he was asleep, Ingrid took the cigarettes from his shirt pocket and moved to the floor. "You've taken my bed," she said to the steady, deep breath. Halfway through her second cigarette, she dozed off. An ember burned through her nightgown to her thigh. She swore and pressed the burn with a licked thumb. Instead of stubbing out the cigarette, she dropped it out the window and watched it land, sending up a thin blue plume of smoke on the street outside the guesthouse. Then she went out to the pillows and made herself a bed.

Sometime in the night, Finn lifted her from where she had fallen asleep and placed her back on her own bed. Ingrid willed herself to remain limp in his arms. She allowed her head to jostle closer to his bare chest and pressed it lightly into him, wanting to absorb the musty smell of sweat and salt. She couldn't remember ever being carried by a man—and so lightly, as if she were a child.

When he came again the next night, she balanced herself on the edge of the bed. She had not imagined he would come back again, and again just to sleep. She didn't fully understand why it did not matter that he neither looked at her nor touched her in the dark. She simply liked that he was there.

In sleep, his elbow extended into her and forced her off the mattress. She lifted the awkward wooden chair close to the bed and draped the mosquito net over them both. Tonight there was no question of sleep. She leaned toward him and examined his face in the half-light. The features seemed beyond rest. Minutes passed and nothing in them moved, no dream played in the eyelids or twitched the ends of the lips. Ingrid held her hand above his forehead and felt the warmth from it. She noticed bits of sand stuck to the damp skin. She bent over his unwashed hair and, finding the smell appealing, inhaled more deeply. Then she sat back and surveyed the whole picture of the man, from the long sheet-wrapped legs to the muscular torso, brown and dense and out of place on her narrow bed.

He woke early and all at once. Ingrid scooted her chair back as he swung his legs to the floor and squinted through the mosquito net toward the door. Without looking at her, he reached for her hand. He held it in both of his, spreading it before him like a map. Her skin, soft and pale next to his, was scarred in places with tiny half-moons and ridges, burns and cuts, because she was both careless and deliberate in the kitchen. He turned her hand upside-down and studied the bluest vein in her wrist, tracing its crooked lines. She could feel his breath on her hand. "Please," she whispered. "Look at me." He kept his eyes cast down, his head bent. She reached out and lightly touched a wave of his hair with her hand.

He stood up, dwarfing Ingrid in her chair. The mosquito net enveloped his head like a mist and he began to gather it up, every part of him in quick motion as the diaphanous material argued and then conformed. The net was now knotted again, and hung neatly above the bed. "Your professor," Finn said. "You've come all this way for him?"

She did not answer directly. "I think you can help me find him."

"But you haven't come for me. Remember that." He paused at the door, as if to say more, and then left.

The Deep Sea

*I*n the hotel office was a broken fax machine, flanked by two file cabinets, a basket of pamphlets and an upright, elderly man encased in a spotless white uniform. He was entering numbers into a ledger. Next to him on a wooden table was a telephone with no dial tone.

"Are the phones often out?"

"Often enough, miss."

Ingrid opened one of the pamphlets. It detailed the recreational activities on the island, illustrated with brief sketches. "These drawings are wonderful," Ingrid said. "Who did them?"

"Mr. Henrik Bergmann, the founder of Salama."

"Interesting. I thought they had been done by a child."

"That is what makes them good, don't you think? No hesitation, no doubt."

"Yes, you're right. Though it doesn't fit my picture of him."

"And what is your picture?"

"I thought he was a hard man. Maybe even cruel."

"He could look that way sometimes."

"You knew him?"

"I was one of the first workers at Salama. I knew Mr. Bergmann well enough. Danny has told you about him?"

"Yes."

"Danny knows nothing of Henrik Bergmann. He knows his son and the bottom of a bottle. The rest is his own creation."

"You speak very good English." Ingrid smiled. "Very accurate English."

"Yes?" the old man tapped his pen for ink. "I have been told this. I had an excellent teacher in Henrik Bergmann."

"Was he a good man to work for?"

"Very good. He taught me many things. After he disappeared, I thought maybe he knew it was going to happen, that he had prepared for it. A wise man foresees his own end."

When he said no more, Ingrid skimmed the activities illustrated in the pamphlet. One could go snorkeling, take a sunset sail on a dhow, sail to the ruins across the channel, go deep-sea fishing.

"Tell me about the deep-sea fishing."

"For one hundred dollars, you go with a professional for the day, way far out in the ocean. Very exciting, this fishing. You fish for big ones, like marlin. You know the marlin?"

"Yes. The one with a long nose."

"It is called a spear and it is very sharp. It could slice you like a knife. But don't worry, lady, this won't happen to you. Our fishermen are safe and very professional. The best is the son of Henrik Bergmann. A very fine fisherman."

"Is he?" Ingrid closed the pamphlet with a small smile. "I think I'd like to go."

"Good, good. You will never forget this experience. You go home and tell your friends how you fought the giants of the sea. How many in your party?"

"Just me."

"Only one? You have no friends?"

"Just me."

"It might be lonely for one to go alone."

"I don't mind. I'm perfectly happy to go by myself. If a hundred dollars isn't enough, I can pay more."

"No, no, miss, that is no problem. *Hakuna matata.* You will have an enjoyable time no matter what. Now you must wake early, very early. Is this a problem?"

"Not at all."

"Good. Then you will go to the beach at first prayer call and Finn Bergmann will be there to take you to the boat. You are not afraid of the sea?"

"No."

"Good, good. That is fine. A brave lady. You can pay me now, if it is convenient."

Ingrid dreamt lightly and woke before the first prayer call, unsure if she had actually slept. Her dreams had been like distorted thoughts, which was unfortunate, because she had wanted to be strong for this day. Instead she felt wobbly and mistrustful of her instincts.

She dangled her hand from the bed to feel for her crumpled shorts and damp bathing suit and dressed in the predawn silence. Pausing before covering herself further, she stretched her bare arms to the ceiling, arching her back like a dismounting gymnast. And then she laughed.

She crept through the sleeping guesthouse and into the gray village, where a single goat bell clanged in the empty street. For a few yards, she swung her hips like a streetwalker. Near the hotel, a spotted cat appeared from an alley and followed her, mewing plaintively when she showed it her empty hands. "I have nothing for you," she whispered. "But maybe later I will have some fish."

The beach was empty, the sand chilled and sodden. Ingrid sat with her knees hugged to her chest. She stared hard at the flatness of the colorless expanse before her, focusing on the point where the sea stopped and the sky began, and waited. She could not judge how much time had passed before the sky began to change and a shape stirred on the periphery of her vision. A figure was walking down the seawall, sandals slapping on the hard surface. It was a small sound, but it carried through the morning like a call to prayer. The sandals were white and the brightest thing on the beach. Her eyes latched on to them as they hopped off the wall onto the beach, willing her focus not to travel farther. Soon the sandals had reached a skiff and were pivoting the boat toward the water. Ingrid rose and moved to stop them from getting in the boat without her.

Finn was startled. "What are you doing here?"

"Going fishing."

"With whom?"

"You."

He bent over to shove the skiff into the water. "The devil you are."

"I paid. You have to take me."

"I don't know anything about it."

"You should have checked your schedule."

He ran his fingers through his hair. She could see he was tired. "Just you?"

"Yes."

"It's not the best day, today. We were planning to go far."

"I'd be happy to go far."

Finn pushed the skiff past the small morning waves. "Get in, then. We're wasting time."

Ingrid waded into the water. "This is your job. You shouldn't be angry."

"I'm not angry."

She stepped into the skiff and sat opposite him. A few deep thrusts followed by long, silent glides brought them to *Uma*'s hull. Jonah appeared above them on the bigger boat, confused.

"Miss?"

"Ingrid," Finn said dourly. "Miss Ingrid."

Jonah whistled as he helped Ingrid out of the skiff.

Jonah trolled a line while Finn steered the boat. Ingrid sat next to him and watched Jonah control the rod with his foot. "Is that how you fish for the big ones?" she asked.

"He's fishing for bonito," Finn said shortly. "Bait."

Jonah yanked the rod with one hand and a bright fish flipped on board. He leaned down and exclaimed happily in Swahili. "It's a female," Finn said. "Means good luck."

"Why?"

"I couldn't say. The belief is older than I am."

"It's interesting that the female brings the luck," Ingrid said. "Your island treats women like bad luck. It must create some confusion for you fishermen."

Finn turned to look at her. She had wedged herself into the only shady corner on the boat, where she stayed as the morning moved into day and the sun beat down. Around noon she wished she had brought a hat. Jonah slowed *Uma* and then cut the motor. With two hands, he lifted the anchor and dropped it overboard. She kept to her corner as Finn set up the rods.

"I suppose you've done this before," Finn said.

"No, never."

"We're refueling. Then we're going to have some lunch." Finn held a rod in one hand and a bonito in the other. "Now listen carefully. This is a rod. This is what brings the fish in. And this here is the bait; this is what they go after. The line is what connects you. It's the thinnest, strongest part of the equation. It seems like it will break but it rarely does."

"I didn't know fishing was so poetic."

He ignored this remark, curtailing his explanation. "Come here," he said at last. "Let me snap you into a harness."

"I don't want to be snapped into the harness."

"Well, then, if you hook a fish, you have to be prepared to go overboard."

"Fine," Ingrid said. "I was wanting to swim."

"Jonah," he called into the galley, "she isn't serious. She doesn't care about the fish."

"I care," Ingrid told him. "I'm just more interested in seeing you catch them."

"She likes to observe," he called to Jonah. "That's what people who've got education do. Have you noticed, Jonah?"

"It seems Jonah's not listening."

"Jonah is always listening."

"Just catch yourself a fish," Ingrid said. "Do what you would do if I weren't here." Finn shook his head. "If it's that bad," she said, "you can just leave me out here. I'll go away quietly, you'll be surprised."

Finn tossed her a flotation pillow. "Better take this with you."

"Okay," she said, standing up. She went to the side of the boat and sat on the edge. "Just carry on with your day." She dropped the flotation pillow in the boat and tipped herself over.

She had two thoughts before she hit the water: that it was good for Finn to be surprised, and that she was scared. *I am doing us both a favor,* she thought.

All thoughts left her as she plunged down deeper. She wanted to continue but the buoyant water was already returning her to the glare of light and air above. She bobbed to the surface and stretched herself out, lying as if sleeping, her face to the sky, feeling calmer than she had felt in days. *Don't make me move,* she thought. *I don't want to move.*

Finn watched her from the boat. Her hair was spread around her like a halo. When she had drifted a certain distance, he pulled his shirt off his back and dove, pushing the water with his hands, moving as quickly as he could toward her. Opening his eyes underwater, he saw her pale form floating. He looped his arm around her torso and pulled her close to him. She opened her eyes and began to cough.

"You're hurting me," she said and tried to push him away. He held her tighter. Their legs tangled, glancing off each other and returning. Finn caught her legs in his and held them. He pushed the hair from her face.

"What is it that you want?" he said.

"I've come a long way to see someone," she said. "I want you to tell me where he is."

"Are you crazy?" he said. "These currents are dangerous. Do you realize how far you've drifted?" She would not look at him. He held her head with his hand and spoke into her ear. "I don't know what your professor is up to, but I can tell you one thing— you should stay out of it. Wherever he's gone, it isn't to do with

what you read about in your books. Now swim with me or hold
on to me. Jonah is refueling, so we have to get there on our own."

Ingrid looked for the boat. She could not see it over the waves.
"If I let it carry me, where would the current take me?" she asked.
"Where would the Agulhas deposit me?"

"We have a long way to go," he said sharply. "Come."

He swam easily with her, as if she were a part of him. She released the lock she had made around his neck, flattening her palms
on his chest and pressing her cheek to his back. She held on to him
with the fierceness of a rescued swimmer. The water rushed by her
and she thought of nothing but how she was relieved to be holding him this way. When she felt the rhythm of his strokes, she
began to kick with her legs to help him, lying on him, moving
with him. She felt herself gaining strength. Her mouth was near
his ear. "You see how easy it is to save someone," she said.

They were gentle with each other the rest of the day. Ingrid spoke
little, read her book some and watched the graceful precision of
Finn's movements. He did nothing for show; his obvious compe-
tence was not for her, not for anyone. At lunch, she ignored her
banana sandwich and drank her beer and half of his.

When they caught a decent-sized fish she came to life, clap-
ping and hopping on the deck. After measuring and recording
the fish, they released it, and Ingrid leaned over the edge to
watch it disappear. Recovering from a glorious splash, it righted
itself with a lash of its tail and wriggled into the depths. "I think
I still see it," she said. "That glint down there." Finn stood next
to her, silent. "Why is that so thrilling?" she asked, leaning so far
over that the ends of her hair dipped into the water.

"Maybe because free things often disappear quickly."

She turned to look up at him. "Will you take me to Kitali?"

"No. Anyway, he's not there."

"Still, I want to see it."

"You won't be welcome."

"If you don't take me, I'll go by myself."

"Fine. You seem to like going by yourself." Ingrid turned back to the water. "If you can find the strength to wait for a day," Finn added after a while. "I will be on that side of the island. I will look for him."

Ingrid placed her hand over his. "Thank you."

"Finn!" Jonah exclaimed from the steering wheel. "Look who we have found." Finn stood and smiled as Ingrid had never seen him smile. "It's Boni," Jonah announced proudly.

What Ingrid saw bobbing in the waves was a pitiful little boat that looked barely seaworthy. As they neared it, she saw in its center a beautiful black man, gleaming in the sun. He stood with his legs splayed, balancing in his tiny boat, his kikoi wrapped like shorts around his thighs. Ingrid watched as *Uma* approached him. Her hand shot out in front of her to wave. Boni waved back, grinning.

"Hello, everyone!"

"Boni," Finn said. "How long have you been out?"

"I don't know. The sea is alive with fish. It's like a lusty woman that won't let me go. And who is this pretty lady?"

"This is Ingrid," Finn said. "She purchased us for the day."

"I would like this job, to be sure," Boni said, laughing.

"What have you caught?" she asked.

Boni motioned to the burlap-covered mound in the back of his boat. "Wonderful fish for eating. I would like to make one of them a present to you, Miss Ingrid, because I think you are fishing for sport today, not dinner."

"That's okay, Boni, you keep your catch," Finn said. "We'll send her home with something."

"You promise? I think she needs a big fish."

"Don't you worry," Finn said with a laugh. "We'll find her a big fish."

"We will celebrate later," Boni said. "A big celebration!"

"Celebrate what?"

"I am going to break a record. Wicks is giving me a magical line made of wire."

"We should talk about that, Boni. Wire lines can be bad magic."

"At the bar over a Tusker!" Boni bent his knees until he was sitting. Finn pushed him off. Boni stayed sitting for a while, happily absorbing the changing scenery as his skiff turned slowly in circles.

CHAPTER

17

The Second Village

Fatima found Finn at the bar, in the clutches of evil. She took him by the hand and led him into town to the market, leaning him against a tree while she bargained for vegetables. Finn watched her go through her routine as he had since he was a boy.

In the last half decade, Fatima's face had acquired laws of its own, finally surrendering to the anarchy of age. Her mouth was hard with resolution. Her eyes could still be scornful. Her forehead was as wise and regular as the waves of the sea. Despite the warring elements of time, her features joined together in the rare instance of a smile. The miracle of her smile occurred in the marketplace, when she finally got her price. Finn smiled too, watching her. He carried her packages to her house and sat on the makute mat inside while she peeled potatoes outside, humming.

At dinnertime, Fatima slit open the belly of a snapper, winding the intestines around her fingers and yanking them free. A slippery egg sack remained. She removed it carefully, tearing the delicate membrane open with her fingernail. The roe spilled onto a dish, which she brought out to Finn. "Eat," she said. "You need the strength." She cut the meat of the snapper into cubes for a curry, stirring coconut milk and herbs over the heat of a fire she controlled with long pieces of wood, pulling and pushing them out of the flames. When the curry was done, she set it at the edge of the fire and patted her chapati dough until it was flat and round. She fried four chapatis in her only pan. The smell of food revived him.

They ate the curry with the flat bread, folding the stew inside like a package. Finn ate three. Fatima nodded in approval and looked pleased until he took out a cigarette and lit it. He avoided Fatima's eyes and blew the smoke straight up into the air so she couldn't wave her hands in front of her face. He knew the smoke didn't really bother her. She objected to cigarettes because they made men feel and act like little gods with their smoke and fire.

Fatima rearranged the sticks in the fire, muttering incomprehensibly. They sat for a while in silence. "Finn," she said at last. "That man Wicks will get trouble with his new hotel."

"Trouble from whom?"

"Trouble from the people who live on that side of the island."

"Ah." Finn lit another cigarette. A cloud of smoke came between them. Fatima did not go into her usual coughing convulsions, and from this Finn guessed the subject mattered to her. "They say Wicks is building a hotel on a sacred site. Maybe an ancient burial place," she said.

"That's nonsense. No one has ever lived there."

"Well," Fatima conceded, "they don't want the hotel." She sat on her haunches in front of the fire and wrapped her shawl around her shoulders. It was getting cooler. "Those people left here when your father's hotel came. They wanted to escape its evil and now, in front of their eyes, is going to be another one. They feel trapped."

"Is it that bad?"

"I have heard, yes, it is that bad. They want to do something. They want to stop it. But Mohammad refuses.

"Because he is unwilling to fight, his village will be ruined."

"There's nothing he can do. Money is money. If Wicks wants to build something with it, he will."

"It's their island, not Wicks'. You tell him that—he's your friend."

"He's not my friend, and it's his money. He can do with it what he likes."

"Get pinkman Wicks to talk to them."

"He doesn't speak Swahili."

"That's why you must talk for him."

Finn dragged hard on his cigarette. "It's not going to make any difference what I say."

"No, but they may not curse the hotel."

"Oh, Lord."

Fatima grabbed a stick from the fire and shook it at him. "Do not 'oh, Lord' me." She jammed the stick back into the coals. "If it isn't your job, whose is it?"

"All right, all right. I'll think about it. I'm going to that side of the island anyway."

"Talk to Chief Mohammad," she insisted.

Finn flicked his cigarette into the fire. "After I think about it."

Fatima glared at him and then laughed. "You are still a boy." The laugh turned into a hacking cough. Finn held her so she didn't lurch forward. He patted her back. "I'm all right." She waved him away like cigarette smoke and sat back in the dirt and hung her head. Her body looked deflated. "Inside the bread box," she said finally. "I have some chocolate for you." Finn watched her without moving until she nodded toward her house. "The kind with hazelnuts."

✿

At the first prayer call, Finn set out for Kitali. The horizon was lightly streaked with the pale bands of dawn. By land, Kitali was eight miles away, but eight miles through soft beach sand was like sixteen on hard ground. Finn felt the muscle in his upper calves harden as he pushed his weight off the sunken balls of his feet. The tide was high when he set off and there was a breeze that, by late morning, would work itself into a wind. He stopped to watch the sunrise and thought about Wicks' hotel and how he would speak to the people of Kitali. After all, one could only negotiate with people who wanted to negotiate.

The villagers of Kitali were more stubborn than those they had split from. They had left because Mohammad, a former village chief, had sensed the unease felt by some of the villagers over the proximity of Salama and its corrupting influence. Mohammad had organized those who gave off silent signals of distress at the changes taking place. He had helped them find one another. A mother and child from one family; a young man from another. As they gathered together, the silent signals sharpened into an alarm that soon coalesced into an active resistance.

It had happened quickly. It was as if the earth had cleaved, dividing the two camps by an unbridgeable rift. Families were fractured; children were separated from fathers who refused to abandon their lucrative jobs at the hotel. It was only a matter of weeks before the resistance gained enough momentum to incite physical action. They left en masse, walking in a long procession, the women's black *bui-bui*s billowing in the offshore breeze, the children silent and somber with the weight of separation. The occasional howling of an infant was the only sound that pierced the trancelike determination of the pilgrims.

Fatima was famous for reminding people that it had all been

predicted by her sister, the white-haired *mganga*. Before life flickered out in her pale blue eyes, the *mganga* had whispered into
Fatima's ear, "The strong will leave, but you must stay with the
weak. You must help them find their way. The boy will help you.
The lion's son will also grow to have sharp teeth, and the strength
to kill. Teach him to use them wisely."

Unlike some of the others who stayed behind in the original
village, Fatima was not afraid to live surrounded by the influences of the unfaithful. She had a God-given purpose, and she
had already survived for years living close to the lion's den.

When she inherited Henrik Bergmann's son, Fatima set about
trying to undo the damage of some of his father's Western thinking.
"So," she often said to young Finn, "Salama is your father's village
and my village is the real village. They are as different as the sun and
the moon, but they are on the same island. Never think that life is
simple, or that only one truth exists at one time. Do you see this
chocolate bar? It is a gift from the new village to the old. I am going
to eat it and think of your father, who brought us a few nice things."
Fatima was proud of the complex awareness she had fostered in Finn
at such a young age. To understand one world was good fortune, but
to understand two, this was the beginning of wisdom.

Unhappily, Finn's response was one of resignation rather than
interest or privilege. Part of his wisdom was the knowledge that
things happened for mysterious reasons. It was Allah's will. To
challenge this nebulous force was both dangerous and exhaust-
ing. To Finn, it seemed a full presence of mind was not necessary
for most acts required of him. Unfortunately (Fatima thought),
the resulting quality of otherworldliness intrigued those around
him. Those who did not know him, primarily hotel guests, were
piqued by his physical beauty, which was both uncultivated and
remote. Women guests in particular were drawn to his calm,
which they never rightly identified as absence.

. . .

Mohammad was sitting in the center of his open hut. Finn knew him from a distance by his ears, which were as wide as a butterfly's wings in mid-flutter. He stood outside the hut until Mohammad motioned for him to sit on the warm sand. His bald head glinted in the sun. "Finn," he said, looking at him with both kindness and reservation. Finn returned his greeting with a bowed head. Mohammad sat in silence before he resumed. "You've been sent here."

Finn decided not to launch at once into the business at hand. "A girl has come for the professor," he began.

Mohammad tilted his head to the sky. "Is this our concern?"

Finn paused. "Not yours. Mine."

"Would you like to speak to him?"

"I probably should," he said.

Mohammad smiled. "You are not eager. Well, do not worry. He's gone."

"Gone where?"

"I don't know."

Finn dusted the sand with his fingers. It was finer on this side of the island, more like sugar. "When will he be back?"

"Why don't you come for the fast," Mohammad suggested. "The next new moon." Then he smiled and looked at the sky, as if listening. "Fatima sent you here."

"Yes."

"Fatima, the peacemaker. She is still strong enough to make you walk all this way."

"She sends you her blessing."

"She is getting fat on chocolate, I hear."

"She is enjoying life."

"Tell her she should come see us. Both of you. Come together."

"Fatima won't travel."

"She is getting old. She will want to come soon." They continued on pleasantly, progressing to the inevitable topics of weather and fishing. The season at Kitali, Mohammad reported, had so far been good. "Of course we cannot compete with you, Finn," he conceded. "Since you were a boy, you have been able to pull fish from the sea."

"Your new neighbor Wicks is giving me some competition."

"Yes, he is causing some disturbance here as well," Mohammad agreed quietly. "God willing, it will pass."

"Will it?"

Mohammad pressed his hands together as if in dismissal of both Finn and his question. "And now, something to eat before you go?"

Finn ignored Mohammad's urging. "If Wicks' hotel is built, will you curse it?"

"We have moved beyond that, Finn. Curses are for the broken. The hotel will go the way it must go."

Finn was uneasy with this answer. "What can I tell Fatima?"

"Tell her not to worry so much."

Finn stood and looked around at what he could see of the village. It seemed to be deserted. "How is he?"

"The professor? The last time I saw him, a happy man."

Over the years, Mohammad's village had prospered. The simple purity of their existence unleashed a bizarre and productive energy. They had designed a hut suited to their new environment that, because of the shortage of mangroves, lacked solid walls. The huts consisted of a thatch roof supported by four mangrove poles. The roof was lashed onto the four poles with sisal and easily removed for repairs. Semipermanent walls could be hung for times of privacy.

Open huts meant a heightened awareness of one another.

With time, an almost effortless communication flowed like air between families. In the middle of their fourth year, communal sensitivity peaked into such a coherence that one day Mohammad stopped speaking altogether. A few others followed suit when they discovered that the faintest impulse of desire was picked up, identified and answered by someone else. Mohammad spoke now only to pray. Finn knew it was out of respect that he talked to him now. As he wove his way through the tranquil collective, he almost envied the life Mohammad was free to lead.

Before he left, Finn walked the grounds of Wicks' hotel. Templeton had also sent him a Christmas letter, though he had not mentioned it to Fatima or to Ingrid. The letter had warned him that, seeking water, Wicks' construction would soon cross the property lines. Templeton maintained that this was unacceptable because Mohammad's land and water were sacred. It was typical of him to foist such a burden onto Finn—to presume that Finn would be the go-between. He did not trust him any more than he trusted Fatima about the sacredness of the land; both had their own reasons for wanting to prevent construction.

Wicks' site was nestled into a protected enclave. The natural clearing in the trees and its placement on a rocky outcrop facing the sea made it seem possible that the hotel was not the first settlement on that location. But between that and an ancient burial ground was a considerable leap of faith. So what was Finn to do? After his brief excursion, he returned to Mohammad's hut.

"Mohammad, is the hotel to be built on sacred ground?" he asked.

Mohammad lowered his head slightly. "Some say so."

"And you?"

"I know it to be so."

CHAPTER

18

The Words of the Imam

Ali took Ingrid to the Riyadh Mosque between the second and third prayers. Because she didn't entirely trust him, she decided not to mention that her interest in the mosque had more to do with the Imam than with Habib Salih. Ali did not need to know more than necessary.

He had brought her one of his sister's *bui-bui*s to wear over her clothes. "This will help you mix in," he said wryly.

"Am I really going to mix in?"

"Why not? It is a mosque for the people. Slaves are people. The lowbred are people. Women are people. This is the right mosque for you to visit."

"And is it a mosque for you to visit?"

"I will come for you after the third prayer. I have some friends to see nearby. Business."

"You wouldn't be caught dead in this mosque, would you, Ali?"

"Dead, yes. It would be a good place to be dead in. The people there are very kind-spirited. The women stand on the left, or is it the right? Well, you'll see where they stand. I think they move around in Riyadh. Stand wherever you like."

But inside they were sitting. A circle of women in *bui-bui*s, sitting so close their black robes touched. Ingrid sat behind the circle, keeping her eyes on the sandy floor. A hand on her elbow pulled her gently forward, to a place they had made for her. Ingrid looked at the ceiling, where something was written in Swahili, a circle of words with no distinct beginning or end. While the walls arched toward the heavens, the roundness of the interior made it feel like the structure was hugging the earth. Ingrid allowed herself to feel liberated beneath her robes. She was looking around the room for the Imam when the music started. Across from her, a pair of dark eyes had locked onto hers as a drumbeat, low and steady, seemed to synchronize the movements of the gathering. A hypnotic swaying transformed the room, so it resembled a dark wind-blown field. Someone started to sing, a soft repetitive melody. Ingrid closed her eyes, allowing her mind to follow the notes. The song grew as more voices joined and crescendoed into a full pitched chorus that encouraged whoops and hollers, punctuations of joy.

One by one, the women rose and others from behind moved into the circle, which had widened, pushing to the edges of the floor. A few women wandered to the middle of the enclosure. With their eyes closed and their heads tilted back, they began to dance, freeing their robes in a solitary spin. They looked like black bells, like whirling seedpods.

A hand found its way into Ingrid's. The figure beside her unhooked her veil and revealed her face. It was Sari. She held a finger to her lips and pointed down. "I borrowed shoes, so no one knows Sari comes to this mosque. They think I am someone else walking through the village."

Ingrid looked down at her sandals. "Is that how you knew it was me?"

"Yes, and I was happy. Come," Sari said, her face radiant, "dance with me."

Side by side, they twirled, catching sight of each other and laughing as they grew dizzy and then passed through their dizziness into something else, where blurs of color floated like fabric over their eyes—but no faces, no people, only the singing and the arched ceilings stretching skyward, protecting, encouraging. Ingrid imagined God instructing the dancers, instructing her: *Reach for me, forget your limitations, your balance. I am bigger than all of it. Lose yourself for a moment and see me.*

She did not want to stop because for an ecstatic moment there was no thought, there was feeling only and toward no one, but everyone, everything awash in a feeling that was large and getting larger, spilling out of her. *I am not big enough,* she thought. *Compared to this, I am nothing.*

Then the mosque was suddenly reeling around her like a film on fast-forward. The words on the ceiling spun into one another. *It's what the world is,* she thought, *so many spinning circles of words you cannot read. But here, down here, there is something inside me that is not moving.*

She closed her eyes to the chaos up above. Below her was the unmoving support of the floor. She pressed her hands into it gratefully, opening her eyes to Sari's voice: "Don't touch her. She is my friend." Ingrid's head covering had fallen away and her hair lay spilled on the floor around her. A child crawled to touch it. Sari covered her up again. The singing, the music had stopped.

"Come"—Sari's voice—"we go outside."

"I don't want to move."

"Try to get up. I will take you outside to sit." Ingrid lifted her head to find Sari. "You let go to God," Sari continued. "But not many *mzungu*s go to God like that. I think it brings fear to them." Sari gestured to those in the room who were staring. "It would be best if we go now."

Above Sari's head was the script on the ceiling, which Ingrid could now make out. The words chased each other around and around: *He who comes here will find what he is looking for.* Then another face appeared above her, a man with a long face and a thin beard. "You are well?" he asked.

"Yes."

"This is the man who translated your verses," Sari said. "He told me he knew you would come."

"I recognized the handwriting straightaway," the Imam said with a smile. "Templeton came to us years ago. My brother sent him." The Imam touched his hand to Ingrid's brow. "And you?"

"I'm still looking for him," she said vaguely, aware now that a small group had drawn around her.

"Don't limit your search," he said, gathering his robes. "There is much to find."

"Wait," Ingrid said, reaching under her *bui-bui* to her skirt pocket. She unfolded her tracing of the amulet's inscription. "Do these symbols mean anything to you?"

The Imam briefly inspected the page and handed it back to her. "These letters here are crudely drawn suras," he said. "The markings of Koranic chapters. There are also what could be indicators of ayats, or verses, within those chapters."

"And the other markings?"

"Script. Would you like me to read it for you?"

The page trembled slightly in Ingrid's hand. "Yes."

The Imam had barely looked at the page before he translated. "It says: *Every slave is a king with God in his heart.*"

"Have you seen this before?" Ingrid asked.

1 7

"Not directly. It is, shall I say, familiar."

"It exists. The amulet exists, doesn't it?"

"There are many stories on the island. This is one of them."

"Tell it to me."

"If you are truly a friend of the professor's, you would know it better than I. Now if you'll excuse me, I must return to the others."

"What chapters do the suras correspond to?"

The Imam smiled at Ingrid's distress. "There are one hundred and fourteen suras in the Koran. Here you have the first, al-Baqarah. In English you call it The Cow. This is al-Qamar, the Moon, followed by al-Rahman, al-Dhariyat and al-Najm—or in English, the Merciful, the Winds and the Star."

He read off a series of verse numbers, which Ingrid scribbled on the back side of the drawing. "I had a feeling they were linked to the Koran," she murmured. "So he knew what he was looking for."

"*La illaha il Allah.* There is no God but God." The Imam stood, a pillar of white above her. "Everything is linked to the Koran," he said, removing himself while Sari helped Ingrid to her feet.

"The Imam is the brother of Mohammad," Sari explained as they ducked under a curtain and found themselves outside. The light was sudden and harsh. "Mohammad is the chief of Kitali," she continued, holding her hand over her eyes. "A great man."

"I think he is with this Mohammad," Ingrid said, as much to herself as to Sari.

Instead of returning to the guesthouse, they found shade under a palm tree. The sand under their bare feet was warm, almost hot. They sat and Sari took Ingrid's hand. "I think he is protecting you," she said.

"Who?"

"Finn Bergmann."

"How is that?"

"He follows you. He was there today, outside the mosque."

Ingrid contemplated Sari's delicate hand in her own. "You're protecting me too, aren't you?"

"You are alone," Sari said. "But you will not be alone for long. I wasn't."

"Maybe Finn is my *pepo*," Ingrid said, watching as Sari's head moved up sharply. "Does your *pepo* have a face, Sari?"

Sari's astonishment dissolved as her lips curved in sweet memory. "Sometimes I see him like a flash! But then he is gone. He is afraid, I think. I don't think he is bad. There is a ritual that will kill a *pepo*, but I don't want that. I want to make it better for both of us, so he is happy in me and I am happy with him."

"How do you know it's a man?"

Sari smiled. "Because I am a woman. Women do not haunt other women. If I am lucky, I may sometime make my *pepo* into a *rohani*."

"A *rohani*," Ingrid repeated. "Isn't that a spirit husband?"

"It's the best husband a woman can have. Only she can see him. To everyone else a *rohani* is invisible. But he is loving and kind and he brings her gifts of silk and rosewater and he protects her. This is the kind of husband I want to have."

"And what about Abdul?"

"Abdul has another wife. He has three daughters. He will not know of my *rohani*." Sari reached to adjust Ingrid's veil. "Maybe you can pray for your *pepo* to become a *rohani* too."

The next morning, Sari was sitting on her bed, staring at the wall. Ingrid knocked on her open door and she started. "Are you conjuring your *rohani*, Sari?"

Sari made a sign and lowered her eyes. "I was doing nothing."

"I'm going away for the day. I didn't want you to worry."

"You are taking a holiday from your work?"

"Yes, sort of."

"I hope you enjoy yourself."

"Thank you. Don't wait up for me. I promise to come in quietly."

Ingrid knew from the morning sun which way to walk. She brought a bottle of water and a sandwich from the hotel and draped a kikoi over her shoulders to protect herself from the sun. It was good to walk away from the village, the hotel, her roof: the bizarre microcosm that had become her world.

The island changed quickly when she left the village boundaries. Coconut palms and sand, and no other life. The sand sank deeply beneath her feet. Simply walking should not have been so arduous, but she was tired. She had spent the previous night reading the Koran and the suras the Imam had directed her to. As she had suspected, they were the same passages she had read in Templeton's notebook. She read the verses over and over and then transcribed the lines from the amulet in her notebook, thinking about what, in light of these verses, the amulet's symbol might mean.

The verse from al-Rahman, in particular, kept coming back to her. *He has let loose the two oceans: they meet one another. Yet between them stands a barrier which they cannot overrun. . . .* She considered Templeton's map with its two arrows connecting at the shore. Another pilgrim before her had made his way through the desert back to his people and led them to the mouth of a new spring.

As in Templeton's notes, water was a recurrent theme in the Koran; it was represented as a reward for the righteous—from the faithful Moses striking a rock to have springs rush forth, to the garden paradise reserved for true believers. At the moment, she could appreciate that to peoples of the desert, water was literally a blessing, one of God's greatest gifts. And water on an island? Sometime during the night, the lines at the bottom of the amulet had given her an idea.

When the sun was high, she tucked her hair into her hat and removed her sandals, which kept filling with sand. She rested in the shade of a palm and checked her watch again. It could not take longer than three hours. She had been walking for two. Later, when the skin on the soles of her feet felt tender, she strapped her sandals back on and picked her feet up as she walked like a wading bird, which tired her further.

She decided it was wiser to rest while the sun was strong, and found a spot of shade between two palms where she ate her sandwich, sipping water she wanted to gulp: it was already half gone. When she resumed walking, she was no longer sure which way the sun was moving. It seemed not to be moving at all. It was planted directly overhead and had been, she thought, for the last hour. Maybe if she walked to a high place, to the top of a dune, she would be able to see the settlement.

What she saw, after trudging up the nearest dune, was more dunes. Off in the distance was the ocean. As she walked, she began to feel groggy, unhappy to be so far from the sea. She was sweating, and the loss of moisture made her irritable. She should have tried to go by the beach, she thought, though judging by the map it was longer and the morning tides were wrong in any case. At least on the beach she would have had the comfort of fishermen.

By three o'clock, the terrain had changed: the dunes were not so high and there were fewer palms. The afternoon wind had picked up. Ingrid could now feel an ocean breeze in the air. When she saw water ahead, she quickened her pace.

The beach she came out onto was deserted. She stood for a while and stared out to sea. She was lost, but how lost could one be on an island? Unprotected by the reef, the waves were larger here. Some rolled into a break; others pushed into a frothy wall. Still others seemed destined to meet the shore calmly. Farther out, currents and crosscurrents ran against each other like rivers, so that the sea seemed to be both in motion and stationary. It was possible to see all of it only by focusing on no one point in particular. The sun was beginning to set. She knew that there would be a moon that night. She would sleep until it rose and then start back the way she came.

She scooped sand into a mound and placed a palm frond over it for her head. Above her, the sun slanted through the trees; insects circled in and out of the golden light. The night came, and with it came hunger. At least it was not cold. She thought of Sari and her *pepo* and attempted to imagine a *rohani*. The first manifestation was said to come at night, after days of praying. It appeared as a lion or a great snake or sometimes as a human being. If she was not afraid, the vision would transform itself into a wonderful man.

Sleep came quickly, only it was not like sleep at all. It was like floating. A weightless journey over sand and rocks and finally a pool she could swim in. Then in the dream someone was talking to her.

"I saw you from the water," the voice said. She opened her eyes to a world that was both dark and bright. She could not see the moon or any other source of light. She was confused. Then he touched her arm.

"Why are you always so nearby?"

"Come," Finn said. "I'll take you back by boat."

"I'm going to Kitali," she protested.

"He's not there," he said. "There's no reason for you to go."

Ingrid sat up and gathered her kikoi around her shoulders. "Tell me something. How do you suppose Mohammad gets his water?"

Finn stood up and looked down the beach. "A spring, I imagine."

" *'Behold, there are rocks from which streams gush forth,'* " she recited. " *'God provides for the faithful, issuing sweet water from rock . . .'* I have been thinking there must be a place there where water springs from rock and sand."

"And?"

Ingrid took out her sketch of the amulet. "I am not going to ask what you know, because I don't think you'd tell me. But do you see how roughly these suras are drawn? I believe they were etched by a king who lived on Pelat. Water brought him here, water kept God in his heart. I think he wore the amulet as a reminder, as a talisman, which is why I ask where Mohammad goes to drink. Maybe the king lived near there."

Finn reached for the sketch. "You are beginning to sound like your professor. You make things up out of air and then pretend they are real."

"Have you seen this before?" Ingrid asked. Finn ignored her, studying the faint lines in the moonlight. "I don't know what you're hiding from," she added. "I don't know why you can't talk to me."

"Who are you, anyway?" Finn thrust the map back at her. "An accident. What brought you here has nothing to do with me."

"Just tell me if he's all right," Ingrid whispered.

"I don't know." Finn turned toward the shore. "But no amount of walking in the sand will get you closer to him. Now, come."

When they got to the boat, conversation stopped. At one point, Ingrid shouted another question, which Finn also ignored. It could have been because of engine noise, but she doubted it. She watched him covertly, envious of his stubborn reserve.

The Beginning of Silence

*I*ngrid found she could not talk about Finn.

Nor could she talk directly to him.

Twice since he found her on the beach she had sat next to him at the bar and drunk the sweet drinks Jackson mixed for her, absorbing with strong doses of alcohol the fact that conversation between them was impossible. Finn refused to abide by the contract of language. He was like a terrorist who blew up bridges between them; fragile, rickety beginnings. At first it made her angry, angry at herself, if this was her fault, then angry at him because it was ultimately his fault. Coward! The malady of isolation didn't mean you had to forever boycott conversation with the rest of humanity. Because he refused to speak about Templeton she persisted in the impossible task of extracting personal information from him. "And your mother?"

"I didn't know her."

"And your father?"

"No more questions now. Shh."

But she continued to lob words at him like rocks from under her broken bridges, amazed that they did not hurt him. "Danny told me how your father died," she told him.

"Did he?"

"Why are you smiling? It's an awful story. But it sounds like he was in the wrong. He was the foreigner, after all. He was the guest. You must have noticed, colonial behavior and thinking can be very inhospitable to its hosts. Anyway, you must miss him."

"Not exactly."

"I don't believe you. I miss my mother even though I barely remember her. Maybe you don't miss him because the island is being ruined by his hotel. Look at them. They're sitting ducks for this *mzungu* bacchanal." The words didn't touch him. He didn't even flinch. She changed her approach. "When was the last time you drank a nice bottle of wine with a woman? My father says—"

"Your father's daughter talks enough for three."

"He would laugh to hear you say that."

When she finally sat next to him without trying to speak, he touched her hair. She felt a shock and turned away, afraid that if she looked at him, she might cry at this small reward. She felt like a child again, learning how to behave in a world she didn't understand.

"I won't make a habit of touching you," Finn said.

The words jolted her. "Why not?"

"Because you can't look at me."

"I see."

"Most women don't. They create things that aren't there." *He's trying to hurt you,* she thought. "You think you're different?" he asked.

"I am different, aren't I? You sleep with me without fucking me, don't you?" Saying the word made Ingrid's courage surge. It was like a sharp pebble in her mouth. She wanted to say it again. When Finn chose not to answer, she opened a book on the bar, quietly pleased with herself.

❦

Danny replaced Finn as the afternoon wore on. "Oh, my. As I approached you I thought I saw a dream on your face. A wish, a want, a yen. Something flimsy and unnameable. What a lovely sight: the softening of hard, Nordic rigor."

"I was thinking about Islam and how it got to this island," she said.

Danny signaled to Jackson. "Do you ever let your mind wander, or do you always steer it?"

"I find steering more productive."

"Well, I recommend a good wander."

"Don't worry." Ingrid closed her book. "My mind wanders enough in this heat."

"Good. It's the secret to happiness here."

"I think alcohol has more to do with that."

"Well, now, you've got to make a few concessions to your new hemisphere, don't you? First off, no one works *hard* here, not even your professor. Let's give it some thought. How hard can he be working? For one thing, he's managed to forget all about you. Bloody fool for doing that, I say. So put that nasty book away and let's have a drink. Later we can wander companionably to some dark place and have a look at our beloved Southern Cross."

Ingrid slid her book into her bag and watched Danny drain his first beer. "I think I'll take that walk now, while it's still light. Would you like to come?"

"Heavens no! A proper beach walk is very hard work."

Ingrid stood and smiled. "You know, Danny, in spite of your efforts to horrify me, I'm starting to like you."

❧

She left the bar and walked down to the beach, leaving her sandals on a rock. The tide was low and the clouds were close to the ocean and moving fast, picking up light from the sea and the sun so it seemed they were lit from the center. She walked until she lost sight of the hotel and the village, until it was just the sea and the sand and the sun-misted air.

There was something between Finn and Templeton that she couldn't get near, and something in Finn himself that kept pushing her away. She thought of what she could say to him, to get him to talk to her. *Let me in, I won't spy on your solitude.* No, that was a lie. His solitude intrigued her. She wanted to get closer to it, to him. But she did not know how to operate without the protection of words. As if amused, he watched her struggle. She turned and started back for the hotel.

When Ingrid reached the rock where she had left her sandals, one sandal was missing. She circled the rock to see if it had fallen, but there was nothing but sand. Who would take only one shoe? Carrying her lone sandal back to Salama, she bought a fifth of whiskey from Jackson and retreated to her roof. She put the sandal in her suitcase. She would go barefoot now, like Ali. She poured herself a glass of whiskey and felt fortified. *Screw Finn Bergmann and his marinated heart.* Keep thinking, Ingrid. Think your way past him. He's not really a part of this, not a part of you.

She sipped her whiskey and studied the night sky, cycling ideas through her head until one of them caught. Cultures that lived under clear skies, Templeton had once said, incorporated the stars into the fabric of their lives. Desert cultures shared the complex clarity of the nighttime tapestry that blanketed them. In Egypt, Osiris and Isis shone into the hollow shafts of the Giza pyramids, lighting the way for the dead. Ingrid remembered standing with Louis in the burial chambers of the pharaoh, and in the smaller chamber for his wife.

The tyranny of the present was its lack of interest in the past. She had learned to be calm in spite of her fury. In her brief century, sacred deserts had been irrigated and the blinding dimness of artificial light had blotted out the beauty of the night, the revolving sky. Ingrid poured herself another glass of whiskey and stirred it with her finger, dunking her only piece of jewelry into the glass. She removed and dropped her mother's ring into the tumbler and looked at it from below. She held the glass to her mouth, draining the whiskey until the ring slid into her mouth. She held it between her teeth, remembering the story of a desert poet Templeton had told her about, who had languished in the insanity of so much clarity.

Christ and Mohammed had also fled to the endless space of the desert, chased by those who feared their vision. And they were delivered there, by more visions. Under its piercing nights, they had seen something they believed was true. It was the strength of their belief that saved them, the human heart grasping at the possibility of the divine.

She reread Templeton's note by candlelight, tipped a corner into the flame and watched as it burned. When it got close to her fingers, she dropped it and let the embers extinguish themselves on the ground.

Ingrid decided she liked being drunk in her new environs. She moved inside as if Finn's eyes were on her, watching her as she undressed. She walked around the room as if dancing, as if this were the way she always walked, the beauty inside her fighting to get out. She slipped on her cotton nightie as if it were silk. This is who I am, she said to him silently. Watch me. *This is who I am.* She turned up the flame in her lamp and made her shadow dance on the wall. Consider it, she instructed her shadow. Consider the possibility that your beauty has strength, a soul.

The latch to her door lifted and Ingrid spun around. Ali's face flickered in the light. Ingrid reached for her shawl, too startled to speak.

"I did not see you at dinner," he said.

"You cannot come into my room like this, Ali. Do you understand?"

Ali smiled and stepped inside. "Finn comes to your room."

"What?"

"Because he is white, you let him come."

"No, Ali, *no*—he sleeps here, that is all."

"He sleeps only. Yes," Ali nodded and smiled his lupine smile. "I understand."

"Why am I even explaining to you? You are *trespassing.* I will tell Abdul."

"Abdul let me in."

Ingrid moved toward him, shaking, and shouted, "Out!"

Ali retreated, placing a small envelope on the doorstep. "He said this was left for you."

Ingrid picked up the envelope and shut the door, propping the chair under the knob. After closing the curtains, she opened the envelope and removed a single sheet of paper. The handwriting was faint and unfamiliar. She held the note close to the candle. *"Stop your searching. It would not be hard to prevent you. There is little you understand, and a fool is a danger to everyone."*

Alarmed, Ingrid went down to the courtyard and called for

Abdul. He emerged from his room, irritated. "Who left this letter?" she asked.

"I don't know," he said. She could hear the lie in his voice. Feeling the impulse toward violence well up inside her, she forced her face into a bitter smile. "You don't scare me, Abdul."

"I do not scare you because you are made of fear," he said, smiling back with a kindness so false she had to turn away from him.

The next day, Ingrid couldn't eat. The air was heavy with storm. Clouds gathered but did not break; her clothes clung to her body, damp with sweat and humidity. She wrapped a kikoi around her waist, the way the island men did. The thin cotton fabric flapped around her legs, allowing the air to circulate. She surveyed the village from the edge of her roof and realized that she did not want to write about the island. She pressed the palms of her hands together and remembered herself before Pelat, remembered her strength, her clarity. Then she went inside and opened her laptop.

Dr. Reed:

No sign yet of Templeton, but I am making some headway of my own in his absence. The Swahili brand of Islam is fascinating: tolerant of paradox and open to a world we confine to the imagination. The Arab/African roots of Swahili culture have spawned a pairing of meanings, terms and rituals which manifested in everything from vocabulary—words like *pepo* have Bantu roots, whereas *rohani* is Arabic—to calendars; the African calendar (considered local—i.e., what the fishermen use) is solar and the Arab calendar (more orthodox, or Islamic) is lunar. There are even two kinds of settlements; the Stone town, which houses the more orthodox (and coastal) Swahili, and the Country village, where the

more local, or African, population live, usually farther inland. These towns are economically mutually dependent and
are enmeshed on many levels, including marriage. Not surprisingly, there are two names for God—Mungu and Allah.
What's striking is that such disparate worlds have peacefully
coexisted for centuries.

I have been studying the Koran. Classical Arabic is impossible to translate into English; we are missing the sacred.
To hear it spoken, one can believe the sufic claim that it is
based on mathematical formulas. It has both dimension and
truth. It is replete with etymological stems that, instead of
attempting to describe God in words, reflect his infinity.

> *And do not drive away*
> *Those who call upon their Lord*
> *In the morning and the evening*
> *Seeking the essence of God:*
> *You are not accountable for them,*
> *And they are not accountable for you.*
> *So if you drive them away,*
> *You will be an oppressor.*

You see, it's a smart religion. Outside of Araji, not all the jack-
asses in the department would understand it. Its power is
daunting, perhaps too much so for your mighty Western
mind. . . . I have nothing to say to you, really.

Ingrid deleted the last paragraph. Before she could restart the report, her laptop battery went dead. She called Abdul upstairs to
help her. Without looking at him, she held up the plug in a re-
quest for a socket. "I cannot help you," he said.

"Of course you can't," Ingrid said bitterly.

. . .

In the hotel office, Ali looked on as Ingrid plugged in her computer and her adapter exploded. He jumped back and whistled. Ingrid kicked the garbage can.

"I think there was at one time," Ali offered, "a typewriter on the island."

Ingrid sat on the hotel terrace and waited for him. By the time he returned with the typewriter, the sky had blackened with clouds and the motionless air began gathering strength.

The storm broke violently; the village roofs streamed from their gutters. Ingrid wrapped the typewriter in her shawl and hurried past rivulets of rainwater that ran alongside the path. She had not noticed the irrigation system before. Bits of garbage were washed away and a stench arose, as if weeks of crusty filth were being loosened and released. Quite suddenly, the rain stopped. The sun was brighter than before, with no humidity to divert its force. It banged against Ingrid's rooftop like a cymbal. She wrapped a damp T-shirt around her head and sat down with the typewriter.

> *Templeton, damn you, where are you.*
> *I am typing on the world's oldest typewriter.*
> *It's too bright to think, too hot.*
> *I feel I am falling apart in this sun and rain. I am*
> *afraid.*
> *I need to find you, you whom I no longer know,*
> *can barely understand. I can hear you laughing.*
> *How many times have you told me*
> *you need to lose your bearings to find new ones,*
> *to understand a new place you must lose yourself in*
> *its people, its god, its plants, its poisons.*

I think now that I have never done it before and
comfort myself by thinking you would approve.
Come back. I need you.

Ingrid could feel that Sari had entered the room. There was no change in the atmosphere, no presence announced, just a darkness at the periphery of her vision, moving closer tentatively until Ingrid raised her head. Against her black robe was an envelope that seemed unnaturally white. She held it out like an offering. Sari's forehead was wet with perspiration. "Poor Sari," Ingrid said. *"Kali sana." It's too hot for what you're wearing,* Ingrid wanted to say. *Take that robe off and sit here with me on the cool floor.*

Their fingers met on the blank frontier of the envelope. Sari's fingernails were bitten down to the skin: red strips had been peeled from her fingertips. Ingrid held one of her fingers in her own and smiled. "Poor fingers," she said in Swahili. "Sad fingers." Sari inspected them, holding them close to her face. "Ooglie," she said.

"No, not ugly. Tired. Sari's fingers are tired."

Inside the envelope was a frond with an invitation etched on it. A party for Finn. He was going to be thirty. Please come to Salama at seven for dinner and celebration as Danny's guest. Wear something little.

A Suitable Party

*I*ngrid wore her only clean dress. A T-shaped table had been set for twenty under the trellis on the sand of the outdoor grill. Torches had been lit and the table was littered with jasmine petals. Cocktails were being poured from a pitcher by a black American named Rudy who came from a yacht in the harbor. Ingrid had met him through Danny at the bar. He was a bald, bearded man with a round belly and thick glasses. He smiled at Ingrid. "Have some *miraa* tea, but first remind me of your name." A lithe tanned woman in very short shorts rubbed up against him. "This is Janine, my crew."

"Ingrid. Pleased to meet you."

"Oh, I know about you." Janine smiled. "This is the one Danny was talking about yesterday."

Ingrid smiled into Janine's bloodshot eyes. "What did he say?"

"Nothing but wonderful things. Have you met Lady Emily?"

Janine asked, gesturing toward a svelte woman with mangrove sticks in her hair. Tonight she had an animal hide pinned around her waist and floated past them in a cloud of perfume. Ingrid stared after her, mesmerized by the slits in her pelt that revealed, for anyone wondering, that she wore no underwear.

"The island's landed lady," Rudy said. "Supposedly she came here on vacation three years ago and hasn't left. That fellow over there is her lover. He's a dirt-poor Kenyan but now he's got English nobility backing his safaris. They lead boat trips up the coast, looking for elephants or something." Lady Emily's lover had white-blond hair to his shoulders and an angelic countenance. "Now, if you'll excuse me, I have to distribute some goodies. I'll seek you out later. Oh, meet Onka. Onka, this is Danny's American friend."

"I feel so free." Onka smiled, touching her tiny torso. "I've just given birth. This is my first time out of the house in days. I haven't met any of the new people. Have you been here long?"

"A while."

"There's Sabo." Onka led Ingrid toward a heavyset black man who was deep in discussion with a large white woman. Onka stood next to him and leaned her blond head against his arm. "He's my love."

Sabo smiled at Ingrid and held out his hand. "I'm chatting with a novelist," he said in the queen's English. "Judy, isn't it? This is Judy. And you are?"

"Danny's American friend."

"Ah, well, Judy's American too," Sabo said.

"I haven't lived there in years," Judy corrected him. She was draped in some kind of muumuu. "I spend my time here or on the Continent. I hardly consider myself *American.*"

"What are you writing about, Judy?" Onka asked.

"I never talk about my work. It interrupts the unconscious creative processes."

Onka laughed. "Isn't she wonderful?"

"I've brought some friends from London." Judy gestured to a cluster of three women who were talking with bent heads. "We're here for another few weeks at least. One of them is a spiritual healer. She has us doing sun salutations at dawn. You can't believe how powerful her energy is."

"Ingrid!" Danny bellowed. "Extract yourself from those beastly women and come over here at once."

"You're a friend of Danny's?" Judy asked, failing to mask her distaste.

"From America," Onka added. Danny hooked Ingrid with his arm and pulled her close to him. He was surrounded by more European Kenyans, some of whom she had met before. "This is little Miss Muffet," Danny said. "The woman who's going to bear my children."

"Yes," Ingrid said, smiling brightly. "We're expecting."

"Congratulations," one of them said.

"Good Lord, Danny, are you going to be a father?" another asked.

"That depends on Miss Muffet. Look, it's time for dinner and still no Finn. We'll just have to carry on without him."

"You're sitting next to me," Rudy whispered in Ingrid's ear. Stanley Wicks sat across from her. His feet quickly found one of hers in the sand. She winced at the pressure and pulled her foot away.

Wooden bowls full of soup were placed in front of them.

"No cutlery tonight," Stanley explained. "They seem to enjoy eating with their hands." Later, he touched the tips of her fingers with his. "I hear you're looking for someone."

"Everyone must know by now."

"He was lurking around Kitali for a time." Stanley forced a smile. "Is he supposed to be working there or what?"

"I don't know. I thought he was there, but he seems to have disappeared."

Stanley's eyebrows raised. "Really?"

"It's not that unusual."

"Perhaps he's gone home," Stanley said hopefully.

"That would be unusual."

Stanley stopped smiling and tipped the bowl to his mouth. "God knows what's in this. The tea was lethal enough."

"Was it?"

"Never trust what people give you at these parties. You might not make it to the main course."

"Stanley, darling," Daisy called from down the table. "Have you got my smokes?"

"We just came from Malta," Rudy said, sitting next to her. "Janine learned to make Maltese lace. That's what we do. We sail to a place and set up shop; learn the language, learn the local craft, indulge in the local drug. But this is the best place. We always stay here the longest. Look at these people! Have you ever seen better-looking people in your life? The gene pool is incredible. And now they're having babies. I can't wait to see how they turn out. Onka had a baby four days ago and look at her. Onka, show her your stomach!" Onka stood up and raised her dress above her breasts.

"Shame your boobs didn't get any bigger," Danny said.

"Big breasts today, sag-bags tomorrow," Rudy said. "I like 'em small and pert."

"Is this really dinner conversation?" Judy asked.

"Where is Finn, for God's sake?" Stanley asked. "Isn't this his birthday?"

"Of course Finn wouldn't actually attend his own birthday party," Judy said. "There's a delightful perversity to this island," she told the woman next to her. "Rudy, have you brought your black bag?"

"I don't come to shore without it, not here, anyway."

"I'd love a shot of B vites. Paradise is so unexpectedly taxing, don't you find, Stanley? You should have one too. It really boosts the system."

"One for everyone!" Danny announced. "We'll all be pep pep peppy!" He stood up and did a jig in the sand.

Stanley's hand was back on top of Ingrid's. "You're not like them, are you?" he asked quietly.

"I might be."

Stanley looked at her closely.

"You're mocking me."

"It seems everyone mocks everyone here."

"It's quite sad, isn't it." Stanley took her hand. "What lovely hands you have. Long, lovely hands. Oh, that tea has done me a disservice. May I look at your palm?"

"Your wife is not pleased," Ingrid said as Stanley drew her hand to him. "Here she comes."

"Do you mind?" Daisy asked Ingrid. "Stanley, my smokes, please. I asked for them ages ago."

"Sorry, darling. That tea has me a bit loopy. Here they are." Stanley smiled contritely up at his wife.

"That was turtle soup," Rudy announced. "For all you vegans."

"Thank heavens I didn't touch it," Stanley muttered.

A small child appeared at the end of the table. She was holding something in her dress. "Rudy," Danny said. "Your brat's here."

"What have you got there, sweetheart?" Rudy asked. The child moved next to her father and opened the folds of her dress. "Where did you get that, sweetheart?"

"I found it under a bush. All alone."

"Its eyes aren't even open."

"What's she got?" Judy asked.

"A kitten. Newborn."

"Oh." A few sympathetic sounds came from the women.

"Put it back where you found it," Danny instructed. "It was abandoned for a reason."

"Danny's right, honey," Janine said. "It's probably sick."

The child's features hardened as she stepped back, out of the torchlight.

"It won't live," Danny announced. "Wasn't meant to. Dead by morning." Without a word, the child disappeared.

Conversation resumed and Finn had still not appeared. Rudy circled his arm around Ingrid's waist. "On a personal note, I'd like to know how you feel about swallowing," he said. "I can't tell you how important it is for a woman to swallow. It's about trust. Remember that. Janine knew that, right from the start. You don't know how devastating it is for a man when a woman spits out; it's like she's spitting out his deepest love."

Ingrid picked at the lettuce in her salad. "Are there really no forks?"

"Eat with your fingers. You can wipe your hands on me," Rudy said, slapping his thighs. "The hair picks up the particles and the skin absorbs the grease. I'm a walking napkin." Rudy put his mouth to her ear. "And if, by chance your hands want to go walking farther north, well, they're welcome there too."

"Ingrid, taste this flower. It's delicious." Stanley held some kind of blossom to her lips.

"Adolpho!" Daisy yelled. "Come over here, my shoulder is killing me." A muscular young man rose and stood behind Daisy while she positioned his hand. "Right here. It feels like a bloody rope knot. See if you can work it out."

"Have you got a masseur with you?" Lady Emily asked, her lethargic features roused with a half-smile.

"He's divine," Daisy confided. "I don't know how I lived life without him."

"May Staz and I borrow him sometime?"

"Of course, that's what he's here for. Though he's not really for public consumption. But that doesn't apply to you, Lady Emily."

"He may never go back to his employer after he sees your Greek perfection, Emily," Danny said. "Incidentally, are you still waging war with those nasty pregnancy pounds, Daisy?"

"Thank you, Danny," Daisy muttered. "That was a nice little dig."

Danny shrugged. "You've got some competition in the leg department, Em. Miss Muffet down there is sporting some fabulous limbs. Stand up, Miss Muffet, show us your gams."

"Yes," Rudy agreed. "Show us."

Ingrid stared at a button on Stanley's shirt.

"Don't be such a brute, Danny," Lady Emily said. "Can't you see she's shy?"

"Stop harassing her," Judy chimed in. "She's done nothing to deserve it."

"She was born and somehow she made her way here. That's enough. Tell you the truth, your gams are enough for me, princess Em."

"I'm honored."

"Sit on my lap, won't you?"

"Not tonight, Danny, I'm being good."

"Well, then, for chrissake, let's drink to Finn!" Danny raised his glass. "And then let's smoke to Finn. And then let's shoot up to Finn! And then let's bonk to Finn!"

"Let's bonk *with* Finn," Judy added. "The rest of you I wouldn't bother with."

"If only he knew of your love, his heart would be going pitter-pat, pitter-pat."

"Stuff it, Danny. You're only jealous."

"Oh, yes, that's it. How astute you are. Why, you must be a writer. A genius of human nature."

Ingrid stopped following the banter. It was coming from all ends of the table and converging above her head in a merciless web she felt would snare her if she raised her eyes from the table-cloth. Then anything could happen. Danny would force her to strip and parade up and down the table naked. She would be molested by sweaty, corpulent Rudy while his skinny wife looked on. Daisy Wicks would burn her eyes out with a cigarette. If she couldn't leave, she had to make herself disappear. Think about something else, she told herself; think about Templeton.

Instead, Ingrid thought about Sari and what she might wear to bed at night. Did she cover herself there too? She remembered that Sari had no windows in her room. It seemed impossible that she slept at all in such heat, especially if Abdul paid her night-time visits. Withered old Abdul on top of lovely, perspiring Sari.

A sauce-covered lump was placed in front of her. She looked around the table to see if others were eating it and how. Down the table, Judy had gotten hold of a spoon. "If you weren't so hor-rid," she was saying to Danny, using the spoon to point at him, "you'd get laid more often."

"Another pearl drops from her lips!" Danny cried. "Quick, out of my way so I can catch it."

"Don't let him bait you," one of Judy's friends said. "Remember what we talked about today."

"He's not worth resisting," Judy said. "Such blatant misogyny needs to be stamped out."

"If you're doing the stamping, Lady Beluga, I shan't live long."

"Bastard."

"A quick, painless death. Some would agree you'd be doing me a great favor." Danny held his lighter to a bowl of hash. "Death by stomping," he said, inhaling. "I always wanted to be remembered for something. Pity we can't choose these things."

Lady Emily laughed. "Staz darling, how about a little lap dance?" She walked in the sand to her lover and straddled his thighs. He pulled the animal hide up over her bare buttocks.

"Oh, no," Stanley muttered.

"She's not wearing anything," Judy hissed.

"Isn't it glorious?" Rudy said. "We should all be so wise. The closer we are to animals, the better." Lady Emily began gyrating her hips. She rested her head on Staz's forehead, covering them both in a cascade of shiny hair. Ingrid stared at the flame of a candle.

"To the fall of Rome!" Danny yelled. "Finn will be sorry he missed this."

Ingrid slipped away to go to the restroom and found her feet turning away from the lights of the party and taking her back to her guesthouse, to where Sari slept.

She slowed soon after she left, when she felt a presence along the path.

He was sitting on the stairs to the upper bungalows of Salama—she could see only a pale stripe in the pattern of his kikoi. He spoke her name softly. She stood on the path and waited for him to say it again, louder. A small demand; but he could not give her even this.

Their silence was corrupted by the sounds of the party, by drunken laughter in the distance. She imagined he was someone else, someone she had never seen or heard, and continued along the path.

His arm encircled her from behind, walking her backward to the steps, his face against her cheek like a brace to keep her steady. The stubble dug into her skin. She pivoted around while he caught her hand in his. He sat on a stair and held her in front of him. His fingers stroked her hair back from her face. She knew he was drunk.

"Are you enjoying my party?" he asked.

The parts of her not touching him melted into a liquid state of wanting. She ran her hands slowly up and down his thighs and arms. "Why is Wicks afraid of Templeton?"

Finn laughed softly. "He's a frightening fellow."

She leaned her head against his chest. "Someone left me a frightening note at the guesthouse."

"Frightening how?"

"It said if I didn't stop my activities, they would be stopped for me."

"Yes, well, your activities might be offensive to some. I've been trying to tell you that. Perhaps it's time you pay attention."

"And sit here and do nothing?"

"What is there to do?"

Above them a woman's voice called his name with modulated urgency and suddenly they were apart.

"Who is that?" Ingrid asked.

"A guest. An old friend."

She looked up into the darkness, seeing only his outline.

"No," Ingrid said. "Don't leave me. Don't open me up and then leave me."

He leaned down to kiss her. "I think a little silence is good for you."

Ingrid watched him appear briefly in silhouette as the lights of the upper gardens found him and took him away.

Part

Four

The Safety of the Sea

U*ma* started with a bang and a rumble and headed out to sea, passing the dhows of the night fishermen on their way in. Boni steered near them and stood in his dhow. With his foot on the rudder, he held up a snapper as long as his arm and shook it at *Uma.* Finn saluted him with a fist.

"Bravo, Boni!" he yelled over the engine.

By lunchtime *Uma* had reached Kifi Island, where the night fishermen sometimes slept. The few who lived on the island dried their catch and sold it in town every month. Without the gentle rise of smooth rock where the fish were left to dry, the island, thin and round as a coin, would have been invisible to everyone but the birds. Finn and Jonah anchored *Uma* and swam ashore to see what they could find on the rocks. On the beach, they passed a carcass of a large tiger shark surrounded by tuna and snapper. Finn whistled through his fingers and a man appeared from behind the rocks. "Habib!" He greeted the man in Swahili. "How is it?"

Habib scratched his head and looked at the sky. "Not bad. The fish are biting."

"I can see. And the shark?"

Habib turned to look at the fly-covered carcass. Next to it was its jaws, huge and gaping. "It's big."

"Very. The biggest I've seen in a long time."

"We found it on the beach. The tide brought it in."

"Propeller?"

"No." Habib picked something off the bottom of his foot. "It had a hole in its head."

Finn looked at the shark. "A hole? How big?"

"Not big." He made a small circle with his fingers. Finn squatted, picked up a handful of sand and sifted a little at a time.

Back on *Uma,* they ate cheese sandwiches and bananas. "Where have you been sleeping at night?" Jonah asked. "You are not in your bed when I come to wake you."

"But have I been late?"

"No."

"So you know I have not been exerting myself with nighttime activity."

"Then where do you sleep?"

"Abdul's guesthouse."

"The American girl!" Jonah grinned.

"It's not what you think," Finn said, lying down. "She is alone here."

"Ah, noble Finn. My faith in you grows with this information. Finn, the guardian angel."

"You're laughing."

"Only because no one would believe it."

"Our finest acts, my friend, are witnessed only by God."

"Well, I hope he is watching you."

Finn groaned and put a hat over his eyes while Jonah cleaned up and brought him a glass of water. Finn took it and held it on his chest. "Drink it," Jonah said. He waited until Finn had propped himself up and begun drinking before going to the back of the boat, baiting a hook with squid, spitting on it for luck and throwing the line. Finn closed his eyes while Jonah trolled out a kilometer and threw another line, running the engine just above idle.

While Finn slept, Jonah caught three bonitos and a snapper, working both lines.

The sun was sinking toward a sliver of land to the west and the heat was beginning to die when Finn finally awoke. He stood, looked around, and then sat down quickly. "Bait?"

"Four bonitos. Female first."

"Good." Luck was with them, and it had put Jonah in a good mood. He took a cigarette from Jonah's shirt pocket and sat next to him. "And for supper?"

"Snapper."

Finn ran his fingers through his hair, still wet with perspiration. "Too much time on land," he said. And then, after a pause, "I got hold of a konahead." Jonah scoffed and made the sign for bad luck. "What the hell, Jonah, it used to work for us."

"Those were small fish. We used rubber bands."

"Same idea."

"And the bait?"

"We'll use the bait first." Finn held his cigarette between his lips and adjusted the strap on his hat.

When Finn tossed the konahead up from belowdecks, Jonah let it go by and land with a thud, eyeing it from the wheel. It was half a meter long and had one large eye and neon orange stripes.

It lay there untouched until Finn came up with two mugs of tea. "Where's its body?" Jonah asked.

"Doesn't have one." Finn handed Jonah a mug. "Doesn't need one."

"And this color? What fish would bite this color?"

"It's the way it moves. The color doesn't matter. It fades twelve meters down anyway. Thirty, thirty-five meters down and it's gone completely."

"That's nice, but marlin feed on the surface."

"Not after they hit the bait." They sipped their tea. The sun was disappearing and the horizon around it glowed.

"Does *Tarkar* use konaheads?"

"That's where I got it—it's an old one of Nelson's." Finn met Jonah's eyes. "Look, we won't know until we try. You didn't want to use rubber bands either." Jonah was unmoved. Finn went in to cook the fish.

The sea was calm. A few stars pierced the sky as they threw small bait overboard and drifted, eating the snapper with bread. *Uma* bobbed gently in the still air. After they had eaten, Jonah wiped the rods with varnish and Finn took the wheel. He steered south by the stars. Past midnight, he grew tired. He sang to himself and chewed a few sticks of *miraa,* thinking of Boni.

Had a shipment of *miraa* not arrived from the mainland every afternoon at three, there would have been a riot, led by Boni, who chewed the natural amphetamine into the dawn. After a bundle or two, *miraa* had mind-altering effects. Boni would report communications he had witnessed between schools of snapper and the constellations: their movements were affected by cloud cover, eclipses, meteor showers. Boni detected patterns and repetitions. They were quick, but often predictable. They couldn't lose him, for he, Boni, relied on something more powerful than any instrument: an intuitive sense of where, within his domain, the fish would be.

When he was drunk, Boni bragged. He sat at the Salama bar and spun tales. The white women were drawn to him, and he played them the way he played his fish. His haul was always the largest, he told them. And it was true. When the morning sun filtered through the baobabs on Tomba Island, Boni could be found angling his dhow along the seawall, where people were waiting to buy fish from him. He grinned up at them while they stood on the narrow stone wall, the frayed edges of their kikois fluttering in time to Boni's loosened sail.

When he had sold half his fish he would head, pockets full of shillings, to Salama, the only place he could get a drink at day-break. He told himself he would sell the rest of the fish later. But by lunchtime, he would be lunging at passing women. By late afternoon, when he became obscene, he was invariably kicked out of the bar. Boni then stumbled off to sleep somewhere in the vicinity of a woman. Sometimes that woman was his wife: often by accident or habit he crashed onto the floor of his own home. His wife left him lying there until dusk eased her shame into pity and she tipped a glass of water to his parched lips.

"Boni," she said. "You are a bad man." He avoided looking at her eyes and instead nestled his gaze into the deep folds of her black *bui-bui*. Only occasionally did he have the urge to discover the shape it hid. It wasn't for lack of beauty; it was what she knew.

"Have you brought me money?" she asked. "We need food." Boni's eyes climbed the soft hills of her cloth to find her round, solemn eyes with his own drunken stare. He did this to avoid words. By dinnertime he was back at the hotel bar, washed and rested and chewing the night's first bundle of *miraa* with Jonah or Finn.

Finn woke Jonah just before dawn, when he was too tired to stand. After a quick bread and tea, they headed for the blue water northeast of Malindi. Finn had made good time. He dropped a bonito at sunrise and hooked a small spearfish almost immediately. He netted it and flipped it on board, where it twisted and slapped against the deck. Jonah cursed the spearfish, which was no good for anything. Finn tossed it back and rebaited the hook.

By ten, they were almost in blue water. "Get something to eat," Finn said. "I'm following gulls." Jonah climbed up to the lookout with bread and jam. Single gulls didn't constitute a flock, but if they were headed in the same direction, there might be something. Jonah wrapped his kikoi around his head and squinted out beyond the gulls to a horizon of swells. A marlin feeding would ride the swells, showing its fin as it glided down into a trough.

The sun was directly overhead when Jonah shouted and clambered down on deck. Finn slowed the boat. They each reeled in a rod to check the bait. Finn picked strings of seaweed from the mouth of his bonito, and they threw them back. Jonah took the wheel and angled the boat in the direction of the dark shape he had seen just below the surface.

Finn hooked himself into the harness and waited, his eyes trained on the area right behind the bait. A few minutes later, a black fin broke the surface. "Marlin tailing!" he called to Jonah. "Keep her at four knots." Finn clipped himself to the starboard rod. The marlin swam up and struck the bait with its bill. The line jerked from the outrigger clip, and suddenly went slack. Jonah cut the throttle. "Take it, take it," Finn whispered as the bonito disappeared below the surface. The marlin turned and went for the bait. "He's got it," Finn cried out. The line fed out as the fish swam off, giving it enough time to swallow the bonito. Finn counted to ten and then struck.

"Go!" he yelled. Jonah gunned the boat forward. The hook set, the line whirred. Finn let the fish run for a few hundred meters, and when half the line was out, he started reeling it in, guiding it onto the spool with his thumb. The marlin let itself be pulled in a few meters and then ran again.

"Shit," Finn said. It ran a hundred meters or more before he started pumping it again. The fish came in slowly: it was at least three hundred pounds. When it jumped, Finn tightened the line as soon as it started to come down, throwing it off balance so that it landed with a whack.

"Try that again," Finn murmured. "It'll make this faster." The line went slack and the rod jerked to the right. "He's circling," he called out, pumping the line in quickly. "C'mon, up you come . . ." He held the fish on a short line, so it could feel the pressure. The marlin jumped to the port side of the boat. Finn tightened the line again while Jonah tied a slip noose in a heavy rope and put it around Finn's legs.

When the fish was played out, Finn pulled the leader toward him, hand over hand. Jonah grabbed the flying gaff. The marlin's bill surfaced again and Jonah pulled the slip noose up Finn's body and over the rod. It slid down the leader, onto the bill and over the fish's head. Jonah laid the gaff over the head and pulled it tight. The fish was lifted and suspended. Keeping the rod tip high, Finn pushed the rope over the dorsal fin to the tail and yanked it tight. Then, together, they pulled it over the deck.

It was a magnificent fish. Ten years ago, they would have taken it with them. Now it was against the rules. Some white man had taken to calling it a "sport fish," and now it was something you caught for competition. A fleet of boats cruised the coast for these sport fish so they could capture a title. The competition, the title, had meant nothing to Finn at first, but since Wicks came to the island, that had changed.

"Quickly, Jonah," Finn said. They tailed and measured the fish and let it go.

❧

The next day they refueled in Malindi and headed south to Turtle Bay. They kept along the continental shelf, a couple of kilometers offshore. Finn dropped the anchor at the edge of the shelf and fastened a buoy to the top of the anchor line. They cast two lines and pulled in a kingfish and two tuna. The sea was ragged with wind.

"Do you see what I see?" Finn said.

"Of course." *Tarkar* was coming toward them at high throttle, smooth as silk. Finn and Jonah pulled in their lines. Nelson sidled up alongside *Uma,* a Walkman on his ears. "Take that thing off!" Finn yelled. Nelson slid the headset to his neck and leaned over the side to look at *Uma*'s deck. He pointed to the buoyed anchor line. "Expecting something big?" he shouted.

"Never know," Finn said.

"Any luck?"

"Some."

"We hit a shoal of snapper fifty kilometers north on the way down," Nelson said. "Sailfish. Couldn't bait it." He grinned and spit. "They're out there, all right. A boat in Malindi got two marlin last week—two- and three-hundred-pounders."

"Should be a good season." Finn took off his hat and adjusted it. He saw only one crew member on deck. "How many do you have on board?"

"Four. Need every one. We're running up to five lines."

"I guess she's big enough to handle it." He put his foot on the edge of the boat and leaned into it with his knee. "What are they doing down there?"

"Wicks got us some high-tech rods. They're putting them together." Nelson grinned. "We'll be hauling some big ones."

"Uh-huh. Don't get all those lines tangled. You using wire?"

"No, not this time around."

"Good."

Nelson rearranged the pouch of tobacco in his cheek. "Got a new girlfriend, Finn?"

"No."

"Word is you're sweet on someone."

"Not unless she's got dorsals."

Nelson grinned again. "You tried that konahead?"

"Not yet. Just bait so far."

"Wait till you see how fast those konas are picked up. Easier to swallow too, they slide right down." Nelson took off his hat and scratched his head. "Seems this area is being fished pretty well. We're headed down to Kalifi, stop at Mnarani, see what's doing. Wicks is primed for this season, wants to keep the title. Where you headed?"

"Blue water. No farther." Both men looked around. It seemed to Finn that Nelson was imitating Wicks' accent. "Good luck, then. See you back on the island."

Nelson was right, the shelf was being fished and Finn preferred to stay clear of other boats. When they lost sight of *Tarkar,* Finn's mind started to calm and he was able to think about Nelson with less anger. High-tech rods, wire lines, Walkmen. Like Finn's father, Nelson was unconsciously dangerous. The thoughtless actions of such men offended God's order, if there was one. Fatima's voice sounded in his ears; it was her thoughts he heard when he considered the question of God.

You are luckier than your friends, she often told Finn. Am I? He asked. Of course, she said incredulously. They know nothing of God.

And what do I know?

But Fatima had long stopped answering such impertinent questions.

Finn had never known his mother, but Fatima said she had died for a reason: Finn was meant to know God and Fatima was the mother Allah had sent to teach him. But there was a great distance between God and Finn. Occasionally, God came to him at sea, when Finn had both the time and space to consider him. The rising pulses of the waves lulled him, and for a moment the aggravated *majini* were expelled and a larger presence settled in. Something like peace came over him as the sound of *Tarkar*'s engine grew distant. He held the wheel lightly, and the boat moved ahead on her own. Every time he thought he might bring God back with him to the island, and every time God deserted. With each kilometer that brought *Uma* closer to home, he shrank inside Finn. By the time they were anchored in the bay, God had been reduced to a wisp of an idea that he could only sometimes grasp. Then Danny was there at the hotel bar, ready to escort him straight to hell.

Jonah yelled. Finn closed his eyes. Then, over his shoulder, he saw a marlin tailing the bait. He kept *Uma* steady until the fish struck. Jonah, bare-chested and smiling, was hooked in and ready. Finn slowed the boat and the line fell away. "Wait," he said. Jonah was an early striker. They waited. The line continued to sink. "Has he taken it?"

"Not yet."

"Just wait," Finn said. "He's deciding." Jonah was poised, legs and arms tense.

"Damn fish," he said. "He doesn't want it." Then the line started to move.

"He's taking, don't strike yet," Finn said. By now the line had fed out a few hundred yards. "Now!" Jonah struck. Finn pushed the throttle forward. The line sang as it spun from the reel.

"He's a big one," Jonah said through his teeth. "Very big." As soon as he turned it, the marlin jumped. "Finn!" Jonah gasped. "Five hundred at least."

The fish fought for an hour, jumping, arcing, tailwalking. Jonah, drenched with sweat, started pulling the fish in. Then, thirty meters out, the line went taut.

"He's moving again," Jonah said.

Finn went back to the wheel. "Where's he going?" he yelled.

"I don't know!" Jonah's rod bent down into the shape of a hook. "He's sounding!"

"Oh, Christ. We'll plane him!" Finn gunned the boat forward. Jonah fed the fish line until it was far behind the boat. As Finn slowed *Uma* down, Jonah stopped feeding the line. "Don't break too much," Finn warned. He pushed the throttle forward to pull the fish up from below. Jonah's rod bent low. "Is he coming?"

"I think so."

"Hang on to him." *Uma* moved forward against the weight of the marlin. The angle of the line evened until there was no resistance, no fight at all. A fin broke the blue surface of the water. "Shit," Finn said. "He's playing dead."

After they had it slip-noosed and gaffed, the marlin suddenly came back to life, swinging wildly from the support. Finn and Jonah threw themselves to the side of the boat to stay clear of its bill. Then a shot rang out and the fish went limp.

The two men stared at the lifeless body. Finn crouched down beside it and slowly fingered a bullet hole in its head in disbelief. "What the hell!" He looked around. *Tarkar* was off his port side. Finn waved her over.

"What the hell are you doing?" Finn shouted when the boat was within earshot. Nelson drifted up next to *Uma* and cut the motor. He stood at *Tarkar*'s port side, hands on his hips, legs splayed.

"That fish was going to kill you," he said. "You were too close."

"You could have killed one of us, you idiot."

"I'm a good shot, Finn. I've been practicing. And the fish was too big. It could have sliced you in half." *Tarkar*'s waves rocked *Uma.* Finn steadied himself with one hand on the fish. "It could have killed you both. Almost did."

"Bullshit!" Finn pushed the marlin away from him. It swung port and starboard. "Does Wicks have you carrying guns too?"

"Relax, Finn, it's a record fish. You should thank me. Measurements that big are hard to believe. Better to have the fish."

"It's against the law, or have you forgotten? Who do you think you are on that boat—Stanley Wicks?"

Nelson spit and then smiled. "Cool down, Finn."

Finn turned away from *Tarkar* and stared at the planks of the boat. Nelson started the engine so that Finn had to shout over the noise. "What the hell are you doing with a gun?"

Nelson smiled and waved as *Tarkar* pulled away.

The marlin was strung up on the waterfront, where it was surrounded by boys and men. Behind the crowd was Ingrid with Stanley Wicks, who was saying something about the fish and gesticulating with his hands. Ingrid was listening intently. Wicks slipped his arm around her waist in what seemed to Finn like a gesture of ownership. Finn ignored them and squatted about ten meters from the fish. Its bill almost touched the ground; its eyes stared vacantly into the dirt. A boy was trying to pry its mouth open. Finn should have chased him off but he didn't move. By afternoon the marlin would be hacked to pieces for dinner steaks. Finn stood and circled the fish until he could see the bullet hole, which one of the boys was fingering. "It was a real fighter," he explained to his friend. "Finn went 'bang!' like to a fierce lion to kill it."

Finn headed for the hotel, disgusted. Danny, who saw him coming, had a beer waiting.

"Nelson has gone mad," Finn reported.

"Poor little pea-brain. It wasn't long before his cranial fluid came to a boil."

Finn drank his beer in one swallow. "Wicks has moved in on your girl."

"What girl?"

"Ingrid."

"Ah well, that's all right."

Finn pushed his empty beer bottle away. "I need something stronger."

"You like her," Danny mused. "Don't you?"

"No more than you."

"I don't. She's just another woman."

Finn looked around for Jackson, who had momentarily disappeared. Annoyed, he lit a cigarette. "It's Wicks that bothers me."

Danny affected a Swahili accent. "And why should one such as this affect one such as you?"

"Because he makes it his business to interfere. And he's married."

"She's not stupid, you know. No ingenue, our girl."

"But she trusts people."

"Criminal!" Danny banged the bar with his fist.

"Just dangerous."

Two double shots of tequila arrived. Danny rubbed his hands together and nudged one toward Finn. "Drink this down and then tell me if this is protective brotherly love talking or something else."

"Tequila, is it? You're bringing out the big guns. Is it brotherly love you have for me, Danny, or is it something else?"

Danny tilted his glass and winked. "Wouldn't pay you the insult of calling you family."

Finn held his tequila to the light. "This stuff messes with my head."

"I pay good money for that mess. Bottoms up."

Finn closed his eyes tightly as he drank.

The Last Visit

*I*ngrid had seen Finn at the waterfront. He had looked away from her before she could distance herself from Stanley's encircling arm. Finn would misunderstand about Stanley just as he had misunderstood about Templeton. Her own judgment of Templeton depended, it seemed, on her mood. In her darker moments, she had come to suspect her professor of orchestrating the anonymous note. He was, she was beginning to realize, unorthodox enough to do such a thing.

From the hotel terrace, Ingrid watched Finn rowing in his skiff and drank him in without moving a limb, afraid he would see her and alter his routine, his morning worship. She wanted only to keep looking, to somehow absorb him. She had developed a hunger for him that she hated because, while she did not understand him, she understood that Finn did not think about her. She taunted herself by imagining what it might feel like to be in his arms again. They would not, she thought, try to make her feel *safe.* There was no complicating this man. The defeat, the anger she felt, came with the realization that his terms, the laws that governed him, were stronger than hers.

That night he came to her again and Ingrid's heart pounded so hard she could not sleep. He was drunk and slept through the night without touching her. In the morning, he left before dawn. Ingrid said nothing, did nothing to stop him. *Let him go.* It was a war of attrition; soon enough he would hold her. Soon enough he would speak. *Then let him go. Be strong. Stronger than he is.*

The following night she waited for him and slept poorly, listening for his step. He did not come.

Then he was there again, touching her, his fingertips on the small of her back, the curve of her hip. Ingrid could not sleep with him next to her. "I'm going to talk to you," she told him. The room rose and fell with his breath. With her head on his chest, she moved with his breathing and pretended they were at sea. "Just for a while. I don't know what you think of me. Do you think about me at all? I don't think you do. Here's a confession. I think of you when you are somewhere else. On your boat. I think of you there."

His arm moved around her shoulder and held it. He was half-asleep. "I think you think about many men," he mumbled.

Ingrid pressed her cheek into him. "What men?" she whispered, but he said nothing more. His arm around her loosened as he left her for sleep.

In the morning, Finn sat up and put his head in his hands. Ingrid pressed herself into the hollow between his shoulder blades. He was holding a photograph that had fallen from the chair. It was the picture of him and Templeton with the marlin.

"Why do you have this?"

"He sent it to me."

"This does not belong to you." Finn was looking closely at the photograph. He seemed on the verge of saying something and then, thinking better of it, put the photograph back on the chair and turned to go.

❦

Then Finn stopped coming. *Uma* was still in the harbor, but he did not go to the bar at night and he did not come to her room. Ingrid slept badly for two nights, waiting for the latch on her door to lift. In the day, she was weary and unfocused. She tried to nap and instead drifted into a nervous state of anxiety.

She saw him finally, at the hotel. She had told herself when she found him she would be gentle, although she did not feel gentle. He had deserted her and she was angry because she could not find him when she was sure she finally had something to say. When she saw him, all she could think of saying was come to bed with me again; lie with me in your silence. I promise not to speak.

He was eating lunch on the terrace. His face was stony, his eyes rimmed with red. Without me, you sleep badly, Ingrid thought. I sleep badly without you. He told her it was the sun that had burned his eyes. *Another lie,* she thought, hardening herself against him. He pairs his truth with lies.

Inside, she drank a breeze like a milkshake and waited for him. By the time he came in, she was drunk. She held out her sunglasses. "Take these. They'll help your eyes." He left them on the bar. Jackson gave them back to her with a quiet shake of his head and took away her empty glass.

"Where has he gone?"

"Maybe down to the beach, Miss Ingrid."

She found Finn crouched over a fishing net on the sand. "Why can't you take anything from me," she demanded. "Why is it so hard for you?"

"I never asked you for anything."

"Didn't you?" Ingrid floundered. Hadn't he?

"You're drunk," he said.

"It's so I can talk to you." She sank to her knees in the sand. "I want you to tell me about your god."

Finn smiled stiffly. "Is that really what you want to know?"

"Yes! Tell me *who he is.*"

"Why? Because I am not acting as you want me to act?"

"Yes, I want to understand."

"If it helps you understand, I will tell you that the god I believe in made men without shame. The fate of man's soul is in his own hands, not God's."

Ingrid did not see how this was important. "What about women? What does he say about the women?"

"In Islam there is no blaming anyone else. To me, that's a better god than some."

She stood and dusted the sand from her legs. "Maybe God has nothing to do with it. Maybe Templeton wanted to punish me with you."

"For what?"

"Who knows." Her thoughts were clear: this man was a confused drunk, a fundamentally crippled human being. He could not think, feel or talk. She smiled as politely as she could. "I'm sorry to have caught you in my confusion."

"Don't concern yourself with my opinion of you," Finn said. "I have none."

Ingrid put her hands together in a mute clap where they stayed, clinging to each other as Finn returned to his net. There was nothing to do but walk away.

That night she finished her bottle of whiskey and jotted a sloppy course outline in her notebook. By the time she finished, she had reclaimed enough of her dignity to fall asleep.

She woke the next morning with a dry mouth and a headache and for one terrible hour she was too weak to force her shame into anger. *I'm worn out,* she thought. Since she had arrived, every direction she had pushed on this island had shoved her back. How could one expect so little and still be so hellishly denied?

She rolled out of bed and swore as a mosquito bit her arm. Ending its miserable life with a slap, she decided she'd had enough of bullying and evasion. Templeton could continue on his mysterious path alone; his king would remain a figment. She had enough material for her course to leave the island that day. She got dressed and combed her hair. How surprised Finn would be if she just up and left. The idea was irresistible. She was now convinced that every moment of grace she had witnessed in him had been made possible by her own deluded generosity, that he knew nothing of her.

"I need to get to Nairobi," she told Ali when she found him at the hotel. "Tell me how."

"You are leaving us already? No more professor?"

"He doesn't want to be found. In any case, not by me. And I think I've seen enough of this island."

"There are no planes for a week, at least."

"Why not?"

"The runway is under repair. There is an office for buses in town, by Friday Mosque. But the buses are not regular and to get to where they come you must take a dhow if the tide is high, a donkey if it is low. It takes time. They say the rains are coming early and soon the roads will be bad. A bus is not the best way to leave. Better to wait for a plane."

The bus office consisted of a single room with a desk and a calendar on the wall. The man sitting outside was either petulant or stupid and despondently denied any association with the office. Flies collected on his unflinching face. Yes, the office was open. No, no one was there. Do you know where the man is? When he'll be back? You're useless, Ingrid told him. The man's mouth curved into a smile as he reached beneath his kikoi and scratched his groin. Ingrid turned and stalked to the hotel bar.

"I can't seem to get off the island," she said to Danny when she sat down.

"The only thing to do is take a dhow to Tomba in a week and wait on the airstrip. Something will turn up before too long. But the rains are coming early this year, which is bad luck. Maybe you could stay for those too."

"Absolutely not."

"Well, the airport giveth, the airport taketh away," Danny mused, lighting a cigarette. "Do you know who said that? I can't remember at the moment."

"You're all so useless," Ingrid said.

"All but Finn."

Ingrid did not respond. She was doing her best to put herself into a trance by watching the smoke from Danny's cigarette rise into the air and curl back on itself when Stanley Wicks walked in through the French doors. "Ingrid! I was beginning to think you'd left us!"

"Unfortunately," Danny said, "she can't."

"Oh, dear." Stanley seemed genuinely distressed. "Trapped by the rains."

"I'm sure you'd like to devise traps of your own," Danny said. "Poor little rabbit."

Ingrid rose. "I was just leaving."

Stanley took her elbow. "I'll walk with you."

"Now, now, Stanley," Danny warned. "No touchy-touchy."

Stanley stared at Danny.

"Thank you, Stanley," Ingrid said, pressing his hand with hers. "I'd love the company."

They walked in the general direction of Abdul's guesthouse. "I spend too much time in there," Ingrid said.

"We all do."

"I wish I could get off this island."

"Well, until you can, I find a project helps. Since I started work on my hotel, I haven't had the time to be homesick. I haven't even had time to think."

"I'm envious. My projects have all run out."

"A good book, then. That can do the trick."

"That's an idea," Ingrid said without enthusiasm. They had reached her guesthouse. "Thanks for the suggestion."

"Yes, well, not at all." Stanley held out his hand for a formal handshake, which, for some reason, warmed Ingrid's heart. "It's nice to see you again."

"You too, Stanley."

Ingrid dozed into the afternoon with a T-shirt wrapped around her head. Sari woke her to announce that Stanley Wicks was downstairs. A spirited, henna-painted hand danced into the air and seemed to cradle the question before it was asked.

"Your hands look beautiful, Sari."

Sari responded with an elaborate curtsy that featured more lovely hand movement. "Then I tell him to come up?"

"Yes."

❧

"I've brought you some Forster," Stanley said, leaning a long cardboard tube against the wall. "Forster is good for this place. I find him a comfort when I'm feeling far from home. You could always be farther, you know. You could be lost in the Marabar Caves. Are you feeling any better?"

Ingrid flipped listlessly through *A Passage to India.* "I'm not sure I could survive here the way you have."

"That's why I'm building my own place—so I can set up different rules. No drunken debauchery in Kitali. Well, limited debauchery, anyway. And a good library." Stanley surveyed the tiny room, his gaze pausing on a small stack of books. "My wife doesn't read."

"What's in the tube?"

"Oh, I brought some drawings of the hotel, in case you were interested."

Stanley spread the blueprints out on the bed. They knelt on the floor and as he described what was to go where, Ingrid realized with amusement that a possible key to what she had been looking for had fallen in her lap. As she studied the plans, looking for a familiar landmark from the maps she had already seen, she could smell Stanley's clean skin beside her, his freshly laundered clothes. She stole a look at his smoothly shaven cheek. Stanley noticed and a blush spread beneath his tan. His voice softened as he described his designs. "You see, here's the main dining room. It's got a retractable roof, which will close during the rains. Otherwise it will stay open to the sky, even at night."

"How lovely," she said, and then motioned to the far corner of the map. "What's this?"

"These are the guest bungalows, all on the ground level. They don't like building higher than that in Africa. They feel it's unnatural."

"Are the rooms round?" she asked, struggling to engage him long enough to find what she was looking for.

"Yes, isn't it brilliant? There will still be private bedrooms extending from the main communal area. But don't you think it would be grand to have windows all round?"

"And no corners to sweep." Beyond the bungalows, just outside the property lines of Stanley's estate, was a river intersected by a few quick lines. Ingrid glanced at the map long enough to make a mental picture of this demarcation she thought she had seen before.

"I'm convinced that life is wondrously altered by roundness," Stanley continued. "The experience of living in a round structure. I can't wait to see how they turn out. You really should come and see it when it's ready." He was looking at her now. "I would love to take you round." Ingrid shifted her position so she could see him as he spoke and noticed his eyes, which were kind. She was, she realized, vaguely attracted to him. This did not change when he touched her face and then leaned forward to kiss her. The kiss was so tender it felt more like a blessing. Stanley took her hand in his and held it tight, bringing it to his lips before returning it to her.

"Can I show you something?" He fished into his back pocket for a folded, soiled envelope and gave it to her. "From your professor."

"From Templeton?"

"I carry it around with me. I don't know why. Finn told me he's not quite right in the head."

Ingrid held the letter in front of her. The handwriting caused something inside her abruptly to shift. *To Stanley Wicks: Do you know about the power of belief? Here they believe in witches and ghosts and curses, and more than any of it they believe in the existence of evil. Not devils with forks but invisible wisps that easily pass through solid matter. These innocuous little wisps begin to cloud the soul. It is when God is no longer visible that the presence of evil is known. Evil takes the form of an obstacle. A roadblock. We in the West would not necessarily recognize it, but for these people, evil is as frightening for what it takes away as for what it can become. It is surprising what can become evil. . . . Do not continue to build . . .*

Templeton's tone was alarming. She tried to keep her expression neutral as she read; the ominous wording made Stanley's agitation a studied underreaction. She smiled at him over the letter. *This is a friendly warning but I would suggest you heed it as a threat . . .*

She handed the letter back reluctantly and sat back so she could again see Stanley's face. "I don't blame you for being frightened. He's very convincing when he wants to be. If it's of any comfort, I received one of these too."

"From him?"

"Anonymous. More or less telling me not to meddle."

Stanley smiled. "Part of me thinks it's just smoke and mirrors, these letters and curses. The island is changing. It's the way of things. While it may be hard for some, there's nothing they can do." He began rolling up his plans. "I suppose threats and letters are their only recourse. Maybe Templeton is their scribe."

After Stanley left, Ingrid lay on her bed, struck by Stanley's last statement.

❧

At sunset, Ali touched her shoulder and laid a plate with a chapati and beans next to her. The sky was a glorious electric pink, the air between them so infused with color that it seemed possi-

ble to touch it, to shape it into something you could hold. Ali
sat cross-legged and ate from his own plate, folding beans into
the chapati and eating with his fingers. She copied him, eating
quickly, wiping her mouth with the back of her hand. Ali nodded.
"It's better to eat with your hands," he said. "Food tastes better
when it's closer, not delivered with cold metal utensils. This is
how we eat in the village. It's how the prophets ate. After, we
can go have coffee on the street. Maybe you will like our coffee,
too."

The men in the village sat on wooden benches outside the coffee hut. Ingrid was an object of general interest as she sipped the
thick, sweet liquid. Some of the men nodded in her direction,
others stared openly. One of them left his bench and sat next to
her. Ali introduced them. "Habib wants to read your fortune.
Give him your cup when you are finished." Habib's smile flashed
gold and rotten teeth when she handed him her empty cup. He
took it, turned it upside-down on its saucer, and waited for the
residual grounds to drip a pattern down the sides of the cup.
Habib turned the cup over and then around and around, speaking in rapid Swahili. He finished the reading with a look of con-
sternation and what seemed to be explicit instructions.

"What did he say?" Ingrid asked Ali.

"He said you will be a teacher when you are finished with
your current business. Then you will go home and have many
children."

"That's not all he said."

"No, but it's nonsense anyway."

"Tell me."

"He says you should be careful with your health."

"My health?"

"He prescribed teas and such, probably he wants to sell them to you himself and make a little money." Ali smiled dismissively at Habib. "But these old men are charming, no?"

"It seems they have an act," Ingrid said. "Like you."

"How else can it be? But I like you, Miss Holes. You are so far my favorite American." These words, accompanied by his eyes and slow, raffish smile, made her want to slap him.

The next night, Ingrid went down to the street alone. She had been entertaining the idea that Templeton's letter to Stanley was a harmless scare tactic. The letter, after all, had been written weeks ago and nothing had happened to Stanley or his hotel. She was not convinced that Templeton was the force behind these communications. She had never heard him expound on the question of good or evil—or God, for that matter. If Stanley was right, and he had become a voice for someone else, the tone and content of the letter made more sense. The question was, how deeply was he involved in this resistance and why.

Ali found her eating on her porch. He fell into a hammock. "I want you to stop coming," Ingrid told him.

Ali was silent, considering this. "You will eat?"

"Of course I will eat. Now go."

"When can I come again?"

"I don't know. A few days."

"Very well. I will pray for you."

"Nonsense, Ali. You don't pray."

"You are wrong about that." He hoisted himself out of the hammock. "May peace find you."

The afternoon rains had started in earnest. There was constant talk about their early arrival—it was generally thought to mean bad luck. The holes in the airstrip yawned and filled with fresh water. Mud overflowed on the tarmac. Dry cement for the repairs was creeping its way up by dhow, from Mombasa, but no one expected it for a week or more. Ingrid stayed on her porch during the day and picked up the Koran frequently, persisting against its bizarre verse in an attempt to draw closer to the thinking behind Templeton's notes. The letter he had sent Stanley had revived her interest in this maddening puzzle—and Stanley's blueprints had given her a missing piece. She took out the map and her sketch of the amulet, and turned again to the first entry from the Koran:

> *In the water which God sends down from the sky and with which he revives the earth after its death, disposing over it all manner of beasts; in the disposal of the winds, and in the clouds that are driven between sky and earth: surely in these there are signs for rational men.*

This must have been what Templeton had been waiting for, she thought, looking out to sea. Something would happen with the coming of the rains. *We opened the gates of heaven with pouring rain and caused the earth to burst with gushing springs, so that the waters met for a predestined end.*

At sundown, she dressed and went down to the street for chapatis and beans. When her candle burned down to nothing, she left the guesthouse for the bar to look for Stanley Wicks.

The bar was empty except for Finn, who was nursing a warm beer. She sat down beside him, feeling remarkably calm. "Still here, are you?" he asked, without looking up from his beer.

"I seem to be stuck."

"You must be getting lots of work done."

"Have you seen Stanley?"

"Now why would you be wanting him?"

"You're drunk."

Finn looked at her, his eyes dead. "And this surprises you?"

"No. Jackson, can I have a breeze?" Ingrid asked, her calm leaving her for a sensation of heat. "Seeing that you can still construct a sentence, why don't you tell me why you came to my room in the first place."

"Because the professor asked me to look after you."

Ingrid felt her chest constrict like a fist. "Did he say why I needed looking after?"

"You were naive. I didn't think so at first, but then I saw it."

"Why did he pick you?"

"He thought it might come naturally."

"But it didn't?"

"I'm not a watchdog."

"It didn't cross your mind to say something like, 'Be careful, Ingrid, this island can be a dangerous place for a woman'? It would have been much simpler."

"Wouldn't have worked."

"Because it's common knowledge that I don't heed warnings? Because everyone knows I am perilously naive?"

"Because the island's more complicated than that. And a woman like you needs protection no matter what you think you know."

Ingrid found self-control by looking at his feet. "What is a woman like me?" she asked deliberately.

"You know what I'm talking about."

"I don't. Tell me."

"A good-looking white woman."

"Oh, please. How wonderful that you're all trying to *protect* poor white me. So tell me, why don't I feel protected?"

"Also," Finn said into his glass, "Kip dropped her kits. I've given her and the little ones the run of the house. The place is crawling with cats. I needed a place to sleep."

"That's bullshit."

Finn's eyebrows raised. Still he did not look at her.

"You're a bad liar, Finn." Ingrid took his face in her hands and turned it toward her. Jackson dropped something behind the bar. "The only reason you lie is because you're afraid."

He leaned close to her so the heat of his face touched hers. He whispered, "I am a little afraid of you."

"Well, that makes things much better. What a hero you've turned out to be. I thought you were going to *help* me."

"Are you listening?" Finn's voice was hot and gritty. "I am going to help you now. On the island there is something we call *ghaflah*. It is a great sin. It means forgetting your divine origin. Losing your self-respect. *Ghaflah* makes a man dangerous. A man who thinks he is innocent. But when he has lost his sense of divinity, he no longer acts with responsibility. He becomes dangerous to everyone."

Ingrid turned to leave.

"Listen. I am speaking seriously. You need to remember your divinity, your strength and goodness. Not me. You don't need me." He held her arm. The tension of his grip shot up and down. "You cannot become my responsibility simply because you have forgotten yourself."

Ingrid spoke into his chest because she refused to bend or twist to look into his eyes. "I thought we were alike," she said. "I thought you felt alone like me. You are lucky to have such clarity in your life."

"Lucky," Finn repeated. The word unlocked his grip from her arm and he spoke harshly now. "I can live nowhere but here. This island. I see no one but those who choose to come here. Those who choose to come here live a life of *ghaflah* and they infect the island with it. My home, my island is dying. It's because of my father and now it's because of me. There's nothing I can do but watch. This is my luck."

It was over. He was her enemy again. "So you drink," she said. "You watch and you drink."

"I am also trying to forget."

"Templeton saw that in you, didn't he?"

"Your professor saw too much. I am glad he's gone."

After Ingrid left, Finn sat very still. Jackson replaced his beer. Lighting a cigarette, he waited for the silence to erase the sound of her voice. When he had finished the beer he felt better. Halfway into the next he thought of how it would be to kiss her, really kiss her. Even drunk he couldn't see what would come after, where the end point with a woman like that would be.

Wicks passed through on his way to the office. "The telephone is still not working, Mr. Wicks," Jackson reported.

"Damn! Things are falling apart around here."

"Someone was just in here looking for you," Finn said.

"Who's that?"

"I've forgotten. Maybe Jackson remembers."

"It was Miss Ingrid," Jackson said. "Miss Ingrid was looking for you."

"Just left," Finn added.

"Did she?" Wicks said hopefully. "Maybe I can catch her." And he was gone.

"You see, Jackson," Finn said. "When you know what the fish is hungry for, you can control him. The less I see of that fish, the better."

Finn stayed until he was drunk enough to think about the white men he would like to see go home. Wicks first, then Templeton. They were the same to Finn, both with obstinate heads full of grand ideas. Recently, Fatima had forced him to listen to Templeton rave about what had to be done in the face of Wicks' hotel. Like Salama, it would bleed far beyond its property corners, infecting everything around it. Something had to be done, and Finn had to help. Fatima agreed, smiling to herself as she poked the fire and listened to the bearded white man, melting a square of chocolate against the roof of her mouth. Finn wanted nothing to do with any of it.

Templeton had for years pressured Finn to shut down Salama—as if that were possible. Last on the list of Templeton's concerns were the lives and the livelihoods of the hotel workers, the young men who knew nothing but the hotel and would be lost without it. Too many years of his pigheaded instruction had left Finn deaf to talk of change. It was Finn's downfall, Templeton said, this belief that the world took care of itself without the effort of those who understood it. Finn had shrugged and remained silent until the professor left. "He's a preacher," he told Fatima then. "Worse even than you."

"He is right and don't be so stupid. How have you gotten so stupid?"

"It's you who've changed, Fatima. You've gotten crazy."

"Don't change the subject. You are a part of this island. You understand this. I see you see it so forget your bloody fish and do something useful for us humans."

How much Ingrid knew about her professor, Finn didn't know. She was both too strong and too weak; just being close to her confused him.

The Sloppy Art of Seduction

*B*y the time Ingrid felt brave enough to return to the hotel, Finn had gone to sea again. She stood in the bar and bit the inside of her lip until it bled. Danny watched her from his stool. "Have a drink, Miss Muffet." His smile was lazy. "You're looking particularly lost. Is your work going smoothly? Have you *discovered* anything?"

"I have discovered that the women on this island create their own lovers and husbands. I'm beginning to understand why."

"Isn't it wonderful to understand?" Danny crooned. "I love understanding, though I have no idea what you're talking about."

Ingrid sat at the bar while Danny went behind it to the phonograph. "I think we should celebrate your prolonged stay on the island." He was flipping through the records with a cigarette between his teeth, the smoke unfurling in front of his face like a cobra. "The funny thing about Finn is that he loves Sinatra. *Songs for Swinging Lovers,* here it is. Don't you find that odd? He's hardly the romantic type. Still, there are the rules he breaks so unexpectedly. He's a strong, smart fish, isn't he, Ingrid? And now he's sounded on you. You've lost sight of him. He's somewhere under the boat. You don't think you've lost him because there's still tension on the line, but he could have wrapped the line around something. It could be tangled in the propeller. There's no way of knowing." Danny rested the needle on the heat-warped disk. The record crackled over the speakers. "Maybe one person you meet in life surprises you. Not just once, but often. There may not be anything quite as exciting. And you haven't been surprised much, have you, Miss Muffet? I think you may be worrying that you'll never be surprised again and it terrifies you because you like it, don't you. You like the possibility of being outsmarted."

"What do you do with yourself, Danny, when you're not here?"

"You see, I've made a direct hit. Bleed a little, Ingrid. It's good for you." Danny poured himself another whiskey. His voice dropped to a whisper. "Another thing that scares you is that I'm the only one here you can talk to, the only one who understands your little problem. It's a bind, Ingrid. You're in a bind."

"You're wasting your intelligence on me."

"I disagree." He smiled. "Stay a while longer."

A few off-season hotel guests trickled in for their predinner cocktails. The bar felt empty, like an actorless stage.

"Where is everybody?" she asked. "Onka and Lady Emily and the rest."

"Off to Nairobi."

"How did they get there, for God's sake? When did they go?"

"They got out in time."

"God, I feel trapped."

"Oh, sad day. I was pretending you were enjoying my company."

Ingrid did not see Finn until she got up to go to the bathroom. He was standing by the door with an older woman, a hotel guest, a tall, thin brunette with a coral necklace and a strapless dress splashed with bright color. Ingrid watched from across the room as Finn bent his head while she spoke into his ear. There was no expression in his face as he listened. The woman pressed something into his hand and folded his fingers over it. Her polished nails glinted on his skin.

Ingrid returned to her seat next to Danny and watched Finn leave the bar. A few moments later, the woman with the strapless dress followed him. "Finn is back," she told Danny.

"Is he, now?"

"But he's gone off again." Ingrid stood up and gathered her shawl around her shoulders.

"Going to chase him, are you?"

"I need to speak to him," Ingrid added. "The last time we spoke I was rude."

"Yes, well, diplomacy has saved the modern world. Best of luck on your mission. If it fails, you know where I'll be."

Ali was at his evening post at the outdoor bar, drinking beer with his brother. Ingrid asked him to show her the way to Finn's house. He did it reluctantly and they wound through the village in silence. "Leave me," she told him at the door. "I can find my way home."

The front door was ajar. Ingrid stepped into the dark house, quiet save for the sound of surf from the open veranda above the beach. Then a woman's laughter from inside. Ingrid squatted by the door and peered in. At the foot of the bed, the woman was on her knees in front of Finn. Her bright dress was in a heap next to her. Finn stood with his hands on her head while it moved up and down. "You're salty," she said to him. He looked down at her and then away. The woman's hands pushed up to his chest, closing on his nipples. She rose like a vulture and pressed her lips to one and then the other nipple, stepping out of her panties and moving her lips to his neck. She took Finn's index finger and urged it back and forth between her legs. Ingrid stepped back as the woman turned around and pressed her buttocks into his crotch. He gripped her waist while she bent over and placed her hands on the bed, bracing herself as he moved into her. "Oh yes," she groaned. "How I've missed that." His thrusting was long and slow at first and then it shortened. He told the woman to be quiet. "Hold me," she said, clasping his hands to her breasts. He moved them slowly in circles. When he came there was no sound, just a heaving that was hard and final.

"Finn has a lover," she told Danny back at the bar. "You didn't tell me that."

"Have a weentsy drink, Ingrid."

"She's staying at the hotel."

"Is she? Well, bully for her."

"Who is she?"

"You haven't been listening to me, Miss Muffet. Listen closely, Finn has lots of lovers. They pay him for sex. Charging for it is Finn's way of being honest. He likes it, but without any of the accoutrements." Danny twirled his hand in the air. "Attachments and that sort of thing."

"Does he need the money?"

"Good God no. Really, he's just like the beach boys, just a different flavor. More lemony, like a cleaning agent. If it was sex you were wanting with him, that little tidbit might help you out."

Ingrid stood up and walked away, holding her stomach with her arms. She went to the terrace and stared at the ocean. The night was moonless, the water black. Ingrid took the image of Finn and his woman and plunged them into the black water. When she sat back down next to Danny she counted the bottles of liquor behind the bar by twos. "I know," Danny said. "It's abominable."

"It isn't. It makes perfect sense."

"Perhaps that's why you haven't performed the carnal act with him yet. It's possible you couldn't afford him, being a poor academic. The fact that he hasn't told you is interesting, however. That could mean any number of things."

"Maybe he has an ounce of compassion."

"I've seen mothers pay him to deflower their infatuated daughters. Better to know the devil than to guess. And Finn is safe and clean. Did you know he's Swedish nobility? It's a good selling point for our boy."

"I have to go, Danny."

"Yes, of course, you have work to do. Come to my house for dinner tomorrow. I'll have Hamilton cook some fish stew. You're getting too thin, you know."

Ingrid paused at the door. "Is there anyone you love more than him?"

Danny smiled and then winked. "It's doubtful. Don't tell him, though. He despises being loved."

On her way back to the guesthouse, Ingrid sliced her foot on something in the sand, a piece of glass or a broken shell. It was a deep cut that abruptly changed her direction, a stab of pain that blocked out thought.

She tracked blood into Finn's house. He was sitting on the veranda, bare-chested, smoking, making small white clouds against the flat, black plane of ocean in front of him. The room was lit by a single hurricane lamp. Her shadow was long. Even from as far as the door, it touched him.

"I just wanted to tell you I understand." She could feel the blood, the sand sticking to her foot. "I know you don't care, but I thought you should know."

"Come, sit. Tell me what you understand."

"I watched you in here with that woman, that guest."

"Now that surprises me a little."

"I thought I had something for you. And you had something for me—something I needed. But everyone thinks that about you. That woman. Other women. Danny, even. I'm no different from them." Ingrid stood on her good foot. A sleepy kitten jumped off a chair and came unsteadily toward her. "You don't like people. They all want something from you but they have nothing to offer in exchange. Nothing you're interested in. It drives people crazy. It has been driving me crazy, but now I understand. Maybe you want a little revenge. Otherwise you want to be left alone."

Finn flicked his cigarette off the veranda. "And here you are."

"For the last time. I can take care of myself now." Ingrid lowered her other foot and stepped backward until her shadow left him.

She stood outside for a moment and watched through the window as Finn moved the kitten from the place she had been standing and put his hand over the wetness on the floor where she had been, pressing his palm to his cheek afterward and then setting the kitten on his chest and lying down on the cold stone surface.

❦

The next evening Ingrid went back to Salama, her foot bandaged. By the time she sat down the throbbing had started. "Even here you won't be able to keep the sand out," Danny told her. "Soak it in Detol when you get home."

"It's small but it hurts like hell."

"Bacteria breeds in this humidity. If the red spreads up your leg, get off the island. We're not equipped here for infection. Incidentally, I'm sorry about last night."

"Sorry why?"

"I don't remember exactly. What a nuisance this memory business is. You see, mine is fading, like a photograph in the equatorial sun. I could forgive anything of that sun, and maybe I have. Yes, I think I have." He spoke so quietly that Ingrid had to lean to hear him. Their heads were almost touching. "Do you think you could love me?" he whispered.

Ingrid pulled away and placed a finger on the rim of his glass. "Pour me some of that, will you, Jackson?"

Danny smiled. "There are some who consider me before Finn. Rarely the best."

"I considered you."

"Oh, Ingrid, you're slaying me."

"When I first met you I thought it was possible to know you." Ingrid swallowed half her whiskey and leaned close to him. "What do you think about, Danny?"

"Isn't it obvious? I was sure it was obvious. I think about bonking women. I'm quite decent, you should give me a try. It might be just what the doctor ordered. When was the last time you had a good bonk, princess? Look at you, you're blushing. What a fragile flower you are. I had no idea."

Ingrid swallowed the rest of her whiskey and closed her eyes to the burn. With enough liquor, she could forget about her foot. "Why didn't you finish your degree at Oxford?"

"Oh, well, now." Danny laughed. "Things happened."

"What *things*?"

"I learned the fine art of cooking, for one. In prison, I'll have you know. So I'm a tough bastard."

"Why were you in prison?"

"One of my favorite stories. A wretched Italian girl stashed her dope in my bag on an international flight. I had gone back to finish school like the good boy I used to be. Just like you, Miss Muffet, I used to love school. Used to love eye-tyes too."

"Was she your girlfriend?"

"Shameful, isn't it? Nasty woman left me high and dry. Marched right through customs and didn't once look back. My heralded return to Oxford stopped at Heathrow security. Here's a lesson from old Danny: life can turn very quickly in the wrong direction." Danny flicked his lighter and produced an enormous flame.

"Jesus, Danny."

Danny winked. "You know what they say about a man's flame."

Ingrid moved his hair away from his drooping cigarette as he searched for it with the flame. After torching the end of the cigarette, he puffed happily. "But all was not lost. I went to prison and became an exceptional cook. So you must join me for dinner sometime."

"I'd love to."

Danny belched. "Does this mean you want to get bonked? Because that's really what I'm interested in."

Ingrid smiled. "Why do you do that?"

"Because it's the truth. And all women really want is to get bonked. We'll have a lovely time. We'll get to know each other over dinner and then bonk all night."

"I take it you don't want me to come for dinner at all."

"Objection!" Danny pounded the bar with his fist. "May I inform the court I was merely engaged in the fine and sometimes sloppy art of seduction. If my subtleties were lost on the lady, I can only plead innocent—and if you find me guilty let my punishment be the nearly unbearable knowledge that I have failed." He rested his head on his arm. "Only a few really good ones in a year and what do I do in my excitement? Self-immolate. It's the hideous self-loathing of a lonely drunk. Don't leave, Ingrid, sweet Ingrid. Stay with me. Take me home."

Danny leaned on Ingrid as they walked away from the lights of the hotel. He was taller than she had realized. His house was only a few hundred yards from Salama and when they got to the front door, he paused in the dark entryway and cursed quietly. Inside were scratching, mewing, crackling sounds. The floor was alive with patches of color. There were cats everywhere. Danny lurched toward the kitchen and returned with his spidery arms raised. A large plate came crashing down on the floor, and then another shattered into a feline scream. A single cat lay motionless while the rest scattered through open windows. Danny snatched its tail and flung it into the night. "Bloody felines. They got into my curry." On the way back in, he tripped on the doorway and landed hard on his elbows. His hair hung in his face. He made no move to get up. Ingrid was on her knees. "Let me help you."

Danny leaned on Ingrid as she led him up the stairs. Halfway up he folded into a spasm of choking sounds that could have been weeping. He grinned, vomit down his shirtfront. "Oh yes, fine mess. Hamilton!" he bellowed. "Where's my sweet slave when I really need him?"

Ingrid moved behind him and raised him by his armpits. "Come on, we're getting you to bed."

"Yes," Danny mumbled. "High time for a bonk."

Ingrid removed his shirt and left him facedown on his un-made bed. She took off his shoes and covered him with a light blanket. She paused in the doorway before leaving. He was so still, he might have been dead.

Ingrid woke early and bathed her foot. The crimson of the infection faded at her anklebone. She wrapped the widening cut in gauze and then worked the foot into a sock. Down in the harbor, the spectral shape of *Uma* was still gone. Finn was at sea. She went to the fishermen's beach and looked for Ali, but Ali had gone by dhow to Mombasa.

She set out for the hotel to see if the phones were working and instead found her way to Finn's house. The door was wide open and the ocean air blew in from the veranda. The pages of an old paperback rustled on a table, its cover torn off. The only other paper she could find was a pile of receipts for *Uma*. No letters, nothing. If Templeton had instructed him, he had done so verbally. How had he phrased it? *Take care of her, she loses her way.*

Ingrid walked around the house, stepping carefully. In one of Finn's drawers was a stack of folded kikois. In his bathroom of raw rag coral, she dug to the bottom of his hamper, pressing his damp, soiled clothes to her face. She rolled a T-shirt into a ball and carried it under her arm back to the guesthouse. Back in her room, she laid the shirt flat under her pillow.

The next evening Danny invited Ingrid to eat dinner at Salama. "To make up for my bad behavior," he said. "And to get some real food in you." Nearby were Stanley and Daisy Wicks, having a silent meal. Stanley was reading a newspaper, Daisy studying her fingernails. Danny paused at their table to bow. "Good evening. Meet my dinner partner, Miss Ingrid Holtz."

"You've introduced her to us at least five times, Danny," Daisy said.

"Have I? Well, have a lovely evening. Stop reading and talk to your wife, Stanley. It's bad manners."

Stanley's eyes were on Ingrid and they drifted rhythmically throughout the meal from his wife to the table where Ingrid and Danny sat.

An improperly dressed and malodorous Nelson joined them after he had talked to Stanley and Daisy, who yawned instead of greeting him. "Danny, old man," he said, pulling up a chair and straddling it backward.

"Hello, Nelson. This is Ingrid."

"We met at the bar once but hello anyway. What's on the menu tonight?"

"Ingrid's having lobster and I'm having a bloody rare steak."

"I may have both. I'm hungry tonight."

"You're not dressed for dinner, Nelson. Here in the hotel we dress for dinner."

"We were out late." A smile broke across his face.

"And?"

"Came damn close to Finn's record marlin. Sailfish on the way back, not so big."

"Have some wine, Ingrid," Danny said.

Nelson leaned to take a glass from another table and filled it to the rim. "Didn't see *Uma* at all. She was gone before dawn. Any idea where Finn was off to?"

"It's a common enough question."

"I think he might have gone north. I had a feeling about it this morning. Thought we'd see him."

Across the room, a wineglass shattered on the tile floor and

Stanley's cautionary voice droned beneath Daisy's titter. "Don't be so em*bar*rassed," Daisy brayed. "I'm sure she's not watching you as closely as you're watching her. Let's find out, shall we?" As she stood up, Daisy dropped her water glass to the ground. "Oops, I've broken another one," she said, laughing. "Danny, I'm getting to be like you."

"I'm afraid I can't approximate your grace."

"Well, thank goodness." Daisy rested her hand on Nelson's shoulder. "And your new friend, the one my husband is having wet dreams about, what's her name again?"

"Miss Muffet," Danny said.

"Well, she's got a rude habit of encouraging married men. Don't they teach you manners in America?" Daisy took Nelson's wineglass out of his hand and gave it a perilous swirl before smelling the wine. "Rotten wine. But then you're cheap, aren't you, Danny?" She set it down on the edge of its base so it toppled and spilled toward Ingrid. Burgundy dripped into her lap. "Pity you're wearing white. Cheap red wine leaves such a beastly stain."

Ingrid smiled too sweetly.

"Oh, look, Prince Stanley's here to save the day. I'll say my good nights. Ta."

Stanley had gathered napkins from other tables and dipped them into a pitcher of water. He offered the soggy mass to Ingrid. "This may help. Salt as well." Ingrid pressed the napkins onto her skirt. She allowed Stanley to sprinkle salt on the pink stain.

"What a lovely night it's turned out to be," Danny said. "Daisy should be paid for her performances. Our conversation was on the verge of becoming dull."

"Please accept my apology," Stanley said to Ingrid. "I don't know what else to say."

"Poor Stanley," Danny said.

"We did well today, Stanley," Nelson said through a mouthful of bread. "Those new rods are magic. We got one almost as big as Finn's."

"Fine, fine," Stanley said. "Keep up the good work." He leaned down and put his hand on Ingrid's knee. "My apologies again."

"Nonsense," Danny said. "We enjoyed it."

Ingrid had deposited the damp napkins on either side of her skirt. She was hunched over, patting the stains.

Ingrid left Danny at the bar. Outside, Stanley was sitting on the terrace. He smiled when he saw her. "I've just opened a splendid old bottle of wine. Could I persuade you to share it with me?" Ingrid sat down next to him and accepted a glass. She drank it quickly and let Stanley refill it. The sea was bright with the moon and they watched it as if it were a stage. "Sometimes at night from my veranda I see dolphins playing," he said. "They swim in circles and leap out of the water. Now I have started looking for them." Stanley refilled his glass and was silent for a time. "I don't know if Daisy's exactly happy here."

"Take me to Kitali with you," Ingrid said.

"Perhaps you think me a coward . . ." Stanley trailed off. "Something strange happened at the construction site."

"What?"

"It sounds silly, but a plate of food was left in the main room. A nice-looking three-course meal, all laid out. More food than we normally have. But no one came near it. The crew drifted around it for a while and then half of them simply left."

"Was there anything else?"

"Not that I noticed."

"In Swahili culture, there's something called *Kafara,* a ritual where food is taken to a polluted place and takes the pollution, the evil, with it."

"So my hotel is polluted and evil."

"Someone seems to think so."

"My damn driver won't even take me there. He pretends to be sick. So now, as I refuse to go alone"—Stanley raised his glass—"I'm as stuck as you."

Ingrid put down her empty wineglass. "Come swimming with me."

Stanley laughed. "Now?"

"The water is beautiful at night. I went once before and I haven't had the nerve to go by myself."

"What about your foot?"

"I can barely feel it."

On the beach, the sand was cool. They carried their shoes and walked away from the lights of the hotel. Stanley chatted about the progress at Kitali and then fell silent.

After a while Ingrid said, "I don't think you're a coward."

Stanley looked back toward the hotel and then at Ingrid. "I have an urge to kiss you again."

As he took her hand, Ingrid pushed out thoughts of Templeton and the *Kafara* and Finn and his female hotel guest. Then there was only poor Stanley. She let him press against her, realizing there are few things as urgent or as unthinking as a man's desire. But the depth of Stanley's trouble opened her to him. He was even more helpless, more lost than she. She held him closer, thinking it had been too long since she had acted on her own desire. Briefly recalling Finn's woman in the floral dress, she dropped to her knees. Hardness wanted to be soft. She could, she thought, do him that favor. It's what women did for men. Stanley moaned and held her head. "You're divine," he whispered.

Ingrid pulled him down to the sand.

"I'm sorry about the wine," Stanley continued. "I'm sorry

about your foot. When it comes down to it, I have a lot to be sorry for."

She watched as he carefully worked the buttons on her blouse. "I have a weakness for your manners, Stanley."

"This is not good manners, I assure you."

Ingrid took his hand and placed it on her breast. "Don't be sorry." She closed her eyes. "But remember you're married and we're a little drunk. I'm doing this partly so you'll reconsider Kitali. We could go together."

"Is that a good idea?"

"Is this?"

"All right, then, I'll think about it."

Lying on her veranda the next morning, Ingrid watched the deep green of the palms finger the sapphire sky and touched her breasts and abdomen gently with her fingertips. She had no desire to move. She no longer cared about the things she had cared about yesterday—Templeton, Finn, Kitali. There was nothing she needed to do or know, no right action to take. She sensed that in this surrender she would find some sort of lasting victory.

At prayer time, she went to the Friday Mosque, the island's most orthodox mosque, forbidden to women. The sound of the chanting and the warmth of the afternoon lulled her. She closed her eyes, listening for repetitions, for words she had learned to recognize, for the spaces in between in which she felt she could swim.

She stood in the doorway, letting the sun loosen her muscles and joints while she watched the backs of men sway in unison. Soon the afternoon rain would release the moisture from the air.

The spit landed on her forearm; an old woman she had never seen hissed at her and shooed her away from the doorway. Shame burned in Ingrid's face. She turned abruptly from the mosque and back toward the village, searching for the path that led to Templeton's old room. She walked in a circle, recognizing nothing. By the time she found her way to the seawall, the clouds were cracking above her and the rain came down with a fury that seemed intentional. The rain made crying easy, a slow grief that caught in the back of her throat and tore into her chest. She sat on the seawall with the rain like a room around her and wept. Beyond the walls of rain she imagined a clear day and, somewhere in that day, the mother she had never known, a woman who might have helped her understand her heart better than she could.

She moved blindly along the seawall until she reached the hotel, where she went directly to the office. She was soaked; a hotel worker raised an eyebrow and went to find her a towel.

"Are the phones fixed?" she asked when he returned.

"Sorry, madam, not yet." He resumed placing papers into a file cabinet. Ingrid wrapped the towel around her shoulders and sank into a chair next to it, absently running her eyes over the file headings. They looked like financial statements, separated by year. From what Ingrid could see, they dated back twenty or thirty years. A name on one of the headings made her straighten. "What's this?" she asked, pointing to the file.

"Our records," the worker said.

Ingrid was now straining toward the open drawer. "Why would Mr. Nicholas Templeton be in your records?" The hotel worker placed his hand on the drawer and closed it.

"Templeton takes care of the hotel's finances?" Ingrid pressed.

The worker was now standing guard in front of the cabinet. "He used to oversee them," he said tersely. "When Finn was small."

When she entered the bar, Danny saluted her. "You keep coming back," he said. "You don't know what else to do." Jackson offered her a clean bar towel for her hair while Danny studied her with what seemed like kindness. "He's got you, hasn't he? Who knows where he is or when he'll return. It's not something to run your life by. I, on the other hand, am as regular as the rain that drove you here. I can be counted on. It's a modest attribute, but I claim it proudly as my own. You can always find me, Miss Muffet. It gives you a shred of stability, something to build upon."

"Oh, please," Ingrid said.

"I'm being quite sincere."

"After two drinks you're very sincere. I'm not looking for anyone."

"Now, now, let's be nice."

"It's my father's birthday," Ingrid said as she finally sat down. "I was going to phone him."

"Beastly thing's not working, I hear."

"Speaking of fathers," she asked tonelessly. "Who ran Salama after Henrik Bergmann died?"

"Come to think of it, I think it was your Templeton."

Ingrid paused. "And why do you think it might have been Templeton?"

"Probably because he's Finn's legal guardian." Ingrid stared. "Neither man promotes the relationship, so it isn't talked about much." Danny added, "Clean forgot about it myself."

"Did you, now?" Ingrid said acidly.

"I don't think Templeton relished the job, but the alternative was Fatima, and she would have shut the place down."

"Fatima?"

"The woman who raised Finn. She despises Salama because this is where Finn gets his booze." Danny pushed Ingrid's hair back from her face. "Look at you, melancholy creature. Do you miss your papa?" Ingrid moved out of his reach. "What does he do, your father? Is he a lawyer? I hear most American men are lawyers."

"He's a professor," Ingrid said flatly.

"Another professor! Well, well, he must be very proud of you, and all the professorial work you've done." Danny cupped his hands to light a cigarette. The cigarette seemed to animate him. He straightened up and smiled. "He must love you deeply, beyond imagining. You must be his jewel. Or perhaps he's sitting at a bar this very moment, a bar like this one where he can forget his work and think instead about what he's done to get you on the wrong track. Childless, wasting away on a remote island." Ingrid stood up. Danny's eyes drifted to some point above her shoulder. "Don't leave. You want to say something, say it. You think I'm abominable. Come on, girl, where's your mettle."

"What happened to your father, Danny?"

"Henry? You know what happened to him. He's been getting pickled in Nairobi for the past twenty years."

"Your real father."

"Henry is my real father, for better and mostly for worse."

"That's not what he told me."

"Oh, he's telling tall tales again, is he? Well, I suppose it runs in the family. Comes naturally, actually." Danny laughed as she left the bar. "Who knows what the truth is, Miss Muffet," he called after her. "It's unfortunate for you that it's become so important."

She was too tired to walk carefully. On her way home, she put her full weight on her bad foot, feeling the chafe of sand in the wound. The pain was sobering.

Instead of soaking her foot in Detol when she reached her roof, she sent Sari to find Hamilton, Danny's houseboy. Before lying down, she folded her pillow under her foot and then turned her cheek to rest on Finn's shirt.

The fever had started. It moved up, slowly attacking her

ankle, her lower leg. *It's not my fault,* she would tell Finn, *I have been hobbled by your island.*

Very soon, it seemed, Hamilton was at her door, smiling broadly. "Miss Ingrid, are you well?"

"Well enough. Give me a moment."

"Your foot is bad?"

"A little. Thank you for asking. Can you take me to the professor's room?"

"You can walk?"

"If you help me."

"Later I will find you a cane. Now take my arm."

On the street they met Boni. "Hey, Boni!" Hamilton called. "Have you sold all your fish today?"

"Only half," Boni called.

"Save me a tuna. Not a big one. Can you take me out with you tomorrow?"

Boni grinned. "I am going alone. Wicks has given me a wire line." He turned to Ingrid. "Tell me your name again, pretty lady. I saw you on the water with my friend Finn."

"She's Danny's friend," Hamilton said protectively. "Miss Ingrid."

"Yes? Good man, Danny. I'll have a nice tuna for you later, Hamilton." Boni bowed his head. "Miss Ingrid. I hope you can share this tuna with Danny."

"Thank you."

"Good man, Danny." Boni rested his hand on Hamilton's shoulder as he passed.

"Danny's well liked," Ingrid said.

"You think it is strange?"

"He's a drunk."

"One cannot hate him for that."

"I think I could."

"Have mercy, Miss Ingrid. He will not live for long."

The pain in her foot drove all mercy out of her. She could feel nothing else. She turned to Hamilton at the professor's door. "Leave me alone this time."

Hamilton nodded in consent. "I will return in one hour."

Ingrid lay on the floor and propped her foot on the bed. The blood ran out of the infection and, for a moment, eased the throbbing. She thought about the depth of Templeton's collusion in managing the hotel's finances. Years of aiding the institution that would eventually destroy the thing he loved most. How had he done it? And who knew what he had done? How much did this explain his present course of action?

She turned to the bed and noticed that the briefcase was not where she had left it. It had been moved, and now lay closer to the edge of the mattress, so that its binding was in full view. She pulled it out and held it to her chest. Closing her eyes, she tried to feel the presence of good or evil around her. The normal relationship between cause and effect did not seem to exist on this island. There were other forces at work, invisible wisps. *Listen to yourself,* she thought. *You're losing your perspective just like Templeton lost his.*

She reread the entries, parts of which had started to make sense. F. told him that leaders are sent to mend the tears between men, that his king was not the first and would not be the last— that he could not possibly understand the great pattern God weaves. . . . They were searching for a new leader. And the mysterious Agulhas, not only a current, but a palace, a haven, a warning and a revelation—*a revelation.* Mohammad's denial burned in him like a prediction of fire. *The place must be protected, with or without his consent. . . . This is a declaration to mankind: a guide and an admonition to the righteous. Take heart and do not despair. Have faith and you shall triumph.* Fire, water, enemies, triumph and defeat. Templeton's notes contained within them a complete moral universe governed not by God but by the will of man.

She turned once more to the early pages from the Koran. *He stood on the uppermost horizon,* she read, *then, drawing near, he came down within two bows' lengths or even closer, and revealed to his servant that which he revealed.* Ingrid rose to her elbows. The inscriptions were some kind of instruction. Templeton's map and scribbled calculations were an attempt to decipher directions to an actual location. Sitting up and forcing her mind to calm, she began to study the words more carefully, trying to envision them as a place.

He beheld him once again at the sidra tree, beyond which no one may pass. At a distance of two bows' lengths from the horizon was a tree beyond which it would be difficult to proceed. . . . *He has let loose the two oceans: they meet one another. Yet between them stands a barrier which they cannot overrun.* Her mind worked feverishly—the two arrows, the current, the river—the intersecting lines on Stanley's map. But where was he? Where was Templeton in all this?

Ingrid lay back down and studied the ceiling, following a crack to see where it ended. When the crack moved, she suddenly realized it was a trail of ants. Craning her head backward she spotted a bag that had been secured on the ledge above the window. She hopped over to it and pulled it down, instantly exposing a vast and seething army of ants. Somewhere underneath the commotion were chocolate bars. Ingrid threw the bag out the window and returned to the bed, wondering what else she might have missed. She ran her arms under the mattress again and this time found something else. She grasped it, hesitating before pulling it out because she recognized it instantly. It was her left sandal. She held it dangling by its strap. The leather was stained with something. She dropped it to the ground.

By the time Hamilton returned, she was fighting to stay calm. "Where is Fatima?" she asked.

"Which Fatima? There are many Fatimas."

"The one the professor knew. Finn's Fatima."

"Oh. She lives in the village."

"Take me to her."

"I can't take you to her. I am Danny's boy and she won't see Danny."

"Then point out her house."

"I must first ask Danny."

"Don't ask, Hamilton. Just show me."

"I think this is bad, that we have come here and entered the professor's room. And now Fatima. It's not good. Danny must know."

"Nonsense."

"No, not nonsense."

"Well, then, hurry up. My foot hurts."

"Oh, your foot!" Blood had soaked through her sock.

"Forget the foot, just take me, Hamilton. I'll never ask you for anything again."

Hamilton helped her to her feet and then stepped backward. "Excuse me, Miss Ingrid, I cannot take you. You don't realize what you are asking for."

Again, she tracked blood into Finn's house. She searched more carefully this time, looking for anything that might help direct her toward Fatima. She found nothing more than packets of herbs tucked at the back of a drawer. Kip was lying at the base of the bed, on top of the mosquito net. Her kittens lay curled in a basket. When Ingrid approached, Kip opened her eyes halfway and closed them again. Ingrid got beneath the net and scratched the cat's ears through the material. Finn's cat. Finn's Fatima. Even Templeton belonged more to Finn now. She fingered a hole in the mosquito net and lifted the net for Kip, who ignored the invitation. Ingrid lay back on the pillows. She slapped a flea on her arm. Next to her on the white pillowcase were countless hopping flecks. Finn's fleas. She swore and sat up. "Not fair," she said to Kip. "Not fair."

Ingrid found Ali sitting at the outside bar, drinking beer with his brother. "Ali, I need you," Ingrid said. "Half an hour."

"Yes, of course." They walked around the hotel the other way to avoid a dinner party. When they could no longer hear the voices and laughter, Ingrid stopped. "Take me to Fatima's house."

"Fatima?"

"The Fatima the professor knew. The Fatima Finn knows."

"For what reason, may I ask? She is not someone to disturb, especially without warning."

"Just show me her house. Then you can leave. Please, Ali."

"It's late."

"It's only eight o'clock." Ingrid took his hand. "Come, show me."

The House of Fatima

*F*atima's house was ordinary from the outside. Ingrid's courage swelled slightly at the doorstep; if no one was there, she would go home to bed. Ali vanished as soon as she had knocked. Was one knock enough? She knocked again and a voice sounded from inside. "It's Friday. *Friday.*" Two beats of deep resonating timbre. An instrument more than a voice.

"I'm sorry," Ingrid said. Her voice sounded like a child's. "I'm so sorry."

Silence and the smell of roses. Ingrid had never seen a rose on the island. There were no flowers, indeed there was no growth at all, around Fatima's door. Yet roses and more roses seeped out of a crack in the door. "Excuse me," Ingrid said to an eye in the crack. "Hello."

"Who are you?"

"Ingrid Holtz. I know Professor Templeton. I know Finn."

"Do I care who you know? No!"

"Please, will you let me in?"

"I don't want to let you in. I am entertaining."

"Just for a moment."

"A moment! One such as yourself could not understand the importance of a moment to my guest."

"Well, then, I'll come back. But I only have one question."

"I don't believe you." Ingrid didn't move. Then, "You can stay for five minutes."

Ingrid entered the cave of Fatima's house. Candles were lit on a table set for two. Pillows of rough silk covered a carved chair that looked like a throne. Across from it sat a simple wooden chair. "You may not sit," Fatima said.

"Standing is fine," Ingrid complied. "I've just been sitting anyway, sitting for hours. You see"—she motioned to her bandaged foot—"it's become hard for me to stand."

Suddenly Fatima was laughing, her round form shaking with mirth. "What a day has arrived. That I have something a *mzungu* woman wants, what a day." Fatima continued to laugh. "Forgive me if I am amused."

Ingrid stared at her. "What do I want?"

"You ask me this? We are strangers. I have had a joke with myself only. Allah knows what you want."

"Where is Nick Templeton?"

"Who?"

"You know him. Finn's legal guardian. I imagine you raised him together." The mirth left Fatima's face. "Where is he?" Ingrid demanded.

"Gone."

"Gone where? To the sacred site at Kitali?"

"That you think I know such things . . ." Her voice crackled into silence. Then she resumed, almost in a whisper, as if to herself. "We cannot follow them. It is not meant. I have a son, my soul, my *pepo,* I cannot follow him."

"Follow him where?" Ingrid spoke quickly so she would continue.

Fatima gestured impatiently to the ceiling. "You are not as stupid as you act. I cannot help you, miss. I cannot change the path of things. All I do is watch. You see there are no windows here, but I watch. To me you look sick. Go to bed and stay in bed for three days. Drink this tea and take this. Take it all. Make yourself strong." Fatima stood close to Ingrid and peered into her face. "Yes, there is a battle going on." Fatima took a pen and a jar of ink and sat down at the table and made quick, precise movements with her hand. Ingrid listened to the hypnotic scratching of pen on paper. Before the ink dried, Fatima ripped the words from the page and dropped the scrap of paper into a glass of liquid. The ink left the page and floated up in the glass in feathery yellow clouds. "Here, drink this."

"What did you write?"

"Something that will make you remember, if there is any memory left in you." Fatima retreated to a shadowy corner of the room and sat on a stool.

"Where is your guest?"

"He is right in front of you, smiling because, unlike me, he is too kind to laugh."

"I don't see him."

"Because you are one of the blind. I see you are gaining in numbers."

"You say that because I am white? A Westerner?"

"Any number of reasons."

"You don't think I understand you. Does Finn?"

"What did you say?"

"I'm asking about the boy you raised."

"Who are you to speak to me of this?" Ingrid watched Fatima's face as the expressions changed. Finally it settled into an expression she had seen on Finn. "I know who you are," she said, her face a wall. "I knew before you came to this island." Fatima turned to the throne at the end of the table. "Are you listening, *rohani*? It's disgraceful."

"Who are you talking to?"

"My husband. We were having dinner."

"You have a *rohani*?" Ingrid stared at the throne and saw nothing. "What does he look like?"

Fatima snorted. "Just drink what I have prepared for you."

"Tell me what I'm drinking."

"Words. May they find a place inside you. Now go. A splendid man awaits me."

Ingrid was light-headed walking through the village. She could no longer feel her foot. She felt only a vague texture beneath her. She watched villagers approach from a great distance and then rapidly pass. Instead of looking down as she had trained herself to do, she met their eyes. It did not matter: she was unfaithful. There was nothing to hide. We're all unfaithful, she thought. Full of *ghaflah* and shame.

At the guesthouse, Abdul followed her up the stairs, chattering behind her in Arabic. She did not turn until she reached her door. His face was pinched with anger. She closed her eyes and backed into the room, feeling the vibration of his voice push her away. By the time she bumped up against her bed, he was gone and the world was silent.

Death at Sea

*F*or the third night in a row, Finn found Jonah sleeping on his doorstep. He shook him out of sleep and together they rowed out to *Uma* in the blue-gray stillness of dawn. "Jonah, aren't you ever sleeping at home anymore?"

Jonah shook his head sullenly. "You know why not?" he asked. "Because I have the mark of the devil." He unzipped his pants and held his limp penis in his hand. At the base of the shaft was an open sore. "If I'm lucky it will kill me."

Finn stopped the oars mid-stroke. They hung, dripping bright tears of seawater. "What is it?"

"A disease from Europe. A disease from sex."

"You've been with a *mzungu*."

"Like you, brother. A beautiful white woman."

"I use protection. Never without. *Never*." Finn took up the oars again and slammed them into the water.

"A rubber stocking on your penis?" Jonah laughed. "Not very nice."

"But look at you, Jonah." Finn pulled the oars too hard and wished he had farther to row.

"At least I am honest. Listen to me tell you what I have done. I had sex with a white woman. A guest. Something you do all the time but you cannot say it. It may kill me but I have time to beg Allah's forgiveness."

"You're stupid, Jonah. And you're not going to die." They had reached *Uma,* but neither made a move to board her. "Tell me what happened."

Jonah put his head in his hands. "She was far down on the beach. She had no clothes. I was returning from the reef and she saw me. I looked away—I was sorry to have seen her, sorry for the shame she must feel—but then she waves to me to come to her. I thought maybe she had questions, a problem. So I kept walking and stood not far, looking at the sand. 'Come closer,' she said, 'kneel down. Don't be afraid. We're perfectly alone.' Perfectly alone, she said. I could do nothing. She was very hungry and then I was hungry too. Never before have I been with a woman in this way. She was a stranger to me, like a whore. I prayed the next day for Allah's forgiveness. I was sick twice in my stomach—food will not stay in me." Jonah looked up at Finn with tears in his eyes. "I am afraid of what I have done."

"Jonah," Finn said. He could find no words of comfort. "You'll be okay. Time will go by, you will forget."

Jonah spat over the side of the boat, suddenly angry. "She gave me money."

"Did she?"

"It makes me feel like a bait fish. I am not worthy of my wife. I cannot walk into my house. I cannot sleep with my own wife because now I am the whore."

"I'm sorry, Jonah."

"How is it with you and all these women? How can it be in your soul?"

Finn looked at the water so Jonah could not see his face. "It is nothing."

The next night, Finn drank at the bar with Nelson but not as much as Nelson. After walking him home and listening to his maudlin manifesto on his new rods, Finn again found Jonah sleeping on the doorstep of his house. Jonah's wife had locked him out this time, leaving him a thin blanket. Jonah explained it was better for him to sleep outside when he was drunk.

"Sometimes I confuse my two selves by speaking to my wife as I speak to you. Not only this, but when I am in bed with my wife, she puts her hand on my chest to invite me to touch her body and she knows something is wrong because my desire for her does not harden."

Finn paused before he asked, "Why not?"

Jonah shook his head. "She would see my shame. When I am away, at the hotel or at sea, I forget her." Finn was silent, listening. "She no longer speaks to me, she just looks. I think she is searching for what has been taken from her. What has been stolen."

"How long has it been this way, Jonah?"

"More than a year. I don't think I want a child anymore. I would not know how to raise it."

The two of them rowed out to *Uma* in the darkness, Jonah half asleep with his arms wrapped around his torso and his chin tucked to his chest as if he were a sleeping gull.

They headed southeast. Finn steered until the sky lightened. When he woke Jonah they were a mile off the coast, just above

Malindi, and heading straight east for deeper waters. Jonah took
the wheel while Finn fixed breakfast and tossed up a sweatshirt.
Jonah was afraid of the cold; he tensed his thin body against it,
which, Finn said, only made it worse. You must try to relax, Finn
told him, imagine the sun at noon soaking into your bones.

Jonah stood next to him by the wheel. "Where are we going,
the Seychelles?"

"No. Just farther than normal." Jonah was silent. "I want to
see something new. Those islands Boni spoke about."

"Boni's islands? You must be joking."

"I believe him."

"In any case, we don't have the fuel."

"We have the fuel."

Jonah crossed his arms. "So this is what we are doing. We are
looking for Boni's islands."

"Yes."

By dawn, they had lost sight of land. The air smelled different with the briny warmth chilled out of the water, which was
now black and bottomless. Hanging over the edge, Jonah reported he could see nothing.

The first deep red smudges of dawn appeared in the swirls of
clouds low on the horizon behind them. In front, the sky was
empty and pale. Jonah was certain they had lost their way. When
Finn encouraged him to climb to his roost, he refused, lying
down instead with his arms wrapped around him. Finn let him
sleep until late morning, when he threw some line out for bait,
nudging him to wake and watch the rods. Jonah shivered, his
arms around his knees. When one of the lines began to sing, he
was slow to reach it. Finn reeled the line in from the wheel. A
bonito flopped onto the deck. "Look, Jonah, a female."

Jonah scowled and began preparing a rod for marlin. "We'll

see if women are still good for something," he said, gouging the live bonito with the hook and tossing it over the back. The fish flipped and sank into the frothy top of a white cap.

They motored until noon, when Jonah came down from his roost and demanded they turn around. "We are tempting Allah. Besides, there are no fish." Finn nodded to the east, where one gull and then another flew above the waves. "Birds." Jonah spit over the side of the boat. "What do they know."

"Go back up," Finn said resolutely.

Jonah waved wearily from his roost, indicating a direction southeast of their course. Finn pushed the throttle forward and whistled for Jonah to come down. He set up another rod with a konahead while Jonah steered. They could see the birds now. Finn tied his leaders quickly, his eyes on the water. "There are two flocks," he said. "Did you see them?"

"Where?"

"Circle around, hit the right first and then come back for the other."

"They may not be marlin," Jonah said.

"What else would they be?"

"Allah knows."

"You and Allah are keeping close company these days. Where is he—below, napping?"

"Don't be disrespectful. We have enough trouble as it is."

"What trouble?" Jonah stood at the wheel impassively. He wrinkled his brow skeptically at the flock of gulls in front of them. "Are you sick?" Finn asked, leaving him for the back of the boat. He called from the harness. "If you're sick, you better tell me." Jonah didn't respond. Finn faced the water behind the boat and braced himself as *Uma* rode a sizable swell into the trough where the gulls were fluttering. "Nothing!" He yelled to Jonah.

"Get closer." Whatever the birds were focused on wasn't moving. One of them appeared to be standing on the water. As they came closer, Finn caught the reflective gleam of a creature floating just below the surface. "Jonah," Finn said. "Slow down." Jonah craned a look over the edge at the fish and whistled through his teeth. "He's hooked," Finn said. "Jesus, he's hooked." He reeled in one rod and then the other and then moved to the port side to where the other flock was hovering. It was almost a kilometer away. Ramming the rods into their holders, Finn picked up the wheel and yanked it west.

Under the second flock of gulls was a familiar boat, slightly larger than a dinghy, one bench in back and one in front. Boni lay between them, his strong body splayed on the bottom of the boat. At Finn's calls, he tried to speak and instead hacked, smacking his parched lips. He raised his hand in greeting. It was caked in dried blood. He was smiling, his bare torso drenched in sweat. "Man, I still have him on," he rasped. Wrapped around his right hand was a wire line that had looped and coiled around his fingers, where it dug into the flesh so deeply it was lost from sight.

"Boni, your hand!" Finn shouted. Boni held his hand in the air. Two of his fingers were nearly severed. They dangled below the others, restarting the flow of blood that had dried from inactivity. The blood dripped onto his shorts and disappeared into the thirsty planks of the boat. He continued to grin, lowering his hand and carefully placing it on his thigh. "I've got him," he said.

Finn grabbed the lead rope and tied the dinghy to *Uma*. Boni closed his eyes in the shadow of the larger boat. Finn lowered him a bottle of water, which he ignored. He raised it back up and unscrewed the cap, splashing some on Boni's face. Boni's eyes opened. "Have you seen him?"

"Yes. He's huge. *Kubwa sana.*"

"I knew it."

"You're coming with us, Boni."

"Are you stealing my fish from me?"

"You'll get your fish. Sit up now, help me out." Finn lowered himself down into Boni's boat. He wrapped a wet towel around his head and then one around his hand. With a pair of clippers he cut the wire line and clipped it into a commercial reel. "Jonah," he said, holding up the reel. "Transfer this to the other rod. Come on, big man. Get that stupid grin off your face. Where did that wire come from?"

"Pinkman Wicks," Boni said as Finn hauled him to his feet. "Do you have any Tusker, man?"

"Put your arm around me. Reach up to Jonah. He'll pull you up."

"You're going to tie me on?"

"Of course. We're taking you back to the island."

"No more fishing for you today, Finn brother. I'm sorry."

When they had carried Boni into the shade, Finn tied the dinghy to the back of the boat. "Give him some water," Finn said.

"You are a fool," Jonah told Boni. "You've lost your hand."

"I have the fish."

"You pray to Allah you have your life."

"I would give my life for another night like that. Me and him. Alone. He pulled me for hours, pulled like the devil. He's a strong one. Finn, are we close?"

"He's here," Finn said. "Barely alive. What do you want me to do?"

"Bring him on board!" Boni roared.

"It's not legal, Boni. This is a game fish."

"But what game were we playing, any game you've ever seen? This has never happened before. Never. Wait till Wicks sees this. Just you wait, Finn." Boni's eyes closed and his head lolled to the side.

When Boni lost his hand, his wife lost her last reserve of strength. Folding her *bui-bui*s, blankets, henna, undergarments and an extra pair of sandals into a woven bag that she slung over her shoulder, she told her husband, "Now you are truly useless." It was unheard-of for a woman to speak to her husband this way, but Boni had married a woman with spirit. This had turned out to be a risk, because while he loved her, sometimes he loved other women too. "Only when I cannot find you," he pleaded with her unseeing eyes.

"If you could walk straight from your boat to me you would find me every time. But your real mistress is in the bar. The other women, Allah will take care of them. But you are less of a man than I married. Your soul has shrunken so much it could fit into a Tusker Beer bottle, where it belongs. And look now"—she gestured to his gauze-wrapped stump—"you are shrinking in your body, too. I am going to the other village, where I will continue to be faithful to you. Allah willing, I will bear your child by Ramadan. Or maybe this is how he will curse you—by stopping your seed from growing in me. In any case, you can come to me when you leave your other mistress for good." She paused at the door and looked back at her husband. "You love her and she will kill you. How can I choose a man who chooses death?" And out she walked.

Boni slipped into a rapid delirium, a fevered response to his physical and emotional state. He was seen once more, the next day, wading naked into the waves. On the beach two European women from the hotel propped themselves up on their elbows to watch him. Boni had an awesome physique; everything about him was large. Leading the rest of him into the water was a sturdy, fearless erection, which is what caught the ladies' attention. He proceeded into the sea as if to his marriage bed. The women giggled, and when he disappeared from view, his black head bobbing between the waves, they lay back down and replaced their sunglasses. Later, it was guessed that the blood-soaked gauze on his arm had given the sharks a scent. It was birthing time on the reef. "Death would have come slowly," the fishermen speculated. "Many small sharks. Many small teeth. It would have taken hours, maybe."

For three straight days Finn trolled the bay, dragging his largest net. He was unconvinced. Boni was not the kind of man to die at sea.

Part
Five

Deliverance

$\mathcal{I}$n the stillness of her room, Ingrid could smell things she couldn't before: the sweet rich coffee brewed in the street below, the jasmine scent Sari wore, the smell of rain coming. Occasionally the scent of rose petals. She waited in bed for these smells to reach her, imagining what lay beyond her room, beyond the cracked ceiling and the narrow walls. When she blurred her focus, she wandered into the world of her mosquito net, an extraordinary substance, she decided, designed for daydreaming.

Finn had visited, sent by Fatima. He had left packets of herbs and given Sari instruction on how to administer them. He held his hand to Ingrid's forehead and rebandaged her wound. He did not try to make conversation. After he left, Ingrid liked him better; liked him maybe for the first time. From under her mosquito net, the world seemed to be rearranging itself.

When she realized she had finally lost her bearings, she was overwhelmed with a sense of relief. As she felt herself being inched away by the current, she lost memory of her moorings, of what it was she had been afraid of. Instead, she let the heat permeate her and stopped considering her well-being and what she should or shouldn't be doing. No reins, no worries. No decisions to make.

There were moments of terror when she recognized the symptoms of her weakening, but the terror passed. In the fever and the heat, she was on the front lines of a war she might be losing but couldn't step out of long enough to know for sure. War was war. While it was happening, nothing else existed. Only later could it become a regret. So there was no question about how to proceed. She ate what was brought to her, drank the bitter teas that were brewed for her and settled into a part of herself she had almost no knowledge of.

She wrote with difficulty on her side in handwriting that slanted drunkenly.

Pelat Island

January 29th

Doctor Reed and members of the department,

I am currently immobilized on Pelat. The landing strip is in disrepair and the rains have washed the roads away. The phones are out. All normal for the island and impossible for the Western mind to comprehend. I begin to understand Templeton's difficulties with communication. It seems clear that I won't make it back for the start of the term. I am, however, including a reading list and an essay based on my own research here. A suggested syllabus as well. If possible, have Henry Klingle take over the class. This letter, I am told, will travel to Mombasa by dhow, where it will be picked up and taken to Nairobi. Hopefully the phones will be working before it reaches you. I cannot adequately express my apologies.

Ingrid Holtz

Sari brought her soup in the afternoon and tea in the evening. She was respectful of the mixtures and kept to Finn's schedule exactly. "He will be pleased," she told Ingrid. "We are doing just what he asked."

"Please, Sari, can you take me outside to the pillows? I want to see the water." Ingrid leaned on Sari, who felt strong under her weight. "This is perfect. I can see the whole village. You'll see, I'll heal more quickly this way."

Below her were the houses of the village. She could see Danny's house and, next to it, the hotel bar's thatched roof. Salama grew bright with lights after sunset, while the rest of the village faded in the bluish dusk. Sari returned with hot tea, which she watched Ingrid drink before helping her back inside.

"Abdul thinks you should go to Nairobi."

"Yes, of course he does. Tell him the airstrip is under repair and the rains have stopped the buses."

"He thinks you should find another way."

"There is no other way. Does he want me to leave?"

"I don't want you to leave."

"Is he treating you badly?"

"No," Sari smiled. "I have a *rohani* now. Abdul cannot hurt me."

"So you're free. This *rohani,* has he made you free?"

Sari paused and held up a white petal for Ingrid to smell. "Here, I've brought some jasmine petals for your pillow. They will sweeten your sleep."

The next day Sari brought something wrapped in soft felt, a pair of heavy old Leica binoculars. Curled up and wedged between the lenses was a note: "So you can see me from up there. I am performing wonderful bar tricks to entertain you. Come back down to Bedlam as soon as you can. Yours, Danny."

The world on the roof became more intricate and appealing with the Leicas. Ingrid could see the heads and bodies of people flashing between houses, racing children chasing balls made of tape and rubber bands, the white hats of men hurrying to prayer, the black heads of women toting hand-sewn shopping bags heavy from the market. She could count coconuts on the palms and, farther off, gulls circling above the water. She saw a sea eagle swoop down to the waves and snatch up a fish with its talons. She studied the activities on the boats that came and went: the dhows and their various captains, the tourists who paid to go sailing on them, portly old Nelson bumbling around on *Tarkar,* having what looked like tantrums, screaming at his crew, who stared at him without expression. She watched the heat mingling with the ocean and the flat white clouds that formed over the coral reef by afternoon. The rain-bearing clouds seemed to come from the southeast, over the dunes. They appeared suddenly like huge dark castles, piled one on top of another, in the middle of their fierce ocean journey from India, from the arid interior, from who knew where.

"Sari!" Ingrid called. "Come quickly!" Unaccustomed to a raised voice, Sari bounded up the stairs two at a time. She stood breathless as Ingrid trained her Leicas to the west of Tomba Island. "I saw an airplane. Over there, it landed on the water."

"On the water?" Sari squinted to where Ingrid had pointed.

"It's possible. Some planes are able to land on the water."

"I see no plane."

"It's behind the island. Can you go to the hotel and ask Danny who is coming by seaplane? Ask if there is anyone he knows with a seaplane."

"Abdul is in the courtyard."

"Tell him you are looking for a way to help me leave. He will let you go."

Sari smiled. She returned within the hour. "That man is drunk always," she said. "He says you are to ask Finn Bergmann. But he smiles like he knows the answer."

"He does that to tease you."

"I asked twice. He only drinks and smiles."

"Thank you, Sari. He's an awful man. I'm sorry you had to talk to him."

"He wanted me to give this to you." Sari produced a man's gold ring from her folds. "He says he will marry you, one foot, two foot or no foot. He made me say it back to him to remember it correctly. Now wait here and I will bring you some soup."

Ingrid was looking through the Leicas again, this time at *Uma* chugging toward shore from the open sea. She had pushed the gold band over her thumb. "Ah," Sari said. "Finn Bergmann comes back. Maybe now you are not so anxious to leave."

All afternoon, Ingrid waited for him. She didn't eat her lunch. Sari was disappointed. "You will not improve this way."

"No, Sari," Ingrid lied. "I feel much better."

When Ingrid heard his step on the stairs she folded her pillow in half so she could see the doorway. He was wearing one of his fancy kikois from Somalia, thicker and more tightly woven. The Somalian kikois were what he wore to the bar. When he came closer she could smell that he had already been there. A wave of nausea drove heat into her face.

"How are you feeling? Have you been taking Fatima's teas?"

"Sari hasn't given me a choice."

"Good. I've brought you some more. I will leave it with her. Now drink this."

She did not mind so much when he left. The teas made her drowsy. When she woke, he was there again, sitting on the chair reading. "We are friends now," she told him before closing her eyes. "I think it's better." When she woke he was gone. She slept again and he returned. He was watching her this time. She put her hand out, to see if he was real.

Finn studied her foot. "Your infection has spread."

"I've been thinking, when he wasn't with me, he was with you."

"Who?"

"Templeton."

Finn opened a paper bag and brought out a plastic container. "Fatima's prepared some soup," he said. "Try to drink some."

"I won't ask any more questions. I understand it all better now."

"There's nothing to understand." Finn held his hand to her brow. "You have a fever."

"He would like that. My thinking will be original. You should listen to everything I say. It will all be very interesting."

"Ingrid, drink this. It will help you sleep."

Ingrid held out her hand for the cup. "Imagine if I were to ask you to promise not to leave me. Promise me you'll stay until I get better. It would disgust you. And it would disgust me because it is being so *afraid*." She took two sips of the soup and put the cup on the floor. "I will never ask you to promise."

"I will be here as often as I can," he said.

"Don't say that. I think I am ready now for whatever's coming next. You or not you. It doesn't matter. I don't need a promise." Ingrid closed her eyes. "I'm so tired. This is all making me very tired."

. . .

"I need to pee," Ingrid told Finn the next day when she woke. She leaned on him to hop to the bathroom, where she sat on the toilet and felt faint from the height. "Nothing's happening," she said from her perch. "Take me back to bed."

Finn negotiated with Abdul to get some hot water for Fatima's herbs. When he returned, she motioned to her foot. "I think this is who I am now. This weakness. It's interesting, isn't it?"

"No. You are not that foot."

"Everything changes. I don't mind so much."

"Shh, go back to sleep now."

Then she was alone for a long time. A long, quiet time that carried her up and up like a feather on the wind. She hovered bizarrely, almost pleasantly, between realms: home, Egypt, Pelat. Her memories rose too, one after another, until they were indistinct and she had the elated sense that they had fused, that her life had congruence.

It ended in darkness and a sudden heavy weight on her chest. Heat and hardness, a voice in her ear. A familiar voice that was replaced by a probing tongue and then a frenzy of grasping and ripping and the feeling of skin and hair on her bare abdomen, a pushing in her groin and the tongue that was down her throat now, almost choking her.

The hands were rough on her breasts and then on her arms when she tried to push away. They were holding her down, pinning her to the bed. She opened her mouth to scream. The strangest of sounds came from her throat, not like her voice at all. Then there was a scuffle and more voices—sharp, angry—and quickly she was free and light and cool and there was another hand on her face. A different hand. She held it in her two and pressed it close to her.

"Are you all right?" Finn's hand was moving down her torso

to her panties and her body flinched involuntarily. "He didn't," she said, suddenly tearful. "He didn't."

"Shh. You're all right now." The hand was removed. "I'm sorry," he said.

Ingrid reached out to pull him closer. "Don't leave."

"I'm not leaving. I've brought a dressing for your foot. Some more tea from Fatima. Lie still and put this piece of wood between your teeth. When it hurts, bite down."

"Nothing hurts anymore," she whispered.

"I should have warned you about Ali. I saw it coming."

There was a sensation around her foot. "I had a friend," she said. "My best friend. One night she died, drove off an embankment into a tree. My foot hurt then too. It was colder there. We were in the snow." She reached for his shoulder. "Have you ever seen snow?"

"I was born in the snow," Finn said. "I remember it."

"You remember it?" Ingrid asked, amazed.

"The wound has healed around the bandage," Finn said. "I have to take it off to clean it. I'll do it quickly."

"A good general policy for someone like you. Shit. Shit. Shit."

"I'm pouring iodine on a pad and I'm going to dab the wound. It will hurt."

"Bloody bloody hell."

"You learned that from Danny."

Ingrid lifted her head. The tendons in her neck rose with the effort. "I want to see it." Finn lifted her foot. "I can't see anything."

"There's not much light. It's just dawn."

"What does it look like?" Finn didn't answer. Ingrid drank a bowl of bitter liquid and watched him sideways as he read in his chair. "Read to me."

"This is Arabic."

"I like Arabic. Why are you taking care of me?"

"Because you are sick. Now close your eyes." He began to read. Soon she stopped him.

"What did that mean, what you just read?"

"It says, *'We never sent a prophet to a city without affecting its people with misery and distress so that they might become humble.'* Fatima pointed it out to me. She's becoming optimistic. Things have become worse and she's happier."

"Don't stop."

"Just sleep. I won't stop."

"What has gotten worse?"

Finn looked out the window, toward the sea. "Boni lost his hand."

"How?"

"Fishing. It's Wicks' fault."

"How can that be?"

As Finn started to read again, she was distantly aware of the stops and starts of his voice. "Translate, please," she said. "I am trying to understand." The passage did not grab her. She stopped listening as soon as it began. She held her hand in front of her face. Her long hand. The hand Stanley liked. "Maybe Stanley didn't like Boni's hands," Ingrid suggested, remembering that Stanley was her friend. Finn only felt responsible. "I spent the night with him," she said. "It was like medicine. Good clean sex. I thought of you—please don't stop reading." Ingrid folded her hands on her chest like an Egyptian corpse. "You're a slippery and cold man."

Finn closed the book. "Boni's dead."

Ingrid wanted to reach for him, but she was frozen. Finn stood up. "I'm going to get some food," he said. "You need to eat."

. . .

When she woke again, Ali was kneeling by her bed. The sun was high. He was almost close enough to touch. He was all in white. From above, he looked like an angel, which made her suspicious. She held her hand out to touch his curls and felt only air. Perhaps he was a figment. "Why are you in white, Ali?" she tried. "It's daytime."

"I have come from Friday Mosque," the figment answered. "I have been praying for my soul."

"Why are you here?"

"Finn told me to come. He told me to kneel with no prayer mat until my knees bled."

"How clever of him to tell you what to do. I didn't know that was all it took. Can you leave if I tell you to?"

"I would like to pray for longer."

"You see, this is how Finn and I are different: you listen to him."

A warm cup was pressed into her hand. Finn's voice was above her. "Where has he gone?" she asked.

"Who?"

"Ali."

"Ali hasn't been here," Finn said. "He won't be back."

"He was praying right here, all in white. He looked like an angel." Finn had his hand under her head. He was holding another cup to her lips. "See how trusting I am. This could be arsenic. Pure poison."

"You've already been poisoned."

Ingrid tried to smile at him. "Can you get me some whiskey?"

Finn squeezed her arm. "No."

"Please."

"I'm going to read to you now."

"When you see Danny, tell him to visit. He and I are simpatico on some things."

Finn opened his sea-warped copy of the Koran.

"Finn," Ingrid said. "What are you going to do?"

"Be quiet now," he said, and once again began to read:

> *And We will set up the scales of justice*
> *For the day of reckoning:*
> *And no soul shall be wronged in anything.*
> *And be it the weight of a mustard seed,*
> *We will bring it forth:*
> *And We are well able to take account.*

"On the day of reckoning," Ingrid said. "The good will have water. It will spring forth from rocks and sand. The bad will have fire. Not just fire, but scalding fire." Ingrid smiled. "In the water which God sends down for the strong and with which he revives the earth after its death . . . Water in the desert. It's where he is. I can almost promise it."

When she woke she was alone, burning, and the room seemed strange. Her hair was limp from not washing. Her scalp itched. Something smelled hideous. She pushed her way out from under the mosquito net and put her feet on the ground, one after the other. It was the difficult time of night. The air was thick and still as death.

As soon as she stood, she fell hard to the floor. A scorching pain burned through her and for a horrible moment she felt every cell in her body. There was wetness around her foot, the moisture of infection leaking into the bandage. It was she who smelled. She was rotting. She crawled out of her bedroom to her sink and held her head under the feeble faucet until the water ran down her neck to her shoulders. She arranged a bed of pillows on the porch, shivering from the damp, determined not to burn alive in her room.

Finn came in the early morning. She wanted to know where he had been and with whom but she couldn't manage to ask. He carried her wordlessly to her bed and laid her down gently, arranging her wet hair around her. Still, she was shaking. He laid his chest across hers, hoping to press the cold out of her. She chattered, barely breathing.

Finn held his face close to hers and brushed his lips against hers. "You've got malaria. I'm going to give you a pill. It's going to make you sick but then you will get better. I will stay with you tonight, but tomorrow I have to leave."

Ingrid shook her head. "No. Not yet."

"You will get stronger now. Remember that."

Finn did not try to stop himself. He kissed her forehead and then her lips.

Pelat's Son

The next morning, Finn left Ingrid in Sari's care. At the bottom of the stairs was Abdul, positioned to intercept him. He darted out of the darkness like an angry mongoose. "She cannot stay here any longer."

"She cannot leave. She is sick."

"This is not a hospital. Or a brothel. And she spreads her disease of promiscuity to Sari. I cannot have her here another day."

"Well, I'm afraid there's no alternative."

"I would not let a woman of mine behave this way."

"She's not my woman."

"Your whore?"

"No, not my whore."

"Then what?"

"Abdul. I will come back for her. I'll move her to the hotel."

"Soon."

"As soon as I can."

Abdul stepped aside and motioned to the door.

Finn found Fatima outside, doing her washing. "I need to sleep," he told her. "Just for a while." He lay on the mat he had lain on as a boy. With his eyes closed, he looked almost at peace. There were some things, Fatima thought, that hadn't changed. When her washing was hung, she sat down and watched him.

"This girl of yours," Fatima began when he woke. She waited for him to correct her wording but he only covered his eyes with his arm so Fatima could not see his face. "What does she want?"

"What does anybody want."

"I had hoped she would recover and leave the island."

"I had hoped the same. But," Finn added, "probably not for the same reasons."

Fatima rose and began preparing tea. "And," she finally said, "what are those reasons?"

"She is my responsibility."

Fatima dismissed this claim with a honk of laughter. "Responsibility! If you're saying you've made her pregnant, I can make you a tea for that."

Finn shook his head. "I've never been with her in that way."

Fatima abandoned her tea preparation and sat down again. "Tell me what knot has tied itself inside your head, so we can begin to untie it."

"Wicks has gone to Kitali."

"Do I care about Wicks' movements? I wish the man's blood would dry up and he would stop moving altogether."

"That's a very unchristian sentiment, Fatima. You may remember I was born a Christian. It's a Christian war that's being fought on this island. Wicks and Templeton are like my father, all Christians, all men who have forgotten their God in their wars of ownership and superiority."

"Your father is not someone you might want to imitate."

"My father was a man who lost his God. I am the same."

"You are *not* the same," Fatima protested.

"I have ignored his teachings."

"Whose teachings, your father's? You're talking like a madman!"

"Even if you understood, you would pretend not to. You would like me to act, I know. You've been waiting for years. The trouble is, I may not be able to act in the way you would like."

"It is not for me you should act."

"Who, then?"

"You should act for your people. You should lead them and help them to understand what is happening around them."

"Who are my people?"

"Don't be foolish."

"All I know is that I should have acted for Jonah and Boni. They were my brothers. They followed my example and you see what's happened? They've lost what little they had." Finn removed his arm and rubbed his eyes. "But you know, they had more than I ever did."

Fatima was holding the edges of her chair. "This is not good for sleep, this talk."

"Forget sleep. Do you know what I believe, Fatima? I believe that actions come from pain, or maybe it's love. But I believe that fate can be changed by them. I think this is a Christian belief."

"Actions *are* fate, Finn. Every day you are fulfilling yours. It's Allah's will—"

"And what about my will?" Finn interrupted.

Fatima was silent. "And the girl?"

"The girl has done nothing. She simply asked for my help."

"There is nothing simple about that."

"No, I don't agree. Helping her would do me great good. I

told her about *ghaflah.* I accused her of this sin so she would leave me alone. What I should have said is that I am the best example of it, that it is I who have forgotten my divine origin."

"Finn—" Fatima held her fist toward him. "You are a flower just about to bloom. You have been tucked inside of yourself, in darkness. You cannot blame yourself for a late arrival. You must accept the plan for your unfolding."

"Fatima, there is no plan," Finn said, and then he rose. "In all your talk of God, you never talked to me about love. Not once."

"Love is Allah. He is all around you."

"He is not in this heart."

"Then you must open it and fill it with Him, my son."

Finn knelt in front of Fatima and took her hand in his. "But you see, I am not your son."

CHAPTER

28

Plans and Blueprints

Stanley Wicks was frustrated. The progress he had made aboard *Tarkar,* utilizing the products he had researched, purchased and brought thousands of miles from Europe and America to the African island, had been erased with one random mishap. Boni and his damn hand were being blamed wholly on the wire line Stanley had given him. He had been doing the man a favor. Was it his fault if Boni had no common sense? It was brutally unfair that he should be regarded as some kind of criminal. Even his boatman, Abdul, was looking at him with shifty distrust.

The island experience was changing for Stanley. The worst immediate consequence of all this was that he was driven back to his house, which he had happily managed to avoid for the past few weeks. In its rooms, he was forced to think about what he knew was happening under his own roof, the indiscretions that everyone on the island was aware of, that Stanley himself had managed to dismiss until they were under his nose. Now he was sure he could all but smell the juices of sex that were flowing between his wife and her ridiculous body worker. For all he knew, the nanny was in on it too, all three of them rolling around while the baby howled in the next room.

Domestic displacement and stalled progress at Kitali had resulted in even later nights at the bar. Stanley was beginning to see himself in the regulars there, drinking to dull fears of impotence and various failings of character. It had not taken long for him to become like them. He could think about this now only because, by luck, chance or divine intervention, he had stepped back over the line into safety. His recent interlude with Ingrid had given him the strength to reclaim the future he had almost forfeited. Simple human contact had been enough to galvanize him, to jolt him from his stasis. He was ready to be a part of it again, a warrior prepared for battle.

Stanley flung himself into plans for the new hotel, which were hopelessly behind schedule. Instead of accepting Gus' excuses for the third world (the man was so passive, so defeated!), he was going to turn up the heat where it would have some effect. His good behavior was lost on these island cretins anyway. Gus was too stoned to care, the workers paid absolutely no attention to him and the Salama entourage was too self-involved to notice if he was or wasn't being a gentleman.

Stanley decided to set up camp on the other side of the island, to keep an eye on construction. Nelson took him over on *Tarkar,* loaded with provisions. In preparation for a long stay, Stanley had brought with him the blueprints, flooring and kitchen designs, everything he needed to allow himself to dream. This would be no Salama. It would be a place for thinkers, writers, gentlemen and ladies. Academics, even, like Ingrid Holtz—if she had been staying at his hotel, she never would have taken such a bad turn. This would be a healthy place, where old wounds were healed and no new wounds were incurred.

Excited, Stanley got up and paced around his shelter. People would come at transitional junctures in their lives, the way he had first come to Africa, and they would be gently steered in the right direction by the warm waters of the Indian Ocean. A diet of fish, strong in protein for mental stability, and fresh produce, the stuff Mohammad had in his village. He wouldn't need to make airplane runs to Mombasa for lettuce and tomatoes—he would use what was already here. Still to be resolved was the question of water. They would need it for the produce, for drinking, plumbing, laundry, irrigation for the grounds and God knows what else. Stanley left his shelter and found Gus driving stakes into the sand.

"How are we coming on the water issue?"

Gus looked at Stanley from beneath the rim of his hat. "Bad news there, I'm afraid. The water is not actually on your property."

"I'm sorry to hear that, Gus, because someday this hotel will be finished, and then we're going to have to think about things like faucets."

"Mohammad said we were welcome to dig, to divert the water at the source. We tried."

"And?"

"It dried up. Just sank into the sand. Used pipe, same thing happened."

"Then we'll have to divert it farther down. Mohammad seems to have it all worked out over there. Talk to him."

"Well, that's the other part of the bad news. They've got something of a live-and-let-live policy as far as your hotel."

"What's that supposed to mean?"

"You don't bother them, they don't bother you. That includes digging around in their village for water. They say it's on sacred ground."

"Then I'll buy it from them, if that's what it takes. I can tell you one thing, they're not going to run me off this land. I can see that's the intent."

"I don't know if brute force is the answer here. Sit down, Stanley. Take a load off."

Stanley was too exasperated to sit. "You'd have to be a brute to see this mystical posturing for what it is and steamroll right on. Well, Gus, I am a brute and I'm past caring about the gods they worship and their legions of spirits and goddamn curses."

"This is a side of you I haven't seen," Gus said. "The English terrier." He lit a cigarette and offered one to Stanley. "How's Daisy faring?"

"Daisy's fucking her masseur."

"I see."

"I'm one step away from shipping her back to England, but God knows what damage she'd do there." Stanley sat down and dragged heavily on his cigarette. "To be honest, I'm worried about Harry. What sort of childhood is he having? Perfectly awful sourpuss of a nanny and a mother who's fucking Attila the Hun in the next room. You know, children notice these things. They're not insects, for chrissake."

"Bring her here. No trouble in sight. Old Mohammad might be able to teach her a thing or two."

"The Gandhi of Pelat. He puts on airs, if you ask me."

"He's done his share of thinking."

"Well, I'd like him to think about a little profit sharing. Get smart, Gandhi. Join the modern world. Tell him I'd like his help, will you?"

"Help with what?"

"Once we resolve the water issue, there's the question of produce. We're going to have to feed our guests. Does he understand that? They're coming from the first world, where this stuff is easy to come by. Here it will have to be plentiful as well as extraordinary. You don't fly halfway around the world to be served wilted iceberg."

Gus stubbed out his cigarette in the sand. "I believe Mohammad's clan grow enough only for themselves."

"Well, they can grow more, can't they?"

"They're superstitious about it. They think if they ask for more than they need, they might be denied everything."

"Tell them I'll pay them."

"Your currency means nothing to them."

"What has value for them? I'll convert it. Talk to the man, will you?"

Gus left Stanley and conferred with Mohammad. When he returned, Stanley was napping on the sand. "Mohammad says he didn't know you were a magic man," Gus said, nudging Stanley with his foot.

"He has no idea," Stanley said, yawning. "Tell him he has no idea."

"He wants you to convert your money into peaceful silence for years to come."

"Wily rascal."

"As it turns out, there's nothing they need."

"He speaks for everyone? I don't believe for a moment that no one in the village is in need."

"Unless you can provide pure joy."

Stanley raised himself to his elbows. "This man is impossible."

"He wants you to know that he's very practical. He worries about what he is responsible for, no more. He looks to gain nothing from others."

"Well, tell him I've got a problem. I've bought this land and I've invested money to build a hotel and it's too late to change any of it. It's going to happen. Tell him it's going to happen."

"Mohammad says everything can and does exist in potential. Power lies in manifestation."

"What are you, his spokesman?"

"He's made his views extremely clear."

"So he's challenging me. Fair enough. The conversation is over. The next time I see him he will have no choice, none of this mediated talk. I'm going back to get the rest of my things. Tell your workers not to kick off to sleep yet, I'll be back later today."

Back at Salama, Stanley sat on the veranda and ate a club sandwich. The hotel bar was deserted, and Stanley let his mind wander to Ingrid Holtz. The panic of his adulterous act had already been overtaken by the possibility of another night with her. He found it hard to remain stationary. The sandwich he was eating was as dry as a napkin in his mouth and, though he did not usually drink during the day, a beer now seemed essential. He motioned to Jackson for a Tusker, using the interruption as a way to refocus on the more practical issue of the hotel. The immediate image of half-built walls supervised by stoned and apathetic Gus made him finish his beer in one swallow. Thinking would achieve nothing. He simply had to get back there.

He decided that before returning to Kitali, he would pay Ingrid a visit. From talk at the bar he knew she wasn't well, that she couldn't, for the time being, leave her guesthouse. He would bring her dinner and spend some time in that little room of hers. He would carry up a fresh candle and offer her some of his fancy painkillers. The idea of her pain distracted him; he knew there was something he could do to relieve it. The past days he had found himself running through his mind the details of her face and body, the few things she had said.

Stanley ordered another beer. Was he falling in love with her? He didn't know. A choice lay before him. Either he could move toward Ingrid or retreat back to Daisy and try again in earnest. The idea of being with Ingrid was enticing for obvious reasons. And with him, her chances of recovery would be considerably improved. He would start by getting her off the island, taking her to Nairobi to have her foot treated. They would get to know each other better. Besides, she might need someone like him. He stopped himself there. Beyond what she could do for his ego, did his interest amount to anything more than novelty and lust? Impossible to know. It was like an experiment in quantum physics; you couldn't find out the answer without first ruining the experiment.

Once more he tried to rationalize his desire. Ingrid was his Adolpho: his healer. He had needed something for so long. Why should he deprive himself of such a therapy, such a nice girl? Stanley regarded himself as a noble, moral man, but had he ever been tested? If marriage to Daisy was his first test, he had failed. He had committed adultery and now he was finagling a way out of the marriage for good.

The thought of Daisy made him crave a cigarette. After finding one at the bar, he sat down again to consider the possibility that this juncture presented the marriage with a second chance. He could go to Daisy and confess. He could lay himself bare: Come, he could say to her, my neck is unprotected. Break it if you like. I may desire another woman, but I haven't given up on you. After this pronouncement there would be nothing to say, nothing to do but to look at the woman he had married, watch the expressions travel across her face as she decided what to feel. He wanted to retrieve the softness he had seen in her in the beginning. Then he might be able to forget about what had come between them and stay. They would start over . . .

Danny wobbled by on his way to the bar. "Stanley! I've heard talk that you have designs on my girl Ingrid. Now that's not fair, as you have a wife. We may be in Africa, but those legal attachments count for something, I think."

"I agree," Stanley said.

"You seem very serious today, Stanley. Are you brooding about something?"

"I was just having a sandwich."

"A *sandwich*. How peculiar for you."

"I did find it a bit rough going. In any case, I'm off to Kitali for a spell."

"Give my regards to the natives."

Yes, he would go to Kitali before making up his mind. There was nothing there to distract him from his decision.

Stanley stopped by Abdul's guesthouse after lunch. As he reached the house, the door swung open, expelling Finn onto the street. Finn raised his eyebrows at the sight of Stanley. "Hello, Wicks. After more of what you got last week?"

For a moment, Stanley was speechless. "Just taking a walk, Finn."

"Well, I wouldn't brave the gauntlet of Abdul, if getting to his roof is what you've got on your mind. Ingrid's too sick for physical exertion anyway."

This provocation was so unlike Finn that Stanley was more puzzled than angry. "I intended nothing of the sort."

"You intend nothing," Finn said. "Which is why you destroy so much."

"What have I destroyed, Finn, that you haven't?" Stanley asked, his confusion giving way to anger.

"You seem to feel entitled to take what does not belong to you. Some would call it stealing. What's odd in this case"—he nodded to Abdul's roof—"is that I think she actually likes you. It must be because you're such a . . . gentleman."

"I'm not interested in arguing with you, Finn," Stanley said. "Anyway, I'm on my way to Kitali."

"Are you now?" Finn asked, turning away. "Well, then, we may meet again soon."

Guidance from the Dead

$\mathcal{T}$hat afternoon a dhow deposited Henry Chisham on the quay. He had, he told the captain of the dhow, come all the way from Nairobi by bus. When the bus broke down, he'd hitchhiked with three hash-smoking hippies from Australia driving a twenty-year-old Land Rover with no shock absorbers and only the remnants of seat cushions. "Nearly killed me," Henry told the captain in Swahili. "You've never seen a road more full of potholes. I tell you, my insides feel *pureed. Ninasikia maumivu.*"

"It's Allah's will that you survived," the captain said as he nosed his dhow against the stone steps. Henry stumbled onto the stone wall and headed immediately for the hotel bar, where Danny was feeling so pleasantly drunk that he had skipped lunch.

"Hello, Henry. What are you doing here?"

"I've come to tell you your mother's fallen ill."

"You look a little sickly yourself," Danny told him. "Pale and damp as a diaper." Henry pressed his cold beer bottle to his forehead. "They want her to go to London for treatment," he said. "She won't go without seeing you."

"Bloody hell," Danny said. "Get her on the phone."

Henry shook his head. "She wants to see you."

"This is the best trick yet."

"They're saying it's some kind of cancer."

"Rubbish."

"Talk to Kipo if you don't trust me."

"And trust Kipo! Don't make me laugh."

"He's running the Chichester while I'm here."

"So the natives have finally taken over," Danny said. "It was only a matter of time."

"I think you must come, Danny," Henry said. "Your mother's ill."

"Anyway, I can't go, ill or not ill. I've cut my feet."

Henry finished his beer and stood up. Aside from an initial greeting, the two men had not looked at each other. "Well, then. That's what I'll tell her, that you couldn't come because you've cut your feet." Danny scowled. Henry had his hat in his hand. "I'll be on my way."

"Bloody fucking hell," Danny said. "All right, all right. You win. I'll go."

"I've brought a letter for Ingrid Holtz," Henry said. "It came to the Chichester a few days back. I assume she's still here."

"Better give it to me," Danny said.

"Actually," Henry said. "I'd like to see her. How is she doing?"

"Splendidly. This climate really suits her."

❧

Henry was almost not allowed into Abdul's guesthouse. "Too many men!" Abdul exclaimed. "Is my house a brothel?"

"I can wait outside if you'll just tell her I'm here." Abdul swung the door closed and Henry found himself alone in the swelter of the dusty street. He set his hat back on his head and resumed sweating. When the door opened again, there was a young woman behind it. She beckoned him with a henna-painted hand. Henry removed his hat again, his eyes on the swirling, intricate design on her hand. It looked like a subversive lace that brought to mind women's underclothing. Henry felt flustered, unsure of whether he could meet her eyes. He blotted his forehead with a handkerchief as they crossed the empty courtyard, noting happily that the short-tempered old man had retreated into one of the rooms. At the top of the stairs, Henry shut his eyes against the blinding white of the roof.

He could smell Ingrid's illness at the doorstep of her dark room. She had no idea who he was. "Stanley?"

"No, it's Henry, from the Chichester. In Nairobi," he added.

"Oh!" She struggled to sit up. "The light—I thought you were someone else."

"I just popped in to see how you were." Henry took a few steps toward her bed. "I see you've become acquainted with my son."

Ingrid closed her eyes. "Your son?"

"Danny."

"Danny!" she exclaimed. "Why doesn't he ever visit me, damn it?"

"He seems to believe you're in good health."

Ingrid laughed feebly.

"I've been trying to convince him to come to Nairobi," Henry said quietly. "His mum's taken ill."

Ingrid raised herself on her elbow. "Nairobi? Are you going to Nairobi?"

"I'm going as soon as I can get off this damn island. The

phone's been out for more than a week. Had to come myself to get a message to Danny about his mum." Henry paused. "You remember Christa?"

"Yes." Ingrid was confused. "She's sick?"

"It's happening quickly, I'm afraid."

"Oh, Henry, I'm so sorry. There's a chair in the corner, there. Please sit."

"If you like," Henry said as he dragged the chair to the bed. "I can try to arrange to take you back to Nairobi with me."

"Did you come in a seaplane? I saw a seaplane."

"God, no." Henry nearly fell into the chair. "It took me bloody forever to get here."

"If I left with you today, I wouldn't be able to come back, would I?"

"Not for a while anyway."

She smiled weakly. "I don't think I can go with you now."

"I think you should, you need to see a good doctor."

"But I'm not done here. I still have work to do."

"You are in extremely poor health. I can't imagine what work you'll be getting done."

"No, you see, I'm used to it." She smiled more strongly. "I've gotten used to it."

Henry held up his pocket watch. "It's so dark in here. I can barely see."

"Give it to me." She held the watch face in front of her. "It's just past noon." Henry traced the rim of his hat with his finger. "Danny told me you were his real father," Ingrid said.

"Did he now?"

"You're not, though."

"No."

Poor Henry looked hot. His shirt stuck to his chest. He wore brown leather shoes and white socks and looked like an aging schoolboy. "Tell me about Colin," she said. "Is he still looking for worms?"

"Poor chap's dead, I'm afraid."

Ingrid sat up. Henry stared down at his hat. Over Henry's shoulder and through the open door was the sea. Dully she thought, the sea is big, Colin was small. I am small too.

"He's dead?"

"Yes."

There was nothing complicated about it. The sea was big. Colin was dead. It was so easy to die in Africa. Death had the inevitability of a downward swing in a dance that undulated continuously. Up and down and up and down. Life and death. It was so natural, so fluid, so easy. There was no reason she shouldn't be the next downward swing.

At least in Africa, she thought, death was part of a bigger dance. Maybe that was why Colin had stayed. Knowing he would die, why would he return to a country that would never join dancing to death, a country that stood and walked and lay down at night, migrating through time with no dance at all.

She thought with sudden urgency that Colin had been extraordinary. Who else had witnessed him as she had? Who else could attest to the goodness of his soul?

"He read the Bible," she said.

"Did he?"

"I think he liked it. It's a good thing you had them in the rooms."

"He was a lovely boy," Henry said. "I shall miss him."

Ingrid realized that she had no one like Henry. If she died, there would be no witness. No one to bear the news. She wanted to ask what had happened to Colin's body. Had there been a service? Had his wife in England been notified? Was the body buried or burned? Did they keep his glasses on the face, his shoes on his feet?

"What did he—" she began. "It seems so fast."

"He helped himself along a bit. Can't blame him for that."

Ingrid looked out again at the sea. Maybe the only real choice you had was the moment of your death. Colin had chosen his. Had he thought about going to hell as he did it? Henry cleared his throat and her eyes drifted back to him. He seemed infused with pain. Or maybe he was just hot. Poor Henry. He had lost two sons and now his wife was dying. He was a good man. Ingrid was glad he had come.

"Maybe I could come with you," she offered.

The suggestion seemed to enliven him. "Well, I'm to meet some chap at five o'clock on the quay. He's going to sail me down to Malindi, where I can get the bus back. It would be jolly smart of you to come along."

"All right," she said, working through the idea in her mind. "I will try to be there at five."

"Good girl. Now I've brought you some mail that came to the hotel." Henry handed her an envelope and she recognized her father's writing.

"Thank you, Henry. Thank you so much."

"See you this afternoon, then. Five o'clock departure."

Departure. She laid the envelope on her stomach. She had a few hours to consider it. Her thought process had become as unpredictable as cloud formation. Departure. The word itself had taken on an abstract, shape-shifting quality. Departure from what, toward what? *She had already departed.* How could she depart more or further? She wanted to think about Colin, pay him the brief, superstitious homage one would pay the body of a soldier who'd fallen in front of you, instead of just stepping over the corpse.

At last, Ingrid tore open the envelope. Inside was a note attached to a letter. The note was from her father—*Happy birthday, Ingrid. Hope the work is coming along. Much love, Dad.* The handwriting on the letter inside was different. The date in the corner was September 16, 1975. Ingrid's eyes skipped to the bottom of the page. The letter was from her mother, written twenty-three years before.

My darling baby girl,

Baby no more, for you are soon to be thirty! The few helpful words I have for you would not be pertinent until now— you see, I have never raised a child. I have lost one and am abandoning the other. Your father has done it instead and if you're reading this, he must have muddled through it on his own. Perhaps, as I have urged him to do, he has remarried and you have the all-important two fountains of wisdom from which to drink.

The only counsel I can offer is in regard to marriage. Treat your husband like he is a beloved child who cannot speak. It sounds silly, but I have found it to be a useful approach. Try not to visibly doubt his authority. Instead, do what you want to do quietly without fanfare and you shall both be happy. I have found it is possible to live fully even when you are one half of a whole. Treat yourself gently, like you would treat your own daughter.

I'm sorry I will not be there to see this day or any others. While I have grown uncomfortable with this illness and am resigned to my passing, it is not seeing you I regret the most. I hardly know you, sweet child, but I miss you already, and all that you will become.

Be strong, but not too strong. Strength can be its own undoing. There is much to be learned from surrender. That's very
old-fashioned in these changing times, but it is what I
know—what I have come to understand.

If I could, I would tell you all this myself. What a delight
that would be! Be happy, sweet girl. Live life as if it will always end too soon.

> My love always,
> Your Ma

Ingrid folded and then unfolded the letter. She let her eyes drift
over the words, picturing the woman who had written them
seated at her desk in front of the bedroom window, absently tapping the glass owl next to the lamp with her pen. By then she
was grounded by her disease yet still gracious, still loving. The
phantom memory of this woman's love created in Ingrid a de-
bilitating ache. She read the letter again and then again, submerging herself in a sorrow that hardened only when she
glanced at the inscrutably brief words of her father—and for a
moment she hated him and Henry for allowing her mother's
memory to find her now. She folded the page and stuffed it back
into the envelope.

She called softly for Sari and when she did not come, crept to
the stairs, where she could see down to the courtyard. Someone was
cooking lunch below. The aroma of food brought moisture to her
mouth and then, like a mirage, the memory of food. The hunger
came after, intense and urgent. She folded and refolded her
mother's letter. Somewhere she had money. She could send Sari out
to get a chapati. Thinking about where her money was and how
much she had left and if it was enough to get to Nairobi, and if she
actually could get herself to go to Nairobi money or no money, she
leaned her head against the wall and dozed off in the sun.

When she awoke, Sari was standing below her on the stairs. "You are sick?" she asked.

"Sari, can you get me scissors? A knife?"

"If you return to your bed. Abdul would not like to see you here."

Ingrid went to her bed of pillows on the roof and lay on her back, trapped under a dome of blue.

Sari returned with scissors, a glass of water and something folded into a small piece of paper. "Finn has brought these pills for you, for the malaria. He says you must swallow them with water. They will make you very sick but then you will be better."

Ingrid swallowed the three pills. "It's my birthday," she announced and she began to cut off her hair. It dropped in hunks to the ground where it stirred in the breeze.

"Why are you doing this?" Sari's voice rose sharply in pitch as she knelt to gather the bright hair in her skirt.

"It is my gift to myself. Take it and burn it," she said. "No, bury it. Then I need you to help me."

With Sari's help, Ingrid made her way to Fatima's house. Sari was frightened and left before the door opened. Fatima was barefoot. Ingrid leaned painfully in the doorway, staring at the spread of her toes, the ridges of tendons running to the arch, the stability of their surface area and the toughness of the soles uncompromised by shoes.

"Where is your hair?" Fatima asked. "You look like a plucked chicken."

"Where is Finn?"

"You can't follow him."

In the *rohani*'s chair was Templeton. He looked strange, not quite like himself. Ingrid looked at Fatima. "Where has he been?"

"Who?"

"The professor."

"The professor?"

"He's sitting in your *rohani*'s chair."

Fatima laughed. "See what the island has done to you?"

Ingrid turned to the chair. "I wasn't smart enough to find you," she said to Templeton's image as he became transparent and the fabric of the chair showed through his loden coat. "I think he's cold."

Fatima stepped forward and slapped Ingrid across the face. "Stop it, now. Finn has gone. There is no one in that chair." Ingrid stared at Fatima as her eyes filled with tears. "What are you looking at, you crazy girl? Why are you here?"

"I wanted to say good-bye."

"Good-bye, then. You should have left weeks ago."

"To Finn."

"Well, you can't. As you can see, he's not here."

"Tell him good-bye for me, then. Tell him thank you. I would thank you, too, except I think your teas made me worse."

"Off!" Fatima shooed Ingrid toward the door. "Not only crazy but ungrateful!"

Ingrid held her hand to her cheek and silently shook her head. She limped back to Abdul's, where the thick door was closed to the street. She grasped the metal ring to free the latch, but it was locked. She knocked and when there was no answer, beat the door with her fist. He had locked her out. "Bastard!" she yelled, wanting Abdul to hear.

Sari's sweet, cautionary voice came from above. "Take this," she said. Ingrid visored her eyes and watched as Sari dropped a *bui-bui* from the window in Ingrid's room. It caught the air and floated to the ground, like a bird that had been shot but not killed. "My money, Sari. Throw out my money. There is a bag with my passport and money." Sari put her finger to her lips. Her head shook imperceptibly in refusal. "Please!" Sari's head disappeared from the window and was replaced by a curtain. Outraged, Ingrid went back to the front door and pounded. "You can't do this!"

When it was clear she was never going to gain reentry, Ingrid put on the *bui-bui* and forced herself to walk to the hotel. The bones in her body ached with a searing sharpness; she could feel the fever spreading inside her, burning and looting in its path. Her foot, thankfully, was beyond pain. It was not even a part of her anymore, she thought bitterly. She had *surrendered* it. Though it made her hotter, Ingrid attached the veil over her face.

By the time she reached Salama, the blood in her veins felt like fire. Finn's pills, she realized, were working their destruction inside her, killing everything, good and bad. *Taste the torment of the fire, in which you did not believe . . .*

There was no one she recognized at the bar. She moved past patches of bleached-white napkins to a solitary chair at the edge of the terrace, overlooking the water. Behind her, an English couple laughed over a game of backgammon. Their drinks clinked with ice.

"Should we swim after lunch or take a nap?"

"I don't care, darling, I'm happy just where I am."

"A little on the warm side for me."

"That's just to help you relax. Think of the heat as having hundreds of tiny fingers working on your muscles and joints. Soon you'll feel no pain at all."

Thoughts were coming to her slowly and out of order. To make the situation worse, she was surrounded by what she needed and could not have; no money for food or drink, no way to fortify her body to stop her mind from its dangerous flutter. She couldn't even judge how awful it would be to ask the people behind her for a cube of ice.

She had to find out the time. At five o'clock, there would be Henry to help her. She stood and took a step toward the couple playing backgammon. They grew quiet and averted their eyes. The woman angled her chair slightly and the man raised his hand for the bill. Ingrid suppressed an impulse to laugh at them and returned to her chair. She would wait for Jackson. In the mindless babble of voices behind her, she waited for one she could recognize. When it came, it addressed her firmly in Swahili. "This terrace is for hotel guests only, *mama*."

Ingrid looked up and slid the fabric back from her head. A moment after the surprise, something else registered in Jackson's face. "Is Danny here?" she asked.

"Danny is going to Nairobi."

"Where is Finn?"

"Finn is not here."

"Do you know where he is?"

"I know he is not at sea," Jackson said. "I think maybe he has gone to the other side."

"The other side?"

"To Kitali."

"And Stanley?" Ingrid lay back in her chair and put her hands over her face. Nausea was inching its way up to her throat. "Is he there too?"

"Miss Ingrid, you are not well."

She was drawing stares from other guests. "I'm sorry."

"Your foot," Jackson began. "You should not be here."

Ingrid saw that her foot lay outside the cover of the *bui-bui*. Fluid oozed from the thin, torn bandage. Ingrid rose. "I'm leaving, Jackson. Don't worry. Just tell me the time."

It was two o'clock.

※

In the harbor, *Uma* looked lonely on the water, the only vessel not at sea. Ingrid sat on the sand and imagined Finn moving on her deck, his bare feet meeting her warm planks. She imagined being in his body instead of her own, feeling sun and not pain pressing in on her.

Inside the hot prison of her *bui-bui,* her limbs grew damp. She realized the sun was falling on her the way it sometimes fell on Sari; she was absorbing every ray. *If you stay out too long in these black robes,* Ingrid thought, *you cook.*

Down the beach a few lifeless female bodies sunbathed topless. It seemed better to poach in a *bui-bui* than to fry naked. At least a *bui-bui* protected the private domain of a woman's body. Was it a kindness that the island women did not have to endure the stares and judgments of men? If the body was like land that could be either raped or revered, maybe wrapped in *bui-bui*s the island women were able to preserve the moisture of their fertile soil.

Protect yourself! Ingrid wanted to yell down the beach to the naked women. The sun will bake the water out of you until you are weightless and barren. If anything is to grow, if God is ever to take root, you must keep yourself *irrigated.* She felt the heat sink into her, chasing the moisture out onto her skin. She was about to ignite, to burst into flames. If she continued to sit there, how long would it take for her to vanish, to disappear into rank-smelling smoke. *At least I would move then. At least I would rise above this island.*

From nowhere came Colin and his Gideon Bible: *And if I am to offer my body to be burned, I gain nothing . . . if I have not love.*

She was pulling her *bui-bui* over her head, fighting the soft corners so she could climb out. Underneath, her once white dress stuck to her body. She tore at buttons that seemed to have melted into their holes. Air first, she thought. Then water. I will swim to *Uma.* Then I will swim back to the quay to meet Henry at five o'clock. Then I will go to Nairobi and see a doctor.

The bandage unwrapped itself in the sea. She opened her eyes to the sting of salt and saw it swirling below her, trailing her like a tail of kelp. She swam down, away from it, amazed at her strength and speed, at the infirmity she had eluded. She swam up for air and then down again, traversing like a drunken sea snake to the wooden vessel she felt was either a casket or a crib, pulling herself with her arms and legs up and down, toward and away from the darkness, hugging the water and then pushing it away.

It took the last of her strength to climb over the back of the boat. When she could raise herself again, she stayed low, moving on her hands and knees because it hurt less. Her soggy bandage followed her, catching on corners.

She found whiskey and Detol and a crumpled kikoi. No key. She held the kikoi in her hands—Finn's kikoi, its colors bleached from the sun. Rip it, she thought. Rip it into three pieces. Soak one part in Detol and rewrap your foot. Wrap the thickest strip around your torso. *Cover yourself.* Dip the last strip in the sea and wind it around your head, so you remember what it was like down there.

She almost choked on a gulp of whiskey before she lay down to watch the sky, clouds and birds turning overhead like an enormous mobile. She felt she was for the moment safe, though the crib she lay in was not her own.

Kitali

Finn laid his head on a piece of driftwood and watched the sky. The ocean was loud this morning, the waves angry—as angry as the island had become. To divert the anger he felt for Wicks, he ran his offending products through his head. Wire lines, aluminum rods, guns. Products conceived for a different people—people like Wicks, who wanted the reward most; a bullet instead of a fight.

The beach stretched out before him, curving like a gently bent arm, patiently holding the water that crashed against it. The ocean alone provided no relief, no instruction. Today it was cruel. Finn could smell it: the water and life that was churned up from the deeps and hurled roughly onto the sand; bits of men and boats the ocean had swallowed without a murmur of regret, without a blink of recognition.

Finn rose. As he walked, he thought about what he was capable of doing. Taking life, certainly. He had done that before.

There were different ways to take life. One could do it by looking the other way; he had been guilty of it for years. *I am ready to
leave the man I have become,* Finn thought. That man would not feel
death even if it came with a blunt and jagged blade. And if some
other man is brought to life in his place, I will grant him more
respect. I will not watch the foundations of his life be worn away
until the walls come down around him. I will not do it again. We
are all guests, even within ourselves.

The layout of the village of Kitali was something like a solar system. The shelters radiated out from the communal eating hut,
linked to one another by a weblike system of pathways. Finn
guessed that there were about thirty huts. He arrived shortly before sunset and as he navigated his way through the huts looking
for Mohammad, he noticed that some of them had small gardens,
with flowers he recognized from the old village. On that day,
more than a few shelters had their makute siding in place. Only
a handful were open to the elements. In the past, Finn had been
easily disarmed by the inhabitants of Kitali, who looked at him
differently than the people of his own village. There was no
veiled misgiving, no misplaced trust. Here he had the unusual
sensation of being just another human being. Today, though, his
eye went unmet. It made him uneasy.

The villagers seemed unusually active. The cooking hut was
like a fragrant beehive, children skipping in and out carrying
baskets of fresh fruit and gourds of papaya juice. Mohammad was
standing over a circle of women weaving wreaths of flowers for
the children to wear.

"Ah, Finn," Mohammad said, greeting him. "I was hoping
you might come. I even made a little prayer for it."

"Why, what's happening?"

"It's the day of our beginning. What do you call it? Our *birthday*. Maybe you didn't know in here," Mohammad tapped his temple. "But you might have known in here," he said, pressing his hand to his chest.

"You overestimate me, Mohammad."

"I don't think so. Templeton is here."

"Is he?"

"You must stay for dinner. Tonight we tell the story of how we came to be as we are now. I do not think you have heard this story. I do not know if even Fatima has heard it. No doubt she thinks she has." Mohammad smiled. "It's become important because it seems our food has become desirable to those who know nothing of its origin." Mohammad lowered his voice. "If we tell the story loud enough, maybe even Wicks will hear it."

Finn sat down and began steeling himself for Templeton's arrival. He did not know what to say to this man. As a boy, Finn had been entranced by the phenomenon of Templeton's words—how they led from one thing to another, like a stone skipping across the water. Templeton had appeared not long after Finn's father had died, stepping off the boat in a suit and leather shoes. Finn was still like the other island boys, who would run from their game of beach soccer to surround a man who might pay them to run errands. But Templeton had nothing to offer in the way of money. All he had to offer was the strange consolation of talk, talk that eventually evolved into an education about Salama Hotel, which, Finn was made to understand at a young age, would one day become his responsibility. He wasn't around long enough to provide guidance, and Finn came to think of him simply as the man who talked too much about things he didn't want to hear. Years later, when the memory of his father had been corrupted by stories, Finn wondered if his father had been like Templeton in this way. Once he had asked. Templeton had laughed. "Suffice it to say, Finn," he had said at last, "you are your father's son."

Finn saw him from afar because he was dressed all in white. He walked contemplatively, holding his cane behind his back and tapping it along the sand, making dashes between the imprints of his shoes. When he came closer, Finn noticed that he had shaved and looked again like a respectable European.

"Hello, Finn," Templeton said, his face coming to life. "Mohammed told me you might come. I was pleased to hear it—for many reasons. It seems the time has come for us to converge, for history to stagger forward. I am glad you will be here for it."

Templeton bent down to take off his sandals. "Let me tell you something about your island. One knows where the land ends and where the water begins. There is boundary and containment. This I love."

Finn pushed his feet into the sand. Lately, he could not find a place for Templeton in his psyche where he would rest peacefully. He seemed to rile and threaten everything around him.

"Where have you been?"

"Not so far away."

"People have been waiting for you," Finn said. "Some in particular have been very concerned."

Templeton chose to respond to this indirectly. "I have a story for you, Finn," he said. "Not a long one." He sat down in the sand and crossed his legs. "Centuries ago, a Persian man lost first his heart and then his mind," he began. "He was a poet, a man wedded to the word. He went into the desert to forget his love, Layla, who was given to another man."

Finn's expression was indifferent. Templeton continued. "His pilgrimage, like Moses, like Christ, like Mohammad, was to the desert to purify his soul, to seek an answer, a sign. But there was none. There was only the word *Layla* and the sun and the terrible isolation of his voice. Over and over he repeated his desire, her name. He was alone for days and then weeks, with only the sun and the word, this poet who loved Layla, lovely Layla, another man's wife."

Templeton dug into his pocket and pulled out a pipe. He tapped the pipe against his knee and looked out to sea. "When the miracle occurred and she finally came to him, it was too late. Layla the woman, the idea and finally the word evaporated. When she called out to him, he clamped his hands over his ears. 'Leave me in peace,' he told this awful vision. 'Leave me.'

"She stayed the night, sleeping on the sand. Before the stars faded into morning, she left him, following the trail he had written to her about in his poetry. He had told her that the stars would take her to him, if she followed them.

"They died alone, he in the desert, she back in the city where her husband imprisoned her only days after her return." Finn studied the man sitting opposite him, who he had known for so long and yet did not know. He thought briefly of where Ingrid might be at that moment as her professor talked of fruitless searches, love and madness. "And the meaning of this story?" he asked.

"There are many meanings." Templeton almost smiled. "You more than anyone know how I have relied on words. I have been like the poet, ranting to myself about a king. For ten years I searched for him, I abandoned my life. And when I finally found him, when I finally *saw* him, I also saw his journey. I saw his and then I saw my own—and I realized that all I was left with was the shell of my desire. God's justice, I suppose."

Finn waited while Templeton packed his pipe with tobacco and lit it. "And he is here," he finally said. "This king, in Kitali?"

"It is the silence of Kitali that led me to the truth," Templeton said. He was no longer looking at Finn, but at some point beyond him.

"I don't understand. What truth?" Finn said in frustration. "To the truth of this king?"

"To more than a king," Templeton corrected gently. "Imagine looking for a king and finding God."

Finn was silent. The sun had begun its rapid descent toward the sea. Around them, the air was still and soft with color. "And this God," Finn tried. "Does he live in Kitali?"

"Mohammad has made a home in a place where God has always existed. Without his faith, I would never have found this man. Faith links us, even through time. If you don't understand now, perhaps you will someday." Templeton paused, looking at Finn attentively. "It's interesting how we are all here tonight. Even Wicks must be sensing his destiny."

"Since when have you been interested in Wicks' destiny?"

"I am merely an actor with a role, as are you. Mohammad would rather die than fight."

"Fight who?" Finn asked urgently.

Templeton lowered his voice. "Mohammad's niece was raped." He stared hard at Finn, his eyes lit by the setting sun. "She was coming to see me, following the stream inland and on her way to me she was raped. She won't speak to me about it—she's afraid of me now. It had to be a white man: she used to trust me."

Finn was shaking his head. "I don't think Wicks has it in him."

"No?"

"Besides, he's been busy elsewhere."

"I hold him responsible." Finn stared at the older man, at the stubborn set of his jaw. "Don't make the mistake of thinking I am alone," Templeton added. "I'm not the only one who thinks something must be done."

"So you have enlisted others to further your resolution."

Templeton looked at him quizzically. "I didn't have to. Your confusion is that you don't know if you're one of them." Templeton uncrossed his legs and rose to leave. "I did not ask to play a role in your life," he said. "But we are intertwined and there's nothing either of us can do about it. I am glad you are here tonight. It is right for us to be together now."

After Templeton had left, Finn gripped the handle of his walking cane, which for some reason he had left behind. Eventually he made his way to a shelter at the outskirts of the village and lay down on a makute mat as the light faded and the first torches were lit around Kitali.

When the sun had set completely and the night was dark, Finn found his way easily to the center hut, where a fire had been lit for the ceremony. Men and women gathered, arranging themselves in small groups. Finn hung back, listening to the low hum of conversation. Mohammad appeared out of nowhere and touched Finn's arm. "Come," he said. "Sit with us."

Templeton settled himself across from Finn, his face animated in the firelight as he exchanged greetings. Wooden bowls were distributed, followed by squares of colored cloth woven into fine patterns. The children were excited and fidgeted until a clear female voice started a song of thanks and others joined in.

When the song was over, Finn could not help smiling at the jubilant mood around the circle. "This is a special day," Mohammad said, as platters of food began to arrive and the air grew fragrant with the smell of coconut curry and roasted vegetables. "A day when once, years ago, a great change came to our people. It is said that there will be a time when change will come again. But as is fitting at this time, let me take you back to the beginning."

Mohammad accepted a cup of tea and sipped it, surveying his guests through the steam. He closed his eyes and inhaled the fumes. No one spoke. Soon the sound of the surf and the song of night insects became like conversation, like music, and it was no longer silent at all. At this point, Mohammad began. His voice was soft and low and seemed to find a place between the surf and the night song, so that neither was diminished. Templeton smiled and bobbed his head, swaying slightly as if listening to a fine instrument.

"Our resources have always been limited by the sparse foliage on this dry side of the island. Thankfully, we have been blessed with water. It came to us like a miracle, trickling its way through the sand. The elders accepted this as a sign from God that they had taken the right course. 'See what happens,' they would say, 'when evil is far away.' "

As the food was passed around the circle, Mohammad went on to describe how he had come to decide on the location of the new village after consulting with the white-haired *mganga,* who gave him the tools he needed to find the water. But the final tool, he stressed, was faith. He had been guided by the stars and by faith. "A faith that was patient," Mohammad added. "Not angry or vengeful—a faith that allowed us to see with clear vision God's greater plan and to have the wisdom not to interfere." Finn noticed that first one man and then another leaned toward Templeton and spoke into his ear while he nodded, pressing down on the air in front of him with his hand.

Mohammad blessed the food, which was consumed with joy.

It was a rare meal. Each dish contained a multitude of flavors that arrived on the tongue at respectful intervals, leaving the perfectly sated diners with the impression that every appetite they had ever possessed had been recognized and honored.

"And my friend Templeton," Mohammad said. "You said you have something to share with us?"

"Yes," Templeton said, setting his plate down and pulling a piece of paper from his shirt pocket. "I have long been an admirer of Swahili poetry. Recently I came across a poem that seemed appropriate to the occasion—to Kitali. Some of you may know it. It reminded me of our many discussions, Mohammad. It could be a manifesto for your village, a blessing for this meal. It could be any number of things. The poem was written by Sayyid Abdulla bin Ali bin Nasir almost two hundred years ago." Templeton put on his glasses and began to read in Swahili:

> *How many wealthy men have we not seen*
> *Who in their splendor shone like the sun itself,*
> *Strong in their great hoards of ivory,*
> *Powerful in stocks of silver and of gold?*
> *To them the whole world bowed down in homage,*
> *For them the Road of Life was broad and straight.*
> *They went their ways in arrogance, unafraid,*
> *Heads high in air, their eyes screwed up in scorn.*
> *They swung their arms and tossed their haughty heads,*
> *Retainers went behind them and before.*
> *Wherever they went they took the seat of honor*
> *And many bodyguards surrounded them . . .*

> *Know you, the day will come when over all*
> *The World there will be change: the Seven Heavens*
> *Will be moved from their place. The Sun and Moon*

Will tumble from the sky. And for us men
There will be fire and heat, both without cease.
Where will you turn on that last day, when flames
Rage within your spleen, and from your scalp
The skin is singed—where will you flee for help?
Tell me your refuge, for I would share it too.

Never forget that Day, when multitudes
Will assemble for every deed to be revealed;
That Day when the oppressed will kneel before
Their God and cry, "Decide between him and me!
Judge us, O Lord God! See how I was wronged
By this man—judge us in Thy rectitude!"

And God, by Whom all things shall be disposed,
Shall judge, repaying each his wrongs as due.
Nor can the injured ever be paid back
With golden nuggets, nor with coin of gold.
Money, even were it offered as recompense,
Is not accepted. Compensation must
Be rendered in good deeds performed in life.
And he whose record shows neither good deeds
Nor wrongs incurred from others—he, like a horse,
Is bridled, with bit pressed to his mouth,
And forced to bear the sins of those he wronged.

When Templeton had finished he looked at Finn, who turned away. A murmur arose around the fire as men and women discussed what they had heard, speaking in whispers about this day of judgment, when the sun and moon would tumble from the sky.

The mood of the gathering had changed; tranquility had been

replaced by agitated whispers that traveled around the circle like electricity. Mohammad somberly thanked Templeton and rose to calm the villagers. "He who wants all will miss all," he said, slowly and deliberately. "Let us not forget that this is a day of rejoicing, not a day of fire. Now, after dinner, we will have music and dance." Mohammad smiled at the faces that were now turned to him. "I wish you all peace and God's blessing on this beautiful day."

When the meal had finished, the others gradually rose one by one, a few touching Templeton's shoulder before they left. The platters and bowls were slowly cleared away, and in the background was a low drumbeat and the soft wailing of song.

"I will be visiting Stanley Wicks later this evening," Mohammad said to Templeton when they were at last alone.

"Why ever for?" Templeton asked.

"He wanted to meet face-to-face, today of all days. I sent word that a meeting would not be possible until tomorrow, but he insisted that we meet tonight." Mohammad gazed at the fire. "I imagine it is about the water."

"What are you going to propose?" Templeton asked.

"That if he is patient, perhaps the water will change its mind."

Templeton laughed. "I don't know how receptive he'll be."

"He will not like it," Mohammad said, rising to leave. "But we cannot become enemies." He paused. "The island is too small for anger."

When Mohammad had left, Templeton moved closer to Finn and sought to find out what had brought him there. Finn was distant as he told him about Fatima and her concerns. What he wanted to talk about was the poem. Templeton took some time to respond. As always, there was no quick answer. He talked vaguely about the riches you could see with the naked eye and others you could only sense. He talked about a day of retribution that reminded Finn of Fatima's dramatic proclamations and his mind began to wander until it seemed Templeton's oration was coming to an end. "On that final day, Finn," he concluded, "justice is done. Any life worth living comes to such a day," he added. "Yours is no exception."

"My life?" Finn asked, rising to leave. "What would you know about that?"

"While we haven't seen much of each other these past years, we are not strangers, you and I."

"No. Strangers don't have such high expectations."

Templeton removed his glasses and rubbed his eyes. "If you're referring to my letter," he said, shaking his head in mute protest, "I merely wanted you to know what was happening here. This island is your home."

Finn smiled rigidly. "You forget who my father was," he said and turned to go, leaving Templeton illuminated in the dull glow of the now spent fire.

Not long after he had left Templeton, Finn took a torch and abandoned the warm hub of Kitali to skirt the site of Wicks' hotel. He noticed that the construction had progressed considerably. The site was larger than he remembered it, and some of the structures seemed almost completed. Holding the torch low, he walked inland, to the farthest point of the site. There he crossed back over to Mohammad's property and followed the stream that meandered through palms and sand.

Finn stopped when he came to an obstruction, where the

water had begun to pool. It took him a moment to figure out what it was. Holding his torch up, he could see that Wicks or Gus had started to build a dam to raise the water level high enough to feed a pipe leading back to the construction site. The pipe was raised off the ground and supported by a truss. Finn jumped over the stream to inspect it more closely.

※

Wicks was sitting in the center of the largest of his round rooms, a kerosene lamp turned up dangerously high, surrounded by blueprints. Finn knocked on the wall next to where the door would be. Wicks started at the noise and then hunched back around when he saw who it was. "Hello, Finn," he said sullenly. "What brings you to these parts?" Finn approached the island of paper, noting that Wicks smelled intensely of bug repellent.

"I came to talk to you about boundaries," he said.

Wicks continued to examine his plans. "I see," he said, without looking up. "How can I help you?"

"Have you or one of your crew recently helped yourself to an island girl?"

Wicks looked genuinely bewildered. "I don't know what you're talking about."

"Mohammad's niece was raped," Finn said. "You should know that the evidence against you is mounting."

"I'd never touch Mohammad's niece," Wicks entreated. "You know that, Finn."

"What I know doesn't matter. It's what others believe. In the meantime," Finn continued, stepping now on one of his plans, "you're building on land that isn't yours. We both know this."

Wicks stuck a pencil behind his ear and gazed indifferently at Finn's foot. "We're working on that," he said. "I'm going to

arrange a deal, a little give and take. It will all work out fine."
Wicks broke his stare to look at Finn. "Isn't it a little late in the
evening to be worrying about property lines?"

"You're breaking the law, Wicks." Finn squatted so he was
level with him. "People here don't take kindly to this. We have
different ways of dealing with those who violate our laws than
you do back home in England."

"So you've come to threaten me, have you?" Wicks said as he
gestured irascibly at his plans. "Tell me, Finn, how much can a
few meters matter?"

"What matters is your disrespect for Kitali."

"I have great respect for Kitali," Wicks said. "Particularly its
water."

"If you had respect," Finn said. "You would un-dam that
stream and take your pipes back to your own property."

"I can't oblige you, I'm afraid," Wicks said lightly. "We need
water to mix cement. We're finally going to have some level
floors around here. Are you concerned about competition?"

Finn rose abruptly to take his leave. "I've said all I have to say,
Wicks. Consider yourself warned."

When Finn returned to his shelter, he lit a fire and began honing
a machete. Templeton appeared from the shadows holding two
cups of tea. He paused before coming forward. "I heard about
Boni," he said finally as he set a cup of tea next to Finn.

"I don't want to talk about Boni," Finn said, ignoring the
offering of tea.

"I understand you found him out there," Templeton said.
"Saved his life."

"Boni's dead. I didn't save anything."

"You gave his life back to him. He chose to die."

Finn stopped to oil his whetting stone. "It was Wicks' damn wire line. Boni didn't know any better."

"I'm sorry, Finn. I know he was a friend of yours." Templeton followed the motion of Finn's hand, massaging his own as if to relieve pain. "Do you want to tell me what the knife is for?"

Finn was engrossed in the sharpening of the knife, vigorously shaving it against the smooth slab, filling the silence with the swish and ping of metal against oiled stone. Testing the edge of the blade with his fingertips, he glanced at the man across the fire. Even in the forgiving light, he looked old and defenseless. "What do you see in this place?" he asked evenly. "Another battle no one asked you to fight?"

Templeton was silent. The fire crackled between them. Finn got up to gather more wood, snapping precious branches in half to conserve them. Templeton joined him and when they returned to the fire, sat down stiffly. The effort of gathering the wood had tired him. Finn pretended not to notice.

"I don't think you understand that I love this place," Templeton said at last. "That I have loved it for as long as you've been alive. What I have seen breaks my heart. For years there has been nothing to do but watch. I can no longer watch." Finn continued to sharpen his knife. Templeton took out his pipe. "Tell me about Ingrid," he said.

Finn laid the knife down. "You like to come when there's something to save, don't you? You like playing God." Finn threw a few branches onto the fire so that the flames burned brighter.

"I can't even play godfather, Finn. I'm a man with profound and obvious limitations."

"Well, it didn't work to push her in my direction, if that was your plan. You misjudged. She went the other way, fell backward. Fell into Wicks' arms."

"Wicks?"

Finn enjoyed the wrinkle of concern that appeared on his brow. "What's happened?" Templeton demanded. Finn related a truncated story about her foot, the infection and the malaria that followed. He didn't mention his night visits or elaborate on the subject of Wicks.

"Where is she now?" Templeton asked. "Who's taking care of her?"

Finn ignored the questions. "I'm wondering what your plan was."

"I wasn't aware of a plan, Finn."

"I think you always have a plan. I think your plan was to instigate some kind of insurrection in Kitali to give you an excuse to implement your own ideas of how things should be on this island. I think you didn't want her interfering."

The wrinkle on Templeton's brow smoothed. "I see you've decided to care," he said. Finn did not look up from his knife. Templeton reached for the machete and took it from him, wrapping his fingers around the handle and holding the knife out in front of him. "And what about your plan, Finn?"

"The man who doesn't act is as bad as the man who acts wrongly."

"I see," Templeton said with a smile. "And what 'act' do you have in mind?"

"None of your business."

Templeton was turning the machete in the firelight. The blade flashed. "Have you asked yourself who you are acting for?"

The names sounded in Finn's brain. *Boni, Jonah, Fatima.* "Because Wicks doesn't understand what's at stake."

"What's at stake?"

Myself, Finn thought. Because by not acting, I have continued my father's work. But again, he said nothing.

"A godfather can have many uses," Templeton said, gripping the machete in his hand. The knife made him look stronger, younger even. "He can teach and protect. With you, it seems I have failed at both. But tonight I will try to change that." When the light of the fire died, he rose. "Would you like to come?"

❧

Templeton moved noiselessly toward the construction site, his white shirt disembodied from his brown legs and arms, the long knife hanging at his side. The moon glinted off the machete blade and Finn felt the beginnings of anxiety stir inside him. He followed Templeton as he headed in the general direction of Wicks' sleeping shelter. What was he going to do—scare Wicks into compliance? Finn slowed his pace and watched the white shirt fade into the night. His knife, his act, had been taken from him. The germ of his resolve had been lifted and transplanted and now belonged to another man.

Templeton stopped a few yards away from Wicks' shelter and waited for Finn. "I gather you were going to kill him," he whispered. Finn stared at him in the darkness in confusion. "Here's the first lesson, then," Templeton said under his breath and then slid away. Finn reached out, but it was too late. He stood in numb suspension and watched as the white shirt approached the open-air sleeping shelter.

Finn saw the blade go up and come down. He closed his eyes and against blackness listened to the sound of contact between steel and flesh, the resistance of the bone being met and overcome. A terrible moment of calm was pierced by a harrowing scream. Then a gun fired—once, and again. Templeton was back by his side, his breathing heavy. "Done," he said.

"What's done?" Finn whispered. More shots were fired. Templeton's hand closed around Finn's arm. A paroxysm of bullets and the unrecognizable sound of a human voice convulsing in hysteria.

"Come with me," Templeton said, putting his hand on Finn's shoulder. As the older man's weight came down on him, Finn realized he had been wounded. He grasped Templeton's waist to give him more support.

"It wasn't necessary to kill him," Templeton told him as they limped inland. "A hand was enough."

"You cut off his hand?"

"Part of getting older," Templeton explained, "is that you understand the cost of things. You learn not to overpay. I think it's what he owed."

CHAPTER

31

A Conversation with God

*S*tanley had been sleeping with his gun since Boni had lost his hand. Along with a snifter of Armagnac, he swallowed one of Daisy's Dalmanes to help himself relax. With the drink, he would crash like a broken elevator into unconsciousness and enjoy a kind of simulated rest. In the morning, he'd feel like he'd been hit in the head with a mallet, but he preferred this to the dreams his brain had been manufacturing for the past month.

That night he was especially grateful for his new sleeping formula. At another time, he might have been stricken by the day's events and tormented for hours by insomnia. Even before he had swallowed his second Dalmane, he had been able to dismiss the encounter with Finn. The world was conspiring against him and while he had never felt so alone, he had also never felt so strong, so free of doubt.

He woke with a shock that made him think of the sudden systemic failings that occurred as the body aged: heart attacks, strokes, aneurysm. One of these frightful things had happened to him, a relatively young man. He tried to think of what to do when something unimaginably horrendous like this happened all at once, like a stone falling from the sky onto your head. Should he lie down, run, cover his skull? His father had survived a mild stroke and Stanley had witnessed the progression of thoughts in the moments and hours following. After the shock came the questions, rattling now like loose bolts in his own head. Where did the stone come from? Did God throw the stone? And if so, why did he want you on your knees at that particular point?

But there was none of the disorientation or vague surprise of a mild stroke. A very pronounced sensation was moving through him like a high-speed train, starting at his left hand. *I'm having a heart attack,* he thought. *God has struck me down.* It was his last thought before he transformed into something incapable of thought, a wild animal defending itself. He could see nothing and hear less because now he was screaming, a bloodcurdling sound that seemed to be coming from somewhere else. That he knew the scream was coming from him made him scream louder. His other hand had assumed an intelligence of its own and was firing a gun. One shot after another. Stanley watched his hand in amazement. He himself was finished but his hand wanted to keep fighting. Where was the enemy? Was it God, the rock thrower from above? Would his hand start firing into the sky? Then God sent him a sign: a light, and in the light a gleaming target. God was not the enemy after all. God was directing him toward the real enemy: a man.

Mohammad stood in front of him with his arms outstretched. Stanley did not understand the outstretched arms or the pained expression. He did not understand anything and understanding itself seemed to belong to another world. What Stanley saw in

Mohammad was a symbol of everything that had gone wrong. A glowing bull's-eye, his nemesis in this life and who knew how many others. Stanley experienced an instant of ecstatic release as his right arm, still intelligent and calm, took aim at Mohammad's hairless head and pulled the trigger.

Stanley's gunshots woke Nelson on *Tarkar*. He had dozed off, a glass of brandy balanced on his belly, when the startling sound of gunfire bolted him out of bed, spilling the brandy and shattering the glass. He hoisted himself up to the deck and positioned the spotlight on the shore, scanning the beach with the beam. It was empty. But he could hear some sort of commotion inland.

Suddenly, from out of the trees, stumbled a figure. In the yellow circle of light, Nelson found Stanley careening toward the water. He was doing something with his hands. Nelson lurched toward the driver's seat and started the engine, yanking the radio from its roost while fixing Stanley in the light and sounding the horn. As he maneuvered *Tarkar* recklessly close to the shore, Nelson saw that Wicks was holding his own hand, that it was not attached to anything. He immediately began shortwaving Nairobi, an emergency wavelength to the British Consul. Wicks had given Nelson the code in case of "dire circumstance."

"I think he's lost his hand," Nelson shouted into the radio, edging the boat slowly around a sandbank.

To get a plane from Nairobi would take four hours, maybe longer. They had to find a pilot and it was the middle of the night. Nelson told the man on the other line that money was no object. He read the coordinates of Kitali and then kicked the first-aid chest out from under the bench. In it, thank heaven, were five vials of morphine.

By the time Nelson reached the shore, Stanley had lain down on the beach. He was calm and disturbingly quiet. Nelson realized he had gone into shock. He carried Stanley into the water and heaved him aboard where he sprawled like a drunk. Stanley was mumbling, nearly unconscious now. "You see, God is on my side after all. He is. He is. I'm sorry I don't go to church. I'm sorry my son doesn't. He was baptized, you know. You must have known that, of course, you were there. I must start praying. I will start praying now." Stanley began reciting the Lord's Prayer. When he had finished that, he started on the few graces he knew. Nelson wrapped Stanley's wrist tightly with a kikoi to stem the flow of blood and then put the severed hand in a cooler. Before covering him with a blanket, he stuck a vial of morphine into his arm and listened while Stanley continued, more slowly now, his conversation with God.

The night was cool and starry. A night, Finn thought, like any other night. Strangely still now. Templeton leaned heavily on him, silent with pain. Every few minutes they stopped so the older man could catch his breath. Beneath Finn's arm, Templeton's shirt was damp with sweat. He was leading them somewhere, he said, his face glistening with strain. It was not far now. They had already walked a mile or so inland, following the stream.

A single voice pierced the quiet night. Another joined in, a lamentable wail. Templeton cupped a hand to his ear as other voices joined in the collective howl of grief. "Mohammad's dead," he said. "The bullets after I was gone were for him."

"How do you know?"

"I understand this howl. You understand it too. I will have to go back."

For a moment, Finn stood perfectly still and listened. "I don't think that's a good idea," he said stiffly.

"Not now," Templeton protested weakly. "Later."

They had reached a clearing with a tent that glowed silver in the moonlight. A fire pit had been dug into the ground and nearby were a wooden table and a folding chair. "My second home," Templeton explained, releasing Finn's shoulder and collapsing beside the tent. On the ground next to the tent was a pile of wood and a washbasin filled with water. "There's some iodine inside," he said feebly. "Along with a bottle of whiskey. Little medicine bag in the corner."

Finn tried not to think of Mohammad as he bent over this man who was responsible for so much. Wicks' bullet had bored into the lower part of Templeton's thigh. Finn made a tourniquet from his shirt and tied it above the wound. "Here's your balance. A hand for a hand," Templeton grimaced. "And a leg for a leg."

"Whose leg besides yours?"

"Ingrid's."

Finn cinched the tourniquet until Templeton yelped. "And Mohammad's life?"

"Leaders are sent from God to mend the tears between men," Templeton said. "Mohammad wasn't meant to die."

"Is that right?" Finn left to lay wood for a fire. He spoke to Templeton over his shoulder because he could not yet bear to look at him. "Mohammad was the best man I knew."

"Everything has a purpose, Finn. You must trust that there will be another such man." Finn broke a branch over his knee. "If you have patience, I think life may still surprise you. I know this about you."

"If you know me so well, you might have known not to take the knife from me."

"And have you incarcerated for murder? No."

"Why did you think I was going to kill him?"

"Because your father and I were old friends. While you've been putting up admirable resistance, I think you are partially if not wholly propelled by his rage." Templeton lay back on the sand. "I couldn't bear to see the first act driven by that rage be your last. Rage can create as well as destroy. It can be beautiful, poetic. It can be *just*. You haven't seen that yet."

"And your rage, is it beautiful? Just?" Finn said, going to the basin to wash his hands. "Anyway, those are not qualities I associate with my father."

"As a young man, he *blazed* with them."

"So what happened?" Finn asked.

"Time." Templeton said, grimacing as Finn straightened his leg. "Time is the answer no one can wait for."

"I think you're as crazy as he was," Finn said.

"You're entitled to your own beliefs. But I don't think my first act as a godfather was unsuccessful. I think it was well worth the wait."

"I never intended to touch Wicks," Finn said quietly. "Just his property."

Templeton considered this. "And would that have been enough?"

"We are fighting different wars, you and I."

Finn boiled water over the fire to sterilize his pocketknife and then examined Templeton's leg, pushing and prodding the inflamed lip of the wound while blood oozed thickly down his leg and pooled on the sand. "It's not a splinter, for God's sake," Templeton protested. "You can't squeeze it out."

"Drink your whiskey." Without warning, Finn poured a little iodine on the wound.

"Jesus!" Templeton exploded.

"Hold still, will you? I think it went through." Finn raised Templeton's leg until he could see the other side. Templeton howled. Finn held a piece of wood to his mouth. "Bite this," he said. Templeton dug his teeth into the wood. His brow was damp with sweat. "You're not drunk enough."

When Finn had finished his exploration, Templeton lay in exhausted repose. The bullet had passed straight through his leg, and seemed not to have hit an artery or shattered the bone. Finn fed him whiskey from the cap until Templeton held his hand up misty-eyed, and, Finn realized, drunk. "You know," Templeton began. "I remember you as a boy."

"Do you?" Finn asked, gently cleaning the wound.

"I also remember being as young as you are now and looking into the eyes of age and seeing what was to come. And I remember trying then as I am trying now to feel not terror and disbelief, but comfort. We all join together in the end. In the end, isolation is the dream and the merging of all matter is what is real."

Finn eyed his patient skeptically. "I forgot how drink makes you talk."

"I'm an old man now, Finn. Look at this face!" Templeton patted his hands over his cheeks. "The past is written here, and here, written in patterns unrecognizable to the young. Your father is in these lines." Templeton stroked his cheeks. "I recognize the people in these patterns, like mandalas that are not quite fully erased. I can still make out the outlines of the ghosts who have stayed with me, of what was important. I can see it long after it has been destroyed and is nothing more than a pile of colorful sand. It's all there, you see, just arranged differently." Templeton reached for more whiskey. Finn moved the bottle out of his reach.

"I have to get to *Uma*," Finn said. "There's a first-aid box. We need morphine and clean bandages."

"You're a good boy, Finn. I don't know if your father ever told you."

❧

Ingrid had left the island. She was far away, dreaming from her room in Michigan. The night beyond her dream was white with snow. She was with Jonathan, floating above campus, naked and cold and then, in another beat, she was alone under a hard, bright sun that did not warm her. Finn was there, his face replacing the sun, his features painfully clear. She willed the face closer and realized with a dreamlike lucidity that if she were struck down tomorrow, it was this face she would see: the brown of the skin, the blue of the eyes, the silent mouth. How long it had taken her to know these features. The understanding of this face had changed her.

The dream traveled on in the peaceful world of this single face, bringing her to something else; the memory of love's arrival as a total surprise, like lightning, like a slap. Then they were meeting for the first time. She came to him differently this time. She came understanding more; she knew about the other women, and the God that allowed him these women and then, almost as an afterthought, gifted him with the strange peace of the sea.

Ingrid watched him with the women. He slept with his back to them. He felt them fingering the marlin tattooed on his shoulder. He feigned sleep and shrugged at their questions. It was a fish he liked to catch, a fighting fish.

Then Ingrid was in his sea, her hair still long and covering her like a shawl. Underwater, she could see everything, even the sky. His fish swam all around her. He was so near now. All she had to do was wait.

CHAPTER

32

The Final Journey

Finn made his way quickly to the beach where Gus kept his
motorized skiff. Shoving the boat off the sand, he pulled the
starter cord so forcefully that the engine surged out of the water.
A gaseous cloud formed in the darkness as the noise of the engine
reverberated through the night.

Finn cranked the handle to top speed. He did not try to comprehend the length of the endless night; he would not think
about what had happened until morning, and maybe not even
then. There was a weightless inevitability to the events, and now
that they had happened, now that the violent adjustment had
been made, he felt strangely numb. He supposed he would feel,
at some point, anger. Then maybe something more painful. Mohammad was dead; the island would never again be the same.

Finn tied the skiff to *Uma*. The sky had taken a pale step away
from night. Soon the muezzin would carry to his ears the first call
to prayer: another day beginning. He clambered on board,
clumsy with exhaustion and oblivious to the huddled form

curled under the fishing seat. His initial thought was that it was one of the island boys hiding out as they sometimes did from their parents after a first beer, a first woman, a first betrayal. But this body was wrapped with bits of kikoi and, even in the darkness, he could see the skin was white.

He went to her quickly, kneeling down and feeling her faint breath with his hand. He spoke her name and when she did not answer, he touched her cheek. She was cold. He picked her up and cradled her to him, putting his hand over her cropped head, as if to seal in the remaining heat. The deepness of her sleep frightened him. "Wake up," he said. "Wake up now."

He walked with her around the deck, trying to warm her. When she finally opened her eyes she looked up at him as if he were the latest apparition in a long dream she no longer cared about. He sat down and held her close to him, pressing his warmth into her.

The sky over Tomba was growing light with the dawn when she began to stir against him. "We have to go now," he said into her ear. "We have to get you dressed." He set her down and looked back before lowering himself to the galley. Her face was fragmented with uncertainty. He brought her hot tea with honey and crackers, and put his own shirt over her raised arms and found her another kikoi.

"Are you okay?" Ingrid asked, studying Finn's face.

"I'm tired," he said.

"I took the pills you gave me." She shivered, holding the warm cup.

"And then you went for a swim?"

"No. I looked for you. I wanted to say good-bye, and to thank you." Finn watched her recoil after burning her tongue on the tea. "Then Abdul locked me out."

"He's an old fool."

"I had nowhere to go. I was so hot." Ingrid fought back her tears. "I didn't know what to do."

"I'm sorry." Finn eased the cup out of her hand. "I'm sorry you were alone."

"Whenever I need something on this island, I can't seem to find it," she said.

"Well, you'll be seeing your professor soon," he said. "That's one thing you can stop looking for."

This information left her silent. Finn watched her closely as she hung her head, shifting his gaze as a sliver of sun pierced the horizon. The instant the warm light touched them, he knew what was wrong with the morning: there had been no call to prayer. In his lifetime on the island, in the thousands of mornings he had seen melt into afternoon, he had never heard silence replace the call of the muezzin.

He hurried Ingrid, leading her to the skiff, stepping down into it first and turning to help her. She fell with exhausted faith, almost tripping into his arms. She sat across from him and watched the sky change colors over his shoulder. Finn was disturbed by the too silent morning. He wanted her to speak.

"Is he like a father to you?" he asked, pushing them off from *Uma*.

"Who?"

"Templeton."

Ingrid forced a laugh.

"When I was young I loved a girl, a Moslem girl," he said, shifting to pull the starter cord. "I didn't know it was the wrong thing. Everyone told me. Everything was wrong because of it. I had to surrender finally. There are people you can't love."

"That's not what he is to me."

"What is he, then?" Finn asked, repositioning himself on the seat.

Ingrid looked up as they moved away from *Uma*. "Do you have the North Star here? It's a fixed point in the sky. When you find it you can find north and then the other directions. He has been my North Star."

"He doesn't seem that steady to me."

"No." She paused. "But he's steady in his unsteadiness. He doesn't betray himself. He's like you in that way. It used to inspire me."

"Such loyalty to self can destroy other people," Finn said.

"Like you?"

"Not me," Finn said firmly. "Not yet."

They did not speak for some time, until the sound of sand sliding under the thin wooden floor of the skiff brought her back. Ingrid blinked and straightened as Finn pulled the motor up and jumped into the water. He dragged the skiff onto the beach above Kitali, his mind focused on the continuing silence of the morning. Ingrid helped herself out of the skiff. He let her hop for a few meters and then picked her up. "This is easier, I think," he said.

She looped her arm around his neck. She could not hear the sound of his steps or even feel that he was walking. They seemed to be floating. The light angled through the leaves and flickered against her eyelids like flames.

In a clearing was a man lying with a shirt over his head, blood spattered on his pants. She knew him immediately and stiffened in Finn's arms. Finn held her tighter. She turned her head away and looked back to where they'd come from. Finn laid her down on the sand and leaned her against a stump, kneeling next to her as if for protection.

"Templeton," Finn said. "Come to—you've got a visitor."

Templeton pulled the shirt from his eyes and squinted. "Is that Ingrid?" he asked, working his way up onto his elbows. "Why, you've cut your hair!" He smiled sheepishly and gestured toward his leg. "Look what your old advisor's done now. Got himself shot in the leg."

Ingrid's own wounded leg twitched involuntarily. She stared at it as if at some kind of animal and waited for it to twitch again.

Templeton glanced at Finn. "She's taken some Fansidar and has been without food or water all night," Finn explained quietly. "I imagine she's in a bit of shock." He left Ingrid's side to prepare a syringe of morphine, which he plunged into Templeton's arm. Templeton fell back to the ground and closed his eyes. A smile melted across his face. "Come closer, dear," he said to Ingrid. "I want to see you."

Ingrid didn't move. She thought that if she didn't move or speak, it was possible he would stop talking to her. She was not prepared to contend with his presence, his absence, or anything about him.

"If you have anything to say to him, now would be the time," Finn advised.

"I would like some water," she said.

"Ingrid," Templeton said faintly. "Come let me look at you— it's been a long time."

Ingrid drank from a large container of water and curled up on the sand. Her chill was returning. Outside her sphere of stillness, she could hear their voices and knew they were arguing about her but she could not summon enough energy to sift through their words for meaning.

Then, sometime later, Templeton was at her side, telling her he had nothing to teach her now, that he had nothing more to give her. He offered her some whiskey to dull the pain. When the liquor had fortified her enough to look at him, she searched his face for changes. She pulled herself off the ground and moved toward him on her knees, propelled by the possibility that if she got closer, she might be able to see something that would return him to her. His face revealed nothing. Tears began to well up inside her but she shook her head in resistance. *Don't let him see you like this.* "Why did you want me to leave the island?" she asked, forcing the words out.

Templeton's features finally altered into an expression she recognized. He considered her solemnly. "Because I couldn't take responsibility for what might happen to you."

"It didn't stop it from happening."

Templeton smiled sadly. "So I gather," he said, reaching for her hand.

Ingrid drew back and surveyed what she could see of her surroundings. "Is this where you've been?"

"Mostly," he said.

"I want you to tell me about it," Ingrid said. "All of it. You have to do that for me."

"You make a good detective," he granted. "I was right about that much. I didn't want you wasting those skills on me." Then, as if knowing she needed to hear his voice, Templeton began to talk. He described the difficulties posed by his object of research, the maddening uncertainties and ambiguities of Swahili culture and history. There were three versions of the same story, four different dates, five different centuries. And now, there was this new hybrid spin-off of Mohammad's village, which Templeton had only just begun to observe. "Such a harmonious people," he said. "A people who are both more and less evolved than those they left. But their success is fragile. It depends on isolation." Templeton stared up at the trees, and Ingrid watched as his eyes began almost imperceptibly to fill with tears. "I have lost a friend," he said faintly.

"Tell me," Ingrid urged.

Templeton shook his head and wiped his eyes. "This island is one of the last places where the Swahili still exist in cultural purity. Imagine losing a people who have, over the centuries, managed to survive, keeping their world intact through so many interlopers and plunderings. Losing them will mean losing their wisdom, their spirits, their God. And we will lose them. Not suddenly. They will be gradually absorbed, seduced by the promise of prosperity. Because of Salama Hotel, it is happening quickly. Already much has died, more than Mohammad ever dared imagine."

He continued with restrained passion to explain how the Swahili had maintained their identity through the successive influences of the Persian, Chinese, Portuguese and finally the British. Their history was a testimony not only to the engulfing vitality of mercantile society, but to the flexibility necessary to survive.

"This village—" He struggled for words. "I think I made what you could call a mistake of the intellect by assuming that if I could establish facts about the origins of this anomalous people, their place in the world would be solidified. But what are my tenets, my suppositions, my facts in the face of a disappearing God?" he burst out fervently. "We are here to live. To be present for a short time, to witness the small disturbances and exhilarations, to feel them as they pass. It's the simplest thing in the world, and most of us fail. I have failed. Out here I was rescued, rescued by a drowning people."

Templeton groped for his pipe. "This is the kind of talk that has made Finn loathe my company," he said, settling back finally.

Finn glanced at him and almost smiled. "I know I've disappointed you, Ingrid. Forgive me. I know how strong you are. You may not, but I have seen it in you from the beginning. Now, come, you're an intelligent girl, can't you forgive me? Speak to me, Ingrid—we're all running out of time."

Ingrid was tired. The whiskey had relaxed her and she knew Templeton had already won. He had won years ago, before she had ever thought of coming to Africa, when he had taught a young student to imagine a different world. "Forgiveness," she said numbly. "I have no choice but to forgive you."

Finn began to unwrap the swatch of kikoi from her foot. "It's abscessed," he said. "We'll have to drain it. Give her another drink."

Templeton handed her the bottle of whiskey. "Now we must talk about you," he said. "What's all this about Stanley Wicks?"

Ingrid glanced at Finn, whose eyes dropped to the ground. "He's my friend," she said.

"Nothing more?"

"He's been kind to me. Why do you ask?"

"No reason. I'm just curious."

Finn prepared a second syringe and took Ingrid's arm in his hand. After a tiny prick, Ingrid was flooded with a warmth that shamed the whiskey. She hugged her arms around herself to keep it in and began to rock gently back and forth. Templeton slid around before her as she tried to focus on his words. "It's unlikely they'll be able to reattach the hand," he was saying. "Too much time has passed."

Finn loosened Ingrid's hold on herself and laid her on the sand. "The worst is over," he told her. "This will hardly hurt."

"What hand?" Ingrid asked in confusion. Words and their meaning were once again beginning to zigzag in her mind.

Finn sunk the knife in three times; three short cuts, two on either side of her ankle, the third near the original wound. It didn't hurt exactly. Instead of the dull, throbbing pulse there was a sharp, quick pain and then relief as the infection rushed out, soaking into the gauze Finn pressed to the incisions. Ingrid watched the tops of the mangrove trees, looking for the occasional sunlit gull.

"Now, when this finishes, I'm going to put more gauze in there to keep the cut open so that the rest of the infection can escape." Finn filled an empty syringe with water tinctured with iodine and irrigated each incision. "You've got to keep it clean. It's very important to keep it clean, do you understand?"

"I understand," Ingrid said, and then lost consciousness.

When she came to, several hours later, she had regained a modicum of focus. She turned immediately to Templeton and asked him to explain what he had found. "Your king," she pressed. "Did he exist? Did the amulet?"

Templeton smiled. "What do you think?"

Ingrid pointed at the sky. "I think if the amulet existed it came from the desert up north, where Arab traders used amulets to find water in the desert. The stars I saw in your office."

"And?"

"And if this was where your king lived, maybe he brought it here. It may have been a gift. Someone he traveled with."

"Suppositions. What else?"

"There are suras and ayats etched onto it," Ingrid said. "The verses you transcribed in your notebook."

She closed her eyes and recited. " '*In the creation of the heavens and the earth; in the alternation of night and day; in the ships that sail the ocean with cargoes beneficial to man; in the water which God sends down from the sky . . .*' These are signposts—but for what? There are two hands. The writing is more crude than the inscription surrounding it. Maybe the king added the sura himself. Below it are three lines, possibly a symbol for water. I don't know where it comes from. It's not Arabic."

"Ah," Templeton said. "That is a Bantu symbol."

Ingrid sat up. "Bantu?"

"Etched sometime in the ninth century."

"So the king carved it."

"Or had it carved."

"Where is the amulet?"

"Well, there we run into some difficulty," he said evasively. "I know it exists. Do I need to prove it? To have others believe as I do? I don't think I really care anymore."

Ingrid pounded the ground in frustration. "Where is it, god-damnit?" Templeton reached for the bottle of whiskey and took a long swig. He watched Ingrid and wiped his mouth. She was on her knees. "I want to see it."

"The amulet itself proves nothing," he said slowly. "That's been my problem all along. If you feel well enough, Finn can show you the other piece of the puzzle."

"Of course I feel well enough."

"Take her to the inland pond," Templeton said to Finn. "Follow the stream. Proceed in the direction the Agulhas would have gone, had it not been interrupted."

Finn carried Ingrid and walked through the thick palms to the stream. The jostling regularity of his gait soothed her.

"Templeton whacked off Wicks' hand," Finn announced. "That's what this is all about."

Ingrid raised her head. "What do you mean?"

"Cut, chopped, severed. Took a knife in the middle of the night and hacked Wicks' hand from his arm."

Ingrid felt her stomach turn and thought she would be sick. "Why would he do that?"

"In Islamic law, it's the punishment for stealing."

"What did Wicks steal?" Ingrid asked. Finn didn't answer. "That seems completely insane. Is that how he got himself shot?"

"Yes," Finn said. "I guess Wicks carries a gun."

"My God," Ingrid said.

They had reached a circle of palms unlike those in the village, with clusters of small fruit. Finn put Ingrid down and stooped to pick up a fruit from the ground. He smelled it and then touched his tongue to it. "It's a date," Ingrid said.

"I have only heard about these," Finn said. "I never knew this was here." He carried her into the circle of date palms that stood like sentinels, protecting the inland pool at its center. Ingrid stopped him, wanting now to walk on her own.

They proceeded haltingly to the water. The pool was nearly circular, the water serene and a beautiful clear green. A fine trickle fell from a deep red outcrop, smooth as marble, at the edge of the pool. Flowering plants thrived around the pond's periphery, sweetening the air with their blossoms. Finn left Ingrid to inspect this vegetation he had never seen before. "I do not know the names of these plants," he said.

Ingrid could think only of the water. "I want to swim," she told him.

She stood with her hands on Finn's shoulders while he pulled her shirt off and retied the kikoi under her arms. "It will be easier if you let me carry you," he said.

Finn released her when the water was deep enough for her to float, watching as it surrounded her, softening the stubborn tufts of her hair. "A king lived here," she said. She closed her eyes and Finn allowed his hand to mingle in the bright hair. "Can you forgive him?" she asked without stirring.

"Who?"

"Templeton."

"He has confused my life."

"Love confuses. Almost always."

Finn moved his arms beneath her body until it seemed he was holding her, supporting her without even touching her. Then he did touch her, raising his hands until they found her shoulder blades, her lower back, and he began to turn with her, rotating her around him. She found his eyes in this slow orbit. "If it were night," she said, "we might look like a constellation from above. A wheel. Your arms are the spokes." Finn removed one arm from under her and laid it over her, the way one might in sleep.

Ingrid closed her eyes. *"La illaha il Allah,"* she whispered. "There is no God but God. Maybe this is all that matters."

Finn rotated her once more, thinking that she looked like a mermaid with the kikoi floating over her feet. "I would like to matter to you," he said.

Ingrid said nothing, letting his words fill the silence. For a moment, as she continued to spin lightly, she thought about the God she had felt dancing at the Riyadh Mosque. This God was easier than this man. This God was everywhere and this man was only a few places, and sometimes not even there. His arms pressed around her now from either side.

"And now?" she asked.

Finn didn't answer. He was thinking of the sweetness her words could have and how he had come to desire them and how, when they were not there, the silence was not full but empty. His hands traveled up her body to her face to hold the source of the sweetness, to kiss it, to let it, finally, intoxicate him.

The drone of a small seaplane pulled them apart. To the east, two flares arced into the sky, trailing red sparks as their paths intersected. The plane angled toward their smoky trails and began to descend. They watched it drop from the sky.

"There's Wicks' help," Finn said finally. "We should go now."

Ingrid swam from his arms to the edge of the pond. There she struck a posture that made Finn stare. She turned to him. "There are steps here," she said, kneeling in the water. She placed her hands on the raised surface, where worn stone steps sloped into the water. She ran her hands over the first step, bending to look at it more closely. "Look at this," she said. Finn knelt next to her. Her fingers were outlining a shape. It looked like a child's drawing of a flower. "What is it?" he said.

"I think it's a star." Ingrid swam around the circumference of the pool, pulling herself along by the rocks. "Here's another one," she said.

They found seven stars; some carved into the rough rock above the pond, others in the polished rock just above the waterline. "A map to find the water," Ingrid murmured. "It's a copy of the map on the amulet." She made Finn stay a short while so she could listen to the breeze in the date palms, so that she could, for a moment, become part of the pond's tranquil surface.

Ingrid put her hand on Templeton's arm. He was fast asleep. "Dear girl," he mumbled, when she spoke softly. She put her mouth to his ear. "I saw the stars," she said.

"It would make a lovely story, wouldn't it?" he said, his voice still thick with sleep. "Maybe you should tell it. Go back and tell them about this place."

"Finn is taking me to Malindi," she said. "Where I can catch a plane to Nairobi and find a hospital. You need one more than I do. Come with us."

"No, no," he said, turning away from her, back onto his side. "I've had expert care. I'm home, you see. Someone will come soon to take care of me."

"Who?"

"I have friends here."

Ingrid sat down. "I'm not ready to leave you. I've come too far."

"You have to leave," Templeton said. "Finn is ready to take you and you have a course to teach—you have a life to lead. This is where I belong."

"And what about your king?" she asked.

"The world hears from those on their way to understanding, not from those who have reached it." Templeton coughed violently and held up his hand to prevent assistance. "My life is more here than there. It doesn't matter to me anymore what they understand. They will not believe the story if it comes from me—they will say it is nothing but fantasy. But you can tell them—they might listen to you. And it is just possible that you will convince them to believe you."

He paused, reaching for his water. "I'm tired of all these battles and I can do more here. Now that Mohammad is gone and Wicks has lost his hand there will be questioning. They will need someone to represent them. They need protection and guidance."

Ingrid could feel him slipping away from her. He was in front of her but he had already begun to transport himself to some other place where she couldn't follow him. "Don't be hurt," he said, watching her with tenderness.

"We have to go," Finn interrupted, "if we're going to catch Fatima."

"Fatima?" Ingrid asked.

"She will have heard about Mohammad by now and will want to make her way to this side of the island. We need to see her first."

"Yes," Templeton said. "You can't leave before visiting Fatima. Finn can show you everything you need to see. He understands it all now. Now go," he urged. *"Go."*

"If it's all right with you, I don't think I'll say good-bye," she said.

"No, that would be silly. We haven't said a proper hello. You must write, tell me what happens. I'll be curious to hear how the story unravels. You will be fearless with the department, won't you?"

"Yes," Ingrid said, having no idea what she had to be fearless about.

"I will be thinking of you there," Templeton said, taking her hand. Ingrid studied her hand against his. She pressed lightly on his veins and wondered if he was strong enough to recover. "Where will you live?" she asked. "I would like to picture it."

"In a house with no walls, in a silent village. I will be happy," he said. "Your life will proceed just fine without me."

Unable to picture any of this, Ingrid touched her lips to his cheek and turned to go. The questions he had answered had been replaced with new ones. He was home, he had said. She mouthed the word to herself. There was someone who would take care of him, someone who loved him, maybe as much as she did. Her ache at leaving him was mitigated by the strange conviction that he had reached the end of his journey.

The channel was choppy with wind, and the prow of the little skiff was bashed by oncoming waves. Ingrid clung to her seat and squinted against the spray. Finn raised his voice above the wind. "Are you okay?" he asked.

Ingrid nodded, her face sprayed with seawater. "What happened to Mohammad?"

"Mohammad is dead."

Ingrid wiped her eyes and looked at Finn through the sting of salt. His gaze left hers for the horizon and froze there. He stood up in the skiff. Ingrid turned around. Across the island, the skyline was flushed with scarlet. Black smoke surged upward, scorching the blue sky.

"What is it?"

"It's Wicks' hotel. They are burning it." They watched as flames leapt to the treetops as palm fronds were ignited and quickly vanished into smoke.

They found Fatima preparing a bag, packing items she had set out on her table: a short stack of neatly folded clothes, a bottle of rosewater, the Koran and two bars of chocolate. She was, uncharacteristically, in traditional dress.

After letting them in, she hardly registered their presence. She did not seem surprised or even interested by their arrival.

"Fatima," Finn said. "Where are you going?"

"They are burning the second hotel. It will be Mohammad's pyre. We are all of us going. The two villages united at last. Mohammad's greatest wish"—Fatima scowled—"and this is what it takes."

"We saw the smoke from the water," Finn said. "I will go too."

"You will stay," Fatima instructed. "You did not have to be there for the first pilgrimage. You do not have to be there now." She motioned to Ingrid. "And you have this one now. It seems to be what you have decided. Do not look at me that way, I am not sorry. What I see is two of the same people. It is right for you to be together."

For a moment, Finn was speechless. "I am only taking her to Malindi, where she can get a plane to Nairobi."

"Good for you that you are finally helping others. You do not have to explain to me what you are doing or not doing, it's no longer any of my affair. Now I must go."

"Fatima, before you go, I have a favor to ask of you," Finn said.

"I have no time for favors."

"It won't take time. May we see your necklace?"

Fatima paused and dropped her bag to the ground. "For what reason?" she asked warily. Fatima looked from one of them to the other. "It is mine. You cannot have it."

"We only want to see it, Fatima," Finn assured her.

Fatima plunged her hand below her shirt into the cavern between her heavy breasts. She held out a metal disk the size of a large coin. It was covered with worn markings. "It belonged to my sister and before her to another *mganga,*" she explained, rubbing its surface with her thumb. "It is very old."

Ingrid held her hand out and could see that it was trembling. "May I see it?" she asked quietly.

"I remember the day the professor saw it," Fatima said with a smile. "A day I will always remember. How he tried to get it from me, to *borrow* it. Later he told me he thought it belonged to a king. Of course it belonged to a king! I said. This is not news."

Ingrid took the pendant to the light of the open door. There were inscriptions in two languages, one of them Arabic. On one side was the map she had seen in Templeton's notes. She ran her finger over the wavy lines. She turned the amulet over and smiled. "Do you know what this is?" she asked.

"Would I wear it if I didn't? I know it was worn by a king who understood two worlds and brought them together in greater peace and understanding of God."

Ingrid smiled. "Yes." She offered the amulet to Finn. "It's a map. A way to find water from the stars."

"For reasons you may not understand," Fatima said, holding her hand out for the amulet to be returned. "I was saving it for Finn. I was going to give it to him when the time was right."

"And when exactly would that be?" Finn asked, studying the disk. "When I was the king of this island and everyone was happy and worshiped the same god?"

"I was wrong," Fatima muttered grumpily. "I'm going to keep the amulet for myself."

"Well," Finn said. "I'm sorry I disappointed you."

"It is a responsibility, you understand. It is not just jewelry."

"I understand perfectly," Finn said.

"I don't believe you're ready to wear it," Fatima said. She was still holding out her hand. "You are asking for her, aren't you?"

"No," Finn said, returning the necklace. "I'm asking for me."

"Because you are the same, you two."

"We are not the same. I'm asking for me."

"If we were the same," Ingrid interjected, "would you tell me the truth?"

Fatima refastened the necklace around her neck. "This one plays games with words," she said.

"Did you take my sandal?" Ingrid asked, gesturing to her foot. "Do I have you to thank for this?"

"I see you haven't learned much," Fatima said dismissively.

"Just tell me."

"I will tell you this. The answer is not so easy. This island"—Fatima wove her fingers together—"is like this. And anyway"—she turned to Ingrid—"a wound like that can be a gift."

"Fatima, I am part of this island," Finn said. "So tell me."

"You have changed," Fatima said. "I don't know what you are a part of anymore."

"I haven't changed, Fatima."

"Everything has changed. This is a different island. Even I know it now."

Finn did something he had never done. He crossed the room to Fatima and put his arms around her. She let him hold her, relaxing for a moment against him, and looked suddenly smaller, like an old woman who had lost too much. Then, in an instant, she puffed herself up and pushed him away. Wiping her eyes, she turned away from them. Her hands buried themselves in the nape of her neck as she searched for the clasp.

Finn carried Ingrid back to the boat. "I can walk," she protested.

"We don't have the time," he said. "I have to go to Abdul's to get your things."

Ingrid spoke from inside his arms. "Have you ever thought that maybe your home won't be in a place or a god? Maybe it will be in a person."

Finn waited until they were at the skiff to respond. "A person is not a house. A person cannot protect you from rain and bad weather. A person is not enough." Finn laid her down next to the skiff and placed a water bottle in her lap. "Wait here for me. We will take *Uma* to Malindi, and there you will catch the plane. It will take us five hours or so to get there if this weather holds. Until then, you will drink the water in that container."

Ingrid was unexpectedly glad to see her belongings again. After securing her passport and wallet, she picked through her bag for something to wear. Her clothes were clean and folded. "Sari must have done this. Did you see her?"

"She had your bag in her room. I think she was hiding it from Abdul."

"How is she?"

"She seems fine. She said to tell you good-bye, that you will be in her prayers."

Ingrid went back to her bag and rifled to the bottom of it, where her toiletries were. "I would like to brush my teeth."

After boarding *Uma,* Finn went to the steering wheel and cleaned the gauges with his sleeve. "Good," he murmured. "We have enough gas."

Ingrid sat down with her chosen outfit folded neatly in her lap. She looked like a child waiting to go to school. "I'll go below so you can change your clothes," Finn said. "Would you like some tea?"

"Yes, thank you."

Down in the galley, Finn put on water for tea. He sat down and rubbed his face, his jaw rough with stubble. It was strange not to have Jonah there. He lay down and rested until the kettle shrieked, and then he poured the steaming water into two mugs.

He found a clean shirt and a good white kikoi under the couch. In the bathroom, he washed his face and his armpits. Before picking up the tea, he took a cup of water and toothpaste with him.

Ingrid had changed her clothes. She wore a flowered skirt and a yellow blouse. On her good foot was a sandal. She was sitting in the fishing seat looking straight back up the channel. Except for her hair and the missing sandal, she looked again like a *mzungu* woman. He brought her the cup and toothpaste.

Ingrid glanced at his kikoi. "That fancy kind comes from Somalia, doesn't it?"

"Yes."

"I noticed you like to wear the Somalian ones to the bar. Do women prefer the white?"

"My father had a rule that island men could only wear their good kikois to the bar at night. It is still a rule."

Finn returned to the wheel and started the engine and wondered about her clothes and how they had changed her. Was this what she wore in America? What did she wear in the snow? He looked back at her, sitting there at the side of the boat, brushing her teeth. He felt far from her again, restored to his life, and she to hers. While there was some comfort in this restoration, it made conversation difficult.

When Finn put *Uma* in gear, Ingrid hopped up to sit in the passenger seat. She propped her foot up on the dash and wrapped a shawl around her shoulders. They did not talk. Finn took the amulet from his shirt pocket and held it in his hand. They sat next to each other with the comfortable rumble of the engine and stared at different patches of ocean. Ingrid looked for fish because she had a feeling that if she looked hard enough, she would find one and forget for a moment that her life was moving on, *it was moving back,* without her.

Finn watched the water but saw nothing but its blue-black color. The amulet had grown warm in the palm of his hand. He glanced at Ingrid but her face was turned away. Turning around, he saw dark clouds of smoke hung over the island, an injury to the otherwise flawless sky. Out of the clouds came a small white plane.

Finn turned back to his steering and for a moment thought about nothing. Then the images seeped in. Black smoke, lifeless water, Wicks . . . Finn touched Ingrid's shoulder. When she turned around he held out the amulet.

"What?" she called over the noise of the engine.

"Take it back with you."

"I don't want it."

"Why not?"

"I would only take it if you came with me," she shouted. "And you wouldn't like it there. It's cold."

"Like Sweden."

"Maybe worse."

Finn did not look at her. He counted white-caps to ten, then twenty. "Then you will stay."

Ingrid stared at him and then out to sea. *Then I will stay.* Is this how life went? Someone said something, said four impossibly brief words and the whole construct changed. Ingrid stared dumbly at her feet. Every detail of every choice she had made up to this point led in one direction. He knew it. It was in her skirt, her blouse, her one sandal, her one good foot. It was in everything about her. There was no movement in this new direction, no *doing*. She had glimpsed its path dancing in the mosque, in the height of her fever, in Finn's face, but she could not yet trust it. Looking at him now, she knew Finn didn't trust it either. She had been wrong about him. He was brave.

How brave was she? She could pretend she hadn't heard him. They were just words. Four short words, from a man who did not trust them.

Because she knew silence didn't scare him, she took her time before answering. When she spoke at last, it was to say only three words, as brief as his, wrapped up like a package. "For a while," she said.

Finn tried to see her without turning from the sea. "You will live with me then, for that while."

She did not answer, though this was not so much a question

as a statement of fact. She counted the words in her mind. More than twice as many now, words enough to lie down on. When he finally looked over, her face was tilted to the sky, where the seaplane droned toward them. Without meeting his eyes, she smiled. A small smile. For Wicks? Then her eyes fell quickly enough to catch his and she nodded, a nod as small as her smile.

If Stanley Wicks had been looking out of the plane flying overhead, he would have seen Finn's boat turn around, leaving a wake like a question mark in the blue-green water.

READER'S GUIDE

1. What is the significance of the title? What light, if any, does it shed on the book's themes?

2. Discuss the theme of faith in the novel and the various realms in which it is explored (i.e. spiritual, personal, romantic, parental).

3. What is Ingrid after and how does it change during the course of the book? What does she actually want?

4. What does Templeton represent to Ingrid? What does he represent to Finn?

5. Discuss Finn's relationship to his past, present, and future; why, as Fatima says, is it so hard for him to act?

6. We find both Finn and Ingrid at turning points in their lives; can you describe what those turning points are and why they've come about? Why is Ingrid drawn to Finn—and what reasons does Finn have for resisting/avoiding Ingrid? What, if anything, do they have to offer each other?

7. Is Templeton's act of violence toward Stanley Wicks justifiable? Is Stanley Wicks an evil character? Is he in any way sympathetic?

8. Discuss the oppression and/or freedom of the women in the novel. How are women viewed and treated on the island, and how does this impact life on Pelat? What role does imagination play in the lives of these women?

9. Is Danny innocent or evil? What does he provide for the story in general and for Finn and Ingrid in particular?

To print out copies of this or other Random House Reader's Guides, visit us at www.atrandom.com/rgg.

Suggested Reading

Sebastian Faulks, *Charlotte Gray*

Paul Bowles, *The Sheltering Sky*

Isak Dinesen, *Out of Africa*

Norman Rush, *Mating*

A. S. Byatt, *Possession*

Kuki Gallmann, *I Dreamed of Africa*

Jennifer Egan, *The Invisible Circus*

Michael Ondaatje, *Anil's Ghost*

Graham Greene, *The Heart of the Matter*

Francesca Marciano, *Rules of the Wild*

Acknowledgments

I want to thank the Michener Foundation for helping me to get started on this book, and the Hedgebrook Foundation for helping me to finish it. Thanks to Ed Stackler, whose editorial direction helped me turn a crucial corner, and to Janet McIntosh for her invaluable anthropological input and her expertise in Swahili culture. I owe to John Middleton's *The World of Swahili* any understanding I have of the complexities and beauty of that culture. And thanks to Thomas Cleary, whose poetic translation of the Koran shed new light, and gave me my title.

Thanks to Geri Pope Bidwell and Gail McCormick, who have been supportive from the beginning, and to Holly MacArthur and Serena Crawford for rooting me on even when I abandon my work at *Tin House.*

Thanks to Ann Banchoff for her invaluable support and friendship—and to Joanna Goodman for knowing and loving me so well. Thanks to my amazing family (especially to Thomas Malarkey for his incredibly careful reading and insightful response), and to Mark, for weathering this storm with stability, strength, and love.

A very special thank-you to my agent, Tina Bennett, for her brilliance, intuition, and grace. I could not have dreamed up a better ally. And to my editor, Joy de Menil, for her vision and tenacity and very deep involvement—and for being an editor in the best and truest sense. Working with her has been an honor and an education.

And, finally, thanks to Random House for taking a chance on me.